ABOUT THE AUTHOR

KAARON WARREN was born in Melbourne, Victoria, in 1965. Since then she's lived in Sydney, Canberra and Fiji. She doesn't have a long list of odd jobs to her name, but she did rise to the position of cigarette booth when she was a check-out chick.

From "White Bed", her first published story, which appeared in a feminist horror anthology in 1993, Kaaron Warren has produced powerful, disturbing fiction.

With a hundred short story sales, many award nominations and a number of wins, Warren's fiction tackles the themes of obsession, murder, grief, despair, revenge, manipulation, death and sex.

Her short story collection *The Grinding House*, CSFG Publishing (published as *The Glass Woman* by Prime Books in the US) won the ACT Writers' and Publishers' Fiction Award and was nominated for three Ditmar Awards, winning two.

Kaaron has three novels with Angry Robot Books. The critically acclaimed *Slights* was nominated for an Aurealis Award, made the preliminary ballot for the Stoker Awards, the longlist for the British Fantasy Awards and won the Australian Shadows Award.

Her second novel, *Walking the Tree*, broke new ground in publishing. Warren wrote it twice, once from the point of view of the adult character, once from the child character. The novella Morace, the children's version, is available as a free ebook download on purchase of the book.

Her third novel, *Mistification*, will be released mid 2011.

Her award winning short story "A Positive" had been made into a short film by Bearcage Productions.

Kaaron lives in Canberra, Australia, with her husband and two children. They are recently returned from Fiji where they spent three years in the diplomatic corp.

ABOUT THE ARTIST

OLGA READ graduated with a bachelor degree in fine arts and fashion design in Moscow. She has worked with a wide variety of artistic media in a diverse range of applications, from traditional Russian folk art to modern architectural illustration. These days her preferred media are oil, watercolours and pastels. Olga is inspired by natural beauty and loves painting children's portraits, and studies of fruit and flowers. She works in the realistic manner following the tradition of the great masters of this style.

Olga has produced a number of works inspired by the beauty of Fiji, which has been home to her for the last three years. She exhibited widely in Fiji, and several of her works can be found in the country's resort hotels. Now back in Australia, Olga is preparing for her first exhibition, while settling in a new house with her family.

Dead Sea Fruit

Dead Sea Fruit

KAARON WARREN

TICONDEROGA
PUBLICATIONS

DEDICATION

*To the editors, for caring enough
to do what they do.*

Dead Sea Fruit by Kaaron Warren

Published by Ticonderoga Publications

Introduction copyright © 2010 Lucius Shepard

Cover artwork by Olga Read

Designed and edited by Russell B. Farr
Typeset in Sabon and Dali

A Cataloging-in-Publications entry for this title is available from the National Library of Australia.

ISBN   978-0-9806288-5-2 (limited hardcover edition)
        978-0-9806288-6-9 (trade paperback)

Ticonderoga Publications
PO Box 29 Greenwood
Western Australia 6924

www.ticonderogapublications.com

10 9 8 7 6 5 4 3 2 1

Contents

Introduction

LUCIUS SHEPARD

There has been a tendency among some genre critics to lump writers into two categories, labeling them either stylists or storytellers, as if one were independent of the other. Gene Wolfe, for example, is often spoken of as a stylist, whereas Orson Scott Card, say, might be put forward as a storyteller. The implicit idea is, it seems, that a stylist cannot tell a good story and a storyteller cannot do style. I can think of no one better suited to prove the falsity of this arbitrary premise than Kaaron Warren.

Ms Warren's collection, *Dead Sea Fruit*, contains twenty-seven stories that range and on occasion crossbreed the genre (horror, science fiction, fantasy). They are first and foremost relations, yarns, many having a passing similarity in tone to the informality of tales told in bars or by strangers on a train. Some begin with apparent casualness, without lengthy preamble, as shaggy dog stories often will, while others have almost a tribal quality redolent of legends sung at night and by firelight, passed down from generation to generation. They tend to jump you into the lives of their characters with few referents and minimal description, and go careening off in what may seem a random direction, veering this way and that to a purpose that only becomes evident later, much later than the traditions of the formally told story generally dictate. Yet for all that they are eminently stylish and stylized. Warren is a master of implication, of implied setting and of suggestion, capable of evoking the character of a place and time, the spiritual context of a world, by means of a single detail, a single startling image. She writes with a scalpel to craft these stories, drawing thin, precise lines to create her effects. Most of the stories are nightmares... not the nightmares of classic horror fiction, with the prose equivalent of jump scares. No, these nightmares operate behind a bleak dream logic, carrying the reader along what may appear to be an ordinary path with now and then some curious, barely stated scenery, so that they accumulate in one's brain like dread or a fever. Everything is understated, except for the final emotional impact of the piece. It's a magic act to which very few writers can aspire, and fewer yet can achieve.

In her novella, the marvelously allusive "The Grinding House," Warren starts us off with a strange migration of birds, thousands of them, not flying but walking alongside a highway. We see this through the eyes of a four-person sales team, the sort that hawks magazine subscriptions door-to-door, doing their miserable work for short money and under the eye of an unsympathetic manager. The migration strikes them as odd, a harbinger of something far worse, but they don't remark too much upon it—they have more pressing concerns, among them making enough for food and shelter from the selling of a weight-loss product called Slenderise. All around them horrific things occur—grisly accidents, brutal injustices, grotesque deaths—and in most cases they react with relative indifference, or at best with mild sadness and concern. Before long we realize that the world is undergoing a terrible transformation that threatens all human life. This is not quite our world—it's the future or an alternate universe or some slight perversion of our world—but its people respond as we do to disasters, ignoring them for as long as possible and then dealing with them when the wolf comes to their door. The specific disaster in "The Grinding House" is addressed only intermittently as regards surviving or fighting back—survival is no longer the important issue. The end is inexorable, a done deal, and only a distasteful madman, who wears a white suit and collects the ashes of the dead for scientific analysis, is concerned with finding a solution. Most people have adapted and accepted their fate and are living ghostly, pre-death lives (as characters in Warren's stories are prone to do).

It's difficult to quantify the novella in terms of Warren's work, knowing that her best surely lies ahead of her, but this story seems to me an early masterpiece. Not that the other stories lag far behind in terms of quality—it's perhaps merely its ambition that separates "The Grinding House" from the rest. Each of these stories had a potent effect on me, and reading them over the space of a few days left me a bit disoriented, they held such a profound sway over my emotions. Everyone who reads *Dead Sea Fruit* will have their favorites, but notable for me were the title story, which treats of an anorexic ward and the Ash Mouth Man, a sinister figure whose kisses may have landed the women there; "Ghost Jail", the tale of a DJ who is exiled for her political acts and a woman whose sister's ghost, carried on her chest, helps to quiet the spirits of the dead; "Bone-Dog," about an obese porn star and her peculiar pet; "Coalescence," in which a blogger recruits subjects for a company that provides hosts for the minds/souls of brilliant men and women who have recently died; "The Gaze Dogs of Nine Waterfall," in which a dealer in rare dogs (Puffin dogs, the Calalburun, Tea Cup dogs, Gabriel Hounds, etc.) who travels to Fiji to bring back vampire dogs; the incantatory "Woman Train"; "State of Oblivion," set in a place above the clouds where people willfully forget a world to which they must someday return; and "Cooling the Crows," wherein a cooler (think Patrick Swayze in *Roadhouse*) must deal with a group of bizarrely damaged people.

This is a singular collection and you need to start reading it immediately, so rather than waste your time with an inconsequential closing flourish, a paragraph that would prove nothing aside from my ability to stretch a scene, let me just say that I envy Kaaron Warren's talent and admire her enormously.

Now turn the page.

LUCIUS SHEPARD
PORTLAND, OREGON
JULY 2010

Dead Sea Fruit

Dead Sea Fruit

I have a collection of baby teeth, sent to me by recovered anorexics from the ward. Their children's teeth, proof that their bodies are working.

One sent me a letter. "Dear Tooth Fairy, you saved me and my womb. My son is now six, here are his baby teeth."

They call the ward Pretty Girl Street. I don't know if the cruelty is intentional; these girls are far from pretty. Skeletal, balding, their breath reeking of hard cheese, they languish on their beds and terrify each other, when they have the strength, with tales of the Ash Mouth Man.

I did not believe the Pretty Girls. The Ash Mouth Man was just a myth to scare each other into being thin. A moral tale against promiscuity. It wouldn't surprise me to hear that the story originated with a group of protective parents, wanting to shelter their children from the disease of kissing.

"He only likes fat girls," Abby said. Her teeth were yellow when she smiled, though she rarely smiled. Abby lay in the bed next to Lori; they compared wrist thickness by stretching their fingers to measure.

"And he watches you for a long time to make sure you're the one," Lori said.

"And only girls who could be beautiful are picked," Melanie said. Her blonde hair fell out in clumps and she kept it in a little bird's nest beside her bed. "He watches you to see if you could be beautiful enough if you were thinner then he saunters over to you."

The girls laughed. "He saunters. Yes," they agreed. They trusted me; I listened to them and fixed their teeth for free.

"He didn't saunter," Jane said. I sat on her bed and leaned close to hear. "He beckoned. He did this," and she tilted back her head, miming a glass being poured into her mouth. "I nodded. I love vodka," she said. "Vodka's made of potatoes, so it's like eating."

The girls all laughed. I hate it when they laugh. I have to maintain my smile. I can't flinch in disgust at those bony girls, mouths open, shoulders shaking. All of them exhausted with the effort.

"I've got a friend in New Zealand and she's seen him," Jane said. "He kissed a friend of hers and the weight just dropped off her."

"I know someone in England who kissed him," Lori said.

"He certainly gets around," I said. They looked at each other.

"I was frightened at the thought of him at first," Abby said. "Cos he's like a drug. One kiss and you're hooked. Once he's stuck in the tongue, you're done. You can't turn back."

They'd all heard of him before they kissed him. In their circles, even the dangerous methods of weight loss are worth considering.

I heard the rattle of the dinner trolley riding the corridor to Pretty Girl Street. They fell silent.

Lori whispered, "Kissing him fills your mouth with ash. Like you pick up a beautiful piece of fruit and bite into it. You expect the juice to drip down your chin but you bite into ashes. That's what it's like to kiss him."

Lori closed her eyes. Her dry little tongue snaked out to the corners of her mouth, looking, I guessed, for that imagined juice. I leaned over and dripped a little water on her tongue.

She screwed up her mouth.

"It's only water," I said. "It tastes of nothing."

"It tastes of ashes," she said.

"They were hoping you'd try a bite to eat today, Lori," I said. She shook her head.

"You don't understand," she said. "I can't eat. Everything tastes like ashes. Everything."

The nurse came in with the dinner trolley and fixed all the Pretty Girls' IV feeds. The girls liked to twist the tube, bend it, press an elbow or a bony buttock into it to stop the flow.

"You don't understand," Abby said. "It's like having ashes pumped directly into your blood."

They all started to moan and scream with what energy they could muster. Doctors came in, and other nurses. I didn't like this part, the physicality of the feedings, so I walked away.

I meet many Pretty Girls. Pretty Girls are the ones who will never recover, who still see themselves as ugly and fat even when they don't have the strength to defecate. These ones the doctors try to fatten up so they don't scare people when laid in their coffins.

The recovering ones never spoke of the Ash Mouth Man. And I did not believe, until Dan entered my surgery, complaining he was unable to kiss women because of the taste of his mouth. I bent close to him and smelt nothing. I found no decay, no gum disease. He turned his face away.

"What is it women say you taste like?" I said.

"They say I taste of ashes."

I blinked at him, thinking of Pretty Girl Street.

"Not cigarette smoke," the girls had all told me. "Ashes."

"I can see no decay or internal reason for any odour," I told Dan.

After work that day I found him waiting for me in his car outside the surgery.

"I'm sorry," he said. "This is ridiculous. But I wondered if you'd like to eat with me." He gestured, lifting food to his mouth. The movement shocked me. It reminded me of what Jane had said, the Ash Mouth Man gesturing a drink to her. It was nonsense and I knew it. Fairytales, any sort of fiction, annoy me. It's all so very convenient, loose ends tucked in and no mystery left unsolved. Life isn't like that. People die unable to lift an arm to wave and there is no reason for it.

I was too tired to say yes. I said, "Could we meet for dinner tomorrow?"

He nodded. "You like food?"

It was a strange question. Who didn't like food? Then the answer came to me. Someone for whom every mouthful tasted of ash.

"Yes, I like food," I said.

"Then I'll cook for you," he said.

He cooked an almost perfect meal, without fuss or mess. He arrived at the table smooth and brown. I wanted to sweep the food off and make love to him right there. "You actually like cooking," I said. "It's nothing but a chore for me. I had to feed myself from early on and I hate it."

"You don't want the responsibility," he said. "Don't worry. I'll look after you."

The vegetables were overcooked, I thought. The softness of them felt like rot.

He took a bite and rolled the food around in his mouth.

"You have a very dexterous tongue," I said. He smiled, cheeks full of food, then closed his eyes and went on chewing.

When he swallowed, over a minute later, he took a sip of water then said, "Taste has many layers. You need to work your way through each to get to the base line. Sensational."

I tried keeping food in my mouth but it turned to sludge and slipped down my throat. It was fascinating to watch him eat. Mesmerizing. We talked at the table for two hours then I started to shake.

"I'm tired," I said. "I tend to shake when I'm tired."

"Then you should go home to sleep." He packed a container of food for me to take. His domesticity surprised me; I laughed on entering his home at the sheer seductiveness of it. The masculinity masquerading as femininity. Self-help books on the shelf, their spines unbent. Vases full of plastic flowers with a fake perfume.

He walked me to my car and shook my hand, his mouth pinched shut to clearly indicate there would be no kiss.

Weeks passed. We saw each other twice more, chaste, public events that always ended abruptly. Then one Wednesday, I opened the door to my next client and there was Dan.

"It's only me," he said.

My assistant giggled. "I'll go and check the books, shall I?" she said. I nodded. Dan locked the door after her.

"I can't stop thinking about you," he said. "It's all I think about. I can't get any work done."

He stepped towards me and grabbed my shoulders. I tilted my head back to be kissed. He bent to my neck and snuffled. I pulled away.

"What are you doing?" I said. He put his finger on my mouth to shush me. I tried to kiss him but he turned away. I tried again and he twisted his body from me.

"I'm scared of what you'll taste," he said.

"Nothing. I'll taste nothing."

"I don't want to kiss you," he said softly.

Then he pushed me gently onto my dentist's chair. And he stripped me naked and touched every piece of skin, caressed, squeezed, stroked until I called out.

He climbed onto the chair astride me, and keeping his mouth well away, he unzipped his pants. He felt very good. We made too much noise. I hoped my assistant wasn't listening.

Afterwards, he said, "It'll be like that every time. I just know it." And it was. Even massaging my shoulders, he could make me turn to jelly.

I had never cared so much about kissing outside of my job before but now I needed it. It would prove Dan loved me, that I loved him. It would prove he was not the Ash Mouth Man because his mouth would taste of plums or toothpaste, or of my perfume if he had been kissing my neck.

"You know we get pleasure from kissing because our bodies think we are eating," I said, kissing his fingers.

"Trickery. It's all about trickery," he said.

"Maybe if I smoke a cigarette first. Then my breath will be ashy anyway and I won't be able to taste you."

"Just leave it." He went out, came back the next morning with his lips all bruised and swollen. I did not ask him where he'd been. I watched him outside on the balcony, his mouth open like a dog tasting the air, and I didn't want to know. I had a busy day ahead, clients all through and no time to think. My schizophrenic client tasted yeasty; they always did if they were medicated.

Then I kissed a murderer; he tasted like vegetable waste. Like the crisper in my fridge smells when I've been too busy to empty it. They used to say people who suffered from tuberculosis smelled like wet leaves; his breath was like that but rotten. He had a tooth he wanted me to fix; he'd cracked it on a walnut shell.

"My wife never shelled things properly. Lazy. She didn't care what she ate. Egg shells, olive pits, seafood when she knew I'm allergic. She'd eat anything."

He smiled at me. His teeth were white. Perfect. "And I mean anything." He paused, wanting a reaction from me. I wasn't interested in his sexual activities. I would never discuss what Dan and I did. It was private, and while it remained that way I could be wanton, abandoned.

"She used to get up at night and raid the fridge," the murderer said after he rinsed. I filled his mouth with instruments again. He didn't close his eyes. Most people do. They like to take themselves elsewhere, away from me. No matter how gentle a dentist is, the experience is not pleasant.

My assistant and I glanced at each other.

"Rinse," I said. He did, three times, then sat back. A line of saliva stretched from the bowl to his mouth.

"She was fat. Really fat. But she was always on a diet. I accused her of secretly bingeing and then I caught her at it."

I turned to place the instruments in my autoclave.

"Sleepwalking. She did it in her sleep. She'd eat anything. Raw bacon. Raw mince. Whole slabs of cheese."

People come to me because I remove the nasty taste from their mouths. I'm good at identifying the source. I can tell by the taste of them and what I see in their eyes.

He glanced at my assistant, wanting to talk but under privilege. I said to her, "Could you check our next appointment, please?" and she nodded, understanding.

I picked up a scalpel and held it close to his eye. "You see how sharp it is? So sharp you won't feel it as the blade gently separates the molecules. Sometimes a small slit in the gums releases toxins or tension. You didn't like your wife getting fat?"

"She was disgusting. You should have seen the crap she ate."

I looked at him, squinting a little.

"You watched her. You didn't stop her."

"I could've taken a football team in to watch her and she wouldn't have woken up."

I felt I needed a witness to his words and, knowing Dan was in the office above, I pushed the speaker phone extension to connect me to him.

"She ate cat shit. I swear. She picked it off the plate and ate it," the murderer said. I bent over to check the back of his tongue. The smell of vegetable waste turned my stomach.

"What was cat shit doing on a plate?" I asked.

He reddened a little. When I took my fingers out of his mouth he said, "I just wanted to see if she'd eat it. And she did."

"Is she seeking help?" I asked. I wondered what the breath of someone with a sleep disorder would smell like.

"She's being helped by Jesus now," he said. He lowered his eyes. "She ate a bowlful of dishwashing powder with milk. She was still holding the spoon when I found her in the morning."

There was a noise behind me as Dan came into the room. I turned to see he was wearing a white coat. His hands were thrust into the pockets.

"You didn't think to put poisons out of reach?" Dan said. The murderer looked up.

"Sometimes the taste of the mouth, the smell of it, comes from deep within," I said to the murderer. I flicked his solar plexus with my forefinger and he flinched. His smile faltered. I felt courageous.

As he left, I kissed him. I kiss all of my clients, to learn their nature from the taste of their mouths. Virgins are salty, alcoholics sweet. Addicts taste like fake orange juice, the stuff you spoon into a glass then add water.

Dan would not let me kiss him to find out if he tasted of ash.

"Now me," Dan said. He stretched over and kissed the man on the mouth, holding him by the shoulders so he couldn't get away.

The murderer recoiled. I smiled. He wiped his mouth. Scraped his teeth over his tongue.

"See you in six month's time," I said.

I had appointments with the Pretty Girls, and Dan wanted to come with me. He stopped at the ward doorway, staring in. He seemed to fill the space, a door himself.

"It's okay," I said. "You wait there."

Inside, I thought at first Jane was smiling. Her cheeks lifted and her eyes squinted closed. But there was no smile; she scraped her tongue with her teeth. It was an action I knew quite well. Clients trying to scrape the bad taste out of their mouths. They didn't spit or rinse, though, so the action made me feel queasy. I imagined all that buildup behind their teeth. All the scrapings off their tongue.

The girls were in a frenzy. Jane said, "We saw the Ash Mouth Man." But they see so few men in the ward I thought, "Any man could be the Ash Mouth Man to these girls." I tended their mouths, tried to clear away the bad taste. They didn't want me to go. They were jealous of me, thinking I was going to kiss the Ash

Mouth Man. Jane kept talking to make me stay longer, though it took her strength away. "My grandmother was kissed by him. She always said to watch out for handsome men, cos their kiss could be a danger. Then she kissed him and wasted away in about five days."

The girls murmured to each other. *Five days! That's a record! No one ever goes down in five days.*

In the next ward there are Pretty Boys, but not so many of them. They are much quieter than the girls. They sit in their beds and close their eyes most of the day. The ward is thick, hushed. They don't get many visitors and they don't want me as their dentist. They didn't like me to attend them. They bit at me as if I was trying to thrust my fingers down their throats to choke them.

Outside, Dan waited, staring in.

"Do you find those girls attractive?" I said.

"Of course not. They're too skinny. They're sick. I like healthy women. Strong women. That's why I like you so much. You have the self-esteem to let me care for you. Not many women have that."

"Is that true?"

"No. I really like helpless women," he said. But he smiled.

He smelt good to me, clean, with a light flowery aftershave which could seem feminine on another man. He was tall and broad; strong. I watched him lift a car to retrieve a paper I'd rolled onto while parking.

"I could have moved the car," I said, laughing at him.

"No fun in that," he said. He picked me up and carried me indoors.

I quite enjoyed the sense of subjugation. I'd been strong all my life, sorting myself to school when my parents were too busy to care. I could not remember being carried by anyone, and the sensation was a comfort.

Dan introduced me to life outside. Before I met him, I rarely saw daylight; too busy for a frivolous thing like the sun. Home, transport, work, transport, home, all before dawn and after dusk. Dan forced me to go out into the open. He said, "Your skin glows outdoors. Your hair moves in the breeze. You couldn't be more beautiful." So we walked. I really didn't like being out. It seemed like time wasting.

He picked me up from the surgery one sunny Friday and took my hand. "Come for a picnic," he said. "It's a beautiful day."

In my doorway, a stick man was slumped.

"It's the man who killed his wife," I whispered.

The man raised his arm weakly. "Dentist," he rattled. "Dentist, wait!"

"What happened to you? Are you sleepwalking now?" I asked.

"I can't eat. Everything I bite into tastes of ash. I can't eat. I'm starving." He lisped, and I could see that many of his white teeth had fallen out.

"What did you do to me?" he whispered. He fell to his knees. Dan and I stepped around him and walked on. Dan took my hand, carrying a basket full of food between us. It banged against my legs, bruising my shins. We walked to a park and everywhere we went girls jumped at him. He kissed back, shrugging at me as if to say, "Who cares?" I watched them.

"Why do it? Just tell them to go away," I said. They annoyed me, those silly little girls.

"I can't help it. I try not to kiss them but the temptation is too strong. They're always coming after me."

I had seen this.

"Why? I know you're a beautiful looking man, but why do they forget any manners or pride to kiss you?"

I knew this was one of his secrets. One of the things he'd rather I didn't know.

"I don't know, my love. The way I smell? They like my smell."

I looked at him sidelong. "Why did you kiss him? That murderer. Why?"

Dan said nothing. I thought about how well he understood me. The meals he cooked, the massages he gave. The way he didn't flinch from the job I did.

So I didn't confront him. I let his silence sit. But I knew his face at the Pretty Girls ward. I could still feel him fucking me in the car, pulling over into a car park and taking me, after we left the Pretty Girls.

"God, I want to kiss you," he said.

I could smell him, the ash fire warmth of him and I could feel my stomach shrinking. I thought of my favourite cake, its colour leached out and its flavour making my eyes water.

"Kissing isn't everything. We can live without kissing," I said.

"Maybe you can," he said, and he leant forward, his eyes wide, the white parts smudgy, grey. He grabbed my shoulders. I usually loved his strength, the size of him, but I pulled away.

"I don't want to kiss you," I said. I tucked my head under his arm and buried my face into his side. The warm fluffy wool of his jumper tickled my nose and I smothered a sneeze.

"Bless you," he said. He held my chin and lifted my face up. He leant towards me.

He was insistent.

It was a shock, even though I'd expected it. His tongue was fat and seemed to fill my cheeks, the roof of my mouth. My stomach roiled and I tried to pull away but his strong hands held my shoulders till he was done with his kiss.

Then he let me go.

I fell backward, one step, my heels wobbling but keeping me standing. I wiped my mouth. He winked at me and leant forward. His breath smelt sweet, like pineapple juice. His eyes were blue, clear and honest. You'd trust him if you didn't know.

The taste of ash filled my mouth.

Nothing else happened, though. I took a sip of water and it tasted fresh, clean. A look of disappointment flickered on his face before he concealed it. I thought, "You like it. You like turning women that way."

I said, "Have you heard of the myth the Pretty Girls have? About the Ash Mouth Man?"

I could see him visibly lifting, growing. Feeling legendary. His cheeks reddened. His face was so expressive I knew what he meant without hearing a word. I couldn't bear to lose him but I could not allow him to make any more Pretty Girls.

I waited till he was fast asleep that night, lying back, mouth open. I sat him forward so he wouldn't choke, took up my scalpel, and with one perfect move I lifted his tongue and cut it out of his mouth.

Woman Train

Woman Train

Woman train, the woman train, takes me to the home of women. Takes me home to all the women. Across the aisle my sister sleeps, her eyes half-open, missing nothing. I slowly bend and grasp her bag. Click the locks, gently though, so she can't hear. Fold back the flap to find revealed her lunch, her book, her watch. I take the watch for later use. I read the book, flicking through it, the pages fan and cool my face. The book is dull, just like the girl. I eat the food.

The meat is dry, the bread is stale, the cheese is hard to chew. The food is dry, like we are.

The men flap mouths as we pass by, flap mouths to say, "Dried up." Sparks crackle, as they brave the snapping wires to lean in close. The war's not done, and left behind a skinny few, a skinny few, to live each day as a day and not a life.

Woman train, the woman train. I see men working, from my window. They can't see me as I flash past, woman train, but they all know, they all can tell, there's women aboard. They stop. I see this as they flash on by. A dull cartoon, each man one frame, they move as one, smell as one, they move and smell as one big man. I see a pile of cars.

The train squeak/screeches. My sister wakes in the carriage we share.

"What is it?" she says.

"I didn't speak."

She sleeps again.

Down the passage I hear laughter, voices, and one low scream. My sister snores, I leave her there, the shout, the scream, then silence.

I follow my ears, listen for noise. Nothing.

Then a gurgle.

I peer though the window into a carriage. The youngest woman's place.

I can smell her hair.

She senses movement, lifts her head, displays her throat to show she means me no harm.

She kneels on the floor, thighs on either side of the man. He doesn't move. She waves her arm. I enter.

"Kiss him," she says. "He tastes like milk."

I laugh.

Kiss a man?

My sister would die.

Choke with envy.

I kiss him upside down, my tongue rolling, tugging his till he groans.

"Good girl," says this one. She lifts her skirt, edges her underwear aside, sinks down.

He groans.

"Good boy," I say, stroking his brow. "What is he?" I say when she is done.

"Suitcase boy," she says. She wipes her mouth with her hand, her vulva with his shirt tail. I don't care to follow her work, so we push him off push him off push him off the train. Cartoon men outside the train I see them run, cartoon legs long and stiff, cartoon mouths open to scream.

Woman train, the woman train, it takes us to the woman town. We are safe in woman world. I find some food, steal some food for the youngest one. We should not steal, men steal, but we are needy too. The youngest one smiles and I think she looks weaker. I wonder if already she is wrecked for woman's world. If I told the others what she'd done, we'd drop her at the station and I would see, in cartoon frames, the men attack. That would mean a carriage free, freedom from my sister's gentle snoring.

We travel fast through smaller towns, we travel slow through cities. It's dull out there, and drab and slow. It needs a woman's touch. Our clothes are red, our hair-cuts rough, but we are well, and smart and rich and happy, and the men can't enter our domain unless we want them to. I see a pile of cars.

Woman train, the woman train, days and days without fresh air.

"There is no air," Big Sister says, and she should know, the great balloon. She says there's food and drink galore, but dry, like us. We are safe on our woman train. Let them fight their war and peace. We are safe to rest and plan. Let them fight, I've seen the film of blood and wounds and bandages, dirt and death and that's for them. We didn't choose it, we won't support it. Loyal wives and sometimes fighters, knitting, cooking, staying sober. It's not our way to stay at home for, stop the rot for, keep the peace for, close our legs for, close our mouths for, woman train woman train.

They dig the metal best used for life, they melt the metal, weapons of war. The papers say "wait till we win," they say that women's lives will change, that we will pay for our protesting. Woman train we reach a city, slow down, see the sights and all around are men in costume playing war. They say they fight for god and country but we know they fight for glory. They have forgotten those pre-dawn moments, when we remembered long dead mates, when we remembered stupidity, futility, waste. They will remember in their last moments, dying breath, no knitted socks, no caring parcel, no movie maker fan club clever writer live-to-air. No one's watching. We don't care. All are lies.

My sister's there at the carriage door, her eyes surprised, her mouth so wide. She reaches deep into a pocket and out comes liquorice, black and sweet she waves it like a ticket. I let her in. She can't get used to travel by train. She claims to hear the flakes of rust scraped off the rails as we move along. She claims to hear the creak of joints, the rending of metal. She claims the ship (she calls it that) is fit for scrap and not for queens, as we all are.

City men stare as much as country men. They point, I see, as we go slow, point and nudge and smile.

"There goes the woman train, full of chicken," they'd nudge and say. "Let's stop the train and get them off and have some fun."

I shudder to think.

I am older than all these here. Time is clear and I am history. Time was when before the war we travelled from here to there so fast we had no time to talk or read or knit or eat or think.

Not so far back and then it was when things were good. Our babies lived and we all worked in jobs we liked. We all know this. Not so far back that they don't know. It's further back, the bad old days, when things were hard and people died and men and women lived together.

"In a house?" my sister says, although she knows the truth.

"In a house."

"Not on a train? A house, with room to move and furniture and chairs to sit and dream?"

"Yes, all of that," I say and smile, because I know, cos I've been told, that times were bad and there we were amongst the men as if we were the same.

"Amongst the men," my sister says, and as we talk we look outside and they look in.

We leave the city, pick up speed, then slow again as something bangs and thumps the roof. It happens now and then. Woman train, oh woman train, hunger and pain are not aboard the woman train.

"Supplies," I say. My sister nods. She leaves me then, investigates, comes back to say there's bread and cheese and wine and lettuce.

I smile.

None of it tastes like it used to, when women growers loved the seed and food grew tall and fresh.

My sister drinks her wine and smiles.

"Here," she says, "it's not so bad."

I kept those bottles for a while, a tally of the time, but time passed slow and people died and I grew very tired.

We sometimes wave woman train to be polite, the children there would be so sad if we ignored their tiny hands waving, waving, at an old grey beast and the train too. I see a pile of cars.

"Do you see girls?" my sister says, and sure enough there are some girls, dressed up like dolls and smiling sweetly. Borne by women not on this train, not travelling here to the woman town. The men make signs, at times, to us, big long things with ugly words we do not read but cannot miss. What can we do but travel on and let them fight and then we'll fix the world.

Woman train it never stops. The toilet clogs and all they say is hold on tight and keep it clean and someone cuts a hole somehow and there we go, drop turds and piss onto the ground. My sister says it wasn't hard to cut the hole, and pokes her finger through paper wall, metal red with rust and crumbly.

I laugh because she cuts herself, her finger swells and then I'm sorry. All supplies have gone to war and all we have to disinfect is piss.

Even that, it seems, is in short supply.

"Soon we'll be home," I say to her. She doesn't smile.

"But when?" she says. Her nightmares now keep me awake or else I would have let her share my room. She is not well and now I think I'll miss her when she's gone. I sorrow now before she's gone, sorrow at her leaving.

I give her squares of mint to clear her breath and chewy strips of beef. We laugh to think it's what the men call war food.

We push her body out.

We are just eight. I can't believe it, some new world. Other trains, perhaps, fared well, but we are down to eight.

We sleep.

The cold comes in the whole time now, and chills me to the bone.

"See what it's like?" I'm sure they say, "to suffer?" We've had no news for many weeks and it was lies. Newspapers lie so we read old magazines with "Cooking Pies" and "Knitting Shawls" and how to treat your man.

We laugh aloud. We are too smart aboard the woman train.

My sister wore a poppy dress and we left her dressed in that. It's strange, I mourned by saying nothing, eating nothing, staring out to where she'd been and there she was again.

I want the train to stop. I see it now, at last, what's going on. Six days passed in which I mourned and then I saw her body.

Circles.

To prove my point we watched all day and used the torch at night. We took turns, the six and I (cos one more died, Big Sister, Big Balloon) to watch for her, that flash of poppy. It gave us something to do. Then we would see how far we'd travelled, how wide our circle was. Round and round and round.

It was antique, my mother's torch, from when she was a child. The men have things so slim and good, they have no moments of darkness.

Six days, it took, and now it's clear, there is that hut and that town, and that sign, and that well. Before we knew we thought it was the same because of boredom. I am the oldest, the natural leader, the one with all the anger. They are confused, they say "So what?" It's salt and lack of water, makes these women, once full of fire, seem slack and quiet and dull.

The driver isn't human. It's a box of chips and cells. We know something about these things. We learnt these things as well. We move up there, we've done it before, to find a mark, a contact point, to ask for food or news, or help.

There is no mark, the mark is gone, no way to call the men outside. The box is there, a cheap small lock, we knock it off with a boot heel.

Woman train, woman train. There is no town. This is our home. We have to think now, where to stop, which place to take as our new home. If there are men do we say yes we like your war? Or do we stay strong women? We manage the cells, make the changes. The train will stop and then we'll see how life will be on solid ground.

Down to the
Silver Spirits

Down to the Silver Spirits

The looks of pity were bad enough but it was the advice we grew sick of. Eat this, take that, go there, buy this. And the don'ts, as well: don't have hot baths, don't drink tea or coffee, don't take anti-depressants. All this from smug women with babies on hips.

"Why don't they shut up?" I said one morning after a particularly bad shopping trip.

My husband Ken said, "You shouldn't let them upset you." He showed me some research he'd done on the internet, about eating only eggs for a month to boost your chances.

"I like eggs," I said, so we ate omelette, scrambled eggs, boiled eggs and fried for eight weeks, and still I didn't fall pregnant.

I tried to stay positive. I kept looking. I told Ken, "The Tarot told me that June 12 would be good, if I wear red all day and don't fuss with small things."

Silence.

"At least pretend to be supportive."

"No, it's just that... I wasn't going to tell you about this, but someone at work told me about a woman who might be able to help us at a spiritual level. He and his wife went to her after their daughter was drowned and it was a sanity saver, apparently."

"We don't have any dead children," I said.

"I know," he said patiently. "I know that. But it might help."

It did help.

Maria Maroni changed our lives.

Ken asked me if I wanted him to wait in the car.

"No!" I said. "This is about you, too. This is us." He took my hand and squeezed it, then we walked to Maria Maroni's door.

"You knock," I said.

A tall young man opened the door. He smiled, an open-mouthed smile which showed broad, white teeth.

"I'm Hugo," he said. "Mum asked me to show you through."

His hand warm on the small of my back, he led us along a mosaic-floored hallway.

"It's beautiful," I said. He didn't respond, and I wondered if he was the artist, pretending modesty.

I thought Maria would be matronly, kindly, make us cups of tea and let us talk. But she was tall, blonde hair in a high bun with soft wisps down the side. Her features were sharp but beautiful, highlighted with cleverly applied makeup. She wore a black singlet with a see-through blouse over the top, and tight black pants and high heels.

"You're here!" she said, and took my elbow. Her voice was strong, and she made me think of those women who spruik out the front of dress shops, clothing for every size inside, they say, 50% off, today only. She gave us each a glass of brandy and took one for herself, then led us to a small, white-walled room. There was no furniture; she knelt to the floor and gestured us to do the same.

"Are you okay?" Ken whispered in my ear. He doesn't like anything as esoteric as this. He likes chairs and tables, and doctors with tests.

I looked at him and nodded. "Are you?" I said. He nodded also, but I could see he was concerned. He would never say so, but he thinks I'm vulnerable to vultures, that they can take advantage of me if he isn't there to watch over me. I don't really need his protection, but it comforts me to have it.

Maria tapped on one wall and I thought we were beginning, that she was summoning her spirit. I closed my eyes and waited.

But she was calling her son. "Drinks, Hugo."

"What would you like?" he asked me.

"Just a glass of water, thank you."

Hugo wrinkled his nose as if I'd asked for a glass of pig's blood. I wondered if he was one of those who despised anyone who turned down an alcoholic drink.

As he left the room, Ken said, "You've got him well-trained."

"For now. It won't be long before he's the boss."

I couldn't make sense of it; perhaps it was a mother-son thing, which I would know one day.

Maria Maroni stared at me for five minutes or so. Then she said, "You have three shining silver balls spinning around your head and shoulders." I looked over my shoulder, and up, and she laughed.

"It is a gift I have, to be able to see them. They are vessels," she said. "The spirits have moved on, but the vessels will stay with you always."

"Where are their spirits?" I whispered.

She closed her eyes. "I don't know. It may be they have not yet found a home."

I said, "But I've never been pregnant. It's never got that far."

Maria nodded at me. "Oh, yes, it has." She lifted her chin to indicate upwards. "Three times."

Ken sucked in breath, bracing himself. He knew what was coming. I wept for those lost babies, crying till I was sick and had to run for the toilet. Maria gave me a glass of something green and sweet, and when I'd swallowed it I felt no better, just calmer.

She squeezed my hand and looked into my eyes. "Usually at this point I counsel people about the eternity of existence and the surety of fate. But with you, I am compelled to direct you in a different way. I know a small group of potential parents like you," she said. "Lovely people, every one of them. It might be good for you to meet them."

Hugo came in, the long-forgotten water on a tray held before him.

"Am I too late?" he said.

We had been to groups before, but never found the right one. Some had given up any hope of becoming parents, accepted childlessness and thought us obsessive. Some seemed to think it was fine being around people with children. They could stand seeing happy families.

This group was not like that. We gave each other the strength to do what had to be done.

It was wonderful to be among people who understood. We had all suffered in similar ways, though Julie and Wayne had had four miscarriages and three stillbirths and I couldn't stop crying to hear of her pain. And Nora and John had the record for the most IVF attempts; Fay and Frank, who, at 65, would be considered by most as too old, but not by our group; and Susan and Brent, who didn't talk much about their experiences. Susan usually cried.

It was good to talk, to compare methods and chances taken. But it was sad, too, the failure of us all. That was hard to deal with in a group.

Ken and I had been attending weekly meetings for three months and it was our turn to host. I still saw Maria Maroni on a professional basis every two weeks, just to hear her talk of what could be. She asked me about the group, and shook her head to hear of empty wombs and lost souls. I invited her to the meeting at our house, because she had brought us together and I wanted to thank her with some nice food and brandy. She was reluctant at first, saying strangely, "I'm not sure if you're all ready."

"Ready for what?" I asked, but she shook her head.

"I'll let you know," she said.

She called me on Tuesday morning, saying, "I've spoken to Hugo, and we've decided you are ready. We've decided it's time to try something new."

"What is it?" I said, my heart beating. There had been nothing new to try since the eggs. I had a feeling it would not be anything dietary.

"I'll tell you all tonight," she said.

They arrived at nine, when most of the nibbles were gone and we were close to the end of the brandy. She seemed agitated, excited.

"Sit down," I said. "Have a drink."

Maria accepted a glass and swallowed most of it before looking at us. "How are you all?" she said.

"Maria!" Nora said, "Please! Jen told us you have something new, something for us to try. Please!"

Maria nodded. "I've brought my son today. All of you have met him."

Hugo seemed different, though. There was a magnetism about him, a handsomeness I hadn't seen before. Very different from the sullen, resentful young man.

"What's he going to sell us?" Ken muttered, and if I'd had a knitting needle I would have stabbed him for speaking.

Hugo sat down with a beer in his hand and we made small talk until Julie slammed down her cup in agitation.

"I don't care about how long your taxi took!" she said. "Why are you here?"

"I'm here because Mum has asked me to come and tell you what I know of the place I was conceived. A place called Cairness. You won't have heard of it; it's a well-kept secret. Mum learned of it from an old man who traded the secret for a lot of money."

One of the husbands sighed. I'm not sure which one.

"This is not about money, though," Hugo said. "This is about Cairness, and what it can do for you."

"But what is it?" Nora said. "What do you mean by Cairness? What is it?" The word 'conception' ensured our attention.

"Mum didn't tell me till recently that she'd had trouble conceiving. It's not the kind of thing you inflict on a child." He smiled beautifully at Maria.

"No. I kept it quiet for a long time. But then you wanted to know. You needed to know. And with you, your heritage is everything."

"It is. Knowing where I'm from changed the path my life will take."

"This is making no sense," I said. "What are you talking about? What is Cairness?"

"Cairness lies beneath our lake. Below this very city. It was an ancient city destroyed by flood and built upon, forgotten by the cities that followed. It's down there." He gestured, to help us see.

John said, "I vaguely remember hearing about it, now. When they engineered the tunnel beneath the lake. They didn't get far, did they? Before it flooded?"

"That's it. That's Cairness."

"But it's flooded. All of it. I heard they accessed it using SCUBA gear, but nothing was found."

"There is treasure, for those who will look."

Frank said quietly, "But we are not interested in treasure. You've been misled. Not one of us here has any interest in treasure."

Maria said, "You're telling this badly, Hugo."

He gave her such a look. "There is one great room there, one deep, protected room. This is where the treasure hunters reached. But they returned empty handed and terrified. The bodies were long gone, many, many thousands, they think, all drowned and gone to rot. But there are ghosts. They left their souls behind. No one is sure why. Would you like me to tell you what I think?" Hugo asked.

"Please," said Nora. "Please do." Her voice always sounded on the verge of panic, as if any minute wasted made a difference to her chances. He took a sip of beer and grimaced.

"It's gone warm," Ken said. "I'll get you another." Hugo handed his bottle up.

He said, "I think they are the souls of the babies never born. The ones in the womb when the city drowned. I think they are desperate to live a life."

"And we are desperate to have them," Nora said. We chattered excitedly, the other women and I, about the possibilities of it all. The men slipped away one by one and I caught them in the kitchen, whispering.

Ken looked guilty, kissed my forehead and said, "Hello, darling."

"What are you men talking about?"

They exchanged glances.

"We're discussing what he's said," Ken said.

"You mean Hugo. He has a name." I went back to my friends. I didn't want to hear the husbands' negativity.

I shivered as Hugo spoke. I looked at Maria and she was nodding at him, smiling.

"I've been into the city," Hugo said, "and walked through the first tunnel. I did not believe in ghosts; all I saw was metal, boxes, furniture pieces. Then we entered a larger, more open space. I saw nothing but decay, until my guide said to me, *try to shift your focus, like you're looking at one of those 3D pictures.* I stared at the back of a ragged chair until the room around it blurred. I let my gaze slip and saw them. Hundreds of them, crowded in the room like it was the hull of an old transport ship, squatting on the floor, shifting, moving. They plucked at me and my guide, pulled at us. He said, 'They hate us being here. I think they want women.' "

Fay choked a little. "What is this? What are you telling us?" We are not patient story listeners.

Hugo said, "I went back a number of times. My friends couldn't understand why I went, they'd say, *Aren't you afraid of the ghosts?*"

Maria said, "And what would you say to them?"

"I'd say, *I'm going for the ghosts.*"

"But what sort of a city was it? Do they know?" John said. The men had rejoined us. Ken handed Hugo another beer.

"It was a good place," Hugo said. "A place of great learning and charity. Of absolute equality. I can tell you that much. I took friends there, showing the place off, I guess."

"And just by chance the connection was made," Maria said. "A couple, who'd tried everything for ten years, got pregnant. It was a miracle. It was discovered that the spirits are ready to be reborn. That is, if a woman comes with a womb to fill, there will be a silver spirit ready for her."

We all looked at Hugo. "You?" Julie said.

He nodded. Hugo drank his beer. None of us spoke. "There is no real record of who the silver spirits are, and we cannot guarantee your own children's souls are there. But we do know that these spirits are benevolent, regardless of who they were in life, and that most clients report a moment of absolute knowing." He nodded at us. "Recognition."

The bribes were huge, he told us. That's where most of our money would go. We didn't care, though. None of us cared about the money. We wanted those silver spirits.

We wanted one like Hugo.

My husband squeezed my knee. "We'd like to give it a shot," he said. I loved him for believing, for accepting the possibility. Twenty-five years was too long to wait for a child; soon we'd be fifty-five, too old, too old to start that life.

Maria said, "I just want you all to be clear about what you will be giving up, beyond the financial sacrifice. You will not be the same once you are mothers. The men will notice this and may choose not to care. But you will not feel about them the same way."

We all nodded, barely listening.

Hugo said, "Only those who are truly serious make it, I'm telling you. The dedicated ones. The ones willing to make sacrifices."

I felt proud to be such a person.

We all met the night before in an expensive restaurant right in the centre of the city. Views of the Lake. I didn't like it there, never felt safe, felt ugly and old, out of place. Julie loved it; they lived in the city, hang the expense, she always said.

"Maria?" I asked.

"She won't be joining us," Hugo said. "She wishes you all well."

It was a little shocking. I was relying on Maria for support.

Susan and Brent weren't there. They didn't like the idea. We'd had a difficult meeting when they told us they weren't coming. Brent had said, "I've been asking around about Cairness. It seems that local legend has it the parents trapped the children and then flooded the city. That's what people say. That it was no natural disaster."

"Brent!" Nora said. "Don't ruin this for all of us by listening to gossip."

"Nora, they say the spirits are of the drowned children, not the unborn babies." He looked at us all as if wanting us to understand. "You need to think about why the children were murdered by their own parents. Why would any parent do such a thing?"

Fay's husband Frank was ill. Some men just don't have the stamina. Wayne wasn't there, either, but Julie wasn't bothered. We all knew they had an 'open' marriage. I watched her flirting with our handsome young waiter and cringed.

"We're starving!" she told him.

We all chuckled over our delicious meal. The unity of it made me want to cry. This was how it should be. This was where I was supposed to be.

"The men will need to wait at the entrance. We've talked about that, right?" Hugo said.

"Aren't they coming with us? I said.

Hugo shook his head. "No. No. This is a woman's place. The silver spirits like women. If the men go down I can't guarantee a result."

"I don't know if I can do it without John," Fay said.

"And me without Wayne," Julie said, although of course she could.

"And me," I said.

"It's not up for discussion. As far as I know, it doesn't work if the men go down there. It's up to you. The risk is yours." He looked at the ground. "You will need to leave your men behind."

For a moment I almost gave up. Then Ken said, "There's no need for discussion. This is what we came to do, this is what we'll do."

"So do you want a boy or girl?" Nora asked. My husband and I smiled at each other.

"We don't mind," I said, "So long..." and the whole group interrupted me then, saying, "...as it's healthy." Everybody laughed. Sometimes you laugh for the joy of being the same, those rare moments when a group of people think alike.

We sat up late, talking softly and enjoying the night. We didn't talk much about the next day and I was glad. I didn't want to think about what lay beneath. What we would be seeing. I wanted that part done with, and my baby in my arms. I could almost smell that baby scalp smell.

I woke up in the morning to my husband's bare, downy back. I stroked him gently, his shoulder blades, his neck, his back. He stopped breathing for a moment then started up again and I knew he was pretending for fear of stopping me. It struck me suddenly how wonderful he was, all he did for me. I kissed his back gently and he stopped breathing again. I pulled at his shoulder to turn him over and we made gentle love without speaking.

Hugo was at our door early, making sure we were okay. "You're looking flushed, Jenny," he said.

I blushed. Ken laughed. Sex had been a matter of timing for us for a long time. Spontaneity seemed like a waste. It was as God intended, sexual relations for procreation, not pleasure. My husband made sad little jokes about it to his friends, "We're trying as hard as we can," winking at them. No one ever laughed.

All the husbands except Frank made the joke, we realised when we got together. Not one of them mentioning the hard work of it, the routine. Frank found it all offensive, every last mention.

We spent the day exploring the city, buying presents for the babies, our arms laden with generosity. Hugo didn't join us.

John waited in the bar that evening while we got ready in the hotel room Hugo had booked. We giggled like brides and did buttons and zips. It was odd, such sensible, serious women acting like girls, but we were so very excited. We had all brought beautiful dresses to wear. It was the most important day of our lives and we were going to look our best. Ken was jealous and finally stomped off to the bar to join John. "You never dress like that for me," he said.

"This is not about you," I said.

"It never is," he muttered.

We giggled when he left. It's hard to take men seriously. Julie joined us last; she can't go a day without a run. She thinks her obsession with fitness will help her keep a baby. We had just opened a bottle of champagne when Hugo knocked at the door. We squealed like teenagers and Julie let him in.

"We need to get moving," Hugo said. "It's a long walk down and back up again."

I hate walking at night at the best of times, but here? In this city? I wanted a police escort.

The others kindly told stories to distract me. John spoke about his brother, who bathed his kids at Nora and John's house.

"Can you imagine?" John said. "The whole bathroom smelt of children for days."

"That's so cruel," we said. Most of us rarely saw the relatives with children. They were so smug, so pleased with themselves.

As we walked, we talked a little about expectations. All of us were terrified. We were headed for a community of ghosts, and no matter how benevolent Hugo said they were, we were frightened. We walked quickly to keep up with him. He didn't look down, watch his step, as we all did. He seemed to float, almost oblivious to the city. He reminded me of my Indian Guru, stepping on those who didn't get out of his way.

We reached the lake's edge and Hugo stopped under the ramparts of the old bridge. He seemed to pant like a frightened dog.

"What is it?"

"Not keen on water. It's okay. I'll be fine."

John said, "I love it here. Testament to man's stupidity. Why build on a flood plain? It doesn't make sense."

"Cities have been destroyed by flood here many times. Each is arrogant enough to believe they will be the ones to avert the waters." Hugo shrugged. "This city is over 200 years old. It's doing okay. You live here, John. You chose this flood plain."

"What if the child is like him?" Ken whispered to me.

He could be a hateful man.

Crowds walked by, shouting, and beer bottles landed at our feet. One glanced off Fay's arm, but she rubbed at the spot and said nothing.

Hugo led us down under the rampart. It stank of rubbish, wet dirt. He pulled some gloves from his pocket and squeezed his fingers into them. He swept a pile of rubbish away to reveal a manhole, which he lifted and shifted.

He gestured me inside.

We climbed down. It was quieter. The smell of it: Wet, hot concrete. Urine, vaguely, as if the piss had been mixed into the concrete when it was poured. There were steps, steep, with rusty railings. Nora twittered away, frightened to hold the railings in case they collapsed.

"Hold onto me," her husband said.

Rust covered my hands. I wiped them on Ken's shirt a dozen times.

Hugo seemed jumpy. Eager to please.

The walls felt very near. We began to sing to distract ourselves; it's a long way to Tipperary petered out and someone started on the National Anthem, which made us all laugh.

"Are we close?" Julie said. Her voice was faint. We were all tired. I didn't even want to think about the climb back up.

"I should never have brought you here," Ken whispered in my ear as we stepped over a pile of reddish refuse.

"You didn't bring me" I hissed. "I came! I came of my own accord." He lifted his arms up, a favourite gesture of retreat, and at that moment I wanted him gone. He supported this without really believing it, and I would leave him if he ruined my chance at motherhood.

"Is that the entrance, sealed with the rock?" he said.

This practicality distracted the men, and between them they rolled the rock aside. We didn't talk. Each one of us women knew we would do this; we would walk through a pit of fire for our babies.

We heard a low groaning sound.

"What's that?" Ken asked.

"The air sounds different down there. It's enclosed and there are walls and things. You'll be right," Hugo said.

"I can't do it," Fay said. At our group sessions, she was always the tensest, wanting to know the truth but terrified of it at the same time.

"It's all right," Hugo said. "It's the silver spirits calling. They won't harm you. Ghosts aren't malevolent when they're in the majority. They tend to be calm, and feel like they're at home. In heaven, perhaps."

He looked at us, standing back.

"You're all here because you've been to hell and back. You want children, right?"

We nodded.

He spoke very quietly. "They're waiting. Go find the one you love."

A sound of babies crying and a smell, the smell of babies came to me. I clutched Ken's arm. "Can you hear that? Smell it?"

He shook his head. "I can't. I'm sorry."

I stepped in first. I was tired of waiting; I wanted that baby.

I expected underground to glow silver. Hugo had told us it was cold so we were rugged up, but the iciness of it still surprised me. The smell was bland, a little metallic, a little earthy. Someone had rigged lights up and we could see the rubble and debris of a fallen city.

There were sockets in the wall, where the hinges of the main gate had hung.

"I can't believe the archaeologists haven't cleared this place out," Fay's husband called from the entrance.

"Look at this wall." Nora touched the clear flood marks. "You can see where the water stopped." She bent down and picked up a handful of dirt, then sifted through it to show us a silver coin. "I can't read it in this light."

"We'll look at it later," I said.

"What do we do?" Fay said. "Just stand here?"

"I say we walk. They must be further in," I said.

We moved in close formation, tripping over bricks and rocks as we made our way deeper into the city. The floor was very damaged, but you could see the beauty it once was, the remnants of a magnificent mosaic.

The room was very deep, probably five times my height. On one wall (and again, it was terribly damaged) I could see an amazing family tree, each child below its parents, all with that same broad smile Hugo wore.

There was movement to our left.

"What's that? Is it someone?" Fay said.

It was grey, drab. "It can't be. It's not silver," Nora said.

Then the grey thing lifted its head and we saw a face of such terrible anger we all screamed.

"Move on! Move on!" Nora shouted.

"No, back. Back!" Fay said.

"I'm not leaving without my baby. I've come this far. I'm not leaving," I said.

I stepped forward and shouted, "We're here. Where are you?"

Hundreds of the grey, drab creatures appeared, slouching towards us like wolves. Their faces were drawn, sad.

"This can't be them," Nora said.

The groaning grew louder as they approached.

"I don't want one of them! They don't look like babies," Fay said.

Some of them seemed twisted, bent. I couldn't look them in the eye.

We turned and tried to run, but they surrounded us.

"Maybe this is how they're meant to look," Julie said. "They'll change, won't they?"

Their faces were deformed, ugly. They snarled with transparent teeth and floated above us, spinning so fast we grew dizzy watching them.

I felt drawn to one, it's true. For a moment it paused and cocked its head, as if assessing me. Then it stretched its hand out to me.

"No, Jen, no!" Fay said.

It was too late. The ghost stretched out with both hands and thrust its long fingers into my eyes. I was blinded, but felt no pain. I felt it crawling into my head through my eye sockets, dragging itself through, sliding down my throat and into my womb, where it curled up, waiting for a body to grow into.

Fay covered her eyes, crouching on the ground. "Fay," I said. "You will be so sorry if you don't do this. Come on. Look, I'm all right." I pulled open her arms and she looked up. Five of them surrounded us, peering down. They jostled to reach her, their fingers grabbing at her eye sockets and tugging until she screamed.

One slid its index fingers in and the others flew off, leaving the silver spirit to enter her as mine had done.

I turned to see Julie being filled as well, and Nora. My throat constricted as if swollen, and we walked silently back to where the men waited. The other ghosts flew around our heads, ducking over us, making us flap at them as if they were birds.

The sight of those dear husbands made me cry. Ken looked like a stranger, as if he'd aged ten years since I'd been in Cairness.

"What happened?" they said. "Are you all right?"

We all touched our bellies, feeling life wriggling there.

"We're all right," I said. There was no point telling the men. No point. What could we do? You can't kill something already dead and we all wanted children so much.

"And now you know why my mother will never return," Hugo said, quiet in my ear.

Fay brought her famous potato salad again this year.

"I roasted the potatoes," she said, as she passed me the dish. "Isn't that naughty?" I watched her three year old son, already stripped to saggy spiderman underpants, sawing at my bench with the bread knife. He danced around us, his tiny penis jiggling, his flabby white stomach quivering. I smiled, thinking, "*You look like a worm. Or a fat white adder who's just swallowed a child.*"

He stopped dancing and paused, cocking his head at me. Then he hissed like a snake.

"Very naughty," I said. Fay's husband Frank kissed me drily on the cheek and smiled. He didn't say hello; every year the tiredness takes him more. He placed three bottles of red wine on the bench.

"Are we the first?" Fay asked. Ken entered the kitchen, carrying our three-year-old daughter, flopped as if boneless in his arms.

"Punctual as ever," he said. Fay flicked her gaze to my daughter, then to me. We shared the look, the look we Cairness mothers share, then bustled to get drinks and nibbles ready. Ken bent to place our daughter down but she screamed, as she always did, clawed her way up and onto his shoulders. She stuck her long index fingers into his ears and pressed her face to his hair. He bent with her weight and said, "Who else are we expecting?" He is quiet now, and pale, like he's an extension of her, a growth from under her arms with legs and part of a brain. She likes to be carried. Looked after.

Hugo and Maria, there early to help set up, kissed her.

"Four new families are coming today. Back from Cairness a year ago," Maria said.

"So the children are three months old?" Fay said. We exchanged our Cairness mother's glance again and knew we would not ask the women any questions. We wouldn't say, "How was Cairness for you?" and we would pretend not to notice their babies' eyes, silvery grey, all of them, all of the children's eyes that silvery grey we knew well but that the husbands didn't recognize because they never entered Cairness with us.

Nora arrived with her family. Their son vomited red and purple lollies, half-digested, in the entrance, and we cleaned it up. His arms were covered with carefully drawn naked pictures of his mother. Nora caught me watching and pulled his sleeves down. "He's talking now," she said. "He's got a vocabulary of 15 words."

"That's very good," I said. I didn't ask her if she could understand the words he spoke or if, like my daughter, the language sounded like something not quite English. It started to rain and we watched our children shiver inside, hide their eyes. To a one they hate water. We can't teach them to swim, can't take them to the beach. Fay says it's because of the terrible story Hugo tells them again and again. We can't stop him, though. He says it's family history. He loves the children, each one of them. He gathers them to him like disciples.

"The parents of Cairness were the meanest you ever saw." He spreads his fingers, drawing the children's eyes to his. "And they trapped their dear children, tricked them into a room, and they let go the sluice gates. Those children drowned, chocked with water in their lungs, no air. Can you imagine?"

Oh, the children could, all right. The others hated the story, but Ken saw its importance. "She'll want to know where she came from. When she's older."

"She's our child. That's all that matters."

"It does matter, though. All adopted children want to know."

"She...is...not...adopted." I could barely stand the sight of him.

The new families arrived, bringing store-roasted chicken and packets of chips. Their babies cried and fussed, wriggled and cried.

Fay said, "Don't worry, it gets better," but we watched the three year olds and we knew it wasn't true. Her son crawled around, picking the sleep out of the babies' eyes with his long fingernail.

We'll keep in touch. We see Susan out sometimes, and she looks insane, her furious envy making her shake to see our lovely littlies. Our children are so close in age, and our shared experiences tie us together. Two boys and two girls. All of them difficult in their own way, cold about the eyes and lacking in innocence. But they are our children and we love them. As they grow we will watch them and wonder: What will they do to the world when they are adults, and what are the words we will use to justify bringing them to life?

Fresh Young Widow

Fresh Young Widow

The fresh young widow washed her husband's body. She dipped her cloth into cloudy water and rub rubbed at him, cleaning the pores, washing away dried blood, picking at it with her long, strong fingernails. She closed her eyes as she touched his body but he was so cold she couldn't imagine him alive. She laid her head on his belly and let her tears wet him.

There was a gentle knock at the door.

"Marla, they are wondering if you will see someone. An old woman who walked here eight days from Baristone. She thought the penance would help."

The widow put down her sponge. "Connie, I am washing my husband."

"I'm so sorry, Marla. But they told me to ask. She had a son with her. He's very distressed."

At this the widow walked to the door and opened it. Connie stepped inside, her head bowed.

The widow said, "Did he find his beloved husband knifed to the bone? Did he hold him as he bled to death? Did he wait for last words and hear none?"

"No, Marla."

The widow patted at her wild and unbrushed hair, tried to straighten her filthy clothes.

"Oh, Marla," Connie said. "Oh, Marla."

The sympathy was too much to bear and the widow sank to the floor, weeping great painful sobs. When she quieted, exhausted, Connie said, "I'm so sorry about your husband. We all are. It should never have happened. Why do they even let the tourists in?" Connie began to cry. Marla felt so old around Connie, though the difference was just two years.

The widow knew most girls in the town had loved Brin. He had been funny, handsome and flirtatious. She knew he kissed them, sometimes. Nothing more.

He liked to kiss.

"I'm going to finish with my husband, now," the widow said. She felt no strength in her voice. "Tell the son I may be able to get to his mother. Tell him the stories are not true. There will be no clay walk. No great resurrection. Dead is dead. All there will be is a monument to her. Okay?"

The young girl said, "Okay."

Marla said, "This is new for me, too, Connie. I'm sure we'll get used to each other."

Connie nodded. She placed a box just inside the door. The widow knew it would contain offerings, bribes, and she felt a childish sense of anticipation.

She had three buckets of clay ready, collected as the sun rose. Soft and slippery. She took up a handful and squeezed, loving the squelch between her fingers. The fresh young widow worked the clay. Picked out stones and sticks, any small impurities. She dropped handfuls of clay into a large bucket of water, where small motes drifted to the top. These she skimmed off. She sifted the sludge through her fingers and when it was silky smooth she poured it onto a long flat sieve outside. Cloudy water dripped onto the ground and she left the clay to dry. When it was no longer sticky to the touch she could work it, kneading it until the smoothness of it satisfied her.

Then her real work began.

She added three of her fingernail clippings, a link from his mother's chain, and a pinch of coriander, his favourite spice. She rubbed her fingers together and sniffed them, the smell evoking such an intense memory she smiled. She and Brin had been married only a few days, just returned from their honeymoon in the city, where everything was delivered on the asking; food, drinks, books. She was tired, exhausted, and so was he. He had enjoyed lovers before. She had not. Her learning with the clay was so intense not much else filtered through. She had friends but not close ones. She was popular without people really knowing her.

It had made her blush, returning from her honeymoon to all the attention. All the assumed knowledge. Everybody had smiled at her, nodded.

"How did you go?" her mother said, arriving at their home dusty, clay-smeared, her hair clumpy.

Marla nodded, too embarrassed to speak. Her mother had laughed. "You poor young thing. It's all a bit terrifying, isn't it? What's he cooking you tonight? What are you cooking her tonight?" Her new husband came out of the bathroom, rubbing at his hair.

"Amazing how you forget about the clay when you're away," he said.

Her mother said, "What's for dinner?"

"Oh," he said. "Yes. Aha, can't you smell it?"

The two women sniffed. A rich, rough smell.

"It's my specialty. Ground Nut Stew."

He led his wife into the kitchen and ground some spice for her to sniff. She coughed.

"It's strong. But the flavour is so good. Beef, potatoes, ground nuts, cinnamon. You'll love it. I hope you'll love it."

He kissed her, and she tasted onion.

"He's a good boy," her mother said later. "He understands. Just like your father. We have a little work to do before dinner."

"It's ready now," Brin said. "Can't we eat first?"

"I guess the dead don't travel so fast we can't catch them. I'll leave you to your meal."

"Stay, Mum, eat with us. We'll call Dad and eat together," Marla said, holding her mother's arm.

"What about your parents, Brin?" her mother said.

"They'll come tomorrow," Brin said. "Go call your husband!"

They had eaten together, a happy meal. The men talked, the women, too, but Marla and her mother had thoughts behind their words, thoughts of what lay ahead.

After dinner the women walked to the workshop. It was a large, bright room, angled to let in the morning sun, but not the afternoon sun, so it never got too hot. The floor was slate, easily wiped clean but still ingrained with the red clay they worked with.

They had worked in silence, each intent on the process of covering the body in a way which was beautiful yet would not crack. This was an elderly woman, a resident long gone away but come home to die. Many of them did that.

After a while Marla had realized she was doing most of the work. She rested back on her heels and looked at her mother rocking by the door.

"Are you all right? Tired?" Marla said. Her mother had smiled. "I am, a little." The clay slip filled the small lines in her face, exaggerating them, making her look older and tireder than she really was. "But, mostly, I like to watch you. You're very skilled for one so young."

"You were young and skilled once," Marla said. Her mother had nodded and looked away.

"Your marriage has got me thinking," she said. "Thinking about now, rather than when."

"I'm not good with riddles, Mum," Marla said. She worked a piece of clay and smoothed it over the belly of the woman.

"What I mean to say is, I'm feeling some resentment about this job. This ... placement. I'm feeling I need to get away, see the world."

"And Dad?"

"I'll take him, too," she said. She rubbed at her face. "What do you think?"

"It's not a good job to do resentfully," Marla said. "I know we don't choose it, but I accept it. You go. Let me be the Clay-Maker. It will be okay."

Her mother had fallen to her knees beside her.

"Thank you. Thank you. You kind and beautiful girl."

Her parents had left the next day. They were gone three weeks when Brin was killed.

Marla wiped away the tears brought from remembering that time, dropped a pinch of spice into the clay, then began to cover her husband.

First his toes, feet. The ankles were tough; too bumpy. The shins, knees and thighs. The room was cold to stop the clay drying too quickly.

She covered his genitals, his belly, his back, slapping on the clay and smoothing it, shaping it.

She sat with him, not eating or drinking, until the first layer dried. This needed patience. Each layer needed to dry before more clay was placed on top, or the whole thing would sink, sag, slump. She felt like sagging herself, her weariness was so great.

Then her parents arrived to be with her. Marla never found out who contacted them, or how.

"Marla, my poor darling," her mother said, pushing her way into the workshop. "We came as soon as we heard." Her father hovered in the doorway, his face grey, shocked. Both of them had aged.

"Dad," she said, and he held her while she cried.

"I should never have left you," her mother said.

"This has nothing to do with you leaving. But I'm glad you're back."

"We came to comfort you, but also we need to talk. I have something so important to tell you. Let's go sit by the wall."

Marla and her mother walked together to the clay wall. "I know where I want us to sit. I remember where everybody is," her mother said. She trailed her fingers over the clay faces then stopped. "Here," she said.

They sat down.

"You will need to act. I wish this talk could have waited many years, but this chance can't be missed, as terrible as it is. It is better to make the child with someone you love."

"So who was I born of? Someone you loved more than Dad?"

Her mother said, "No. No. You were born of my mother. She stands behind this clay man." She waved her arm. Marla looked. The man frowned slightly at her, his features a little askew. "He wasn't a very nice man," her mother said. "He bit people." Marla saw his clay teeth, larger than life, like a rabbit's. She closed her eyes and listened to her mother's words.

Marla walked her mother to the house. It was not the biggest house in the town; that belonged to the Chief Mason. The Clay-maker lived in a modest but beautiful home, paved with baked clay tiles, walls of pale terracotta. Beautiful furnishings, gifts from the people of the town.

Marla felt a little dazed. She was not old enough for this information, this task. Yet the task was hers.

"Have some lunch first. Fill yourself," her mother said.

"No. He's waited long enough. I must get to him," Marla said. She walked slowly to the workshop, though, stopping to talk along the way to anyone she saw, accepting their condolences, asking after them. She wondered if her face looked different, now she knew.

Brin grew fuller, thicker. Marla wondered if she could get him through the door, he was so large. She built him into a giant. She built the image of a girl on the clay case; vagina, breasts. Then she smoothed it away.

Knocking came. It was the masons. "Is he ready, Marla? Ready for the Kiln?"

"Not yet. Wait," Marla called out. She fashioned Brin a penis and she made love to her clay man. She sent his seed back to him, kissed his clay lips. She felt the dryness of the clay in her throat, and she coughed and choked as the masons entered. They did not flinch at her appearance. They knew she did not wash, did not change clothes, for the time it took to do her clay work.

For all her hard work, an impurity in the clay gave his face a scowl she had not intended. A downturned mouth she tried to fix but couldn't.

The masons stared in silence at his face.

"I told you we needed to find his killer," the oldest mason said. "You said no violence for violence, but look at his face."

The masons muttered together. There was a clamour at the door. The other mourners.

Two masons lifted the clay man so it appeared he walked, aided, between them.

They carried him outside. The widow staggered into step behind them, tears waterfalling from her eyes. She didn't sob; she was beyond noise.

The wailing around her began. His mother collapsed at his feet. She kissed them, huge sloppy kisses that left small damp patches on his clay toes. She rose, her lips dusty.

"It's wrong, so wrong," she wailed. Her husband and friends supported her so she walked almost like her clay son did.

The widow felt intense pain in her shoulders, her fingers. She had worked feverishly on her husband, making the clay warm between her fast fingers, giving it blood warmth. They carried Brin to the Kiln, a tin shed outside the walls, set amongst the burning sand. Here he would stand in the searing heat until his clay case baked hard. Here her work would be tested; a single flaw and the case could crack open.

As the time came, people gathered by the Kiln. There was a sigh as Brin was brought forth. The case was perfect, uncracked. The procession marched through the streets of the town to the wall. The wall rose just a little higher than the tallest mason, so if he stood up on his toes he could peer over it. It was broad, though, thick with clay people. Solid with clay. There were no gaps. These were filled by the masons as they appeared. The clay changed little in its shading, testimony to the unchanging environment of the town.

Marla was very proud of the wall. There, two more masons waited with cement.

They placed her husband Brin next to the doctor's wife, in the wall two weeks now. Marla could not help noticing how perfect her work was; no cracks in the clay woman, and the expression captured perfectly her kindly nature.

"It should be that tourist here instead," Brin's mother shouted. "He should be the dead one, not my son."

But then Brin would have been a murderer, Marla thought. She held her mother-in-law tight and closed her eyes, resting for a moment.

"Into the wall we cement thy physical being," the Chief Mason said. "May your soul be free to roam until the great clay walk. May your body stay safe within the wall, an empty vessel awaiting your return.

"May your physical being keep this town safe from outsiders and repel evil from within us all.

"May we serve you and you serve us until the time of the great clay walk."

Marla collapsed at Brin's feet, clutching her belly.

"May the seed you planted within me grow, my love. I love you so much. I had so much more time for you." The snot ran down her chin, tears down her cheeks. She felt she was masked with her own fluids.

There were murmurings around her, high-pitched murmurings of hope and excitement. "A baby! A baby! There has not been a baby born here for two years!" They were almost as barren as the clay.

Connie stood staring, a fixed smile on her face. "Congratulations," she said.

"It's all right, Connie. You can care for both of us. You will be with me for life." Although the widow had deliberately misunderstood, Connie still smiled. "Your place is safe," the widow said.

The Chief Mason and the youngest mason came to her. The Chief Mason said, "I can tell you, Marla, that we are outraged by your husband's murder. He was a great man. A good mason." His eyes shifted there and the widow knew he was lying. Her husband had not been a good mason. He didn't have the seriousness for it, the rock-solid dedication needed to build. He was too funny, too rebellious. He liked being the husband of the Clay-Maker. It gave him many privileges and he could shock the others so easily. The Clay-Maker's husband merely had to laugh loudly to be noticed.

"Thank you," she said. She swallowed. "Can you tell me how? What? All people tell me is the tragedy of it, the waste. I want to know what he did."

"It wasn't his fault. He was a funny man. He liked a joke. And the tourist was being disrespectful. He was drunk, and he poked and squeezed at the girls, joked about them being full of clay until he made Connie cry. Brin told him to leave her or he would turn to clay. He called the tourist some names, some cruel names," the Chief Mason said.

"He had a sharp tongue," Marla said.

The youngest mason blushed, and Marla wondered if images had popped into his head of the widow and her husband's sharp tongue. He stammered, "None of us expected the tourist to do what he did. He was skinny, you know? And pathetic. A bully. Brin turned away, we thought it was over, but the tourist leapt on him. Brin was down before we could react. Then we took him to the doctor's and fetched you."

The tears ran down her cheeks and drooled saltily into her mouth.

"Thank you," she said. "And the tourist? Where is he?"

"We'll find him," said the Chief Mason. "We'll find the killer and bring him back. Then perhaps Brin will smile as he watches over us."

Marla nodded. "You know what you will be sacrificing in leaving this place?"

"We do. We are prepared to age a little to see our brother at peace."

"You are good men," Marla said. She allowed herself to be held by the Chief Mason.

They were gone for over a week.

The clay had changed little over the last hundred years. The statues circled the town, staring in, watching the people. Her husband was part of the third row. He stood in front of a child, dead twenty years. The widow's mother was the clay-maker then.

The fresh young widow went to him at night, when all others were asleep.

She fell to her knees, weeping. Then she took a small hammer from her backpack.

She tapped hard at his belly, and the clay cracked. A sighing sound emerged. She lifted out the pieces and reached inside.

A baby girl was in there, gasping for air. She cried with a dry throat. The widow lifted her out and wiped clay dust from her face. Cleared her nostrils. The widow tucked her into the folds of her skirt.

Then she reached into her backpack and pulled out things to fill the clay case with; a dead cat, a sack of flour, some stones. She sealed the case again with new, wet clay.

Then she bundled the baby up and took her home, walking over the rough ground. There was the smell of paint in the air. The ground was green, freshly painted for the newly arrived batch of tourists. The ground was too full of clay for grass to grow. Visitors were advised to bring their own drinking water. The stuff in the town was so full of clay you needed to be born to it or your insides would clog up and you'd be constipated for a week. Washing water was the same; showers were red tinged and gritty. A good rough facial scrub people paid good money for elsewhere.

Marla washed her baby in warm, soapy water and placed the baby into a cardboard box for a bed. Then the grieving son from Baristone arrived.

"Are you busy?" he said. He was an idiot, thick-faced and stupid.

"I'm always busy. Always someone to attend to." She was desperate to lie down and sleep beside her baby.

"I promised my mother I would do this," he said. "She died at the wall. Once she'd seen it. She died right there. I wish we had come sooner. You all look so youthful here. Glowing."

"You should never promise anything which relies on other people."

He hung his head.

"Come with me to collect the clay then. You're lucky; no locals are waiting. My husband is in the wall, now."

"I'm sorry for your loss," he said.

"Not sorry enough to leave me alone."

Marla strapped her baby onto her back. There was a growing hubbub as she walked, "She's had the baby, there's the baby, when did she have the baby?" Her mother had told her not to worry about deception and to forget about trying to fool the people into believing the child had been born naturally. It was part of the mystique of the Clay-Makers. Let the people guess at the process. Let it add to their respect of the Clay-Makers.

She took some of the children with her to search for the clay. It was an adventure for them, outside the walls, and she could send them out clay-hunting on their own, once they knew how.

"We look near river beds, even ones no longer running. Look for puddles; clay holds water so water is an indicator."

One of the children shouted, "Here?" Marla walked over. It was gritty there, and pale. Not perfect, but she saved the best stuff for the locals. This stuff would do for the woman. "Good," she said. She scrabbled with her fingers until she had a palm-sized lump.

"To test it, we roll it into a coil and tie a knot in it. This is good clay—no cracks or breaks when we tie it. Not too much sand or gravel. Well done!" The child blushed with pleasure and the others rushed to impress, too, digging hard and vying to carry the most clay.

They took it back to her workshop. "I will need to prepare the clay," Marla said to the son. "Come back tomorrow."

He was there at dawn.

Marla was awake. "What have you brought to add?" she asked.

The son had a small paper bag. "Some of my father's ashes. A clip of my baby hair. And this is a scrap of material from my sister's wedding dress."

She nodded. "That's good. That's nice. All right. You sit over there. This will take some time."

He sat in the comfy chair while the widow kneeled on the floor and stripped the mother naked. She washed the old woman carefully, treating her as she had her own husband.

The water left a fine sheen of clay on the woman's skin.

The widow mixed the clay with the things the son had given her, kneading, squeezing, squelching.

She layered the woman, took care with her face. She scraped the clay off her fingers into the little opaque pots lined up on her bench. When she had filled twenty and the son had gone out for air, she called out, "Connie! Connie! Some pots!" Connie was still nervous in the workshop. It was so new to her. The Chief Mason had ensured there was no time Marla was alone; he moved Connie in the moment Brin died. "It's all right. Come in. Wipe the pots clean then get them ready for boxing."

While Marla worked, Connie cleaned the pots, found their lids, put stickers on them.

"Is it really magical cream?" Connie said. She rubbed clay between her fingertips.

"They say so. Glowing reports from the women who use it. They pay a fortune for it."

"My dad says we should start a factory and make heaps more," Connie said, packing the pots into a small box. "He says we'll all be rich if we sell more."

"We're rich enough," Marla said. She scraped her fingers off into the next pot. "It's the rare nature of it that makes it worthwhile. You tell your Dad to not be so greedy, like a pig in the mud."

Connie giggled.

Marla worked the clay gently around the woman's face, smoothing the large pores, filling the nostrils. Then the smell of something cooking made her stomach rumble.

"Brin? What are you cooking?" Marla said, and she jumped up, wiped her hands and walked to the kitchen. She pushed open the door, smiling.

Connie stood at the bench, chopping vegetables. She said, "I found a recipe book, and I'm making something from it. It looks very nice." Marla stared at her. For a moment, just a moment, she had forgotten. Just for a moment, Brin was alive again. Marla sat down and cried.

"I can make something else, if you like," Connie said. Suddenly she seemed too wise to be so young. Her eyes filled with tears. "I miss him," she said. "I'm sorry Marla, but I miss him. He made us all laugh so."

"You more than most, I think, Connie. That's one reason you were chosen to be my cook. My helper. You were a good choice to take his place."

"Some of the younger men thought it might be them."

Marla smiled. The thought stopped her tears. "I'm not ready for a new husband yet. Not nearly ready."

"Oh, no, nothing like that," Connie said, blushing.

"But we know what proximity does, don't we, Connie?"

Connie shook her head. "No, Marla."

"No. It's alright, cook what you were cooking, Connie. Eating his food is a good idea." Brin's food was always grainy, gritty. Three weeks of dinners. Twenty-one meals he cooked for her.

The son slept, to her relief. His gaze was very intense. Her child slept, too, growing so quickly she wondered the son didn't run in fright.

Connie whispered at the door, "Are you okay? I'm sorry about the recipe book."

Marla smiled. "Come in, Connie. It's okay. It just made me think of him."

Connie hugged her. "We have an order for four dozen jars."

Marla nodded. "Good. I'll do the rest this afternoon."

"Payment in advance," Connie said. "We've got lots of goodies arriving soon. A feast is planned."

"Bring me a plate," Marla said. "I'm not quite up to celebrations yet."

"No. I'm sorry. It's not a celebration, really. A welcome back for the men returned."

Three masons came to her workshop. "We have the tourist who killed your husband," the youngest mason said. It was not until he spoke she realized who he was. The men had aged dramatically. Far more than she had envisioned.

Marla felt a chill. "You have made a great sacrifice in leaving the walls of our town," she said. "Thank you. I have a woman here ready for the Kiln. Can you keep him till she's done?"

"Yes. We'll keep him."

They took the woman from Baristone to the Kiln.

"There's so much waiting," the son said.

"This gives us time to say goodbye," Marla said. "We can't rush it. You can eat now. Join the celebration while you wait." She led him to where the others had gathered in the Chief Mason's house. Connie paid the delivery man, who brought the food, wine, clothing, all the things ordered for the celebration. He arrived with his smell of the city, his big, loud truck and his air of superiority. He took the money and said, "I know you must like it here, and it brings in the tourists, but those statues give me the creeps."

"Is anywhere else better?" Connie asked.

When the old woman was done, Marla led the son to the wall, the procession following behind them. The son coughed, his throat dry from the clay dust. "How do you breathe with all this dust?" he said.

"We get used to it," Marla said, though she wondered as she spoke if it was normal to feel the air in your lungs, to be aware of the tight filling of the chest with every inhalation.

Maybe other people didn't feel that.

The son said, "Oh, my god, all those faces staring at us. It feels like they're watching everything. Who was the first one covered? How did it start?"

"Many hundreds of years ago, one of the great men of the town disappeared. It was thought he'd left for the city but there was no word. Three years later, when it hadn't rained for most of that time, someone noticed a clay face in the dry creek bed.

"They dug it up. It was our missing man. Set solid.

"No one wanted to crack him open and nobody wanted to bury him like that, so while they decided they placed him upright on the town's limits. Already strange statues stood there, placed before local memory began. A woman died before they decided what to do. Her husband said she was just as important, so he had her covered in clay and set beside the man. They clayed the cracks to keep the statues standing, then an old man died, then a child, and already the wall was emerging."

She left the son trailing his fingers across his mother's face in the wall and went home to her baby.

They brought her the killer. Every centimetre was bruised or cut. His hair was all pulled out; his cheekbones shattered; his genitals cut and scabby; his shoulderbone exposed and his ears sliced to the skull.

They stood there silently, all of them, presenting her with their great gift. The man could not stand. He whispered, "Help me."

Marla bent to him and stroked his hair back from his forehead. She looked into his face and said, "Take him to the Kiln." The masons nodded.

It took five days for the man to die. After the third day all they could hear was a scrabbling noise, like a mouse trying to break through into a food cupboard.

The masons carried him to Marla.

"Thank you," she said. "Would anyone like to stay to honour this man into the clay?" They all backed away.

She stripped him naked. He was blackened. His fingers, the ones that held the knife that killed her husband, were all broken.

She didn't wash him clean. She walked outside the wall, through the gateway made of brick. It was her wall, her family's wall. They had made it. And she was so proud of it. It was raining a little and tears ran from the eyes of the clay people. Rain pooled like piss at their feet. But the clay stayed firm. The mix of cement, gravel and a little fatty soap kept it strong.

Her buckets were light as she walked past the wall. The flowers in their pots were blooming, sending their perfume to her like a generous gift from a stranger.

She swung the buckets. She couldn't help it. Her step bounced, lifted by the warm air like a balloon. She started to skip, the exuberance of the day filling her with lightness.

She passed the masons, resting on this day with nothing to do but repairs. The people believed the wall kept them safe from all evil. And there had never been a calamity. Evil still occurred but it was blamed on external things, or a crack in the wall.

They were always finding cracks in the wall.

"Good to see you looking happy," the Chief Mason said. "You're like a young girl, bouncing along like that."

"She is a young girl," the oldest mason said. He was a friend of her father's. "A young girl with heavy responsibilities." She looked at him to see if he was serving her notice to behave, but he was smiling. "It's good to see you happy," he said. "Here, have some cheese. It's a good one. Imported."

She sat and ate the cheese with them, laughing at their teasing. It felt good to be teased, to laugh.

There was good rich clay around the sewerage plant. She never used it because it stank. It reeked of waste, and she would never use it for good people. She collected three bucketsful for the murderer. The smell made her retch. She carried the buckets back with her nose pressed against her shoulder.

In all her career, she had never been disrespectful.

Marla added nothing to the clay. He didn't even deserve her piss. She didn't prepare the clay as she usually did. Let the small rocks dent his flesh. Let the sticks scratch at him. The baby had awoken and sat up, watching her. They grow so fast, she thought. She gave the baby a piece of good clay, not the foul stuff she was using on the murderer.

The baby ate it. The widow laughed, tears coming. "Funny baby," she said, but the sight of it brought the taste of clay to her mouth, and she thought of her clay husband's kiss.

Marla's mouth felt so dry she could barely close it. Water quenched her thirst, but she had a sudden, intense desire for strawberries. She washed her hands and carried the baby over to the farming district. Here, they carted in dirt from outside, fertile dirt, rich and loamy. They piled it into large flat boxes, like giant's bed bases, and they raised these off the ground, as if the clay would suck out all the nutrients like leeches do.

Beautiful things grew there, tended by talented farmers. Greens, reds, oranges, food which nourished you even by looking at it. Here they kept the clay wetted down, not wanting dust to land on the produce. Things seemed more in focus.

"Marla, Marla, my dear girl. My poor dear, darling, little girl." The farmer held her in a bear hug from which she struggled to be released. The baby squirmed between them.

"No woman should be a widow so young," he said. "It's wrong. It's against nature."

"It is," she said. His sympathy made her cry, and she was caught up again in the bear hug.

"What will make you feel better? Anything. It's yours."

"Just some strawberries," she said. "Do you have any?"

He winked. "Wait'll you see them." He plucked a dozen, deep, dark red, dripping with juice.

She sunk her teeth in, unable to wait. The sweetness brought a bitter thought. Brin. Brin loved strawberries. He would have loved these. The baby clutched at her and Marla fed her a strawberry. The baby cooed in delight.

Back in the workshop, she gave the baby another piece of clay. The baby squeezed it, gurgled, played with it happily. She was already sitting up, getting ready to crawl. Marla thought of her own easy tiredness, her deep weariness, and wondered if this rapid growth did not leave time to build endurance.

She covered the killer with one layer. Then another. She built feet where his head was, a leering idiot face at the feet. Let him spend forever on his head.

If it should be these clay people were resurrected, she liked the idea of him heading down into the dirt.

She called to the mason waiting outside, "He's done."

The mason came in, wrinkling his nose. Politely, he said nothing. Marla laughed. "It's not me, you idiot. I used the sewerage clay for him."

The mason smiled. Marla didn't tell him the killer was upside down in his casing. They took the case to the Kiln and when he was done, the Chief Mason called the mourners.

This was a very different procession. There were jeers and snarls, no tears. There was laughter and chatter.

He was placed in the wall beside the woman from Baristone. "Good he's not next to my son," Marla's mother-in-law said. "Curse you on your clay walk."

There was a celebration afterwards, wine and beer, food and laughter. It was always like this after a procession, even a devastating one. Marla's mother said, "There is a certain satisfaction in what we do. It's like we have settled the answer of death. We've got it sorted out. It's comforting." People stopped to listen and Marla wondered if people would ever listen to her in the same way.

"But will it really happen?" Connie said. "The Great Clay Walk? The Resurrection?"

"It will be many generations away. You will all be safely in the wall, and many more beyond," Marla's mother said.

Connie shivered. "I don't know that I want to be awoken. It sounds terrifying."

Marla's mother smiled. "Frightening, yes. But for the chance at eternal life?"

"Here's to the Great Clay Walk," shouted the Chief Mason. "And here's to the clay, and the great Clay-Makers."

Marla watched them all, the clay dust in their pores, broad smiles on their faces, and she wondered which of them would be able to break free from their clay case on the day of the Great Clay Walk.

Coalescence

Coalescence

Schizo Blogger knew his hair smelt bad but was proud of it. He could sit on its tip and feel it tickle his balls if he was naked.

He made an entry into his weblog and read some of the comments. He felt itchy and irritable but didn't want a shower yet, not until he'd responded to the remaining posts.

Most of the comments on his blog were unreadable, crazy stuff no one should have to look at. He'd always attracted the crazies, right from school when it was like a nose-pickers' convention around him.

So many needy people, wanting free diagnoses. Wanting him to say, "Yes, you've got schizo whatever. You're one of us, now."

They never wrote in if they didn't want to be schizo.

Schizo Blogger had a test, though. There was a certain phrase, beyond, "I hear voices." It was when they said, "The voices said to me," as if stating a fact. That was when he knew he had one. He worked unconventionally, Schizo Blogger. He was effective, though, his bosses knew that. And discreet; no word of the selection process got out. There were fakers enough as it was.

He'd never heard the voices himself, though he'd admit to anyone a touch of paranoia. A certain degree of paranoia was sensible, especially with the bosses he had, the website he ran. They were smart, most of his readers, smart enough to track him down, but he knew that they all struggled with the everyday and wouldn't have the business to make anything nasty happen to him.

A comment flashed in from Ryder 49er, a shy communicator who only popped up once a month or so. Schizo Blogger thought it was probably a lunar thing and made a note to ask the questions which would identify Ryder as a suitable candidate.

"I had another episode," Ryder entered. "On the bus. I had to get off before my stop because the floor was turning to hot tar and no one did anything. Their mouths were shut but I could hear their thoughts and they were praying for me to sink. "Oh please god let him die before my eyes," that kind of thing. I don't know if you're listening today but that's what happened to me."

Schizo Blogger noted the phrasing and returned "Yeah, I'm here. Where else would I be?" and he added a little jumping devil emoticon.

Nudie jumped in: "So how'd you get home? If you had to get off the bus?"

"I had to walk. My feet are killing me. And it was bad outside, too. It was like all the footpaths were talking, saying all kinds of mean things. Told me I was rotting from the ground up."

Being the system administrator had its perks. You couldn't get kicked off the forum for overstepping the boundaries, for one. "Look, Ryder, some of this stuff I know a great guy who can help. I can't give out his details on this forum but send me an email and I'll get them to you."

This was the next step and Schizo Blogger relied on instinct and a little detective work to get to it.

His stomach rumbled and he realised he hadn't eaten in about fifteen hours. It was dark in the room; the rest of them lived similarly, taking control of their own body clocks by shutting out the sun.

He had nothing in his cupboard, not even a pack of self-cooking noodles, usually a last resort food choice.

He was suddenly, ravenously hungry. It worked this way sometimes; he didn't heed the warning signs so his body starved and dehydrated. He tried to drink amino drinks, keep the levels up, but he didn't always think of it.

He tapped into his supermarket's site and ordered his usual shopping. He put a rush on it, and he always tipped well, so the food would arrive soon.

Schizo Blogger entered, "Sorry folks, offline for me for a while." and he logged off. His skin felt thick and his eyebrows heavy, a sure sign he hadn't bathed in a while.

He sniffed around the room until he found a towel which was fairly clean and almost dry. The bathroom was a shared one on this floor, and Schizo Blogger tried to time it so he didn't see anyone.

Nudie threw his door open as Schizo Blogger walked past. "I knew it!" he said. "I knew you'd be going out. You always say downtime when you go out!"

"I'm just going to the bathroom, Nudie. I need a wash."

Schizo Blogger had broken two rules with Nudie. He'd agreed to a meeting, when he rarely had personal contact with the people in his forum. Then Nudie had begged homeless and Schizo Blogger had stupidly got him onto the house manager. So there he was, always ready to harass.

"A wash, hey? Bath?" Nudie was always thanking him, always thanking him. Nudie's hair was wild, curly, full of twigs and lumpy brown bits of food.

"Nudie, you've moved up the list. Don't thank me."

"What number? What number am I now?"

Schizo Blogger rubbed his eyes. "Nudie, I need to wash, then eat. Then I'll be able to think. All right? You've moved up, that's all."

"We'll talk to you while you have a bath," Nudie said. Schizo Blogger smiled. The 'we' was one of the indicators. The absolute acceptance of the other voice.

Schizo Blogger felt bathed in Nudie's adoration and enjoyed it more than he thought he should.

"I'll knock on your door when I've eaten something. Okay? But wrap a towel around at least."

Nudie lived amongst piles of clothes. Stacks to the ceiling in some places. All of it dirty, mouldering. He dreamed of a home with a huge laundry room and plenty of cupboards to hang the clean clothes up. Nudie twitched his lips sporadically, shook his mass of curls. Bits flew off the hair. Schizo Blogger wondered briefly if they'd be able to use that hair, once they shaved it off for the surgery. How many criteria was he supposed to match, anyway? The hair thing was just a side-bar, a bonus. They couldn't go after him for a bad hair job, could they? Sack him? They could have his hair if it came to that. Shave him off baldy weirdo...

Schizo Blogger shuddered. Sometimes he felt that being around people who were fully paranoid rubbed off on him.

"There's three VIPs died this week, maybe four," Nudie said. He fanned out some printouts he'd got off the world net news; deaths. "And probably more, because I'm sure some on the list don't rate a mention but they're still worthy in their own way." Nudie's ear twitched as if someone was whispering too close.

"See, there's this naturalist guy. He gets bitten by a snake, where'd he find it but doesn't matter. He's got a family. I could help with that. And the race car guy, died in a crash. You could be brave, if you were him. And the other guy, did a hundred or something books. Smart. I'd like to share smart."

"Nudie, I've told you the process. When you've moved near the top they'll pick you up. It's all very organised. You get a pension for waiting close by, cos they want you ready to go when they need you. Four hours. You have four hours after the person dies, then it's too late. So you have to stay close to the Coalescence Hospital. You won't know whose lobes you've got till you wake up. But they're all good people. I'd kill to be on the VIP list."

Schizo Blogger wondered if it was naive to fantasise about being placed on the VIP list because of the work he did for them. It wasn't completely illogical. Some teachers made the list, and plenty of artists. Designers. Not all of them wanted to be there. There was one biologist who'd written in his suicide note "Not to be lobotomised under any circumstances," but it wasn't up to him, was it? His lobes belonged to the people once he died; he had no rights.

The VIP list was about life eternal and preservation of brilliance. But the host list would do; it was easy to imagine what it would be like, to have another voice in your head. He knew a lot about how the brain worked, from the people who played on his forum. But these voices were different; strong, powerful, intelligent and verifiably superior to their hosts. They were expected to drive the body and, though this was unsaid publicly, at some stage take over all together.

Nudie rolled a chart onto the table and pointed with a dirty finger. "You see? These people are old, these people are sick. These people are prone to suicide, they've got the risk factors. They'll make the list move along. But it's these ones." He stabbed his finger at a long clump of names. "These ones are holding the list up."

"Yeah, Nudie, you've done well. But I need to get back."

"More recruits? Do they go ahead of me?"

"Your spot is your spot. Don't worry about it."

"Let us know where we are on the host list," Nudie said, waving his papers. "We want to be ready."

A number of world leaders already sat in host bodies. It was thought to be an added benefit, that decisions could be made with two opinions. Yet sometimes hard decisions needed to be made, and these could only be made with prejudice.

One of Schizo Blogger's clients, who'd called himself Lost, used to join in the talk on the newsgroup with a snivelling whiny worm-eating voice which annoyed them all with its self-pity. They weren't allowed to say, "Go fuck yourself" or anything like that. They'd say, "I hear you, brother," and "You are amongst friends," but he wasn't.

Lost made it onto the host list early in Schizo Blogger 's career. He was still a whiny, self-pitying whinger, but now he had the world stage. For the first couple of years after the death of his VIP's body, he struggled to gain any respect at all. As more important people died, though, and more young hosts stepped in, hosts grew in stature.

When the New Zealand Prime Minister died, he was the highest level VIP to seek coalescence. This one bothered a lot of people because he was a morally empty man by most standards. Foreign aid bought his shoes and penile implants while around him children sucked lozenges of drug residue. When he sickened at last there was quiet joy. His grip would be released and the country could find a new leader, one of the modern kind who understood the value of public relations and negotiations.

That was one of Schizo Blogger's early successes, and he hadn't gotten it wrong, yet. He could suss the fakers, and knew the ones who couldn't do the job right.

Ryder had sent five messages to Schizo Blogger's personal email and posted three times to the forum. A massive escalation. Some of the others were talking with him; they all took it very seriously. He'd told them he couldn't remember logging on, he just found himself there. And that he didn't know if he'd been on the forum before, and had lost memory of the day before. They loved to give advice, to help. There were rules on the forum; they could never talk like the voices were real. Voices were delusions, they didn't exist. They were pretend friends or imaginary enemies, but they were not real. In the context of the forum, Schizo Blogger knew from dealing with them off list that many of them didn't believe in delusions. The voices were real. And who was Schizo Blogger to say they weren't?

He answered Ryder in his usual way, though he felt a little bored by the procedure. He was too good at it now, that was the problem.

There were no challenges left to him.

Nudie was taken three weeks later. He came to say goodbye, though his escorts were impatient for him to leave.

"I'll come back, so you'll know who I am, I promise," he said.

Ryder sent through another three messages, each one more distressed than the last.

"There's someone at the window," he said.

"A visitor?"

"I'm on the fourth floor. Is it a ghost? Do ghosts visit? My mother died without saying goodbye. Her last words were, 'Get me some sugar when you're at the shops.' When I got back she was dead, you knew that already. Sorry to repeat myself. Is it her trying to say sorry? Because I can hear a whistling noise like someone tyring to get my attention. And I've got a weird taste in my mouth. Like peppermint cough medicine or something, but I haven't got a cough."

Ryder became more strident in his postings. Schizo Blogger distrusted him; he was too much. Most schizos are so paranoid they never force themselves on you. They mostly ended their posts with "Sorry for boring you. Don't read any more if it's too bad."

Ryder had moved from that to "and then this happened, isn't that weird? Then this crazy thing. And my dead mother rose from the dead to talk to me, and all she said was have sex with your sister. Should I? Have sex with my sister? Is it something ghosts tell you?"

Off list, Schizo Blogger arranged for a meeting with Ryder. Breaking the rules again, but if someone was playing with him, he wanted to figure out how to beat them. He had to know Ryder to figure him out.

Schizo Blogger pulled on some pants then, as an afterthought, tapped out a quick response to Ryder. Some of them got paranoid if you didn't answer straight away.

He pulled on a shirt. He wouldn't know how dirty it was till he got out into the fresher air. His room was filled with his own old smell, familiar to him, plus the dust burning on his equipment and that subtle smell of electricity burning down the wires.

He grabbed his bag and walked outside.

It had been a long time. Months. His last meet had been with a host who now sat on the Board of Education.

It was all familiar, though. There were the reality cameras, set up around the city in public places and you could just click on one and watch from your own room. So the street corner and the people who walked by it were familiar. So was the door to the drinking place (no cameras inside) where you saw them go in sober and come out falling all over the place forgetful of the cameras. He saw two people having sex once, right in the bushes. The girl bent over holding her ankles, the man staring off into the distance. The girl puked halfway through; who wouldn't at that angle? But the man didn't notice. He just kept going.

Schizo Blogger walked the streets, very conscious of the cameras. He wondered if anyone watching wanted him, if they'd fantasise him naked and strong. Or ruling the world.

A young man, very young, with a shaved head, had people staring at him. The brown plug at his temple meant he was newly coalesced.

The stiff-arsed walk gave him away too, like he needed to find a toilet and didn't realise it. Children do it when they're too busy playing; tuck their buttocks in as if to shut the door. The newly coalesced do it, while they're getting used to being operated by two brains.

He stood in the pathway, making people walk around them. He had his hand out, as if begging, but he shook his head to coins.

"Dad! Leave people alone." The woman was over fifty. And she'd done it hard. She didn't smile at Schizo Blogger, and her face was frown-lines. No laughter for her. "Come on, Dad, or I'll leave you on your own."

His fingers clenched slightly and Schizo Blogger could see the age in them then.

"You'll be all right," Schizo Blogger said.

"We sleep in the same bed," he said, blinking. "She calls me Daddy."

"That's not pleasant." Schizo Blogger looked at her, wondering why a woman of her age would want a young lover. Wasn't she tired? Or was she one of those people who sucked the energy out of those around her, thrived on making them tired?

On reality camera, Schizo Blogger had watched pilgrims enter the Salon with hair down to their arses and come out bald, weeping with the great sacrifice. He didn't believe in all that himself, but he admired the concept of sacrifice. You were looked after, when you'd given your hair. Because you were weaker, they believed. You lost your strength. You couldn't cut it yourself and expect respect, though. There was a special chemical branding they did to your bald scalp. Schizo Blogger had seen people with four of five of these scars on their heads.

These sacrifices mimicked the true sacrifice of the hosts.

There were protestors out the front, too, calling the act of hair cutting selfish, self-serving and against God.

Ryder waited for him at a sock bar. You left your shoes at the door, theory being no one's aggressive without shoes.

Ryder had tried to conceal what he was. He wore a torn t-shirt, pants too tight, a foul multicoloured jacket. But his hair was washed. It was messy, but not messy enough to hide the neat edges to it. And it smelt of pineapple, something high class. This man was a VIP or a VIP's aide.

"Schizo Blogger! I knew you'd look like that!" Schizo Blogger had piled his hair into a bun. It threw people, made him look like he had short hair, just for a minute.

Ryder ordered drinks, another mistake. Schizos don't take charge. They let others order. Even three schizos together; no one orders, they all wait wait wait, getting more and more freaked out until one of them flips, throws the table. Or one of the voices makes the order, which is better. At least that way they get a drink.

Ryder ordered scotch and yeah, fine. No rules there. It was good scotch. Schizo Blogger threw his down, letting it numb his temples.

"Another?" Ryder asked.

Schizo Blogger nodded. "You don't talk so much in person."

Ryder swallowed his drink. "I'm shy in person. When you can see me. But my voice says I need to get out. Drink more. Meet people. Thanks for meeting with me. Do you like it here?"

Schizo Blogger didn't answer. A schizo, they'd start to fidget if you didn't answer. Thoughts of 'did he answer and I didn't hear him? What did he say? Did he ask me a question?"

There were no fidgets from Ryder. Schizo Blogger ordered more scotch. Ryder slipped a tiny pill into his mouth between each drink.

Schizo Blogger let him think he was getting away with the sober pill business. Ryder thought Schizo Blogger was a schizo with no cognitive powers. That was an ace.

"So have you put me on the list? You should. Look at me. I'm fit. Pretty strong."

"What about the scotch? They don't like alcoholic bodies."

"Hey, I'm no alcoholic. Social drinker, you know?"

"The thing is, it's not so much the body. It's the ability up here." Schizo Blogger tapped his temple. "You know? Understanding the voice, accepting the voice. Listening. And letting it rule. That's it. A lot of people, their own ego is so strong they ignore the voice. That's not what you want on the host list. You want someone who'll obey. They'll be taking on the personality..."

"The soul."

"Whatever. Soul, personality, whatever."

Ryder shifted on his stool. "But some of them would like particular body types, right? Male or female. Tall, short. Whatever. I reckon some of the uglies wouldn't mind a beautiful body."

Schizo Blogger mentally ran through Nudie's VIP list. So it was someone ugly. Someone egotistical. Could be any one of a dozen.

"You were clever," Schizo Blogger said, tired of playing. He wanted to go home, check his forum, maybe even play schizo for a while. "You almost got me."

"Got you how?" Ryder said, but he blinked too fast.

"There were too many symptoms, gave you away. Rushing them all at the end like that, trying to convince me."

Ryder swallowed another scotch. He forgot his sober pill.

"Who's your boss?" Schizo Blogger asked.

Ryder shook his head. "No boss. That's my problem. Can't hold a job. Can any of us? Hold a job? I get sacked all the time."

"And yet your hair smells like pineapple and you can focus on me without your eyes flicking around the room. You don't check behind your back every few minutes, either."

"That's all details. I am what I am."

"Details are where it works, friend. That's how they're chosen. But it doesn't bother me. If there's money in it, stock, product, whatever, I can help your bloke get the body he wants."

Schizo Blogger did not have that power; he made recommendations for the host list, but that's where it ended.

"What sort of money?"

"I don't know, yet. I'd like to know who he is before I decide price."

"For a virtual shut-in schizo, you're pretty smart."

Schizo Blogger didn't disillusion him. "If you take me to him, we'll sort something out. We can talk about what sort of body he'd like to coalesce with, take it from there."

"I guess that's all right." Ryder hated losing the position of power, that was obvious.

"Let's have one more. Then I need to go shut myself in again."

Ryder smiled.

Schizo Blogger knew how easy it was to play people like him. Play the ego, let them think they were smart, and you won.

A week later, there was a strange knock on the door. A tapping of fingers, like someone rolling all their digits across the door.

"It's me, SB."

Nudie.

"I made it!" Nudie wiggled his fingers in Schizo Blogger's face. "I'm a pianist. He got mauled by dogs. I'm a great pianist." He moved jerkily, still not in control of his limbs. He was dressed in a beautiful pale wool suit and his shoes shone.

"Good on you, mate."

"I came back for some of my clothes, but they don't seem so important now I've seen them again. You take what you want. They're going to let my room to someone else. I've got a house now. With built in cupboards. And someone else does the washing. You get everything, you know. The lot."

"You keep in touch, Nudie."

"It's Jonathon. I decided to take his name."

"Jonathon."

It was two months before Ryder arranged the meeting with his VIP. They met at the sock bar and drove past the old museum, overflowing now with children. The hair in there was rarely oiled; they didn't even have access to a car for the motor oil. Rumour was they used jelly to stiffen their hair, make it shine.

Schizo Blogger had heard there were plans to have lobes implanted at birth, so the skull grows over. But it didn't make sense to him; you couldn't be sure who you were implanting in.

The VIP lived in an old boathouse. Just him there, with his servants. The walls were velvety, padded. Schizo Blogger ran his finger along one stretch but it felt sticky, unpleasant, so he pulled his hand away.

There were soft rugs on the floor and Schizo Blogger imagined his schizo mates loving that, lying on the floor staring at the intricate patterns.

Ryder came to meet him. "He's waiting."

"I'm not late."

"He's been waiting for days. Come on. There's scotch in here, and food."

The room they entered buzzed with screens; reality cameras from around the city. A wall of screens and decks, all the worldwide access you could ever need. Movies daily if there were enough released.

Schizo Blogger recognised some scenes but others were places he didn't know.

"He's got access to every reality camera in the city."

"I thought we all did."

Ryder shook his head. "You see about 75% of the cameras. It's the other 25% which get interesting.

Schizo Blogger stepped closer. "This is beautiful."

"Most VIPs have this access. One of the perks."

The VIP rolled into the room. It wasn't quite a wheel chair, more a little cart with a seat. He looked small in it and Schizo Blogger wondered if he had shrunk will illness and old age or if he'd always been this size.

"A handsome man in my home, welcome," he said. His hair was tied into two long tails and coiled on his lap. It smelt of spices.

He reached out his hand and Schizo Blogger shook it. The old man's hand was weak and floppy.

"Very strong, too. Take a seat, friend. I know you're busy and need to get back to your life."

Schizo Blogger found the charm very shallow. The man was trying to sell himself as a nice person, but Schizo Blogger had done some research. It was not a particularly nice history.

"You understand I can't do anything officially about getting you the body you want."

"I've never bothered with the so-called 'official' There are ways to avoid the 'official'." The VIP nodded at Schizo Blogger, encouraging him to speak. But the twitch of the man's lips, the way his eyes flicked, made it clear he knew nothing at all about illegal procedures, and that he was hoping Schizo Blogger would provide that information.

"I'm always within the law. It's a good place to be. They call it doublemurder, you go outside the law."

"There will be reward. I'll ensure my interim will mentions you generously. As well as my host, of course." The man smiled.

"I could ask some extra questions, find a list of those right for you. Give that list to those who make the decision. They like anything which saves them work."

"I wouldn't ask for more than that." Though of course he would ask for Schizo Blogger's life if that got him what he wanted.

"So you're on the list, Ryder? The VIP list I mean. Not the other."

"I'm not sure. They said they'd put me on."

They walked the hallway to reach the front door.

"No more posting, Ryder. I haven't got time to deal with your fake crap."

"Sorry. It was the only way I could get in."

Ryder was not on the VIP list Nudie compiled and Schizo Blogger realised then that if Ryder didn't make the list, if Ryder was allowed to die without his lobes being transplanted, then there was no way he would ever be a VIP. He could have a VIPs life, though. If he became a host.

On the way home, Schizo Blogger remembered the small junk shop he'd seen on reality camera. Never bothered much with it, because the people in out were nasty, covered with skin, baggy clothes, and they carried dull bundles in out.

One thing of interest though; computers. He'd seen them and thought, "They can't trace a computer like that. It's rubbish."

Schizo Blogger shifted the forum when he got back. Informed all the genuines and shifted it.

He took his new old computer down to the basement where he could more easily post anonymously. It stank down there. There were stacks of long forgotten books, their plastic protective covers beginning to crumble, their pages thick and yellow. They were good for burning but not much else.

He set himself up a new account, with a new identity. He knew what to say to get their attention.

He logged on to his own forum, posted some good stuff.

Then went upstairs and answered himself.

It took a while to make it onto the host list. He didn't want to rush it, so added his fake name after two months, but with a query. A month later, he removed the query and his bosses accepted the recommendation.

He'd been monitoring another group for some time, out of morbid curiosity and a guilty sense of tribe. He couldn't read too many of their posts without feeling ill, but he made sure to post periodically so they'd let him keep reading. He called himself Nervous Newbie, and they tried to convince him that what they did was easy. Worthwhile. There were at least 40 active members on the newsgroup, which meant dozens more who never posted. Once he'd been notified that he was on the Host list, Schizo Blogger gave them the VIP list he'd taken from Nudie. Names, addresses. Only the old, the sick and the suicidal, though. The ones whom death would help. He told the newsgroup, "Feel free," and that's all the encouragement they needed.

Mason claimed the first kill. Jonesy the second. Ryder and his VIP were killed seventh and eighth, though all 92 kills happened in a day.

Mason said, "I did a dawn jobby. I think better then. And their blood is thinner, when they've been sleeping, so it spreads further. One little slice and you'll cover the bathroom floor, easy. Slippery though."

Anonymous managed Ryder and his VIP. "Two at a time. I like it two at a time. They had a wall of screens there, weren't even watching them didn't notice me and they didn't like it when they did see me."

Schizo Blogger received notification that he'd moved up the list. Coalescence News published the newly coalesced; the VIP was amongst them, having been implanted into one of the youngest host so far, a 14 year-old boy with early onset schizophrenia.

Schizo Blogger packed the few things he considered worthwhile into a bag. He left a note for the cleaners to keep all they found. He disposed of the computer in the basement.

When they came for him, he sat waiting with his bag in his lap.

"We're in a bit of a rush. Four hours, we've got. Time of death till the time the lobes fade. There's been another lot of slaughters, all from the VIP list. They're saying that someone leaked the list."

"Wonder who I'll get?"

"You'll find out soon enough. You'll be a hero, you know that? There's a movement to call you all heroes, not hosts."

Schizo Blogger knew they were flattering him to calm him, but he didn't mind. He felt like a hero, marching off to the Salon for his head shaving.

There were some religious groups at the front of the Salon, exhorting people to leave their hair, don't shave it. It's a sin to God to shave your hair.

"This one has to be shaved. He's a hero. He'll take a new soul in an hour or two," one of Schizo Blogger's escorts said.

"Our souls are not in our brains. You can't save a soul that way."

"Where the fuck are they, then? Ay? Stupid fucks. Don't see you saving the world, do I?"

The Salon was huge inside, walls of polished marble. It was once a law court, Schizo Blogger thought, all money spent on making it look grand. There were mounds of hair everywhere, all colours, and the smell of them together made him feel ill. All the oils, all the smells, the spices, the rancid stench of some of them.

Thick hair smelling of motor oil in a great fat plait. The poorer kids greased up their hands and rubbed their hair, hoping for the good shine of those who could afford banana oil. Motor oil attracted the dust, though, which stuck to the hair, turning it pale with fluff.

Dozens of barbers shaving a head every two minutes. It was fast. Most of those being shaved were not hosts. Most were devotees, giving their hair for the sake of their souls. Schizo Blogger was seated before a beautiful young girl, who twitched a small smile at him.

"You can do this?" he said.

"I'm coalesced. I'm the old barber who shaved heads for fifty years." She flipped the razor over his head.

A boy scooped up his hair as it fell, felt it with his fingers. "Treated hair? Dyed? Curled? Anything?"

"Nothing like that."

"It's good hair."

Schizo Blogger had heard rumours that they sold hair for profit, but it had never bothered him before now. To see the hair of his life, the tips of which came out of his skull when he was a young boy, being taken away, sold for the hair extensions of VIPs, was upsetting. "What if I want to keep my hair?" he asked his barber.

"You don't need the hair," she said. He felt a harsh burn in his scalp and knew he'd been branded. She pushed his shoulder. "Done."

He felt so very light. His head was cold; they gave him a hat to wear.

Then they took him away for surgery.

As he went under, he heard the surgeons talking. "Terrible, all these slaughters," one said.

"Yes, but have you heard? The coalesced remember being killed. They remember it! They're giving descriptions of their killers as we speak."

Cooling the Crows

Cooling the Crows

Geoff made two errors of judgment in his life, both in the middle of Winter. Three, if you count the ex-wife, but that wasn't life-threatening.

His first should have taught him, but it didn't.

He was cooling a place down South, a big nightclub with a clientele mostly underage and uneducated. Management wanted to go up market, start charging fifteen bucks for a beer, using glasses for the mixed drinks rather than plastic. That kind of thing. Maybe get a band in sometimes, have the kind of promotion which didn't involve 'chicks drink free'.

They called Geoff in later than he would have liked.

"Once there's an infestation, it's tougher to make a change," Geoff said. They were coming in from the suburbs, taxi loads of them, or they'd drive and make a mess of themselves on the way home. That's why Management finally made the call; three dead, and in the papers 'coming from the nightclub', naming them. Didn't look good.

"Do what you can. We want a re-launch in a month."

Geoff smiled. "You'll need to plan for a little longer than that. Unless you want the stragglers mixed in with your new crowd. Some of them take a while to figure it out. Some of them don't come every week, takes a while for the message to sink in. It's all

— 95 —

about getting the message out, making sure it reaches the right people."

In the end it was easier than he'd imagined. Once he'd told Management to raise the drink prices, and change the music, and send in some screaming queens to fuck in corners. Make it nasty for the suburban bigots to be there. They weren't a smart crowd, and were led by a dozen or so kids who looked good but were all about habit.

Other thing he did was to hand out flyers for a nightclub, other side of town. Give them a place to go, a new spot to go to. Make it seem like their choice.

It went very well, till right at the end. Management was pleased, gave him a bonus. Gave him lifetime free drinks as well, but you never drank at a place you've cooled. Just not on, not safe, don't do it.

The last few stragglers; they came late on a Saturday night. He hadn't seen any of them for a week; it'd been all the business types, drawn by the prospect of cocktails, guaranteed connections, guaranteed introductions at the door, single to single.

He had to use a modicum of force against some of them. One patron, come drunk from another pub, or a party, come thinking he'd find his mates. Geoff'd kicked him out three weeks running, tossing him out on his arse.

"All your mates left ages ago. They don't like this place anymore," Geoff said. He pointed up the road. Smiled. Hoped the guy'd piss off quietly, no fuss, but not really expecting that.

"You don't know my mates, arsehole. I'm going in. I've been coming here months, I'm a regular, you'll be sacked, arsehole." Words didn't bother Geoff at all; it was the elbow in the ribs as the guy tried to force his way in that pissed him off.

He raised his elbow quickly, catching the patron under the chin with a nasty crack. His head snapped back, and he was too drunk to fight the roll so he fell backwards off the step. Most people, that'd be enough. The drunk ones, nothing's enough. He came back at Geoff, fists up. Geoff, tired of it, didn't hold himself back. He laid the blows carefully but aggressively, until the guy bled and could no longer stand. He pointed up at the cross Geoff wore around his neck. "What're your wearing this for? You're a godbotherer? Your lot aren't supposed to beat the crap out of innocent people."

"We're all godbotherers, mate." Geoff didn't tell him he wore the cross to disarm people. Make them trust him, even if only for a second. Sometimes a second was all you needed.

"Fuck you, fuck off to church, go fuck a nun," and Geoff drew back, and, using the crown of his skull, split the man's cheek open like a ripe fruit.

"So they teach pub fighting in Sunday School, do they?"

Geoff turned to the voice. It was young, a woman, but that didn't mean anything. You don't let that fool you; women can carry knives, they can bust a bottle and cut up your face as well as men can.

Geoff looked at her, so skinny her legs could barely hold her up. Huge distended stomach, white and tattooed with small dark crosses.

"You reckon you're coming in here with a baby?" he said.

"Not a baby yet. Still my body." She sucked hard on a fat, hand rolled cigarette which stank of the bonfires his grandfather still made sometimes. Piles of crap in there, all the rubbish he didn't want to cart away. It made Geoff think of what he'd left behind, the pus-pile of a city full of rubbish, fires on every corner turning the sky black and covering your skin with a thin film of grit.

"I'm not letting you in," he said.

But the lack of judgment; he spent too long looking at the girls' stomach, her legs. His eyes stopped flicking, flicking, and from behind a great peck at his skull.

Knocked forward, he steadied himself on the girl's shoulder. She shrugged, trying to knock his hand off, but he squeezed tighter, feeling the collarbone and, in that split second, wanting to crack it clean between his fingers.

He ducked under his left arm, twisted into a crouch while pulling the knife from his belt.

She took the force of the second blow. Geoff knew then that his attacker's reflexes were slow and that gave him time to assess.

Tall. Muscle top (or 'mussell top', as Geoff had seen them sold as in the shops where these people came from). Dirty jeans. A long red scar across his nose; look at me. I'm tough.

The weapon was a hooked stick, long enough to cause harm from a distance, but unwieldy. Geoff wondered why they went fancy with their gear. The basics did just as well.

Geoff stepped up under his attacker's arm and cut the foolishly-revealed jugular.

His attacker fell to his knees, using his weapon to hold himself up.

Geoff felt the dizziness then, the great pain of his head wound. The other patrons had run away, not wanting trouble. All but the pregnant girl

Police sirens, now, one at least. Geoff was relieved. It would be good to sit down, just for a moment.

He felt something stroking the back of his head, probing the wound, and he twisted around to look, strangely calm.

It was a dog.

And the pregnant girl, lying in the gutter, laughed at him.

That's not right, he thought. Waited until he heard the ambulance siren so help for the baby was close, then took a brick and caught her a blow, right to the side of the head.

"She's pregnant," he shouted to the paramedics. "Pregnant! Save the baby!"

He didn't know if the baby was saved or not.

He liked to think so.

He didn't care what Management thought about the incident; his job was done, and what happened to him after that wasn't their business or concern. But he was ashamed to see his trainer, John.

"Your life, and the lives of those around, depends on how you react. You need to make the decision and stick to it. Stay or go? In or out? You can't change your mind. A cooler can never change his mind. Never oscillate."

Proud of the word, its three syllables, its clever meaning. "It's why women can't be coolers. They can be swayed. They listen to reason. You need to watch for the signs. No one else cares, do they? No one cares less about your feelings. What's on the inside.

"Yesterday, one of 'em got to you. It may well happen again. You'll see it 'their way' and you'll have thoughts about the Management.

"That happens, you come to me. Mid-shift. I mean it. You down tools, you come to me. Because if you make that connection, you're done for. You're finished as a cooler, and you won't be able to forget what you've done in the course of your job."

John passed Geoff a beer. "The good thing is, we've identified your weakness. You lost your judgment because of the baby.

Understandable, but unprofessional, right? You can't be swayed by anything. Right?"

"Right," Geoff said. And it was all good, after that.

All good till he was called in to cool the crows. Years in between the judgment calls, and the pregnant girls he saw in between didn't bother him. He didn't let them bother him; he knew his weakness.

Management at an isolated bar wanted the place back for the locals. The crows liked it because it had burnt close to the ground, people dead and their bones still there in the foundations.

The crows would come, driving through the ice with old cars on bald tyres.

"That's what we're talking about," Management said. "This whole death wish thing. It's not like they all make it here; two car loads, dead, spun off the road. Taking others with them, but that's a cause for celebration with this lot."

Management shook his head, as if he was saddened. "The locals can't come anymore. They're not happy. And unhappy locals are not pleasant locals."

Geoff made it a habit to keep the Management depersonalized as well as the group he was expected to cool. No ties, no connections, no bad decisions based on emotion.

He'd learnt that early on, in a bar in the Far North. Management wanted a small group out because they were underage, he reckoned, but after a hard night, the first night always was, Management confessed to fucking one of them and now she won't leave him alone.

Geoff liked working in winter less than other seasons. He didn't hate it; but it wasn't comfortable. In summer, if he wore cool, loose clothes and managed to stand under the eaves, find himself a bit of shade, he was fine. So long as they brought drinks out to him, kept him hydrated, fine. A lot of the job was outside, on the street, checking it out before it entered.

Forewarned.

He listened to them in the queue and inside, later, he'd walk up to one of them and say, "Your mum wants you to know the ring is in the bottom drawer."

And the girl'd freak out. You could see her shut down, shut all else out but that her dead mother had sent her a message.

"How do you know?" she'd say, not remembering ranting on about the lost ring to a friend in the queue, not remembering saying,

"I wish Mum was here. She would have known," and the tears in the eyes wiped away.

Amazing what they'd talk about in the queue.

But winter. Winter you're miserable out in it, your face is cold, your smile freezes on your face so people don't believe it any more. Your ankles ache and the boots you wear; too heavy. You wear more clothes and that makes you clumsy. Patrons are clumsier too, but you don't like the sense of being not quite in control. Your ears are cold. You don't feel like eating. You don't want a cool drink but you don't want a hot one.

Geoff hated winter.

In the cold, his scars shrank in, stretching the skin surrounding them to give him the look of someone with a bad face-lift. Constantly surprised. Granted, it helped to confuse the patrons, make them doubt his stance. But he didn't like it.

Geoff liked to joke that his scars throbbed when danger approached. "Early warning system. Don't always pay attention. They throbbed like hell when I met my ex-wife. Could've saved myself a world of pain, there."

He liked to joke about his ex-wife, but there was nothing funny about it. She said it was about the violence, the way he lived his life, but he never touched her. Never raised an arm at her, or hinted at it. It was just an excuse to cover the guilt she felt for being a crap wife.

She said, "You understand violence. That's the problem. You get why people hurt each other. You accept it into your life like other people accept Christianity. You've got a death wish, a death acceptance. You're certain you're going to die violently, and you just accept that."

"You can't fight fate," he told her.

"Fuck you," she said. He was never sure why that offended her quite so much.

Cooling the crows was a job he couldn't say no to. A challenge. Entrenched patrons Management wanted to cool, and they were an interesting type.

"They got weird fingernails, and they talk weird, like crows going farrrk farrrk," Management said. He winked at Geoff. Geoff hated winkers. They took on your answer for themselves. Assumed your yes without even asking you.

Geoff took a few days, checking them out first. In the meantime, he told Management, get those drink prices up. Sometimes that works, on its own.

Especially with a little bit of bouncing at the door. Second night in; three crows, waiting patiently, too lethargic to fight. The locals stood aside, not wanting to enter.

The smell of the crows (mold, wet wool, oily scalps) turned Geoff's stomach. He gestured one of his flunkies over and whispered, "Piss on their shoes," and watched as the flunky pissed all over them.

"Sorry folks, you can't come in with piss on your shoes. Not the kind of place we're running here."

The crowd laughed, and Geoff chuckled, too. They'd all seen inside, felt their feet stick to the carpet, seen the toilets overflowing, smelt the air in there even at the start of the night.

One of the locals, he'd been pissed on too. The crows weren't bothered, but he was. He stepped up to Geoff, stupid mistake, and Geoff just lifted an elbow up under his chin, made the head snap back and shut him up.

The crowd didn't like it, but that wasn't going to hurt him.

It was clear from the start that this lot were different to others he'd cooled. They were smarter. And they had a reason to be in the place. He found that out by drinking with them, found it out easy as asking.

One girl, she called herself Necro. He said, "What's your real name? Because I'm not calling you Necro."

She played with the chain around her neck. At the end of it; a small crucifix. Not one of the big ornate ones half of them wore as a joke. A real one. She must have got it for her confirmation, something like that.

"Bailey's the name my parents gave me. You think that's any less stupid than Necro?"

"At least it's a name. Necro's just a description."

"Well, you know, that's what we're about."

"What, dead bodies? Death?"

She tilted her head at him. "You knocked that guy out pretty easy."

"Crowd didn't like it."

"Yeah, well, most people don't like violence much. It upsets them."

"You?"

"I grew up with it. It's just another way of communicating," she said.

That was the start of it; when his judgment slipped.

The crows all had long fingernails. They forced small beads under the nails, so that they nails grew over the beads to curve into claws.

They wore their hair short and spiky.

Sometimes people called them carrion crows.

But, Bailey said, "We are not into dead bodies. We are into dying bodies and the place they leave behind. That's why we want this place to be ours."

The scar on the back of Geoff's head stretched. *Could just be the cold,* he thought.

"What is it about this place?"

"Hasn't anyone given you the tour?" She took his hand. He saw Management looking shocked; what the fuck're you doing? You're supposed to be getting rid of them, not fucking them.

He'd have a word later. Let me at them. Let me do it my way. You need to know them before you can cool them. He'd already seen that drink prices didn't matter a rat's arse to the crows. The locals, they were pissing off in droves. But the crows paid whatever the price. They ran a car wrecking yard, pulled in a fortune. Geoff told Management to mix the drinks wrong, water the beer, pour the spirits meanly. That was the next step. The next avoidance of violence.

Bailey holding his hand felt wrong. The part of his brain which made good judgment numbed, but he thought, *so long as I'm aware of it. So long as I know.*

"You know this place has burnt down twice." She started at the massive fireplace. It stood as tall as Geoff, and twice his armspan. "It was the fire, both times. They don't realize a fire this big is like a furnace, and the brickwork gets old, or, like they did the second time they built it, made crappy and cheap so it went up easily." She led him upstairs.

"The first time, fourteen people died. That's on record. Management kept a book. You can ask them to see it; they've got it somewhere."

Geoff had seen the little museum; an old box with books, a charred wine bottle, some keys. That kind of thing.

She led him upstairs. From there, the view of the grounds was clear.

"They buried most of them in the yard, there." He could see small headstones, some of them draped with strips of colourful material. Once colourful. Now faded and grey with cold. Geoff looked at them and wonders; *why do they bother? What is the fucking point of it, remember the dead? Better to forget.*

"The next fire, they found nothing but bones," Bailey said. "They built over them, is what I've heard. So down there, in the foundations, are the bones of the burned. They think it was about 16, that time."

"But you're a Christian, aren't you?" He touched his crucifix. "That kinda death obsession isn't very Christian."

"You should know that we all serve God in our own way. Some obsess with family, or they go out volunteering, making themselves look good. I don't care about looking good. What about you? What about your family?"

"No family. I move around a lot. Don't get much of a chance to form close friendships. It's a lonely life in a lotta ways. You rely on strangers for your relationships."

He told himself he was doing it to get her onside, figure out what it was that would work on them.

Back at the pub, some of the crows barely moved. They were led in by the others, sat down, and they stayed there, barely blinking, until it was time to go. Geoff couldn't figure them. Druggies, he guessed. One man, Carn, Geoff thought his name was, checked them, made sure they sat upright, didn't dribble on the table.

Carn looked like a follower, but some leaders do.

Geoff kept an eye on him.

Geoff upped the basic stuff. Got people in to steal their bags, their phones, their laptops, whatever they were carrying. Had Management put up a sign saying "all care and no responsibility. And we're lying about the care part."

He called the pound on their dogs. They bailed them out quick enough, but he called the pound again, and again.

They left the dogs in the car after that, bowl of water, window open a slit. Up his sleeve, Geoff had poisoned meat.

"Nice dogs," he said. "Hope no one slips anything to them."

"They're worth a lot of money. They're cancer dogs. We gottem from the research institute. They can smell cancer on a person." Carn was always covered in dog hair. He didn't seem to notice.

He got people in to sell them drugs, then called a police raid. That cleared a lot of them, but too many of the locals, at the same time.

The place was a lot tougher than he'd been led to believe. Turned out it was a tow truck drivers' place, too. They were blokes he didn't like to mess with. Management was happy with them, though. They were real men, they drank beer by the keg, they left tips, they spread the word.

It took Geoff a while to realize it, but the crows were there for the towies. Not just for the place.

For the towies.

A call would come in, one of the towies, two, sometimes three, would grab their keys. The crows would follow.

Geoff jumped in with Bailey, one time. "Where're we going?"

"You don't want to come."

"Just this once."

Scene of the accident, and the crows stood back, letting the towies do their job.

Carn hopped around amongst the cars, three of them, there were. He inspected them like a cop, miming note taking. The towies laughed, first minute, then one of them waved a tyre iron to scare him off.

Carn hopped back. "One of them's a write off. Let's get it for the yard. A seller, rather than a builder."

Bailey nodded. "Offer 'em $200."

Carn walked to the owner, a middle-aged woman, cut across the forehead. He spoke; she looked at the towie. The towie nodded. She nodded.

"They get 30 percent of the scrap sales," Bailey said. "If someone'd died in it, we'd offer them a straight thousand, something like that. We don't sell the ones someone's died in."

"You're pretty sick, you lot," Geoff said.

He called his trainer, John, to come out for a look.

"You're okay. You're doing fine," John said. "I can't come out, mate. I've got five on the go here, and the wife's about to piss off, the kids, can't even tell you what the kids are up to, and Mum's sick."

"I'm feeling a little concerned. I wouldn't tell this to anyone but you. I'm not sure..."

"Geoff, you deal with it. Right? You don't need me any more. You're a big boy."

And with that, Geoff was deserted.

In his ear, Management hissed, "Why are they still in the place? Get rid of them. I thought you were the best. That's what I was told."

"I am the best. Some pests take time to exterminate. Two, three doses of poison and they still hold on. Eggs you didn't see. Infestation you didn't find. You need to be patient, pick them off until the last one is gone. Main thing is, if you've got a massive infestation; find the nest. You figure out where they're coming from and you cool that place too."

"Cost?"

"Reasonable for the results. For the chance to say, it's done. No eggs, nothing left to reinfest."

Management nodded. "I'm liking your language, Geoff. I like the way you look at things. Drink?"

It was a mistake to drink with Management. They told you things you didn't want to hear, then made you suffer for knowing.

That was Management, all over.

"And next time you brief someone, it makes sense to give them all the info they're going to need to do the job. Same with anything, your shopping list, mate. You give the right information, you get the job done. You told me crows, just the crows. But the crows come for the towies, don't they? And the towies are a lot harder to cool than the crows."

"And I want the towies cooled because?"

"Because the crows are here for them. You get rid of the towies, the crows are going to leave."

"Well, get to work, mate. This is taking too long."

Geoff told Bailey; "I've checked out the stories, Bailey. There was a fire here, one fire, but no one died in it. They all got out in time."

Bailey shook her head. "We know people. We've spoken to them. We know the truth."

She smiled at him. "You should come see where we live. The old car yard. Every car we use to live in; someone's died in. Guaranteed. You should come see it."

"I don't go to people's homes," he said. "I like the familiar."

He started in on the towies. They were going to be tough; they'd been coming to this pub for years, 20 years, some of them had come as kids.

He'd need reinforcements. There was going to be violence.

Bailey called him. "Geoff. Geoff. You have to help us. One of the towies is here, he's got Carn, he's beating him up. You have to come and help."

"Just one of them?" Geoff said. "You sure there's not more?"

"It's that one who pushed me over last week. He hates us. The others don't care."

Geoff knew he had to get to the nest soon; this was a good excuse.

He grabbed some things; a tyre iron, a knife or two, his baseball bat. Threw them in the back of the car.

Error of judgment. He thought he'd sussed it. Thought he'd figured out the lay of the land.

But he'd been distracted.

He arrived at the dead car yard they called home. The cars. Seen individually, the cars were once luxury vehicles. Some of them were Mercedes, and some nice RVs there, hatchbacks, a convertible or two. Older Holdens, Fords, tough, sturdy, whole sections rusted away.

Once there was space between the cars, room for a man to walk.

Now the cars were merged. Rust and ivy made it hard to distinguish one car from another, though in places a recognizable grille poked out, or an emblem, or one last patch of original colour.

Apart from that, it was one tall tower of metal, rust, ivy, broken glass, fake leather, real leather gone furry and plastic; steering wheels, dashboards, all merged into one.

Bailey ran to the car, reached in to touch his arm.

His arm, brown and strong, against hers, white and weak.

He got out, holding his baseball bat. "Where are they?" The crows stood around him, and he stood with his back to his car.

"You're looking well for a ghost." Carn said to Geoff.

"I'm alive and kicking, buddy. All rumours to the contrary." Carn's nose twitched. He twisted his cancer dog's collar, let the dog sniff Geoff.

The dog whined.

"He knows. Death is in us all."

"Where's the towie? Bailey said you were being beaten up."

"And you came to help me? That's very kind."

"I thought he might move onto her. He'd beat you to death in minutes."

"Would he?"

"Bailey?"

"I just wanted you to come visit me. You're so cautious you wouldn't come when I invited you. I wanted you to see where we lived."

Research, he thought. This is research. The only way I'm going to cool them is to know them. I need to know their nest.

But he knew it wasn't that. Even as he made the error of judgment, he let himself make it. He chose it.

Because he looked at Bailey and saw a woman who understood violence. Who accepted it into her life.

That was a rare thing.

"Have a look round while you're here." She took his arm. "This is the part we live in."

They entered through a doorway, two cars leaning nose to nose against each other to form a triangle. It was like a cave, warm from the cold outside, lined with blankets, partitions there so they had some privacy. He tried to keep track of the turns, but the cars were all alike, the rustiness of them making it seem like one big wall of car.

Geoff felt okay about it; no threat.

Inside, some cars rested on their sides, providing walls of sorts. Some cars had been cut and sliced; they were chairs, tables, wash basins.

Carn sat down on the seat of an old Jag.

"Have a drink, Geoff. Vodka, wasn't it?"

"Not for me, thanks."

Never drink on the job.

"And this," she said, leading him through more cars, though he barely recognized them. "This is where we keep the ghosts."

The smell of it was awful. He'd worked in some places, some absolute pus-holes, but this...

"What do you mean, ghosts?"

As he spoke, he looked up. There were, what? Fifty cars, piled up? Almost impossible to tell, the way they'd merged together. He saw movement in what used to be the windscreens, large white movement he couldn't figure out.

"There are people living in there?"

She shook her head.

"They're dying in there."

She stepped up to one, pulled out her camera. Snapped a picture.

Inside the car, the seats had been removed. Inside, a man, Geoff thought, though it could have been a woman. Tits that big, flabby fat flesh. He filled most of the car. His limbs rested limply; he blinked slowly at Geoff, though didn't seem to see him. Below him, a pile of shit, layers of it.

"What the fuck is that?"

"A ghost. He's dying. We're looking after him."

There was no looking after, though. Geoff could see that.

"You just let him shit in a pile through a hole in the car?"

"We feed them coffee beans and wait till they shit them through. Like those beans people buy which have been shitted by that wild cat. Best coffee you'll ever taste. I'll make you one later."

He shook his head.

She laughed. "I'm joking. Geoff? It's a joke."

"But..." he waved his arm. He could see the cars were full, at least ten of them, ten of them with fat white bodies in there, sitting, blinking.

"Oh, this part's not a joke. This is our life's work. We're keeping a record of their deaths. The moment they die. It's important work. They'll be remembered for it. Otherwise, they'd die on the street and no one'd even move the body." She said this loudly, to the people in the cars.

Geoff could hear nothing from them.

"They don't talk much. Mostly can't."

"But why don't they just get out?"

"Look at them, Geoff. Most of them can't, now. Carn's such a genius. I don't what it is he gives them, but I think it's part that drug they give to keep kids quiet, part something else. You saw them at the pub; those are ghosts in progress."

Geoff thought of the druggies he'd seen hanging out with the crows.

"But...they haven't got any room to move."

"How small is the womb? We have no room there. This is the perfect way to return to the womb."

"But...why?"

"Out of the goodness of our hearts," she said. "They all came to us off the streets, abandoned, ignored, forgotten. They have wasted lives."

She snapped another photo.

"We keep in nice and cold here, so we can see their breath. So we can see their last breath." She packed her camera away. "I'm pretty good at knowing how many breaths they've got left. That one there..." she pointed to a woman with drooping eyes, a greenish tint to her skin. "She's got maybe a hundred, hundred and fifty. She's close."

"Just think of it, Geoff. No more decisions to be made. No more fights to be won. Just giving in to God's will. Allowing fate to take its toll."

"Ready for that vodka, Geoff?" Carn said and finally the instinct kicked in. Geoff crouched, knowing something was coming. Carn threw a jug of vodka at him, following it up with a lit match.

It was a pathetic attempt. Geoff hit the match away, grabbed the jug, smashed it to the side of Carn's head. It shattered, so he had a glass weapon.

"Anyone?" he said. "Anyone?" One of the first rules about being outnumbered (apart from never letting yourself get outnumbered) was to intimidate. Make it seem like you're in control, you're crazier than them.

"This way," Bailey said, grabbing his arm. "You've made your point. Come out this way."

She tugged at him, and it was either stay there, with their big guy bleeding on the ground and any minute they could get up the guts to do something, or go with her.

She led him through the cars, a different way than that they came, he was sure.

"Where're we going?"

"Back way. They'll try to meet us out front. You shouldn't have hit Carn."

"He tried to set me on fire."

She looked at him. "He tripped."

He shook his head. "He doesn't like me."

She led him climbing through an old minivan, fast food wrappers still on the floor from when it was a vehicle.

"That was pretty cool, the way you whacked him."

He'd follow her anywhere, for that. He realised what his real weak spot was; not pregnant women, but women who understood violence.

Women like Bailey.

Then they were out. It was so cold, compared to inside.

"Let's get to the car, I'll put the heater on," he said. She stopped. "You're going to come with me, aren't you?"

"Where?"

"Just away. I can't stay here, now. I'm swayed, I'm done. I need to move on." He was done. The sense of relief, the idea that he didn't have to cool any more, settled him.

"What are you going to do, then? And what am I going to do? Leave this behind?"

"We'll sort that out," he said. "We'll build a new place. You'll work on the road. Make it random." Thoughts ran at him. "There'll be car wrecks along the way, heart attacks, everything happens on the road."

They stopped close to midnight for coffee, an outdoor place, brightly lit, with ice on the tables and mittens provided to hold the mugs.

"How many more breaths would you say you had? Fifty thousand? Maybe sixty."

He laughed. "I'm right for a while."

"We all have to have a last breath." She fiddled with her camera.

His breath puffed out in the cold. He saw her watching it, saw the pulse in her temple.

She'd be counting his breaths; he knew that. He also knew it didn't matter. He had to have a last breath; if she wanted to capture it, fine.

"It's cold," he said. "Let's get going."

She packed her camera away.

"Somewhere cold," she said.

Buster and Corky

Buster and Corky

Some people may not find this story scary. Me, for example. I think it's very funny, but I can't admit that when my aunt is around.

It's not a human food story. The only recipe which could possibly accompany it would be one which involves bones. Beef stock, perhaps, or Osso Bucco. Something with marrow.

I'm not sure if the bones in this story have marrow, though. How long does marrow last once the flesh has rotted off the bones?

My aunt had a much loved and very large dog called Buster. He was one of those dogs with a very impressive arse; muscly and taut. He looked like a tough dog but he wasn't so much; he hated mice, for example and would whimper at my aunt's feet if he ever saw one.

Buster got old, and older, and he got bad-tempered, but still my aunt loved him. Then one day Buster disappeared.

My aunt did all she could to find him, barring spending money on a private detective.

Eventually a dark and nasty smell began to rise from underneath the house and my cousin (who is very tough) was sent below with a torch to find out what it was.

He was very kind as he told my aunt that it was Buster, curled into a ball and gone to sleep.

My cousin was sent below with lime to help with the smell (though I do believe that lime acts as a preservant) and none of us went to visit my aunt for quite some time.

A year or so later, my aunt was given a new dog. This one was small and bouncy, it yapped and barked and delivered great bloody heaps of mice to my aunt's slippers when she wasn't wearing them. His name was Corky and he proved to be good company, if a little greedy.

He was a very inquisitive, diggity kind of dog. He loved bones and my aunt said he must have a treasure map of the backyard to keep track of them all.

One night, my aunt was awoken by an odd sound. In a ghost story, the sound, a scraping, would be accompanied by the words, "Who's got my wooden leg?" or somesuch. There were no words. My aunt, alone in the house on this night, crept down the hall. Scraping, cracking and crunching came to her from the lounge room.

"Corky!" she thought. "He's dug up one of his bones and is having a midnight snack."

Unhappy for this snack to happen in her lounge room, she threw open the door to order Corky out.

The words caught in her throat.

Corky had a bone, all right. A very big one. Corky had been under the house, digging and dragging, and there he sat, on my aunt's good leather lounge, proudly crunching away on Buster's skull.

The Edge of
a Thing

The Edge of a Thing

The killing block fascinated Paul. An obelisk-shaped stone, it was half-buried on his wife's ancestral land so that it poked out of the dark earth like a sentinel. There was a semi-circle of darkened stone stained into the top edge, the blood of hundreds of victims. This was where they placed their necks, and here the blood spilled.

He'd had the idea for the resort, standing with his hand on the old rock. He knew tourists would flock to a cannibal holiday.

If it was going to work, he'd have to get the road fixed from Nadi. You had to drive from the airport, and the single-lane, massively pot-holed road put people off. People wanted to be rustic, authentic, but not when it came to the roads. They wanted big nation roads in a developing country and he would have to try to give it to them.

The potholes were tough; with only one machine capable of repairing them, his stretch of land was way down the list. This area, they got gravel in to fill the hole, but the first heavy rain washed the stones out and more of the road with it.

He knew the road well and hated it more on every trip. Drivers were impatient but didn't have the cars to match, so he'd get ancient, filth-spewing vehicles trying to pass him on a hill bend. If his family were in the car he'd take it easy, slowing down to let the bastards pass, making sure the windows were shut to keep out the fumes. When he was on his own he'd play games sometimes. Slow down, speed up, play with them. They weren't used to it and couldn't figure out what he was doing.

Today he was taking the family to stay at their favorite resort. The trip there filled him with fury. It was a long weekend, the Friday off for Ratu Sakuna day, the great chief who ensured native title of land. People said that on this day his presence could be felt by those where who were not loving Fiji in their actions or their thoughts. Paul used this in negotiations at times, saying, "I've never seen Ratu Sakuna. He knows what's in my heart."

Paul was filled with fury because of all the people building in the villages along the side of the road. Community halls with tall, wonky foundations. Houses made with the porous, cheap grey bricks they liked to use. Whereas his blokes, his 'team', wouldn't work today. It was bad luck, they said.

"Look at 'em," he said. He and his wife exchanged a rare look of mutual understanding.

"Apparently it's not bad luck if you're building for yourself." 'Apparently' was one of her favorite words. She'd use it sarcastically, passive-aggressively, or in fake confusion. He could never quite pull it off the way she did. He'd given the men the day off because he knew what good will he'd receive for it. It still pissed him off, though. He'd managed to move beyond superstition; couldn't they?

The kids were quiet in the back, watching a DVD, using headphones. Some of Paul's European friends resisted this, wanting the children to look out, to see the world as it passed.

"Apparently that's a more pleasant way to travel," as his wife would say. Their kids never complained or whined about "how much longer."

They drove in blessed silence for a while, the route taking them past the turnoff to his building site. As they neared this spot his mind wandered to all that needed to be done. His fury rose again, imagining the stillness of it, the lack of work. He'd rip them to shreds first thing Monday morning.

"You're not going to check on the site today, are you?" Ana said. That was another thing she did; give a command as if it were a question.

"Not today. I might pop over tomorrow when the kids are in kids' club."

He knew her well enough to realize her concern; she didn't want to be stuck with the kids. She wanted to read her crap Clit Lit book, her shitty magazines, she wanted a facial and a massage. She didn't want to be bothered by the kids; that was his job on the weekend.

"Is that a new grave?" he said. He slowed. It seemed new; the dirt bright red against the dark green ferns, the scarves and saris festooning it clean, not yet tattered.

This was Ana's land, her ancestral land, they were developing. It had come to her because her brothers were dead and the chief long gone. Before the kids came along, they'd spent time on the land. Camped out, explored it. That was before they lived overseas, and she turned into a white woman, a kaivelungi, trapped in a Fijian body.

He didn't tell Ana that Mr Roads, the Fijian man who could clear approval for a sealed driveway to Cannibal Casa's reception, and could maybe do something about the water supply, would be at the resort they were heading to, as his guest. She'd be furious; she didn't get how much money it cost to bribe unofficially.

They didn't talk business until the coffee came. They talked golf, rugby, wine, government.

With dessert, Mr Roads said, "My daughter's getting married next weekend. Marrying a local Fijian boy. He's all right. They're going full traditional. You should come as my guest. Bring the wife and kids. You'll like the outfits. My wife can't shut up about them."

Paul and his wife exchanged the second of their knowing looks of the day. "Of course we'll come," she said.

"Come late," Mr Roads said. "They are always late."

With coffee, Paul and the kids joked around about the menu at Cannibal Casa, what they'd serve. What you'd do in Kid's Club. Skull Painting! Gut-Stringing!

"Not funny," Ana said. "This is not so long ago. How long do you think it takes for the taste of human flesh to leave a race?"

"Perfect! That's the tagline. You're a genius."

His son laughed so much juice snorted out of his nose.

Paul arrived at the work site just after 8 on Monday morning. The kids had refused to go to Kid's Club, so he'd been stuck at the resort watching them swim all day Sunday. It was a painstaking run; drivers slowed down as they drove the stretch and not just because of the potholes. There were so many roadside monuments to the dead it made people nervous.

He expected the site to be up and running smoothly. His manager, Taniela, was a bad-tempered man who wasn't interested in making the workers comfortable. He said 7am start, that's when they started.

But all was quiet. The machines where were they'd been left, doors half open, some of them. The ground was wet and muddy, but they'd agreed, they'd already said, that the men would work through the rain or the job would never be done. The men respected Paul. He was tall, broad, used to play rugby.

"Bula!" Paul called. He walked to the service hut, wondering if Taniela has slept the night there, forgotten to wake up.

Inside were three of his men. No Taniela. This was his third... fourth? crew. They'd leave en masse, spooked by ghosts and ancestors, and he'd have to shell out to shift another lot in.

"Where's Mr Tan?" Paul asked

"Mr Tan is in the car, Bosso. Taking Rajan to the hospital."

"Was there an accident? What happened?"

The three men shook their heads. "No accident. The ancestors. He drove forward and they stole his heart beat for moving their bones."

They stood up. "Taniela asked us to stay to tell you. But we will not stay any longer. We will not anger the ancestors. The bad people will have a dream and die. There are many graves along the road. They should never be moved. These are the graves of the great chiefs. They have tried to move them before but you will see the crosses to show how many bulldozer drivers, digger drivers, truck drivers died when they tried to break ground. Bang, a heart attack."

"Fuck the ancestors!" Paul shouted. "Jesus Fucking Christ fucking ancestors. The man had a heart attack. That's it."

"He was a boy. Not a man. Very young."

"Yeah, well with the crappy diet you all eat, no wonder, " Paul said. His diet was good, thanks to his wife.

Next time he'd have to get some Europeans in. They didn't care about the ancestors.

The men packed their things, backed out, ready to run. Paul hit Taniela's number on his cell phone. "Tan? Where the fuck are you? We've another crew about to piss off. Aren't we paying these bastards enough? Give 'em more, for fuck's sake."

He stepped outside and called the men back. Passed the phone to one of them. "Have a chat to Mr Tan."

They stayed. Money given, but the wages were still a joke by Australian standards.

He had to move the killing stone, though. They said they wouldn't work while it watched them.

That night, Paul collapsed exhausted into his armchair. His daughter dimmed the lights to play a game on the screen. Paul quite liked watching the children play computer games; he didn't need to concentrate, or communicate. He had no desire to play the games himself and the children liked an audience. In the village where he grew up, they only had electricity for two hours a night and you could hear it being generated, smell the fuel burning. Here, in his big house in Suva, there was no smell. You didn't notice the electricity until there was a power cut.

He watched for a while then his eyelids began to droop. He heard the children's exclamations and the high-pitched whine of on-screen gunfight. As he drifted, he heard something beneath all that, a low murmur. Unexpected for a computer game, but this one was atmospheric, with dark, ghost-like creatures in the background.

His wife would turn it off if it was too scary for them, he thought. The background noise grew louder, a heavy murmuring sound.

Paul opened his eyes. The room seemed even darker; across the floor he could barely see his son and daughter, crouched over the controls.

There was movement around them, like a shifting sheath of dry sand in strong wind. He said "Turn off the fan," but neither child responded.

The air shifted again and, his eyes now used to the dark, he saw it was not the air but movement. Arms. There were men in his lounge room, sitting cross legged in a circle on the floor. Were they his men? From the site? Or from the village? His eyes were blurry and the light dim; he couldn't see their faces.

"Er, guys?" he said. The men didn't respond. He saw that they sat around the kava bowl, sharing the drink. They did not offer him one. He was always offered first; he was bosso.

"Ana!" he called out to his wife.

"What is it, Paul? I'm on the phone," like he was one of the children.

He stood up; the men ignored him. He walked to her, unwilling to shout any longer. "Um, you let the workcrew in without telling me?"

"What do you want?" she mouthed. He gestured. "I'll have to go; Paul's having a moment," she said and she hung up and walked with him to the lounge room, where she flicked on the light.

The men were not there. The children complained about the light, squinting into it tearily.

"The workcrew...they were here."

"What?" she asked. "Why are the kids playing this game? It gives Emily nightmares."

"Mum, it doesn't. Homework gives me nightmares."

"Shut up, Em," her brother said, but it was too late.

"Homework," their mum said. Paul was left sitting alone. He could smell the kava; it was woody, wet. Yet the men were not in the room. His wife left the light on so she could knit. She was creating a colorful jumper Paul prayed wasn't for him.

"God, I'm tired," Paul told her. "I'm so tired I could crawl to bed." He wanted to cry with weariness, but he wouldn't tell her that.

Ana looked at him, felt his forehead. "Go to bed. Livia can clean up in the morning. I'll bring you a port and a valium, stop you thinking so you can sleep. Can you read a quick story to the kids?"

"Love to," he said. It was true. He was so grateful to her for helping the children to love books. It was a great gift. If she hadn't been to Australia, educated there, she wouldn't even care about books. They never read books in the village. There was too much to do. Fish to catch, yaqona to harvest, stories to tell. Songs to sing. You didn't have to strain your eyes.

The next day, Paul said to the workcrew, "I thought I saw you lot last night. Round my place, drinking kava."

They all laughed. "We were drinking kava. Not at your place, though."

"You're always drinking kava." That caused a big laugh.

"I don't know who these blokes were. Sat around in a circle. Heads down."

The men were silent.

"Chiefs? Were they chiefs?" Taniela asked him.

"I couldn't tell. Maybe."

"If it was the chiefs, they only come in the dim light and when they are very, very ashamed."

Ana called him late on Friday. "What time is the wedding tomorrow?"

"Oh, God, I'd forgotten about that. It starts at ten, but I'd say Fiji Time we get there around twelve."

"Let's leave the kids with Livia. Give ourselves a break."

As Paul and Ana entered the large church hall, a woman gave him a sulu. He tried to hand the thing back; it was hot pink, with Bula Fiji written all over it. She looked at his jeans and tutted, smiling. She took it but wrapped it around his waist, tucking the ends into his waistband.

"I told you," his wife whispered. She was dressed up. Lady of the Manor overdone. She liked dressing European. She'd poured perfume on, saying she hated the smell of people en masse. *If people knew the things she said in private*, Paul thought. *If only they knew what she was like.* A Westernized Fijian, she refused to wear a sulu. Sometimes she'd wear a tight-fitting bula outfit instead, but mostly she chose beige colors. Dull colors. She was tired of color, she said.

He couldn't see the father, Mr Roads, anywhere, the sea of faces blurring around him. "You can't call him Mr Roads," his wife said, covering a smile.

"If I call him Mr Roads, I remember which one he is."

A Fijian woman spoke to Ana, smiling. Ana rolled her eyes.

It was hot in the auditorium. Jeans were a crazy idea, but he never wore shorts. Legs too scarred and hairy. And he'd moved beyond the pocket sulu. Too many years in Australia meant he was no longer comfortable in a skirt. He would wear one in the village, because the men would laugh at him if he didn't, but he hated it.

There were a couple of hundred people in bright clothes, fanning themselves and chatting although the priest went rabbitting on and on. Paul listened to a word in three or four, enough to know he had nothing to say.

Paul was bored shitless. These things could go on for hours. He wondered when they could leave, rehearsed in his head the urgent text he'd receive shortly and how he'd respond to it.

"Why did you make me come back to this country?" his wife muttered, but they both knew why. Here they were wealthy and could have housekeepers. Feel superior.

His wife's own mother had described her as having 'too much learning', tapping her temple. "You know what happens to people when they have too much learning." This ten years earlier, when they loved each other.

Her mother had also warned him about the use of the land. "You must ask the permission of the chiefs and they will say no. This land is for the village."

"But the village doesn't really exist anymore. All moved out. All gone. Just a few stones left behind." He waved his hand like the ocean; sailed the sea.

"The land is tabu and that stone you talk of, that killing stone, that is the most tabu of all," she said. When she died a year later, they were back in Australia. They found out three weeks after, when a relative thought to call them. Paul didn't tell his wife about the morgue and the backlog there. The old woman had been so worried about tabu, yet her body, no one had processed her body in the proper way. No imbu, no mat, no prayers. Paul felt bad about this and paid for a lavish headstone. His wife was pleased with the expense.

The fanning in the Auditorium increased. It was hard to breathe. Below, front row, a shout came up. An older woman lifted her arms up, shouted again, a loud grunting then tipped forward, off her chair, and slithered head first through the railing over the step to the marble floor.

The priest kept talking. It was a minute or so before anyone reacted. *Get a doctor*, Paul thought. *Somebody.*

People stood up, one or two of them. They sat the woman up but she flopped as if she were a rag doll. The priest started to shout, scream as if he were abusing her for lying down while he was talking. "Do not take this woman! She is not ready for your love!"

There was no twitching. Eventually four big men came from behind the stage and carried her out back one each limb so her torso dragged close to the floor. A young woman with a mop walked behind them, cleaning up something Paul couldn't see.

A young girl came after her, hands and knees, sponging at it.

The priest stopped shouting. People called Hallelujah, as if something good had happened because of the priest's shouting.

Paul needed a break, so he stepped downstairs and into the shiny white marble entrance way. He pulled off the pink sulu and dropped it on the floor.

"Paul!" he heard. Mr Roads; not watching his daughter get married, apparently. He had his arm around a thin Indian man, whose shoulders seemed to slump under the weight. "Paul! Did you enjoy the wedding?"

"It's still going."

"These things go for hours," Mr Roads said, smiling broadly. His lips pulled so far back his ears lifted.

"An old woman collapsed in there. Is she all right?"

Mr Roads tapped the Indian man on the shoulder. "We'll talk soon," and he gently ushered the man away.

"Let's find out about the woman. Then your mind will be clear for the job ahead."

"I'm not bothered by it. She just fell over."

"Have a seat, there. Let's find out."

Paul didn't like the position he was in; strange place, where he didn't know who stood where and who was the boss.

A small boy brought him something to drink, a heavily sweet juice which made him thirstier. The boy stared at Paul who wondered if he had something disfiguring on his face.

"Off you go," Mr Roads said to the boy. "Scoot". He sat by Paul. "They were calling to God to revive that woman. She is my new son-in-law's great aunt, I believe. The priest was calling her ancestors to leave her alone. He was saying that there was no need to take her, that she must make her life worthwhile first. He asked them not to cast such a bad omen over the wedding. But it seems as if the ancestors didn't listen. I'll pay for my daughter and her husband to move away. The ancestors can't travel over water. Otherwise the marriage will be cursed."

Paul shook his head. "Whatever." He needed to get back in control; this man worked for him. "Listen, we've got another problem with the water table out at the dunes."

"We thought that, didn't we? But it can be handled on site. Who's out there?"

"I've got Taniela. He's fine. The crew are losing the plot but they'll keep working."

"Why are they concerned?"

"It's nothing. I think they don't like the heat."

"Fijians are not bothered by the heat. You have not told me about the deaths. This is where your problem will be. It doesn't matter about the overseas education. It all goes back to the village once these troubles start. They all remember their superstitions."

After the wedding, a kava ceremony began which would go into the night. Paul's wife didn't like him drinking the stuff; she said it made him revert. But he could see the group dynamic, how they eyed him off, seeing what he'd do. His wife went home, leaving him to it.

As the night dimmed, more men joined the group. Paul didn't see them arriving; they seemed to simply appear. He tried to pass the kava bowl to one but was ignored, and he wondered why the insult. His host didn't notice; in fact, Paul realized, none of the men he began the session with responded to the newcomers in any way.

Deals are struck the same way around the world. In a circle, over a substance, when no deal is discussed. It worked that way everywhere.

He dreamt that night that a bald-headed man stood at the end of his bed. He woke shivering. His wife said, "You've got the guilt, even if you won't admit it. You need to do some good work. Come with me to the hospital."

"I'm not going into that place." His wife's charity was the kind which suited her. "Dress down. Think how pleased the men will be. I can tell the wives; I'll slip it in at tennis."

He smiled at her, feeling a moment of pure blinding envy. The simplicity of her life, the small things she did, the things which worked well.

"Come on," she said, holding his hand. "We never do anything together."

"I'll just check in at the site, see how Arturo's going," he said. Arturo, his nightshift man, an Indian trained in police work overseas, seemed to cope with the dark night site well.

"Forget it, then," his wife said. "Forget it."

There was no answer on the site phone, so Paul called Arturo's mobile, thinking he was doing the rounds.

The phone ran 11, 12 times before Arturo answered. "Mate, how's it going there?" Paul said in his breezy tone.

Arturo mumbled something, and Paul could hear children in the background.

"Tell me you're not at home," Paul said.

"No, no," Arturo stuttered, but his wife, Paul could hear his wife yabbering at him.

"Arturo?"

"Mr Paul, it's the curse. The spirits. They took another worker tonight, lifted him out of his body like he was a banana. Gone and dead, Mr Paul. It looked as if God pinched down his fingers for the soul and lifted it out like you would a hair from your food."

"But what actually happened?"

"This is your curse, Mr Paul. On you and your family. We don't want it. You watch your son. They will take him as revenge, take his soul and leave him evil and vicious. He will never love."

Paul shook his head. "You know my son. Everyone says he's the sweetest. Bit too sweet, for mine. He's not evil."

"You see their power? It will be the end of the line for you. They will make your daughter sterile and take the soul from your son and make him want to die. The end of the line."

"Look, Arturo, I'm coming over."

Arturo led him to the small, mat-covered living room. Tea appeared; the wife was very quiet. Around them, men at the kava bowl. Heads bowed.

"These men..." Paul said. "Who are these men?"

"I see no men, Boss."

Paul shook his head. "Raivatutu. These men are raivatutu, on the edge of my sight. Come back to work, Arturo."

"Not while the chiefs are angry. You have two curses on your head now. You have the weight of chiefs disturbed, and the burden of men killed in your service."

Paul called Mr Roads, businessman, government man, educated man, problem solver.

"I don't need to speak to you, Paul. We have nothing to speak about."

"Help me deal with the superstitions, though. What can I tell them?"

"The old woman dying at my daughter's wedding was a warning to me. The ancestors are very angry. The only way to escape is to cross the water. Leave it all behind. Give it back. The ghosts will not leave you alone, otherwise."

"There's no such thing as ghosts."

"There are ghosts, Paul. I can't help you. You'll need to leave Fiji to escape the curse."

Ana was out at her charitable work and Paul drove in a fury to the worksite. *At least the workers will be there*, he thought. *I pay them enough, bribe them enough to come.*

There was no one. He sat on the step of the service hut and put his head in his hands. He heard his blood pounding in his ears but it was a drum, the lali, pounding rhythmically.

The sun went behind a cloud and there they were, the men he alone saw, dressed now like Chiefs in bark cloth as perfect as that worn at the wedding. They held clubs, heavy-ended weapons with sharp edges for cracking the skull, like the killing stone which had formed this idea so long ago.

The beating of the lali increased. He could feel pressure in his ears, a beating boom boom.

The men lifted their heads and their huge white teeth, one of them said, "Your son's seed will be poison. Your daughter will be barren. We wish great unhappiness to your family. Your wife will come to hate you as the mongoose hates the snake. You will not be an ancestor."

Paul fumbled for his keys but his fingers were useless to him. The men came to him until he stood amongst them.

He thought of his son and his daughter as the chiefs pressed into him. The drumming beat faster and the ting of kava being pounded.

"Your line ends," they said, and they turned their backs on him and walked away.

Guarding
the
Mound

Guarding the Mound

One of the boys came back a man, his arms marked, his feet cut and bloody.

Din looked on as the boy, now a new man, showed the stone he had sharpened and used to kill the meal they would all share. Nobody noticed Din.

"I'll go out next," Din said. "I'm old enough." He said it loudly and often until the new man noticed. "Din, you stay with the women. You cannot be a man when you are the size of a child." Everybody laughed, slapped Din, slapped the new man. Din crouched down and crawled through their legs to get out into the night air. Someone smacked his arse and said, "Hi ho little Din," and he turned to snarl but no one noticed, no one cared.

"I'll do it," he said. He stood by the entrance to his underground home and took up a sharp stick. He scratched markings into his arms and legs. Then he began to run.

The animal howls were louder at night. The noise of them frightened him but he knew that was part of the test. He wondered what he was supposed to do next.

The moon shone a path and Din began to follow it. He felt no hunger; his belly was full of the new man's feast.

He walked, enjoying the freedom.

The moon stayed bright and Din walked till he was tired. He found a stone along the way and chipped at it till it was sharp. Then he found a hollow tree and hid inside behind its branches, waiting for a kill to come. His eyes drooped and the warm air inside the trunk made him sleepy, so sleepy...

He awoke with the sun in his eyes to the sound of voices and smiled, thinking his people had come to look for him.

Then he heard them speak and realised by their accent they were strangers. Din scrunched his eyes tight, thinking they wouldn't see him if he curled up small.

"Look at the size of him," a man said. They poked him with a stick. "Child."

"I'm not," Din could not help but answer.

They laughed.

"Of course you're a child."

"I am a man," said Din. He held his arms out, showing the deep, fresh marks there.

"Only just, hey?"

"Look at the size of him," someone said again. Din shrank back.

"It's all right. No need to fear. We are hunting animals, not you. Why don't you climb out?"

"I'll wait for my family."

The men talked amongst themselves. Then one of them said to Din, "Are you from the moles who live underground?"

Din gasped at the insult. "It is safe there. The animals don't get us."

"But it's dangerous living underground. You're safe from wild animals but anyone could just come and cover the entrance. How would you get out?"

Din heard them sheathing their weapons. He cautiously moved forwards.

"Are your weapons away?"

"You're very observant, boy."

"I'm not a boy."

Din heard the sound of someone drinking.

"Do you have water?"

"We do, my friend. Plenty to share. And meat, too."

Din cautiously climbed out of the tree. He saw six tall men with dirty faces, brown arms.

"Good for you," said one. "Brave." He patted Din on the back. He smelled of burnt meat, blood. "I am the Chieftain's Man. I know bravery. Are you hungry, my friend? Come share with us." Din shared their meat.

"He's very small," said one of the men.

"My father grew not much bigger. I will stay small, too," said Din. He felt brave to say the words, to accept the words.

"And what job do you expect to take?"

"I am very patient. I can watch the lake for the moment the ice cracks. I can watch the sky for the sign of breaking rain. I can watch a sick face for a sign of fever breaking."

The men exchanged glances. One of them said, "Tell me of your people," and Din told them of his home, how close it was. How enclosing and how the people talked little. He could hear the Chieftain's Man talking a distance away. "He seems perfect."

"You would say that. Otherwise your son is in line. You son will be starved to keep him small."

"I know."

Din heard a catch in the Chieftain's Man's voice.

"The Chieftain will not be happy you have used his time for your own gain."

"Spoils of war," the Chieftain's Man said. He came back to Din.

Din said, "My family don't think much of me. They didn't think I could become a new man."

Din's new friend said, "That's no good, boy. You should come with us. You are brave and strong, Din. We need someone like you. We don't hide underground like moles. We have built houses on the earth. The air we breathe at night is fresh."

He put his arm around Din. "I'm the Chieftain's Man and I have his ear. He'll be happy to see you. You should join with us, my friend. Our place is big with plenty of people to talk to. You might like it."

Din blinked. "My people would miss me."

"They might. But would you miss them?"

Din shrugged. "They're my family."

The men exchanged glances again. The Chieftain's Man said, "I'll confide in you. We are hunting animals and we are seeking treasures. Power." He stood over Din, muscles flexing, blood in his fingernails. "Our Chieftain sent us out to destroy those we find. He is frightened of invasion. You family, Din...I'm sorry. But they were like ants, under there. Underground. We just covered up the hole and left them there. They probably just fell asleep."

The Chieftain's Man nodded his head, closed his eyes, dropped his head to his chest, aping sleep.

"Yet you, young man, are alive. By your own actions you saved your life."

Din felt full to his ears. "My mother?" he said.

"Did anybody call for Din as they were buried?" asked the Chieftain's Man.

"No. Nobody called for him. They called plenty of names, but I didn't hear Din."

Din suspected they were tricking him, that perhaps they wanted him for some purpose of their own. But he did not want to go back to find his family smothered. And he wanted to live above ground, with people who thought he was brave, and strong, and useful.

He liked his life with them. He was always much smaller but they didn't notice so much. The Chieftain enjoyed his talk and laughed at him, and Din felt he had a place to be.

Din was uneasy when the Chieftain's Man came to measure him.

"I know I'm short but you don't need to make such a point of it," he said, slapping the man's hand away. "Get that rope away from me. I'm shorter than a man and taller than a child. That's all you need to know. And that you can tell by looking."

The Chieftain's Man smiled at the chatter. He measured Din's chest, his thighs together.

"Sit down," said the Chieftain's Man, and he measured Din sitting on a rock. He measured his hand span.

"What is it?" Din said. "What are you doing? Am I dead? Are you measuring me for burial?" He took up a knife and pierced his thumb. "No, look, the blood, you see. I'm not dead, I'm not sick. The only person in the village who's sick is the Chieftain and he shows no sign of recovery. Him you could be measuring for death, though I don't expect anyone would dare to do such a thing." Din gasped. The Chieftain's Man smiled at him.

"You don't mean..." Din could not speak.

"The Chieftain will see you after evening meal. He's at his clearest then. You wash that stench off. His nose is sensitive and likes nothing to offend it. Come naked if you can stand the cold. It won't hurt you and your clothing is beyond redemption. You may win favour instead. Perhaps one of the ladies may see otherwise hidden talents."

"There is nothing hidden. Nothing surprising," Din said. He slumped.

The Chieftain's Man slapped him on the back. "Come earlier rather than later," he said, and he left the den.

Din stepped out at dusk and walked. Chatter stopped when he came near so he was sure something was afoot. He walked on, wanting to see the horizon at sunset, sit by the aromatic patch of blooms and breathe its scent. He sat for a while, enjoying the silence, when a footfall alerted him to the approach of a large man. Din looked over his shoulder, knowing there was no danger. Even in the falling light he knew it was the Chieftain's Man.

"How is your son?" asked Din, without turning around.

The Chieftain's Man said, "My son is well." He touched Din on the shoulder. "Thank you, Din. You need to come now."

Din rose, brushing seeds from his clothes. "I haven't eaten yet," he said.

"You can eat later. Eating is not important. You will eat well later."

Din felt cold. He shivered. "Well, then, let's go before my belly forces me elsewhere," he said. He stripped naked and left his clothes in a pile.

The Chieftain's Den was smoky and reeked of blood. The Chieftain lay on a pelt-covered slab. Around him were small flames, keeping the room warm. Earthenware jars surrounded him. Din knew these contained all the Chieftain's bodily fluids and waste; nothing would spill to earth. At the time of death, all parts are collected and buried. In the corner the great hulking Brewer mixed his soup. A ladle of the Chieftain's blood. A pinch of dirt from below the ever-living tree. A smear of shit. He looked up when Din arrived and nodded. "Good," he said.

The Chieftain tried to raise his head. Din was shocked at his decline. As his fluids drained from him, he weakened.

"Good," said the Chieftain. "Raise me." The Brewer raised his head, pushing a bundle of clean cloth under his neck. The Brewer gave him something to swallow and his eyes brightened, the blood dripped more rapidly into the jars.

"Din, you are a good man," said the Chieftain. Din heard a rustling, a tearing, and there was the clothes-maker, working in the corner.

The Den was very crowded. The Brewer said, "Forgive me," and pulled a handful of hair from the Chieftain's head. He thrust these into the soup he was cooking then handed the wet strands to the cloth-maker. The cloth maker sewed them into the clothes.

"Do you have a family, Din?" said the Chieftain.

"My family is dead," said Din. He did not remind the Chieftain who had killed them.

The Chieftain grimaced. "Yes. So I will offer you a boon. It seems only fair." He breathed so deeply and for so long Din thought he must have fallen asleep. But then, "You will travel to the five surrounding villages. There will be a woman waiting ready for you in each village. Their Chieftains have agreed, and I have agreed for them. We may not know if you manage to make the babies, you and I. We won't know. But others will. You can make five babies to carry your name.

"This is my boon."

Din nodded. He knew there was more and these words he dreaded.

"For this boon I ask of you something very great." The Chieftain looked Din in his eyes for the first time in his life. "I have chosen you for three reasons. One, your size. Two, your hearing is good and your observation sharp, and three, your patience. I have seen you sit for hours just watching, oblivious to the world writhing about you. I could not wish for a better guard."

Din's throat constricted as if filled with dirt. "Guard?"

"Yes, Din. You will come with me into the ground and you will guard me for all eternity. As long as you protect me, your family will prosper greatly. Any lapse will mean suffering for your children's children. To fail in your task will mean a terrible death for your entire family. You must work quickly. I have only three days."

Din said, "I'm not sure I can father children."

"Your father managed, didn't he?" said the Chieftain. He lay back, closed his eyes. "Be quick, Din. Make your family."

It occurred to Din that if he refused, if he did not sire a family with whom he could be threatened, perhaps he could guard for a few years, then slip away. But the idea of fathering a dynasty was something he found enticing. To think his children would prosper over those of the Chieftain and all those who sneered. Din's name beside the Chieftain's. Din's name remembered.

He travelled by wagon to the other villages. He sipped the foul drink given to him by the Brewer, a drink usually reserved for the nights when the Chieftain was making babies. Each sip gave Din strength, and he began to think in detail about the women waiting for him.

He was not disappointed. The women had vied to bear his seed. They trusted him to guard well. They anticipated prosperity and fame. They dreamed of their great-grandchildren living in comfort and wealth. One woman he couldn't visit; when he arrived her blood flags were hanging by her door. He was given food by the people there then he rode on.

Din tried to memorise their names and a little about them but it was difficult. The youngest one was the most voracious, the oldest timid. The most beautiful woman he had ever seen made him enter her four times to be sure.

Then there was the one he would always think of, in his seat in the tomb. She was short, masculine, her voice rough, yet he loved her voice because she spoke to him and he spoke back and she asked him his parent's names so she would know what to call their child. He did not want to leave her.

"If we leave now we may be far enough away when my Chieftain dies and they will have to choose someone else," he said.

She shook her head. "No, Din. This is our only time together. Now you have a responsibility to your unborn child, to make this the best life possible. That is what you must do."

Din said, "But we could have happy children by being happy together."

"What about our grand-children? And great-grandchildren? What about the children ten generations from now who will not even know of our existence? And anyway, Din," she said, gazing out to the field, "What makes you think we would be happy together?"

Din closed his eyes to forget her face at that moment and he thought instead of her face as he stroked her naked back, and how she had asked him what his parent's names were.

There was loud shouting and she gathered herself together.

"Where is he?" The shouting came to Din and he realised. "Here, I'm here."

"The Chieftain needs you," said the Chieftain's Man.

The clothes prepared for Din were the softest he had ever worn. On his seat there were many soft layers, to comfort him through his years of sitting.

The Chieftain breathed harshly but did not wake. The Brewer collected the last of his blood, stirred it into the soup and said to Din, "Don't spill a drop."

Din swallowed it and it made him think of rats, how a rat would taste if you squeezed it till the juice ran. He spilled nothing on his beautiful clothes.

Around him the wailing, the weeping started. The Chieftain was still. Din stared at him.

"You should fill your eyes with something else," said the Brewer. "You will see nothing but that sight for all eternity."

Din could sense the colour draining from his vision. The smell of the room faded too, the sounds were fainter. All he could hear was a fly walking over the Chieftain's face, and Din leant forward to flick the fly away.

"Good start," said the Chieftain's Man. He led Din to his chair, the first of Din's life. It was a perfect fit. The Chieftain was carried to his burial hole, followed by the treasures, and the jars containing the Chieftain's bodily fluids and waste, then Din, then the woman carrying Din's last meal. He wished he had eaten before the Brewer's draught, because he could feel his tastebuds dying on his tongue as he was carried along.

"Keep him safe," people shouted.

"Stay awake," they said.

"Save yourself," one voice screamed, but Din couldn't turn in his chair to see.

The Chieftain was placed in the deep hole lined with wood and the greatest of materials. His things around him.

Then Din's chair was settled in a perfectly-built alcove. A sword was placed across his lap and he felt the etchings there, detailed pictures inlaid of the Chieftain's life and there, at the hilt, Din thought, was his chair and Din, sitting there with a beard grown past his feet.

"Goodbye, Din. Think of your family," said the Chieftain's Man.

The tomb was sealed off as Din ate his last meal. Feeling it sit heavy and indigestible in his belly, he could hear, very faintly, the sound of an ocean full of dirt being piled on top of him.

Time passed strangely. Din was only aware of the Chieftain, his treasures, his body slowly dissolving into muck, his bones left there to guard. Sometimes the sound of digging and he fleetingly thought of his children, his grandchildren, coming to give him absolution, to tell him they were okay and they could look after themselves. This never happened. By his alertness he guarded the burial mound from all attention and invasion.

He saw generations of insects, millennia of insects. He never slept, never moved. He did not itch and had no waste to be expelled. He did not sneeze.

And then he saw the bones stirring. He watched, thinking perhaps his eyes were tired and he should shut them for just a moment to rest them. No, he thought, there is movement. The jaw. The fingers. If Din was breathing before he stopped now. He squeezed his eyes; that hurt. He felt it.

"Din," the Chieftain spoke. "Din, you are good. You have kept me safe." The skeleton clicked. "Din, one of you has not been vigilant. One of you has slept and let his mound be entered."

The skeleton clicked again, and a sound almost like swallowing.

"Oh, yes, there are others. Other Chieftains, princes, kings, in places you can't even imagine. We all need a guard, Din. Oh, I'm lucky to have you.

"Din, you will leave here for just a moment. You will see the price paid for failure. Then you will return to guard me."

"But how?" said Din.

No words but the Chieftain answered. "You will enter the body of a descendant. You were very successful, Din. You have a very large family."

Din blinked. This wasn't painful. And then...

And then he breathed fresh air. The scent of it almost made him sick. He stumbled over his skirts. His skirts. He was a woman. Running. Running with so many others he was swept up.

Part of him was aware of the deathly stillness of the tomb; his body still sat unmoving. The feeling of movement in this strange body shocked him so much it was all he could think about; elbows and knees bending, eyes blinking, throat swallowing, lungs breathing. Then the dust being raised by his thumping feet, the rocks cutting into his soles.

Around him people ran, some forwards, some back, falling over, shouting, confusion. Din was carried this way and that, "Beware," someone shouted to him, "Watch the baby," and he looked down for a baby on the ground, thinking to step over it and it was his own belly protruding.

"My baby," he said. The voice was that of his descendant. He couldn't tell how many generations spent guarding the Chieftain.

He wondered which of the mothers sent this line forward.

He tripped then, falling over an old man.

"Get off me, woman," said the old man. Blood covered his face. "Get off me, leave me alone to die." People ran about them, screaming, and Din could hear a noise, a crashing, and it was men coming, protected men with weapons. Din understood these things with the sense of his descendent.

"Come on," he said to the old man. "Stand up and come on. If we can get to the side there we can crawl under that wagon and perhaps they will run by us."

The old man shook his head. "I'm too tired." The men with weapons were killing, now, slashing their way through the citizens like they were cutting through tall, sharp grass.

"Come on," said Din. He dragged at the old man till he stood, then helped him through the crowd. Bruised, damaged, uncut, they reached the wagon. There was room underneath for them both, even with Din's huge belly. Heavy jewelry dug into Din as he crawled and he wondered at its worth. They squatted, watching feet running, falling, blood reaching in thick tendrils and threatening to soak their toes.

"They'll find us," said the old man.

"Perhaps not," said Din. He felt there was an irony here, the squashing into a dark place smelling someone else's stench. He felt a kick.

"Oh!" he said. "It must be the baby."

"Shhh," said the old man, but he reached over in the darkness and rested his hand to feel the strength of the unborn child.

They sat like that for a long time.

Then at last it quietened. The bodies were left in piles and the men went away to celebrate, to drink.

Then new feet came, unshod, tentative. They could see a person squatting by this body and that, seeking something.

"Cyrus?" said the old man softly. "Cyrus?" He crawled to the edge of the wagon and dared to peek out.

"Cyrus! Cyrus! Here!"

"Father! Father! You're alive! We have transport, we need to leave now." He paused as he saw Din.

"Yes, yes. She will be coming with us." The old man turned to Din. "You and your child will be well rewarded." He smiled. "Very well rewarded."

"Thank you," said Din. As he crawled out from under the wagon, he felt himself lifting, leaving, and he could have cried for the loss of it, the loss of feeling, and knowledge, the loss of it all.

"You see, Din?" said the skeleton. "An entire family dead, and many others beside. You must guard me with vigilance and never, ever let go. Your family is large now, and prosperous. You should be proud." This last word sighed from the lips of the skeleton so softly and for so long Din felt it like a breeze against his cheek. The breeze felt cool and Din wondered if there was any chance tears had fallen while he had been away.

There were times Din wished failure on other guards. Times he wished for momentary release just to see, to see his children and how they looked. This would mean people dying, though, a family destroyed.

Din still wished for failure.

"Oh, Din, another one gone," the skeleton groaned. He spoke no more, though Din imagined his heart racing. Preparing to see the world.

Din grew to mistrust the words. He stayed still, and watched. Sometimes he heard scrabbling above his head and knew the mound was being explored; he opened his eyes wide and clutched his sword and the exploration stopped.

Din didn't know how it worked, only that if he noticed them they were gone.

Then the skeleton sat up again.

"Oh, Din, Din, so many gone. You are still here, though. Oh, Din, I picked well. Would you like to see how your family is doing? And watch the demise of those others? Oh, there have been so many. I've protected you from so much, Din, much I could have shown you."

Din's heart raced, he squeezed his eyes and he was lying down, lying down, and he stretched his legs for the joy of it. Stretched out and the bed was soft, the covers warm, what animal skin was it? He curled and stretched and moved his limbs because he could. The room smelt dank but not too bad and he sat up to see candles flickering around the walls.

There was a mirror in the corner and Din rose to see his face, how many generations beyond and he was a young man, handsome, one scar over his eye. Din felt proud of it, a battle won.

"Baron! Baron! Step up! The battle is almost lost."

"Who is it?" shouted Din. The voice on the other side of the door said, "It's me, Baron, your servant. We are safe here but we could rise to watch the end of the battle."

"Are many dying?"

"The rider says yes. He says they will all be killed."

"Are we happy about this?" Din pulled a heavy robe over his shoulders and opened the door. His servant was there, small and red-faced. He fidgeted from foot to foot.

"They're saying the blood is running into the river and it will not clear again for many years. We could see it if we leave now."

Din knew his Chieftain wanted him to see but he did not want to waste precious moments of freedom watching others die.

"Is there anyone else here?"

"Your family is asleep, Baron. The children were frightened by your talk but they sleep now."

"I shouldn't frighten them."

"No. But they love it." Din glanced at his servant, wondering at his familiarity. His lack of servitude. He thought perhaps there was a physical likeness, that the Baron sowed his seed quite wide.

"How many children do I have?" Din wondered. "How many of us are there?" He smiled. He wondered if the woman who had asked his parents' names was the one responsible for this part of the family.

There was a great banging and the servant said, "News!" He ran to discover more. Din opened doors and peered inside until he found the children. There were eight, he thought, all of them angelic. Tears from Din.

He wanted to hold one of his children, so he climbed into the bed. His ears and toes were frozen. He climbed in and smelt the child, his child, breathed it in and that was the smell he took back with him to the tomb.

"They will all die if you fail," said the Chieftain. "Your proud line will end. You must carry on."

And time passed and Din waited and guarded and sometimes was released. Glimpses of the world as it changed and grew. The cloth on his body, so different every time, the smells, the things people used to move themselves about. The terrible things they used to kill each other with.

The skeleton crumbled until the bones lay in pieces. The gold, the treasures were safe. The voice came from the pile sometimes and to pass the time Din thought of his family, the millions of them he thought must be his.

And then he was released again, and the world was almost odourless.

It took him a moment to realise he had been released, because his body was still sitting, hands still holding something, feet still flat on the floor.

The cloth of his body felt like skin, not fur, not woven cloth like he had worn before. It moved as he moved, was soft and comfortable.

He sat before a vast window which looked out into the night. The moon shone brightly and it seemed closer to Din than it had on other visits.

Din tried to stand but found he couldn't move.

"Do you have a request?" The voice was in his head.

"I wanted to get up. To move."

There was silence.

"Where to?" said the voice.

"Just to stand," said Din. He wanted to stretch his legs.

"You can move now," said the voice, and the bar he was holding receded into the chair. He stood up. His legs felt odd. Thin and not much use.

He moved close to the window and looked out.

Din recoiled. Below him the ground was so brightly lit it hurt his eyes.

"The lights are so bright," he said. The words hurt his throat, as if his descendant had not spoken for a long time.

The lights dimmed instantly. Din stepped back to the window. He could see himself now, his descendant reflected faintly in the window. He was pale and bald and to Din he looked weak and sick.

"Where are you?" said Din. He looked out of the window now the light didn't hurt his eyes and he could see many thousands of small grey buildings, lined up along narrow paths.

"Do you want to see me?" said the voice.

"Yes," said Din. He wanted to talk. "Where are you?"

"I'm here." Din turned to the voice, not in his head now. A pale, bald, beautiful woman stood before him.

"What is it you need?"

"I want to see out there. What's out there?"

"The people. It's the people," she said.

"They live in those small mounds?"

She looked puzzled. "What is this about?" she said. "What is your concern?"

"I need to see them," Din said. He started to panic. The smell of the tomb was returning and he knew his time was almost up.

"They're okay. It's the others you should worry about." The woman led Din to a screen. There were pictures there, not a war but people dying. Their mouths yawned at Din.

"The illness," said the woman. "It's not safe outside."

"But I'd like to see what it's like out there." He gestured to the small buildings below.

The woman shrugged. "Sit down."

She touched his arm as he settled himself and he saw it, the confines, the fake light, the food provided so bland, the work so dull. Is this it? thought Din. Death or this? He choked. The room dimmed and he was back in the tomb, doing his duty.

"You see, Din? You see what happens to those who fail?" and Din couldn't breathe he was so tired and he closed his eyes, just closed them, and he heard the skeleton whining, and he let his hands fall, he heard digging above and he wondered as he fell asleep who could be left to desecrate the grave he had guarded for all of his eternity.

State of Oblivion

State of Oblivion

We all have things which make the bile rise to our throats. For me it's the smell of cooking meat. More specifically, that moment when it burns.

When it's too late to take the meat out of the fire.

For Leon, loud noises. He gags sometimes, the shock is so great. He tends to spit out the mouthful of vomit, rather than swallow it back down like I do.

Louise swallows, and Joseph. Margaret spat, when she was here. Katya, whose hates the sight of her own reflection, hawks it up and lets it fall out of her mouth, stands legs apart, bends over, just lets it fall out.

And Neal?

Neal I have never seen react to anything in that way.

Has he forgotten so completely?

On the day he arrived I was ill prepared. All I had collected was a small pile of cinnamon bark. I gently filled my pockets, sniffed my fingers for the deep spice smell there and ran towards the tower. The other ingredients would have to wait. All of us were desperate for the supplies he might bring. More cardamom, of course, because they always brought that. Apart from that I couldn't guess. The only supplies we received were those the new people brought. Sometimes it was what we needed. Sometimes we discovered a need for the items they brought.

My cheeks were flushed with rushing. The cinnamon in my pockets tap-tapped. I was the last to arrive.

"Here, Serena," Mata said. "Quickly, the parcels are here." She pushed me to the front of the crowd.

This new boy must be fit, I thought, to carry so much. He was a handsome boy, blue-eyed, thick hair, broad shoulders. He wore a tight, long-sleeved shirt to show off those shoulders.

I wanted to tell him what to do. "Have some food. Sit down. Rest. You're tired." He looked so young.

This was the moment when we almost remembered. When the new person arrived with the smells of the world still clinging to him. We tried not to terrify him, refrained from surrounding him and nestling our noses in his folds. I put my arm around him and smiled. I didn't speak; I was breathing in his scent. It was there, a flash of memory I could almost feel in my throat like uncleared phlegm. He smelled of flowers and fruit but like he'd sprayed them on.

He squinted in the harsh sun.

Katya asked, "Is it sunny below? You are very brown."

"Yes. Though not as bright as here," he said. His voice was gentle. Leon pinched her arm. "We already know that, Katya. Are you so lazy you can't remember?"

"How long did it take you to climb?" asked Joseph. The new boy glanced at his wrist, squinted when he saw a band of white skin, no watch.

"A day or so," he said. His brow wrinkled as if he already wondered what that was.

"Did you see children?" I asked. He blinked. The oblivion was upon him. The others hissed around me. Next time I'd ask that question first.

We were all desperate to know about down the mountain, though we shared our snippets casually, as if they meant nothing.

"No chai?" said Mata. I shook my head and they sighed. They liked to sip while opening the parcels.

The new boy tucked his chin and folded in his shoulders like a bird about to go to sleep.

"They told me not to talk about anything," he said. He tried to edge his way out of the circle. We stepped closer and closer, sniffing at him, seeking clues, memories from his scent.

He was scrubbed quite clean.

"What's your name?" Louise said. She's the youngest here, just fifteen, we think. Blonde, tall. Could have a very lazy time here because all the men are keen to do her work, but she won't allow it.

"I'm Neal," he said.

"So you like to pray," I said. They all laughed. Perhaps they all imaged the same picture as I; the etching of a saint, kneeling at an altar in one of our books. No one is moved by the image. We lost whatever faith we might have had when we lost our past.

Neal brought with him milk and cheese, rice, lychees. Three new hats. Many things.

Neal squinted at me as I squatted beside him. "God, it's hot up here. Trees don't give shade like clouds do." I snorted at the thought of our spindly stick trees providing any sort of shade.

"At least you're already brown so you don't sunburn easily. Some of us went through hell with the burning."

"Really," he said. His tone sneered at me.

"Here," I said, handing him dark glasses. "Wear these."

He put them on and twisted his neck around.

"Can't see too many others wearing them."

"Believe it or not, you'll get used to it. You'll be sitting down to lunch one day and you'll suddenly realise you don't have your sunglasses on."

It was hard, not being able to see his eyes. I couldn't tell if he was looking at me, and I felt shifty, my gaze flickering from one lens to the other, seeking some connection.

"So does anyone remember why they're here?" he asked me.

"Why are you here?" I said. I didn't want him to know how ignorant I was. He didn't listen, anyway; Louise walked from one side of the mountain to the other and he watched her as if nothing else existed. There is something about watching that girl, it's true. I swear she walks more than she needs to. She has a limp she doesn't remember getting and she's worked it into a rolling sexual move, which mesmerises us all. Neal used my shoulder to lean on as he stood. "I might just go see if Louise needs help with dinner," he said.

I watched them flick through the cookery books. "So long as it isn't chicken. It always smells rotten and there's so much different food to choose from," Louise said, "all different using the same ingredients. Whoever wrote these down must have been very inventive."

"They weren't just done by one person," said Neal. Joseph, close by, stopped and stared. He shook his head, said nothing. When Joseph arrived (it seems so long ago now), I had walked him to the edge and asked him questions there. He was very cautious and would not answer in front of everyone. From the moment he arrived, young, fit, shy, the attraction between him and Louise was instant. I hadn't seen her flustered before. Theirs was a great, innocent, short-lived love. Our mountaintop is not a romantic place. They've flattened it out like a mesa to make it easier to settle, to live. We throw buckets of unwanted rocks below the clouds. We use others to build shelters or walls and our tower. The tower we built stands only as high as my shoulders but its walls are smooth and even and it is a good meeting place. We fashioned a bell from a hollowed out trunk and a walnut shell. We are so high we are above the clouds. It's very quiet. It's too high for most things; birds, insects. No snakes or spiders to fear.

Peaceful. Too peaceful, perhaps; Joseph and Louise seemed to run out of things to do, and she got bored. She wasn't bored now, squatting with Neal; I saw Joseph falling back and stepped up to his side to ask him about the livestock.

We could not do without Joseph. He tends our chickens, decides which should die. He is our butcher. No one else wants the job.

Our cookery books are made with pasted recipes, no pictures, no chat. Stir-fried greens, roasted chicken, coal-baked potatoes. Barely necessary to read recipes for those, but it gives us a sense of continuity, if we all do it in the same way. We all know what to expect. Strange how lack of past makes us all so similar.

Louise and Neal began the meal, using the fire Leon so dutifully kept alight.

"I wonder who was the first person to use fire," Louise said.

"That would have been Jaz. She's gone now," said Leon. We fell silent, remembering her nighttime leaving, all of us rising to realise she was gone. She was never one for talking but we decided it was the food. She was hungry.

"Jaz said she wanted soft food and the cookbooks said "Heat over flame," so she dug around in the Box and found matches."

We are all equal here, though we've each taken a role. Leon is the keeper of the fire. Ceaselessly he collects wood scraps. Walks the perimeter. He never lets us down.

"I mean before that, before everything. The first person ever."

No one spoke. We knew nothing of the past. Nothing. All we arrived with was simple language.

"So Jaz left?" Neal asked. "To see what's down there?" No one spoke. One by one we left the fire. We tried not to mention those who left; it was like they ceased to exist for us once they stepped through the clouds.

The last person who went down the mountain was Margaret. She didn't come back; no one does. This is what happened. Margaret woke up crying one morning, then another, the tears just leaking out and puddling on her mat.

She didn't use a pillow, said it made her sweat. This was not sweat, though. This was tears. I watched them form.

"What is it?" she said. "Why am I crying?" She had no enemy on the mountain, nor a lover to make her weep. It made us curious, all of us, about what the dream was, and about her. Scarred fingertips, shiny, a little bit purple.

At tea on the third day, she took more than usual, a huge piled plate. We laughed at her.

"Not pregnant, I hope," said Louise. We laughed at that, too, at the ridiculousness of the suggestion.

"Knowing can't be worse than not knowing," Margaret said. "How can the truth be any worse than what I'm imagining? I would rather know."

"Oh, Margaret," I said.

"Margaret," she said. "Is it even my name? I feel nothing when you say it. Nothing when I say it. Did we even lose our names when we came here?"

Katya said in her slow voice, "We must have chosen this, chosen to have no childhood memories, no recollections. We're not here by force, we know that, because people have left and not returned. What did we want to forget?"

"Maybe the earth is dying and we were chosen as the survivors," said Mata.

"We should be able to have children then," said Joseph.

Louise combed her hair then threw the ball of strands into the fire. "Children must be beautiful," she said

Margaret gathered her things; a soft cloth we wove together, smooth flat stones we heated on top of the sand, a pouch of tea and spices. I cried; I couldn't imagine her not being there. Then she disappeared into the clouds.

"Goodbye, Margaret."

There was silence.

Then we heard the noise. It was far away, further than we could imagine, but we recognized it. High-pitched, we only heard it when people chose to leave the mountain. None of us remembered the sound of machines but we had read descriptions of them at work. Different in tone each time someone left the mountain, always there were those few minutes then the noise. It didn't sound how we imagined a machine sounded like.

"Margaret! Come back!"

Joseph smoothed himself a secluded area well away from the main camp. He squatted there with a book propped up against a rock. "Making Gifts and Treats". How we had it I don't know, why someone thought we needed it I don't know. Still, we all read it, used it. We knew every word of every book we had.

"What are you going to make?" I said. Joseph shrugged. "I don't know. Is there anything anyone hasn't made before?" I squatted beside him and flicked though the book.

"Woven money purse. Don't think this one's been done."

"But what would she use it for?"

"Who's she?" I said, grinning. He grinned back. We both knew who.

"She could keep shiny little pebbles in it or something," I said. He smiled. I watched him work. "Do you like Neal?" he said.

I shrugged.

"I don't trust him," Joseph muttered. He turned from me as if disappointed.

I rose to make the chai and felt the ache in my hip. A pain like a presence, not intense but there for me to be aware of. I peeked in at Katya, but she was sleeping on her back, hands trailing to the floor, snoring. Her medicine cupboard was ajar; I was only looking for pain relief. She wouldn't mind. She could diagnose me later, pull her little healing strings. She liked a patient who diagnosed herself.

I took two pellets and placed them under my tongue. Immediate relief; I forgot I had a hip and went to make the brew. There would be sullen faces if they woke and had to speak before sipping their chai.

Neal stood at the bench already, crushing, sniffing, mixing. Something about the way he stood caught my breath; when I started my work, going through my motions, I realised he was mimicking me completely, even my feline crouch.

He lifted his head and smiled at me in the reflection on the pot. I smiled too, but the sight of the two of us frightened me.

"We're alike, aren't we?" he said. "I've got your nose." This didn't make a lot of sense. I had my own nose and nobody else's. I squeezed it. "It's my nose," I said. "I've got mine, Margaret had hers. She's got hers and he's got his."

"Yes, but none of you are related, are you? Siblings or parent and child."

"We have no children here," I said. I scratched my stomach where it itched, just under my belly button. Neal's face was red. "Take off your shirt, Neal, you'll feel cooler without that black shirt." The sight of the long sleeves covering his arms made me sweat. He hugged his arms to himself.

He said, "Can we leave out the cardamom? I don't like it that much."

I laughed. "You really do say silly things, Neal!"

I felt blessed to be the chai maker.

For each person you take one cup of water. To this you add a pinch each of cinnamon, cloves and cardamom. You boil it. Then you add some milk and sugar and heat, let a teaspoon of tea brew, strain it and you have chai.

We cleaned the water sometimes by straining it through little pebbles. It's an effort but somehow it made the chai taste better. Neal took some care when he helped, but jumped and spilled a little when Mata came up behind us.

"Are you busy, Neal?"

"I was just going to help Louise," he said.

"Neal, you're spending too much time with Louise. We need help moving the toilet walls. The old one is full and needs covering," Mata said.

"Yavohl, Madame Hitler," Neal said.

Mata frowned.

I laughed. "You come up with some weird things, Neal. What's that supposed to mean?"

"You don't know who Hitler was?"

"Unless she's in one of our books, no." Neal's mouth flapped.

I thought of Joseph's jealous comments and began to see how he would be suspicious of Neal.

"God knows where I got it from," he said.

Neal didn't have the innocence of Joseph, somehow. He made Louise shy and nervous. She asked me what he was doing and I wasn't sure, but there it was in the books. Sex. She said he was talking about she hasn't had a period. And babies. We don't have that here, she said, puzzled.

Joseph left his gift by Louise's plate a few days later. She frowned and glanced at Neal. He shook his head. She didn't glance at Joseph.

"Is it a Christmas present?" Neal asked.

"How do you know about these things, Neal? Why do you remember it and we don't?" said Joseph. His face reddened as he spoke.

"Joseph! Don't ask questions!" said Mata.

"No, it's okay," said Neal. He squatted down and we all followed him. "Joseph has been wondering for a while and I think I need to tell you. The thing is, there are people who care about you down there." He raised his hand as we began to babble. "Not necessarily people you know, but people who care about freedom, and memory and difference. They got me in here to convince you all to come down. You don't want to know what I had to do to get up here. And you'll notice I never drank the chai, unless I made it without cardamom."

"Is that it? Is that what makes us forget?" Leon asked.

"That's part of it. The spice masks the drug. Factor in the elevation, and the post-hypnotic suggestion and you have it. They don't want to make it permanent because they want to keep replacing you. They want your places to be filled again and again. It's like a lottery but the prize is a dud."

"Who're they?" I said.

"The Company. They own this space, and all of you gave everything you owned to them to be here. But it's a lie. Part of the hypnotic suggestion is to implant the concept that this is a better place than that. They make a fortune, these arseholes. There's no upkeep; you're almost self-sufficient and any new person has to pay for the supplies they bring. They only supply the drug, the cardamom. It affects that part of the brain which works on long-term memory. We can't let it go on. My group and I. We want to give you back what was stolen. You don't remember your first Christmas when you knew what was going on.

"The pain of childbirth.

"The smell of grapefruit flowers.

"The taste of chocolate icing on birthday cake.

"The sound of the sea—lying in bed and you think someone is breathing next to you then you realise it's the waves, crash and pull, rhythmic. You don't hear the sea at the top of the mountains."

"But why did we pick this? What are we trying to forget?" Leon said

Neal put his arm around Louise. "This is like prison compared to what it's like down there. I'm just glad it's out in the open. It's been hard lying to you all. To you, Louise." He cupped her chin.

"Get off her!" from Joseph, and he knew how to fight, all right, his fist meeting Neal's chin with a crack. Neal staggered back. Using the tower for support he pushed himself forward. "Go down and see, if you don't believe me," Neal said.

"It's not that," I said. I felt frightened talking to someone who knew. Louise didn't take her eyes off Neal. Joseph barely moved. "It's not that," Joseph whispered, and he turned and walked through the clouds.

"I shouldn't have done the bastard the favour," said Neal. "Why give him his fucken life back?"

"What do you mean?" said Leon.

"Sending him back. Should've just gone myself, left him here." We heard the noise, the high-pitched noise.

"What's the noise?" asked Louise.

Neal shrugged. "That I don't know. I only hear it up here."

I realised he had never answered Leon's question. What were we trying to forget?

I watched Neal talking to the others, one by one, earnestly, whispering, smiling, waving his arms. He made them leap up with excitement. Then they started to say goodbye, wanting the world back. Every time one left another arrived, too many to ask questions.

I couldn't keep up with them all, couldn't remember their names or make sense of the smells they brought. They ignored me. I was lonely, old. They laughed, explored, touched and wondered at our inventions, our books, our wheelbarrow, our compass, our clocks

Louise tried to be friendly but they barely saw her. We should have been friends with the new people. But with all of them arriving together, Louise and Mata and I became the outsiders.

When the wheelbarrow broke, Mata said "I think it's the axle," flicking through one of our books. "Look, do-it-yourself repairs. I think I can manage that." She was hanging on by her fingernails. She didn't want to lose the power she had but it was gone. She cringed as the new people crunched through bones as they ate, we never did that, and she went away to find silence.

I taught another to make the chai.

Louise sat at the edge of the mountain, her feet jabbing into the mist which clouded us from seeing down below. I shuddered.

"You look like you've lost your feet," I said. I tugged her shirt. "Come back in and I'll make you some chai."

"There must be something else," she said. As she spoke, I felt a sick ache in my belly, a need I haven't felt for a long time.

"I'm sure there is," I said, "But we don't want it."

I tugged at her again.

"Why haven't the others come back, if it's so terrible down there? They're probably swimming, water up to their necks. Can you imagine how clean they must be? And they are eating at a table, chewy food, soft food, imagine what they're eating."

"How do you know about these things?" I whispered. I felt awed at her knowledge.

"Neal told me," she said. Everything she knew seemed to come from him.

She pulled away from me.

"Come with me, Serena," she said, and ran down the mountain. I waited for her to return but she didn't. There was nothing and then the high pitched noise.

"Louise?" I stuck my arm into the clouds. The air felt damp, cold. What is it, was it all mist, all cloud? I didn't want to wander in that.

I thought I heard words. "No," I thought I heard, and perhaps my name.

I plunged through the clouds.

On the other side the air was warm and scented. Sweet. I saw steps and far-away buildings, huge, tall, looking so big even from a distance I squinted. It seemed darker and I was not used to seeing so far.

A woman waited, squatted. Her face was grey, her eyes stared at me and she stepped forward. She picked up the bag at her feet. "Are you leaving?" she said. The words made no sense to me. "You're leaving," she said, and she stepped through the clouds. I saw other people waiting, and a man dressed in blue, big hands, holding an arm to stop an old man from running forward.

"You can't go back," he said to me. "It's over for you." These words made no sense to me either. I saw Neal. He waved and I stumbled down the mountain.

I couldn't see Louise.

"Louise? *Louise!*" I heard crying and I tried to follow the sound. Each step, though, each smell and I remembered they were buildings, those things, buildings, and you lived in them, under shelter, and food you kept cold there and you got it in bags and carried it heat was there stoves water running water showers books BOOKS to sit and read lying on something soft a bed a couch cushions soft and clothes you could choose any colour and my Mum whose laugh was like a donkey so funny she was small and sweet and laughed like a donkey and Christmas Day presents and chocolates and that day, WEDDING, wedding day... my husband. I touched my hip and remembered, felt my missing teeth and remembered sitting together, drinking, I didn't feel the pain of it if I was drunk, he could hit me and I wouldn't know till next morning a night of ignorance and I turned to go back into the clouds because I didn't want to remember the next thing no no oblivion I tried to step back but the clouds were solid.

"I want to go back."

"You can't go back, Mum," said Neal. He was sitting on a rock. "Once you've left you give up your place. Someone else is there now," and I remembered giving birth to him, how it was going to make me a better person but it didn't god I banged my head against the hard rock I don't want to remember.

Neal stood right by me. He handed me a tiny t-shirt, bright red. "This might help you remember. Sometimes it takes a while for the drug to wear off." He laughed. "Oblivion. You gave everything we owned for it and left us with nothing."

As he talked I could feel an ache in my brain, like when Katya's pain relief wears off and you are left with that specific hurt you started with. That place where memories are. That place was waking up. I vomited and I cried. My body knew before my brain did. It remembered first.

I held the red t-shirt to my nose and breathed in.

"I wanted to see your face," he said. "As you remembered."

I remembered another birth, this one tearing at me, baby cut from me to save its life so I drank for the pain, Neal's little brother. Mike.

"Mike's fifteen," Neal said, and I knew I'd been in the mountains a long time. I tried to turn away Neal grabbed me, and I saw the burn scars on his arms.

Mike's fifteen and I can picture him I know what he looks like someone feeds him and dresses him, he can't piss on his own. I scream, the noise high in my ears the image the smell oblivion o god I beg for oblivion the rock is sharp I run to bang my head smash away the memory of that little boy by the fire, two, nearly two, no birthday party fucken little shit his brother, Neal, Neal watching TV, Mike trying to keep warm, so cold me out cold, blind drunk at three in the afternoon and he gets closer, closer, and the sleeves of his skivvy, four sizes too big, catch alight and he burns, he screams, I hear it, ignore it his brother Neal, Neal hits the flames out, six years old, calls 000 burn scars all over him I remember the number and Mike's alive and he has no arms.

That's what they allowed me to forget.

I stumbled away from Neal. He hated me, he would never forgive me. His brother would never forgive me.

The noise, the noise we always heard when people left the mountain, it came out of my throat, high pitched keening, grieving, grieving no no no.

Louise was further down. She had found a sharp stone or some glass; her wrists were bleeding. She snarled at me, "I didn't know you could make babies like that and I just thought I was getting fat and then it was born and I didn't know what to do with it. It stopped moving after a while and I took it with me everywhere and the smell of it." She vomited, curled up in the vomit and keened. What else? What else did our mountain conceal? I could hear Neal laughing and I knew I couldn't survive this. I couldn't live with it. I ran down the mountain. Neal after me.

"The others are dead already" he said. "Margaret—did you know she was inside fucking her neighbour while her three boys drowned? She came out to find them one, two three, face down.

"She burnt all their clothes, their toys, their bedrooms. She burnt down her home to pretend they never existed."

"Mata?" I whispered.

"Your precious Mata? So smart, always in control? 'She was playing in the driveway,' she said, 'and I didn't see her until I had backed up. Then I thought she was a doll, that crunching noise. I went shopping then drove over her again when I got home and her mum came and said have you seen her. I hadn't. I thought I hadn't but there she was.' Do you see why none of you deserve to forget? Bloody Joseph robbed his own auntie, left her tied up, right? He calls the cops but hangs up too soon, never checks to see if they found her and they didn't, did they. She died of thirst in her own shit and piss. Try living with that. Leon smashed his train and killed god knows how many people, not his fault of course, no, he deserves to forget. My arse. One of the others left her kid in the car while she did some shopping, kid dies. Try living with that. Katya was supposed to visit her twin brother. Couldn't be bothered. She was the one who found his body, much later. He'd OD'd. She could have saved him. Her mother suicided because of it. Lazy cow. Lazy coward."

I cried, I cried. If only if only. That's why we gave it all up for the mountain, to stop the if only. There was no other way to forget, no other way to wipe away that terrible thing. I remembered then that I had tried to die, I wanted to die to forget and this was offered to me, at great cost. You won't need the money, they said, and it's better than dying, and I thought we must have all tried to die, all of us above the mountain had chosen death but been given oblivion instead. The drug was not perfect, though. I thought of the retching we did, each of us haunted by a remnant of memory, just a hint of what we had done and why we had preferred to be dead.

"Where are the others? The ones who believe in our freedom?" I said.

"They don't exist," he said, squinting at my stupidity. "Part of my invented world. If anyone wants you to leave it's because they want your spot." He waved his arm at the people waiting.

"Was it all lies, what you said up there?"

"The concept is true. You paid for oblivion."

"But why did I deserve it?"

"You didn't deserve it, you stupid bitch. You paid for it, everything you owned, anything we owned. You spent it all."

"And it was enough?"

"I'm alive because I fuck an ugly old man. I have nothing. Michael has nothing. Yeah, it was enough."

He handed me a knife. It had been a long time since I handled one as sharp as this.

"It was just an accident," I said. The words were meaningless. It made me feel no better. "Would it make you feel better if I was dead?"

"It really would. I can't move on till you're gone. I'll always be wondering how to make you suffer more."

"But if it was me you wanted to hurt, why talk the others into leaving? Why make them suffer and die?"

He shrugged. "You always were a follower, Mum. You wouldn't have left on your own." He glanced down the mountain. "Shame about Louise."

I looked at the knife and I looked at my son and as I drew the knife across my throat I prayed for darkness.

He stopped my hand and said, "Too easy," and again he stole away my oblivion.

The Softening

The Softening

I noticed the softness in the walls of Grandmother's house after she died. It was my place now, through squatter's rights. My first act was to hang my paintings, black and red depictions my father described as 'horrendous'. The first nail I hammered in felt like it was going into flesh. I shifted positions and tried again, to the same sense of give. It was like pressing the trunk of a paperbark tree; you expect firmness but your fingers sink in.

It made me feel queasy

I walked out to buy new nails, thinking, irrationally, that these had gone soft with age.

I saw Grandmother, beckoning, from across the road.

I stepped back, thus avoiding a wipe-out with a speeding car.

Grandmother scowled and disappeared.

It was not the nails; the walls were soft. I've researched since then, studied, visited, read, and touched. My findings were clear.

The walls of a house in which someone has died are soft. My theory is the soul soaks through the walls like water soaks through clay, leaving no trace but softening the hard substance.

I found a 'death house' chat room and lingered there until it led me to the castle. The castle's graveyard, they said, was full. So was the earth under the flagstones in the great dining hall. I felt sick to think of how soft the walls would be there, but drawn at the same time, like we are drawn to look inside a deep wound to see blood, tissue and bone, although the sight makes us ill.

Finally, I received an invitation to visit the castle in Scotland. "A select few," it said. "Limited to 60 souls."

Grandmother appeared to me, closer this time, nodding her head and smiling as I drank in the airport bar while waiting for my plane to Dundee. A man sat beside me, the sort of man who sits in airport bars next to lonely women. I knew that, but couldn't stop myself from talking to him. So few people spoke to me. He moved closer, leaned in, and that's when Grandmother appeared.

I ran, Grandmother speeding after me like a hovercraft. "Come on, Missy," she hissed. It was the first time I'd heard her speak since she died. "Come on. He's a nice man. Go home with him. Go on." She was never very smart. She couldn't see that her appearance warned me of danger. I caught my plane and sleepwalked the rest of the journey.

The curator surprised me in the foyer. "You're late. The others all arrived yesterday."

I spun and tripped at his voice; my hand sank into the wall to my wrist.

"Do you believe in evil?" He was short, with flecks of debris in his hair, dark patches on the knees of his pants. I pictured him crawling in the spaces behind the walls, then curling up to sleep in a soft, warm crevice.

"Not as an inherent quality," I answered.

He smiled. "Strange you can be in place like this and not sense it."

"I sense *something*." My eyes flicked to the wall where my hand had sunk. It was still dented but filling out again.

He nodded. "Most people do. Most people are a little fearful. As if the ghosts of all the murderers are here still and capable of holding a weapon. Do you believe in ghosts?"

I nodded. "I believe in the essence of a person. A soul."

"Come on. I'll show you the sewing room. It's a wonderful place," he said. "The tapestry tells a fascinating story, and the colours are still bright after these hundreds of years."

I felt fingers in my hair. Grandmother clung to my shoulders, her ghostly fingers clutching at me. She whispered, "Come on, Missy. We're waiting. We're waiting for you." She wrapped her mottled legs under my arms. and I smelt more of her than anyone should smell of their grandmother.

"No, no, thanks," I said. Grandmother's knees clenched, and she hissed in fury.

The curator's mouth fell in disappointment. "Everyone wants to see the tapestries."

I wondered what he had up there. What weapon ready. Or if, perhaps, like Sleeping Beauty, I would prick my finger with a needle. Died of some terrible bone-creeping virus. "Maybe later," I said.

The curator led me into the great dining hall. Others were there drinking and eating, the mess of it making them raucous and uncontrolled.

"The stripper!" someone shouted when they saw me, and they all laughed.

"Eat," said the curator. "Join them."

I heard Grandmother's sharp intake of breath.

"No, no, thank you."

"Here's to the last supper," someone shouted. They were all handed tankards. I heard whispering behind me and I turned.

Grandpa was there, too, his body blotchy with strange black growths. Other ghosts I didn't recognise. Talking amongst themselves.

I stepped backwards, forwards, not knowing what to do. The curator took my arm, digging his fingers in till I yelped.

"You could drink, too," he said.

The diners raised their tankards and toasted. "For the children," they said. They drank. Every one of them. The room seemed to blur. One by one they slumped in their chairs. Some dropped their tankards. Some fell face first into their food. The curator leaned close to me. "For everyone who dies," he said, "a child is saved."

I heard snickering behind me.

The room seemed to soften.

I turned to run. There were a dozen people with Grandmother now, laughing behind their hands, blocking my exit. I shut my eyes and pushed through them, feeling nothing. I stepped through the oozing doorway and began to run. The walls were slumping.

Thickening at the base, sinking down. The ceiling began to tilt, unsupported.

I ran.

The curator laughed behind me.

I could smell brackishness, water left still for too long. I tripped and fell against the wall.

I sank in, then pushed out. I would not die here.

I reached the front door. It was soft to the touch, but the handle still worked. I gently tugged it; the sensation was like removing a bandaid from the flabby thigh of an old woman. I stepped out, leaving the castle hissing behind me.

They would not have me yet.

The
Grinding House

The Grinding House

Albadara: a bone which Arabs say defies destruction, and which, at the resurrection, will be the germ of the new body. The Jewish name for it is Luz, and the "Ossacrum" refers to probably the same superstition.
— Brewer's Dictionary of Phrase and Fable

It was a strange migration. The birds were walking, not flying. Hundreds of them walking, pecking, pecking at dead birds along the way, walking on.

"Shouldn't we call a vet or something? Someone to take the dead ones away?" Sasha asked. They stood in front of the concrete block of flats they called home.

"What's the big deal? They're only birds, Sash," said Rab. "Birds die all the time. They're stupid."

"But there's so many of them," Sasha said. Parrots, rosellas, crows, magpies, sparrows and cockatoos. Dozens of them. "Shouldn't someone at least take the bodies away?"

They heard a rushing, a whispering, then a thump.

A seagull landed with a squelch ten metres away from them.

"Splat!" Bevan said, lighting a cigarette and squinting.

He hated the sun.

Nick squatted down by the split bird. "You're a long way from home, mate," he said. He poked it with a stick.

"Come on, you're late," Bevan said. He fidgeted, shuffled his feet. He wanted them gone so he could have the place to himself. Get his work done. The toilet was filthy.

Sasha squatted beside Nick, holding her huge knitted bag on her knees. "What happened to it?"

Rab said, "Sash, it's a dead bird. It died for fuck's sake. Can we move on?" He ate a peppermint.

Nick said, "Have a look at it. It looks sort of smooth inside. It's weird."

"I don't want to look at it, Nick. All right? Come on. I want a seat on the van today," Rab said.

Bevan wouldn't look, either. "Can you go? Please? Come on, the van'll be there in five minutes. Sell well today. I feel like steak tonight," he said.

"I hope we get somewhere flat," Sasha said.

"Yeah, no hills to walk and people are always fatter in flat suburbs," Nick said.

They reached the collection point just as the van pulled up. A big, white, windowless van that made Sasha nervous. The moonies drove vans like this, full of wild-eyed devotees carrying flowers. Telecommunications companies sent their poor young sales teams out in these vans, too, dropping them, disoriented, in the suburbs.

Sasha, Rab and Nick climbed in and registered. Another team was already there. They sat huddled and silent amongst boxes of Slenderise. Something about the van made them all huddle. A blonde girl widened her eyes when she saw Nick.

"Hey, folks," Nick said. "Where're they dropping you today? We're hoping for the caravan park. People are always fat and lazy there, and they just throw money at you."

Nick threw his fist as if releasing coins. The other team flinched. "Nothing," Nick said. "If you could be sure they were washing their hands it'd be the perfect place."

The van pulled up outside a cinema.

"Team One," the driver said. The silent group shuffled out. The blonde girl smiled at Nick.

"Lucky you," he said. "Clean toilets. And don't forget, there's always spilled popcorn after the movie's over. Sneak in before the cleaners and you'll score a cup full. Wave it under people's noses. Just the smell of that stuff makes you fat."

"Bye, Nick," said the blonde girl. She had tears in her eyes.

Nick winked at her. "Spend some of that cash on me, darling, and I'll make you very happy," he said. She smiled.

Team One walked past a policeman who was dragging a homeless man by the scruff of the neck, and they stepped around to avoid the vomit.

"You've got no chance with her," Rab said.

"Mum says cops used to help people. Sounds like bullshit, huh?" Nick said.

The van dropped them in the city.

"Excellent. No door-to-door today," Nick said. He took off his shirt, leaving a purple singlet that clung to his chest. Sasha tied her shirt up under her breasts. Rab rolled his sleeves to show his biceps.

"God, we're gorgeous," Nick said.

"This is a shit job," Rab said.

Nick squeezed his shoulder. "It's not a job, it's a calling."

The brothers had met Sasha three years earlier, when together they collected for charity. For a while she motivated them to be the top team. Bevan used to sit and watch them, feeding off their energy. Sasha always wondered why he'd hang around people ten years younger than him. It was better with him at home.

No one gave, now, though. They bought; they never gave.

Rab was the star salesperson. He could make his dark-blue eyes leak tears and people bought out of sympathy. Sasha did okay but she was so eager and angry she put customers off a little. She insisted the team give ten percent of their earnings to a charity, which annoyed the others if they wanted to eat.

"It's a tithe, that's all," she said. "It's fair."

The company gave them forty percent. They'd sold books before, and shoes, and services of various kinds. Forty percent was generous.

Nick would leap around like a clown, drawing the crowds in for the other two to approach. His sales figures were always down but the crew worked together. They knew he sold low because he was helping them sell high, so they looked after him.

Sasha tilted her head toward a man telling her he already had Slenderise and didn't need more. That she was no better than a prostitute.

"Fair enough," she said.

"You look like a little bird with your head angled like that. You should turn your head away so you can't hear the arsehole," Rab said.

"I'd still hear him with my head turned," Sasha said.

Nick shook his head. A little later he whispered behind her back, "I love you." She didn't respond.

"Don't tease her," Rab said, though he smiled, his tight-lipped smile so different from Nick's broad one. He thought his teeth were no good. Too many lollies.

"Tease me how?" she said.

"Nothing," they both said.

Rab looked up and down the mall. "There's one. Just getting money out, got a girl with him. He'll want to impress her."

"How can you see that far? I hate your eyesight," Sasha said.

"Here he comes. Look at him. Bloody gold jewellery. You do him, Nick. You're good with rich people."

"You gotta get over hating rich people, Rab," Nick said. "Or else go work for one, making their beds or something." He flinched from a sudden cramp. "Fucking hunger pains," he said.

Rab laughed.

Nick leapt around so fast he looked like a rubber man. "Excuse me, excuse me, sir?"

The man said, "I'm busy."

"Young lady? Are you busy, too?" Nick raised his eyebrows at her. She looked him up and down and said, "Very."

"Too busy to lose some weight? I know you're looking gorgeous, perfection is in the eye of the beholder, but we've got a machine here to tell us if you need to lose just a little. And perhaps lose a little stress, too. We've got it all in Slenderise, the complete weight-loss-mental-health programme. It's even got an anti-cancer agent in there."

The couple stopped to listen.

"It's a free test," Sasha said.

The man rolled up his sleeve. "Why not?"

Sasha held his hand and felt his pulse. It wasn't necessary but men liked the physical contact.

She pressed his forefinger to the small screen Nick held.

It flashed.

"According to this, three weeks will take you to optimal weight for your height and age. And the lithium in the product, which occurs naturally in spring water, by the way, will help you stay happy during the programme. We're all on the maintenance programme."

The three of them smiled gloriously.

"Do me, now," the woman said. They tested her.

"Eight days to optimal weight. I would have said three, but you gotta believe the machine," Nick said.

The woman said, "So, are you two twins?"

Rab and Nick winked at each other. "Believe it or not, no. I'm older by just seventeen months. Never a year and a half, mind you. Seventeen months," Nick said.

The couple bought the recommended dosage and walked away, heads together, laughing.

"Thank fuck for that," Rab muttered.

They sold eight more programmes then got a little bored.

Rab said, "I need a new music player. Let's go buy one."

"We're not spending our money on more equipment for you, Rab," Sasha said. "Nick, give us a song."

Nick started singing, right into people's faces. He got pushed away a fair bit but that didn't bother him. Making people angry excited him in a strange way.

Rab disappeared to buy coffee, but his plan was to have a quick snooze in one of the café's big armchairs. He managed ten minutes before the manager poked him awake and kicked him out.

"This is not a charity place," she told him. The manager was so angry she forgot to make him pay for the coffee.

Rab brought back spring water for them both. "With naturally occurring lithium," Rab said.

"So long as it's naturally occurring," Nick said. He swallowed a pill with his water. "Gotta use your product," he said.

"Excellent," Sasha said. "I'm that thirsty. Thanks, Rab."

They were tired. The performance needed to sell Slenderise wearied them. The bright lights of the mall made their eyes ache. They sat down at the base of a massive flowerpot and talked about going home.

A cop came along and told them to stand up, move along.

"We're just having a rest," Nick said.

The cop got out his notebook.

"Name?" he said.

Nick froze for too long, so the cop angrily gestured for his hand and pressed his finger to the notebook screen.

"Nick Albadara." The cop looked at Nick. "According to this your bank account is empty. You should be starving."

Nick grinned. "I am pretty hungry."

The others laughed.

The cop half closed his eyes. "You'll need to earn some money soon, mate, or you'll drop below the poverty line. You're that close to dropping down a class level. It's hard to get up from there, believe me. Don't try to get money for nothing because you're already marked down for begging." The cop tore at a nail. It seemed to crack away like thin china.

His kindness made Sasha's eyes water. "It's all right, we've made heaps today. We just haven't registered it yet."

They heard crying; low, childish, exhausted crying. They turned and saw a woman, younger than them, really young, and in her arms was the crying kid.

"Help him, help him," the woman said. She spoke quietly. Exhausted.

The cop took off his jacket, and Sasha put her knitted bag on top of it. When the woman put the kid down, he lay still, crying in that terrible way.

"What's the matter with him?" Rab asked.

"I can't hear what you're saying," the woman said.

"Speak up, Rab. You're such a soft talker," Sasha said.

"I said what's wrong with him?"

"His bones hurt. His stomach. His head, his feet. He hurts all over. It hurts to breathe. The clinic says it's growing pains but he's not growing. He can't move anything now. First his feet then his hands, now he can't move."

"There are no tears," Sasha whispered.

The woman bent down to the boy. She kissed his cheek. "I'm sorry, darling, I have to show them." She lifted open the boy's eyelids.

Sasha gasped and turned away. Nick couldn't look either.

The cop said, "Jesus." He picked the kid up. "We've got to get him to hospital."

The woman wept noiseless tears of terrible empathy for the boy. She stood strangely.

"They won't take him until he's dead. Then they want him. The doctor won't see him, I waited three hours, and he wouldn't see him."

The boy struggled, and his breath rattled.

The cop said, "I'll pay. I'll pay for him." He squeezed the boy hard and they heard a cracking. The boy could no longer scream.

"Careful," the woman said. "Oh, God, careful." She reached for the boy and sank to the ground with him. He flicked his eyelids open and they saw bone there, his eyeballs covered with thin bone.

There was a crowd gathered now, muttering to each other, rustling their shopping bags as they jostled for a look. Nick, Sasha and Rab, all of them crying, tried to shield the mother and her son from view. The boy no longer cried. He sounded like he was breathing through a tube, then a straw, then...nothing.

The mother wept. Sasha watched and finally realised what was odd; she'd hunched her shoulders up and never dropped them.

The cop got on his radio and called for help.

"All right. I don't know what's going on, but they want us to wait here," the cop said to them.

"I'm not hanging around here," Sasha said.

"You'll have to wait, they've said," the cop said.

"What's your name, mate?" Rab said.

"You don't heed to know," the cop answered, taking his hat off and scratching his head. "Henri. You're supposed to pronounce it French but I never do. People always get it wrong and I don't worry about it. They think you're a dickhead if you do."

"He's freaking about something," Nick whispered to Rab.

"What'd they say to you?" Sasha said. "Because you know you're in it, too."

"I was instructed to contain the affront. I said there wasn't an affront, we just tried to help. But they hit my number." Henri held up his notebook. It flashed red.

"What is it?" Sasha said to the mother. "Is it something contagious? What is it?"

The woman sobbed without energy, as if she had nothing left inside. "He started getting sore and stiff. He said his bones ached. I said, okay, you need milk and cheese. Build up your bones, and he loved that. It made him happy for a while. A little while. But he got so hungry...then his eyes...and he couldn't hear me. His friend is the same. Why the children? What is it?"

Nick stretched his neck. Spread out his fingers. "It's making my bones ache just to think about it."

The cop looked helpless.

"Can't we get her somewhere comfortable? And the child?" Rab said. He stood with his hands on his hips. "I think we should all go and sit down. We'll go to that outdoor café, over there—we'll have a coffee, we'll wait for them. It's the best thing."

The cop said, "Look, I don't see why you can't just wait. They'll be here in a second."

It was five minutes before the uniformed medical team arrived, "Medical Team" in large letters on their backs, "PD" underneath.

"Police Department?" Nick asked. Henri shook his head. The medical team carried equipment, but they had no interest in the physical well-being of the group. When they picked up the little boy there was the faint crackle of bone and the mother wailed, "Don't break him! Don't break him."

The medics carefully laid the dead boy on a stretcher and covered him. One of them took the mother firmly by the elbow.

"Leukaemia," he told her. "Mercifully fast."

To Henri they said, "Names and addresses. Nothing to worry about here. Leukaemia. A new form. You can't catch it. Names and addresses, and we don't want this family's privacy invaded. We want them left alone now."

Henri turned to Sasha and said, "It's a new form of leukaemia." He shook his head. "Not like anything I've ever seen." He registered their names and address on his notebook.

A crowd gathered, and Nick and Rab took advantage of it. "For the boy," they said. "The mother."

People gave very little and soon Nick and Rab gave up.

Nick fell quiet.

"It's terrible," Sasha said. "We're all upset."

Nick looked at her. "Yeah, but I'm thinking about Dad. He's been walking stiffly. And he's quit work."

"It couldn't be this. Not the same thing. I'm sure he's fine, mate," Rab said.

They looked at the mother. She was quiet now. As they watched she took a deep shuddering breath then flinched, as if her lungs hurt. As the medical officers led her away Sasha tried to hug her but she was too limp.

"Let's get out of here," Rab said.

The cop checked his notebook. "I guess you can go. We'll be in touch if we need to speak with you."

Sasha kissed him. "Thank you," she whispered.

They walked quickly away.

They waited for the van to take them home again. The driver was angry they'd sold so little, didn't care why they'd stopped selling, and he refused to drive them home.

"Most people have already got the stuff, mate," Rab said. "You can't sell what people have already got."

The public bus took forever. Sasha sat in the back, crying, sick with what she'd seen.

Bevan was waiting for them when they got home. "Where've you been? The shops are shut now. I had to cook bloody vegetarian. No salt. I'll add my own later." He waited for a response. None of them spoke. "What's happened?" he said. "Did you lose the money?"

"You wouldn't understand," Sasha said. She stumbled to the room she shared with Rab.

"I might," Bevan said.

"We just saw a kid die," Nick said.

"What? An accident or something?"

"Nah. Leukaemia, they reckoned. I never heard of leukaemia like that."

"Plus it took ages to get home. We had to get the bus and the Rangers won the footy today and there were bodies everywhere," Rab said.

"It's worse when they lose," Bevan said. "I fuckin' hate it when they lose."

"How patriotic," Rab said. "Loyal barracking for the local team from someone who can't even catch a ball." Any child's death made him angry, mostly with the parents for allowing it to happen, as if somehow parents could keep their children safe from accident and disease. Their sister had lost a baby to cot death, and he blamed her. She didn't watch enough.

Nick was sick to his stomach and could barely eat or drink. He wanted physical contact with the others and kept patting them, sitting too close, wanting to be near.

They sat together on milk crates, resting their plates on an upturned box. Old newspapers made the crates a little softer.

Nick, suddenly starving, drank a litre of milk before he began his meal. He always smelt sweet, as if the lactose rose to the surface of his skin and sat there like perfume.

They could hear the TV in one of the flats, the football game replayed. "Kill 'em, Kill 'em," they heard. Football wasn't much of a game anymore.

Sasha held her plate on her knee and ate rice, kelp and steamed vegetables.

"At least have some soy sauce on it, Sash," Rab said. "If you're going to eat seaweed, cover the taste for fuck's sake."

"They put anchovies into soy sauce sometimes. You have to be vigilant." She held her spread fingers to her eyes, mimicking a vigilante mask. The joke didn't lighten their mood.

For dessert, she sat with a bowl of peaches. She never smelt as sweet as Nick did.

They drank beer. Bevan smoked. Sasha finally said, "That poor kid. And his mother. Oh, my God."

Everyone was quiet again. A bird fell out of the trees; prompting Nick to jump up.

"I'm going to look inside that fucker," he said. He lay newspapers down on the grass, put on gloves and found a sharp knife. There were three dead birds in their backyard. Nick picked up one and laid it down on the newspaper. It was smooth under his fingers. He felt no ribs, none of the skinny little bones that make birds so hard to eat. He cut through the skin and came straight to bone.

A smooth plane of bone.

"This is weird," he said. He went inside and put a big pot of water on to boil.

"You makin' soup for tomorrow night?" Bevan said. "Tell me if you are, and I'll have a break from cooking for a change."

"You're the cook, Bevan. I'm just going to boil this bird."

"You're not gonna put the bird in my pot. Fuckin' weirdo." Bevan coughed.

"It's just meat. Like a chicken. Nothing to worry about."

"What if it's diseased?"

"You can't catch bird diseases. You're human."

"What about that chicken flu thing? That killed about a million people."

"It killed about two thousand, and they all had something to do with the chickens' blood. All right? I just want to see what's going on here."

The water boiled. Nick dropped the bird in, splashing hot water and burning his fingertips. While he waited, he laid newspaper out on the kitchen bench.

The smell of wet feathers. He let the bird boil for an hour then lifted it out with tongs. The flesh fell off, and he pulled the rest away. He gagged at the soup he'd made; feathers, eyes, flesh.

He washed the bird's skeleton in the laundry sink then placed it on the newspaper. He stared at it then carried it outside to show the others.

The bird was one bone.

The wings were as smooth as china, with no give, no bend. The ribs had fused to the backbone.

It was like a small football with some of the air let out. Dents, shallow craters. But mostly smooth. A football with smooth wings.

"No wonder it couldn't fly," Sasha said. "Look at it!"

"We should take it to Dad, Rab."

"I'm sure he's got birds there, Nick."

"We're going there tomorrow, anyway, aren't we? Mum's cooking dinner. And I want to see how Dad is. We need the money, man. They're always good for a loan."

Sasha started crying and couldn't stop. Bevan carried her inside and tucked her into bed, then turned on the TV, wanting to distract himself from the thought of her sad little body. The news showed him an apartment block up the road from them, eight small flats housing eight large families. There was a permanent begging place out the front; a table for food donations; a slotted, locked box for money; a bookshelf for books for the children.

The place burnt down. All exits barricaded. All killed.

A terrible accident. "Questions need to be answered," the police minister said, but he smiled as he said it.

"Anything interesting?" Rab asked.

"Nothin'," Bevan said.

On Saturday morning they waited for Nick to get up and finally dragged him out of bed. Bevan drove, with Nick yawning in the back. The bird skeleton was wrapped in paper and packed in the boot.

"You don't all have to come, you know," Nick said. He read the paper as he spoke.

"Your Mum'll cook us a meal. It's worth it for that," Bevan said. "Better than the fried crap we'd get at my parent's place." They all had a momentary flash of Bevan's parents, huge, both of them, sitting on the couch eating fish fingers.

"Well, thanks, guys. For coming," Nick said.

The road was paved with rubbish; adults, children, cats and dogs picking through it.

"Watch out for that kid, Bevan," Rab said.

"What?"

"The kid," Rab said, louder. The child stared at them then moved out of the way.

When they arrived, they saw a family was camped across the road, socks hanging from a rope strung between two trees. Mrs Albadara answered the door.

"Ah, your father's not so well today. Not so well. He'll be okay. Me, I've just got a little headache."

Mr Albadara emerged then, smiling. He was as beautiful, really, as the boys, Sasha thought. The dark hair, black eyes, dark skin. Perfect teeth. Perfect smile.

"Hello, Mr Albadara," Sasha said. She hated feeling so respectful but she couldn't help it around Mr Albadara.

Nick said, "Dad? Something to show you. Something weird. You won't be able to figure it out. It'll stump you for sure."

"You'll show me in the study," Mr Albadara said. He liked his challenges to be private. Nick followed him to the book-lined room and placed the bird on the large, cluttered desk. Stiffly, Mr Albadara leaned over and unwrapped the bird. "I always said you should have been a vet. You're so good with animals. Ha ha."

"I didn't kill it, Dad! It just landed in our backyard."

His father poked at the bird with a pen. "Hmmm. It brings to mind the eternal bone, which won't burn. You can't crush it. You can't grind it or suck the marrow out, which will disappoint you. I know you can't see a bone without wanting to suck it."

Nick laughed. "What bone?"

"You don't know? Albadara? It is the name of the eternal bone. The bone from which the body will be resurrected."

"That's what our name means?"

"I'm afraid so."

"You know we saw a kid die yesterday. His eyes were covered with bone. And inside the dead bird it's the same thing. And you, Dad. You seem so stiff. This boy was stiff."

"Yes. I'm a little worried, too. Sudden onset is always of concern. I will see the doctor very soon." Mr Albadara stood up, stretching high to reach an ornate treasure box. He winced a little. "My ribs," he said. "Ah, in here. I had forgotten." Mr Albadara scrabbled around the things in there; a golden piece of cloth; a string with knots tied in it; a miniature eyeglass, a small rock.

"Here," he said, handing Nick a dusty, blue, perfect glass globe the size of a clenched fist. Inside sat a pearl gray triangle.

"What is it?"

"That's an ancient bone. Very old. It's an indestructible bone."

"It can't be. How old?"

"That I don't know. But it proves to me eternal life. I used to show this to you and Rab when you were children. I'd almost forgotten it existed."

"But you don't believe in religion."

"I believe in that." He gazed at the globe. "Jeremiah would be fascinated by this. I must show him."

"Who's Jeremiah?"

"Oh, just a friend. A most unusual man. You'll meet him. Another time, when we're all at the farm. You think this house is full of junk, you should see his home. Old books, antiques, anything with information from the past. He doesn't think enough information is being passed from generation to generation."

"I didn't know you had any friends, Dad."

His father smiled and nodded. "You tease me," he said.

The others were in the kitchen. Mrs Albadara was making tabouleh and spicy rice, stuffed vine leaves and spinach fingers.

Bevan watched intently.

"You're so fast," he said. "Sasha, even you'd like this stuff. Hey?"

There was no answer. Sasha and Rab had stolen away.

"Let's go spying. Show me your old room. Something to take our minds off this bone thing," Sasha said, tugging at Rab's hand.

"Let's find a place to lie down," Rab said, grabbing her, kissing her. Peppermint passion.

It was a big, old house, full to squeezing with books, specimens, models. Sasha loved it. She could spend hours in that house, if she didn't have to talk to the parents; they made her feel stupid. She loved just looking and wanting half the things she saw. There was a wax skull. A candlestick made of ebony. Books, unsorted, in piles. Dusty glass statues; a horse, a girl, a wishing well. Ornate pens. Cards of all kinds. Empty pewter frames.

In the upstairs study, the library, which was his childhood bedroom, Rab said, "Come sit with me." He pulled her onto the couch and stroked her face. Thrust his fingers into her hair and pulled her towards him.

She kissed him back, crawling onto him, wanting to absorb him. She moved about, finding a position until he said, "Keep still."

She slapped him gently. "Don't tell me to keep still. I hate keeping still." She rolled onto the floor and crawled around, looking for things.

"There's treasure everywhere here," she said. She pulled out a silver bookmark from under a chair.

"Keep it," Rab said. "They'll never miss it."

Bevan said, "I can watch the cookin', Mrs Albadara, if you've got things you need to do."

"You're such a nice man," she said. "You need a nice girl." She smiled. "Let me think of someone for you."

Anyone with a hole, he thought. He stirred the pot, checked the oven. There wasn't a lot to do. He opened her spice jars to sniff them, understand them.

Just to see what was inside, he lifted the lids on the containers lined up on the pantry shelf.

In a tin marked 'bread' he found a mess of things; tiny bells, a ring, three fake tattoos, four silver balls and a voucher for free coffee, many years expired. And money. Notes and coins, dirty and crumpled.

Bevan looked over his shoulder. She hadn't returned.

He took a quick count; two hundred dollars in notes, twenty-five dollars in coins. He took one hundred dollars.

"Petrol money," he said. "Toll money." Money of his own, not money the others had earned. He put the tin back and checked the dinner, hoping Mrs Albadara would come back soon to tell him what to do next. He tried to imagine his own mother teaching anyone to cook.

Never.

Mrs Albadara caught Sasha coming out of the bathroom. She said, "So, Sasha, come sit with me. I feel I know so much about you. The boys never shut up. Sasha this, Sasha that. I've met you all these times but we've never talked, dear, and I've got photos, would you like to see photos?"

Mrs Albadara squeezed Sasha's hand as if they shared some great secret. She pulled out baby photos of Nick and Sasha realised she thought she was Nick's girlfriend.

"Mum! What're you doing? Sasha doesn't want to see those!" Nick said, catching them together.

"I don't know. Any chance to see you naked," Sasha said.

Mrs Albadara slammed the album shut.

"Maybe another time," she said. "I smell burning. What is that Bevan doing to my kitchen?" She limped away.

When they were alone, Nick said, "You shouldn't talk like that in front of my mother, S."

"Fuck your mother."

"It's not her. It's me. You give me ideas. Dirty little ideas I should be spanked for."

Sasha laughed. "Just good friends, Nick. Just good friends." But she smiled at him, confusing him.

"Dinner!" shouted Bevan.

They sat down at the large table laden with food. Sasha felt a little guilty, thinking of the family across the street. But this was food she could eat, and she gave into it.

"If only your sister could be here, too," Mr Albadara said. The others exchanged glances.

"She doesn't come here anymore," Rab said.

They all helped to clean up.

Mrs Albadara wrapped the leavings in newspaper then gave the parcel to Rab. "Bin's out the front."

The end of the parcel was damp and leaked over his shirt.

"Jesus, Mum. I've got rubbish juice all over me."

She sighed. "Sometimes I wish we still had plastic bags."

Rab rolled his eyes. "The Good Old Days."

His mother snorted. "They were good. People cared about each other. Wealthy governments gave money to poor countries. You could go to the doctor even if you didn't have the money to pay. The government would pay."

"Why would they do that?"

"And they'd help you if you couldn't find a job. Not throw you in jail."

"Doesn't make sense, Mum," Rab said.

His mother turned on him. "You don't care! It made sense. But the more it became about money, then it didn't make sense."

Bevan said, "I would've hated the tax payin' business. I wouldn't want any of my money payin' for some loser to get his cold fixed up or whatever."

"People used to do it, then they got the idea they shouldn't."

"We're all right, anyway, Mum," Rab said.

"And that's all that matters, isn't it?" she said. "Take a clean shirt of your father's. In the drawer. There's a nice wide-striped one that will make you look older."

"Can't we give the leftovers to the family across the street?" Sasha said.

"They'll take it if they want it," Mr Albadara said.

"So you've never taken a plate to them?" Mrs Albadara said.

"I cannot lie to you. Once I did. Maybe twice."

"Perhaps you'd like me to take it over to them, served on a silver platter?" Rab said. Sasha wrinkled her nose at him. Nick ignored it all, reading the newspaper.

They were back selling Slenderise on Monday.

"God, I hate Mondays," Sasha said. "People are nasty on Mondays."

"People are nasty every day, Sash," Rab said.

"But everyone walks so much faster on Mondays. It's like they feel guilty for their weekends and want to make up for it."

They watched an elderly man limp by.

"Like him. God knows what he got up to," Sasha said. As he passed them they saw his coat was slashed to shreds and the back of his head was covered with blood.

They all turned away.

Nick jumped in front of three young girls.

"Girls? Girls? Good, are you?" They laughed. One covered her mouth with her hand and Nick saw grime in the knuckles and nails.

"No bath at home? Don't your parents wash you?" The girl hid her hand behind her back.

"We don't live with our parents."

"But where do you sleep?"

"Who can sleep?" the girl said.

"You be careful, girls. See?" Nick pointed. In the distance a teenager kicked a woman who was bent over clutching her stomach.

"See? There are bad people about. You be careful," Nick said.

The three girls walked away. "We need to keep moving. They told us to keep moving," the girls said to Nick. His attention was lost, though; he'd found a dead rat and was wrapping it in newspaper.

Rab grabbed his arm. "Come on, time's wasting," he said. "Let's go find a doctor's shop. That's easy money."

They found a queue that went around the block, the poor waiting for a doctor who'd see them. They sold forty-two weight-loss programmes to the people shuffling, standing patiently.

That night they had steak. As Sasha was washing up a woman came to the door, collecting for charity. Rab answered; Nick was immersed in the newspaper and didn't hear the knock. The woman recoiled from the smell in the house; Nick had boiled the rat then tried to burn its bones and the stink was all-pervading. Trying not to breathe through her nose, she said, "We are returning to the terrible days of asylums. This is what they found on a recent raid." She handed Rab a photo; an emaciated, twisted child lying under a putrid sink on filthy tiles, pants around his ankles, holding hands with another naked child.

"They were both moaning when they were found," she said.

"How come that kid's got a beard?" Rab asked.

She looked at the photo, then at Rab. "That's faeces," she said.

"I can give you ten cents," Rab said. "That's about all I can manage."

The woman said. "There are women being raped in these places. They need medical treatment and they won't get it for less than ten dollars. Some of these women are torn from anus to vagina. They'll never have children."

"Shame," said Rab, and closed the door on her.

"Hey, Sasha, I'd like to tear you from arse to cunt," Bevan muttered to himself. He heard Sasha, sometimes, in the room next door, in the house they all shared. She loved it. She worked Rab till he dropped and still wanted more. Bevan'd give it to her if she let him. Fuck yeah. He'd give it to her. Bevan watched her skinny arse as she washed the dishes and fantasised grabbing it, her turning around and laughing. He fantasised she was his wife. Young, but not too young. Not too innocent.

"Stupid woman. What does she think is going to happen?" Rab said.

"Do you always have to be so negative?" Sasha said. "Just because you only think of yourself and what money you can make doesn't mean everyone else does."

"Look around you, Sash. No one gives a shit about anyone."

"You certainly don't."

"Hey, enough with the bitchiness, all right? I've had it with you." Rab turned and left the house.

There was a cat on the footpath outside. Motionless. Only the tip of its tail moved. Rab gently shoved it aside with his foot and it felt smooth. Hard.

Nick put his arm around Sasha and kissed her head. "Don't worry about him, S. He's more stressed by this whole thing than he'll admit. Come on, I'll take you out for a drink. Mum gave me some money for 'us time'."

Sasha said, "How did she get the idea I was your girlfriend, not Rab's?"

Nick kissed her hand. "No idea." They dressed up a little, laughing. Sasha put lipstick on.

"Where're youse goin'?" Bevan asked.

"Just out for a while. You can come if you want," Sasha said.

Bevan looked at her. "Nah, promised to go see me olds. Have fun."

Sasha and Nick ran out of the house. Free. A van marked "PD" was parked nearby. The medical team emerged, carrying a body bag.

"Another one? What the hell is it?" Sasha said.

There was a hum like electricity in the air, and she realised moaning was coming from houses all around them.

Bevan stayed away for two days. His parents took more time than expected. Things to sort out. Rab also stayed away, tired of feeling in the wrong all the time.

Bevan arrived back first and noticed nothing different.

Sasha said, "How are your parents?"

"Arrested. Dad can't move, and Mum can't look after herself. And the two of them eat more than they earn. I left 'em some Slenderise last time but I don't think they took it."

"Oh, no," Sasha said.

"They're so fuckin' fat they had to get wheeled out." He poured down a beer. Grinned. "I'm livin' off beer from now on." He was glad the onus of caring for his parents was gone from him.

"And their eating habits differ from yours how?" Nick said.

He sat close to Sasha.

Rab returned the next day to find his belongings alone in the bedroom. He said nothing because the phone rang. Their mother.

Nick wouldn't get out of bed. "My stomach hurts. I can't eat. Bring me some milk, a milkshake, chocolate, come on, S," Nick said. He pushed Sasha.

"You seemed okay last night," she said.

Nick tried to smile but his face was stiff. "Are you sure about this?" he said.

"No. But it's what happened so there you go. I'm happy. Rab'll be fine. You can share me." Sasha felt her heart beating faster most of the time. Like it was matching the beat of unheard music.

"Best of both worlds, huh?" Nick groaned. "I really feel bad. My ribs feel like they're sticking into my lungs."

"We should take you to a doctor. They might be able to help."

"I guess."

Sasha got up and made him a milkshake. Rab was in the lounge room, packing music into an overnight bag.

"What's going on?" Sasha said.

"Funny question, coming from you, Sash," Rab said. He smiled and kissed her on the cheek. "Dad's not well. Bevan's going to drive me out to the farm to see him."

"I want to come. Nick's sick, too. We could nurse them together."

"We could."

Sasha took the milkshake into Nick. "We're going to visit your Mum and Dad. They've gone to the farm. Wanna come?"

"I guess. I want my Mum."

"I can be your Mum."

"I doubt that, S," he said. He pulled her on to the bed and kissed her. His mouth felt hard and tasted of milk.

Sasha took Nick to the doctor. She sold her favourite necklace to pay for it.

Nick came stumbling out. "Lithium," he said. "It's just the side affects of the lithium. Nausea, drowsiness, tremors."

"So stop taking the lithium."

"They want everyone to keep taking it," Nick said.

Nick sat in the car while the others packed bags and filled the boot. They took their last supplies of Slenderise. Bevan drove; he always drove. Sasha joined Nick in the back.

"Changin' of the guard, I see," Bevan said. He looked in the rear-view mirror, seeing Sasha stroking Nick's head. "Must be my turn next." He coughed.

Sasha ground her teeth. "I hate clichés, you know, but...last man on earth and it wouldn't happen."

Bevan was silent. Rab could see his gaze flicking from side to side and worried about his concentration.

Nick said, "What about your olds, Bevan?"

"What about them?"

"Is it this bone thing they've got? I heard something on the radio about it and there's stuff about it in the papers," Nick said.

"Wouldn't know. Can't get in to visit them. All I know is, they're gettin' fed so they'll be happy. Why, what is it?" He coughed.

"This bone thing. Sore bones. Symptoms from some hormonal thing, I don't know."

"The doctor said it was the lithium," Sasha said.

"It's gotta be more than that," Nick said. He fell asleep with his arm tucked up under his chin. It took two hours to get to the other side of town. Traffic was heavy and there were accidents, more accidents than usual. People were walking along the freeway and it looked weird, like the walking birds.

A strange migration.

They reached open ground and drove through the lush greenness of it. There were milking sheds.

Nick sat up. His arm was tucked under his chin.

"What are you doin'? You look creepy," Bevan said.

"I can't put my arm down," Nick said. "I can't move it."

Fused.

"We should get a job here on the way back," Nick said. "It looks really nice here."

Rab had to turn down the music to hear him.

Bevan drove without talking, smoking furiously.

As they passed through their third toll booth, Rab said, "How's the petrol going?" Bevan looked down. "We'll have to stop soon." He lit a cigarette with one hand. The smoke reached over to the back seat.

"Bevan!" Sasha said. Bevan wound down his window and hung his right arm out. He drove left-handed. His arm was covered with a long-sleeved top; he rarely bared his skin to the sun.

Bevan pulled into a petrol station and Rab said, "Where did the money come from?"

"I borrowed it from your Mum's bread bin," Bevan said.

"Stole it!" Sasha said. "You stole it!"

Rab was quiet.

"It's petrol money," Bevan said. "Wanted to pay for it myself for a change."

"Mum loves you. She would've given it to you, if you'd asked."

Bevan grinned. "I didn't want to be under obligation to your Mum." He squinted at the gauge. "That should do. That'll get us there." He stuck his head in the window to reach for his wallet.

As they neared the Albadara's farm, Bevan said, "So I'll just drop you off, will I?"

"You gotta come in for a while," Sasha said. "Weren't the fields different last time we were here? When was that?"

"We came two Christmases ago. Remember? We hated it," Rab said.

"Are you sure we haven't been since then? I can't believe we haven't been out of the city in all that time."

"We've been busy."

There were fields of flowers. Dozens of different kinds. Lush purples and reds.

"Let's stop and get some flowers for your Mum. They're so colourful," Sasha said.

"I need a piss anyway," Bevan said. He got out and urinated one step away from the car. The smell of ammonia made Nick's eyelids snap open but he closed them quickly. The light hurt him.

Sasha ran into the fields and picked some flowers. Their stems were white and seemed brittle; they snapped easily.

"What sort of flowers do you think they are?" she said.

"No idea," Rab said. "I don't know stuff like that. Nick is the romantic type. Ask him."

Nick was answering no questions. He'd seen a dead rabbit beside the road. "Get that for me, Rab?" he said.

Rab shook his head in disgust. "You're a fucking lunatic, you know that," he said.

Sasha breathed in the scent of the flowers.

"It's rich. It reminds me of something. Smell them." She thrust them under Rab's nose. He pulled away.

"I know it's not a good smell, but aren't they beautiful?" she said.

"I can smell them already, thanks. Too strong. Let's get away from here." His urgency startled her into movement.

Minutes later they reached the Albadara's farm. There were a dozen cars parked out front.

Mr Albadara came out to greet them, walking stiffly, slowly. He watched as they took Nick out of the car.

"Him too? He can't move his arm?" Mr Albadara asked.

Sasha tried to hand him the flowers. He waved his hand at her. "I don't want them, silly girl. Throw them away. And wash your hands. Did you breathe the pollen?"

"Aren't they beautiful?" Sasha said. She smiled, willing him to smile back and make it all right.

"They smell of flesh," Mr Albadara said. "Don't you realise that? The sweet smell of flesh just before it begins to rot. They're burying the poor over there. Lining them up, piling them in. These flowers grow overnight and they stink. Go dig one up and you'll see. Try to pull it up by its roots and you'll feel a tug. Those mutated flowers grow straight out of the bodies of the dead. Pollination spreads the flowers everywhere else. They grow like weeds, this mutant breed."

Sasha threw the flowers away and blew her nose. The stench was there, now she knew what it was. There was a sick feeling in her stomach, as if she'd eaten meat and enjoyed it without knowing it was meat. She'd sniffed so hard at those flowers, wanting to identify the smell.

Mr Albadara said, "There is more than one graveyard. So many people die, of so many things, with so little money. They plant the flowers to cover the fact. They don't hide it but the flowers are there to make people forget the bodies are there, forget people are dying of hunger and deprivation."

"But there were no graveyards or signs or anything. What're they doing? They can't bury people like that."

"They're dead, they're poor, they have no one. Anything's possible when no one cares," Mr Albadara said.

Sasha thought of the dozens of fields they had seen. Hundreds of these flowers, with bone-brittle stems. She thought of Rab's disgust in the flowers. "Did you know this?"

"I thought everyone did. What else are they going to do with the bodies?"

"I can't believe you didn't tell me."

"I can't believe you didn't know, Sash."

Mr Albadara said, "Roots travel down to where the nutrients are."

"We saw a kid die. Actually watched him die," Sasha said.

"Ah," Mr Albadara said. "Yes. Nick told me."

"He was all stiff, like you and Nick. He couldn't see, though. His eyes were all closed over. They told us it was leukaemia."

Mr Albadara snorted. "Doubtful. Very doubtful. I bet they snapped him up. Raced him off."

Nick nodded and hugged his Dad with one arm.

"The proof will be found in the bones of the children," Mr Albadara said. "Come in."

Sasha held back, watching the others help Nick through the door. It was too strange. Mr Albadara was too strange. She was scared of it all.

"Come on, Sash," Rab said kindly. He put his arm around her. The strength of him made her feel weak.

"I'm all right," she said.

"You've come on a good day," Mr Albadara said as they walked through the house to the backyard. "We're having a little party."

Bevan stepped forward. The backyard was full of women thirty years his senior. Some men but not so many. All the guests were stripped to bare skin and underwear. Rab had noticed this in the city, too, in the public parks. People spending as much time in the sun as possible. They craved it. Bevan usually covered up, with his red hair and white skin. People didn't trust him, so white. The darker the skin the healthier.

The guests had taken off their hats and thrown away the sunscreen. They were getting naked.

Bevan smiled. "Ripe for the pickin'," he said, and walked with his ape's walk to the table of drinks; arms out from his body, fingers spread, legs a little bowed.

"He's such a sleaze," Sasha said.

"At least he's leaving you alone," Rab said.

Bevan did okay. The older ladies liked him, and he liked any woman who liked him, old or young. He could flirt with them, the old ones, and they believed it, because he was gap-toothed, scar-skinned, short-bodied. Their self-esteem was so low, most of them, they could believe an ugly man with BO would flirt with them. They wouldn't have believed it from Rab or Nick.

Bevan slicked his hair down but it sprang straight back into a mess as he walked up to a woman with fat ankles and dry, brittle hair. "Gidday, love," he said.

Nick groaned. They helped him to sit and Sasha found him a glass of milk and a straw.

"God, all these boring people," Sasha said.

They sat together, clustered on chairs, perching on table edges. Nick, intent and curious, sat beside his father near the pool. "What do you think it is, Dad? This bone thing? I boiled a rat the other day. It was like the bird. Creepy. Tried to burn it."

"I'll tell you what's creepy," Bevan said, standing with his hands on his hips between them. "No beer! Where's the beer?"

"There's plenty of whisky," said Mr Albadara.

"I want beer!" Bevan's face reddened like it usually did after a dozen.

"Beer won't help you," Mrs Albadara said, coming over to calm her guest. "Here, have some milk. Energy milk," she said, pouring whisky straight into the carton.

Nick walked stiffly to the table.

"I smell cheese," he said. He picked up a handful of cheese cubes with the unfused hand and filled his mouth with them. He chewed. The pain went away just a little. He took a carton of milk and sculled it, dribbling milk down his chin.

Everyone was doing the same.

The sight of them all with milk moustaches and beards made Sasha laugh.

"Want one?" said a white haired woman. Her face spasmed and twitched as if she was amused. "You look like you could do with one."

"Sasha, this is my Great-aunt Terry," Rab said. "Not bad for her age, is she?"

"I don't eat any animal products," Sasha said. She felt like she needed to apologise for her food choice.

"None?" said Great-aunt Terry.

"I'll take it, Terry," Rab said. He sculled the milk.

"You know what they're saying," Great-aunt Terry said, "It's not the side affects of the lithium after all. Tiredness, and body ache and that. They're saying it's hormonal. And you can only treat it with calcium and Vitamin D. Studies have shown the more sun the better. Don't you just love it?"

Bevan drank straight whisky. He hated milk. He coughed as the liquor hit his throat.

"There's nuts, on the table, and more cheese," Mr Albadara said.

"Cheese is an animal product," Sasha said. She hated the way she sounded but what could she do? She took a kelp pill. Sometimes it was all she had to eat. She whispered to Rab, "You do realise your Great-aunt Terry is insane, don't you?"

Nick was still eating the cheese and drinking milk. Sasha thought he stank of it.

Rab watched her.

"Happy with your choice?" he said.

"I haven't made a choice."

"Really?"

"Why? You bothered?"

Rab laughed. "Is it all completely meaningless to you?"

"The sex part is. The morning part isn't. And the talking part."

They were quiet. They watched Mr Albadara, livelier than he'd been in a long time. He wandered around squeezing and stroking people, saying, "How are you feeling *inside*?"

"Your Dad's scaring me. What's up with him?" Sasha said.

"I don't know, Sash. I guess he's just worried about people." They watched him walking stiffly amongst his guests. His arm movements were stiff and jerky. His smile seemed bigger than usual.

"Did your Dad get false teeth?" Sasha asked.

"Leave him alone, would you? You've done nothing but criticize since we got here," Rab said, staring at her.

Sasha turned her back. "I'm going for a swim," she said. She dropped her clothes at the side of the pool. Her bright yellow bikini brought gasps of envy from the guests.

Rab and Nick watched her for a while, then Nick said, "I want to talk to Dad. Help me in."

Rab took his arm and they found their father standing in the corner of the sunroom. Just standing. Rab helped Nick to a sofa and sat on a stool.

"Dad," Nick said. "How are you feeling?"

"Fine, fine," their father said. "Same as you, I suppose. Not so good. You?"

"I'm a little scared, to be honest. You should have seen this kid die, Dad. It was horrible. The medics took him away so fast. They wanted him for his organs. For other kids."

"They'd have to crack him open like a lobster. He's all one bone, now. Spurs, they're calling it. Yes. I've been hearing a little about this new disease. The bone grows at an alarming rate, they say."

"That's what it feels like. It feels like I'm all bone and my blood can hardly get through my veins," Nick said.

His father nodded and said, "They should name the disease after us. Don't you think?"

Rab frowned. "Why?"

"Because our name means the eternal bone. You boys have forgotten everything I've ever told you. It is an ancient name meaning the eternal bone."

"So this has happened before?" Rab asked. "It must have happened before to have a name."

"That's a point. A good point. I wonder if this did happen millennia ago. If the bones fused, the bones strengthened. And the mythology sprung from that. I'll get back to you. I've got some literature because of our name. Let me read and then I'll call you. Go now and leave me to study." He stumbled as he turned. Rab leapt up and grabbed his arm, helped him to sit beside Nick.

"Dad?" Nick said. "Are you all right?"

Mr Albadara shook his head. "No. No. I don't want this to be over. I don't."

"What, Dad? The party?"

"My life, Nick. My life. I'm not ready to go."

"Who says you're going? You'll be all right."

"I won't, you know. It's too late. For me. Maybe they'll figure it out in time for others. Lord, I hope so. But Nick. Nick, you too. I'm sorry to frighten you. I'm so sorry," his father said.

"You always tell us the truth."

"I try to," his father said. "I'm not too good at lying."

Rab looked at them, their limbs held stiffly. "I'm feeling it too," he said.

"Not like this," Nick whispered.

There was the sound of girlish squeals below.

"Ah," Mr Albadara said. He smiled, satisfied. "Come on." He shuffled downstairs and struggled to open the back door.

"Jeremiah! My friend! You old misfit," he said. "I always know when you arrive because the women make a noise!"

"Here at last. At last!" the man said. He was dressed all in white. Close-cropped white hair and a broad brimmed white hat. The heavy scent of aftershave. He smiled, snarling his damaged, ivory-yellow teeth at them. His face was smooth and tight, too much fat squeezed into too little skin. He held up a bottle of white wine like an Olympic torch.

"Glasses, my friend? Glasses!" he said.

"Come, let's sit inside. Away from the rest. Rab. Nick. Sasha. You too, Bevan. Let's visit with my friend," Mr Albadara said. Mrs Albadara sighed and collected huge glasses for them all. Mr Albadara couldn't hold his properly, and he splashed wine all over his pants and shoes.

"You're getting wine on the carpet," Mrs Albadara said. She was exhausted from being hostess to so many visitors so much of the time.

"That's why we're drinking white," Mr Albadara said. "No stains." He and Jeremiah found this very funny.

"I'm sorry. Sorry. I'm here to make the arrangements. I'm so sorry for your loss," Jeremiah said. He stood up to clasp Rab's hand but Rab just stared at him. He went for Nick then gave up, putting his hands in his pockets.

"What arrangements?" Rab said. "What loss?"

"He's already made mine. So he's here to do Nick's. Normally you'd have to go to see him," Mr Albadara said. "But the moment I called him and said it was an emergency, here he is."

"I don't normally make house calls," the man said. His mouth twitched as if he was trying to be serious but couldn't help seeing the funny side. "My place is up at the top of the hill. I call it The Grinding House. I'm hoping the name will catch on. The Grinding House."

"Are you a doctor? We don't need a doctor. We've already seen a doctor," Sasha said.

"He's the funeral director," Mr Albadara said softly. "We need to decide what we'll do with Nick. They're asking that most people be cremated. It allays the fear of infection. People who can't afford it are going out to the fields. I know what I want to do, and your mother, but we want to include you in the decision. We want to be part of the research, so our deaths are not in vain."

"You want that. I do not," Mrs Albadara said. "This is wrong."

"It can't be wrong if it is for the greater good. The Greater Good. What *is* wrong is burying bodies which could help save humanity," Jeremiah said. His voice was soft, clear, determined.

"Ah, hello? Still alive here?" Nick said. He tried to smile and said, "I'm tired."

"And me. Come, I'll lie with you, my darling," his mother said. Rab helped Nick to rise.

Mrs Albadara curled up in bed with Nick, and cried softly. Rab went back to Sasha, sitting nervously with his father and Jeremiah.

"Rab, we need to talk. This is happening and I don't want the decisions left to you," said his father. "Listen, I want to be honest. I want to describe it to you so you will have some understanding. The stomach pain is first. That ache, and a loss of hunger. Or great hunger, ravenous, accompanied by terrible nausea. You can feel the smoothness inside your belly. The fat hangs there like a pouch."

Sasha tucked her legs up and squeezed her eyes shut. She tilted her head away.

"This is what happens. First the feet feel stiff and the heels sore. You can't bend your toes. Then your ankles feel stiff. It is worse overnight. You wake up in pain. As you walk you feel the bones crackle. Like walking on eggshells. Your fingers, too. You can't move your fingers. When you sleep you try to lie with your fingers comfortably held. You try not to point your toes. Because one morning you wake up and your fingers have fused. You can't bend them. If your toes are pointed they will stay that way."

Instinctively they all curled their toes.

"You know then that you don't have long," Mr Albadara said. "Your knees and elbows stiffen. If you fall asleep with them wrapped around yourself, you will have to break them to move them.

"Your neck stiffens. Your groin feels painful. When you walk it is like your pelvis is mortar and your spine a pestle, grinding, grinding.

"Your breathing becomes difficult. You no longer feel your ribs, just a smooth breastplate, like armour.

"You urinate sitting down, a thin, painful, stream. You can't defecate. Small pebbles eke out.

"Then your ears. You can't hear. There is bone across your eardrums. This happens very quickly. It can happen in a day with the worst growth happening at night."

Rab got up and moved next to Sasha.

"When the bone grows over your eyes you need to make yourself as comfortable as possible. You need to lie down. Before your throat closes over you need to take a drink. Remember though that you can't urinate. Your bladder will be full, and there is no way to release it. The poisons of your waste will be absorbed back into your body, but this is not what will kill you.

"You will know the sensation of bone growth by now. You will be able to feel the bones growing and fusing.

"Your sinus cavities close.

"You lie there. There is a sinking feeling, like you are about to succumb to anaesthesia. You feel like your eyes are open but you can't see. Maybe just a sense of light before the bone grows too thick across your eyes."

His father cupped his eyes with his palms.

"It is very painful. You remember growing pains now."

He dropped his hands to his lap, clenched his fists.

"Your skeleton smoothes into one plane and the top of your throat seals as the base of your skull closes in. If you don't panic you have maybe an hour of breathing before this closes altogether, the last bones merge and you can't even struggle for breath." Mr Albadara sank back in his chair, tears wetting his cheeks.

"Rest, now, my friend," Jeremiah said. "Rest." Mr Albadara closed his eyes. Jeremiah moved closer to Rab and Sasha and whispered, "I've seen a skeleton. They're not telling people. It looked like an alien. An alien! Like the aliens people say they see. It looked like he had one bone. He was smooth. Smooth. No joints or gaps. Some bumps—ankles, knees, hips, elbows. Some bumps on the head. All else was smooth."

Rab got up and stood by his father. "Dad?"

"It's almost inevitable. The fusion," Mr Albadara said, blinking rapidly. "We're born with four hundred and fifty bones, which fuse to two hundred and six by the time you're an adult. The top of your shoulder is still not fused at sixteen. It's the last to merge. The skeleton is so very separate from the man. Almost anonymous. You know who a man is just by looking at him, but a skeleton you need to study and guess." He closed his eyes. "I'll rest, now. Nick is resting, and your mother. Rab, I want you to go with Jeremiah, just so you understand."

Jeremiah stood, his fingertips pressed together in a triangular shape.

"Come on, then," Jeremiah said. "No time like the present. I'll take you with me, then bring you back a little later. Come on!"

"We might as well see how bad it is," Rab said. "Come with me, Sasha?"

They travelled in the hearse. The blackness of it made Rab and Sasha whisper. Jeremiah drove to the top of the hill. A professional sign, painted black letters on a pale blue background, said The Grinding House.

"Does he think it's funny? I don't get it," Sasha whispered.

"He's just a fucking lunatic, Sash. There's nothing to get," Rab whispered.

Sasha shook her head, then scrabbled in her bag. She picked out a bottle of Slenderise. "I thought it sounded familiar. The place where they make Slenderise. It's called The Grinding House. You don't suppose..." They stared at each other in horror, then snorted with laughter. "Surely not."

The Grinding House was an A-frame building. A triangle on a hill.

Rab and Sasha followed the funeral director inside. They didn't hold hands, although Sasha wished they could. She knew she had to be the strong one this time, and tried to pay attention to Jeremiah. She angled her head toward him like she always did when she was listening carefully.

"How's your hearing?" Jeremiah said. "Is it slipping away? I notice things. I've always been like that." He reached over and picked a piece of lint from Sasha's sleeve. Flicked his own shoulder.

"It's only that I see you tilting your head to listen. It's one of those funny things. I don't know if it's a type of aping behaviour or if it helps them listen. I know it's one of the first signs that their equilibrium is going. Body, soul, spirit." He smiled as if they should know what he was talking about.

Rab said, "She's always done that. She doesn't want anyone to know she's a bit deaf."

Jeremiah ignored this as if he were deaf himself. He led them through a passageway lined with books. "You could start at that end and work your way to this and you'd be educated when you finished. All the necessary knowledge. All knowledge. Schools teach you nothing. Nothing. No parent should send their child to school. It should come from the older generation. Passed on. The Grandparent, the Parent, the Child," he said. "Did you hear about the children sent to a school of known, very wealthy paedophiles? They are taught the beauty of big/little love. This is true."

Sasha said, "We actually knew someone whose little brother went there. They took him out the other week."

Jeremiah nodded. "You see? No parent should trust the system. No parent! So what do you think of my sign? Enticing?"

"This isn't a hotel," Rab muttered. Sasha waved the bottle of pills at Jeremiah. "The place that makes these is called The Grinding House, too."

Jeremiah frowned. "Hmm. I was hoping nobody would notice. I stole the name, I'm afraid. I liked it. Seemed a waste on a chemical company. Pure waste."

"So you don't make Slenderise here using dead bodies?"

Jeremiah laughed until tears came. "No. No, I don't. I think they're based off-shore. That's where their naturally-occurring elements are to be found."

Sasha yawned. Rab said, "About Dad..."

"Ah, yes. Yes. And Nick, too, if I'm not mistaken. Both of them before long. They'll be sadly missed. We always say that but for him...he is a good man. Sadly missed. He is very proud of you boys. And your friends. You're good for him, you young people."

"He isn't that old," Sasha said.

"No, no, he isn't. Terrible loss."

Jeremiah led them to a little chapel.

"If you'll wait here, I'll check his notes. He is very clear about what he wants and he wants me to make it clear to you. Sit and let the atmosphere take you. People say it's very calming here. Very calming."

"But most of your customers are dead," Rab said.

Again, the funeral director seemed to be deaf. He nodded at them and walked out through the chapel door.

"What an awful man," Sasha said.

"If you had to choose, sex with him or sex with Bevan, who would you choose?"

Sasha stared at him and didn't answer. She walked around the room, reading the names of the many dead. The room seemed to be sound-proofed; there was a kind of muffled roar which made Sasha think of trapped air.

There were ceiling-high doors cut into the walls.

"Where do these go, I wonder?" she said.

"Don't open them," Rab said. "God knows what's there. Bodies or something. I really don't want to know." He crunched a peppermint.

"They're just cupboards. Can I look? I hate that man. I want to know his secrets."

She tugged at the big silver handles but the doors were locked.

"What has he got in there?"

Rab shook his head. He sank into a pew and put his head into his hands.

"It's still all about you, even with Dad dying and Nick nearly gone."

Sasha stared at him. She sat beside him, held him.

"I don't want to think about it. I'm gabbling. I'm sorry."

She squeezed him, pulled him close. He cried then. It took his breath away.

"I can't breathe properly. I feel like my lungs are going." He cried.

"Good," Jeremiah said. They had not heard him come in. "I was concerned that man wasn't to be mourned."

Rab said, "Just because you don't see the tears doesn't mean they aren't there. You don't need to witness things for them to be real. And he's not dead yet. I'd appreciate you not acting like he is."

Jeremiah passed a small folder to Rab.

"He's very clear, here. Very clear about his remains. His bone-ash to be used for research purposes. Though it's the children they say hold the answers. The bones of the children."

"Mum doesn't want that," Rab said.

"It's the only way we're going to fight this terrible disease," Jeremiah said, rattling his keys in his pockets. "The Pathology Department know my eye for detail. That's why I was asked to help. The Department knew I could manage the work. I am the record keeper. The chronicler. I have everything ready for the Pathology Department each week, and I'm given a receipt. I've been asked to store it all here." He opened the cupboard. Lined up, row after row on cheap plywood shelves, were baby food jars filled with grey ash.

"Four thousand, eight hundred and ninety-three," Jeremiah said. "All catalogued." All with stickers saying "Property of P.D.."

"You're very organised," Sasha said. Jeremiah took her hand and she felt him squeezing hard, assessing the bones in her fingers.

"It used to be there was always one bit that wouldn't burn. Not always the same bit. But always one small chunk. Now, these latest bodies, sometimes it's the whole thing. The whole thing." He mimicked grinding. "Usually we grind any left-over bits down and add them to the ashes. It's an art, you know. The fire needs to be incredibly hot to burn the bone."

"Nick tried to burn a rat's skeleton after he read in the paper about it," Sasha said. "They were right. It wouldn't burn."

"It stank, though," Rab said.

Jeremiah showed them a small pile of triangular gray bones. "These need to go into the grinder. Animal, vegetable, mineral," he said. "Three."

"You've burnt a lot of people," Rab said.

Jeremiah chuckled. "Oh, I didn't burn all of those! No. Those have come to me from around the country. I am the record keeper." He took Rab's hand, squeezed it. "Men are more solid in the bones. They absorb the calcium better than women do. That's why women are more likely to suffer osteoporosis and broken hips. That sort of thing. Broken wrists. Broken arms. A broken finger. Broken toes."

"Are you going to name all two hundred and ten bones?" Sasha said.

"Two hundred and six," he said.

Mrs Albadara was waiting anxiously when they returned. "I wish he hadn't made you go to that man. Why go to that Jeremiah? I don't like that man. He makes my friends nervous."

"That doesn't stop them fighting over him," Mr Albadara said. "It's disgusting how they behave. He's not interested. Can't they see that?"

"He only likes them when they're dead."

Mr Albadara snorted at his wife then turned to Rab. "Now let's see how Nick is," he said. "Take me there." Rab helped his father to the room where Nick rested.

Nick cried when they entered. "Dad. Dad. Dad."

"Your grief makes me feel my life hasn't been wasted," Mr Albadara said.

"What is it, Dad? What is this thing?" Nick asked.

"It's the end of life as we know it," his father said. He placed one hand on Rab's shoulder, one on Nick's head.

Rab laughed. "You're such a drama queen, Dad."

"Are your bones aching yet? Can you feel it? Come to me when you're like Nick," their father said.

"I'll never be like Nick. Sorry to disappoint you."

Nick stared. "Spurs isn't that bad, Dad. They're saying only a small percentage of the population will be affected. We're not talking the end of the human race. Not even close. Just the end of you and me."

"You don't think that's the end of the world?" his father asked. He tried to smile but his cheeks and jaw were stiff. He could only talk quietly.

"It's very comforting having you here," he said.

"That's good, Dad. But I feel like I need to get out a bit. Just to get some air. I can't breathe. Take me somewhere, Rab," Nick said. He called out, "Mum? I'm going out."

"You're not going anywhere," his mother said, coming with a cool cloth for his forehead.

"We'll just take him out for a drive, Mum. Just for a little while. Okay?" Rab said. His mother tutted.

Bevan loaded Nick in the back. "God, he's heavy. All bone and no flesh," Bevan said. He got into the driver's seat.

"Anybody want anything before we go?" He cleared his throat.

Nick cried in pain and with frustration. "Milk. Get me some milk." Nick couldn't stop drinking the stuff. It was like breathing. If he stopped for a minute he felt like he was choking. He lay reclined to drink. Sasha poured the milk though a funnel into his mouth. It sickened her; the sound of Nick gulping repulsed her.

"Start driving," Nick said. His voice whistled, like he was talking through a straw. "I want you to drive."

Bevan started the car. "Where to?"

"Just drive," hissed Rab. Nick sighed as the car started. Already the rumble had eased a little of the pain.

"You might as well take him to Jeremiah. The ghoul. Save us a trip later," Rab said. Nick whistled, then laughed like nutshells crushed underfoot.

"Shut up," Sasha said. "Just drive," she told Bevan.

She felt Nick's neck stiffen.

"I can feel tears. It feels like they're dissolving my eyeballs. I can't even see light anymore, S. My eyes have fused over. I can see a whole new world. Strangely attractive."

His sinuses had filled in so he talked in a strange, nasal voice. Rab looked at Nick until his neck ached. He rubbed at it, grimacing.

"Is your neck sore, Rab?" Sasha said. "Is it stiff?"

"Cry while you can," Nick said.

Rab flexed his fingers. There was less give than there had been.

Bevan slowed for some cows blocking the road.

"See you for the Sunday roast, you stupid cunts."

Nick made a noise like laughter. Sasha and Rab laughed, too.

"Don't stop," Nick whispered. "Keep moving." Bevan backed up, going slow at first then faster. He turned the car in a spin and took them back the other way.

Sasha reached out to put her hand on Bevan's shoulder, to thank him for understanding.

They got back to the farm well after dark. The party was still going; people in the lounge room laughing with their white teeth showing. White-haired Great-aunt Terry looked at Nick then said to Rab, "Shouldn't we call the medical team for Nick? They've asked everybody to let them know."

Sasha sat beside her and held her hand. "Can we leave it for tonight? They can't do anything for him."

"We'll have to call them tomorrow. Okay? They like to be informed. P.D, you know," Great-aunt Terry said knowingly. "At least let us get him a doctor. I just read about this new thing they're talking about, where your bones don't dissolve like they're supposed to. You can get help for it, I heard. He needs help."

"I'm okay," Nick muttered. He was propped up in a chair. His mother fed him and wiped his chin. As they ate dinner, noodles with kelp for Sasha, fish and chips covered with salt for Rab and Bevan, bread soaked in milk for Nick, Sasha whispered to Rab, "The idea of those medical team people coming makes me physically ill. Are they still telling people it's leukaemia?"

Rab said, "I guess it's beyond that. I don't know. Maybe we should leave tomorrow, early, before anyone can call the medics."

"But where? Where are you thinking of going?" Sasha said. "I don't want to go back to the city."

Rab said, "We'll think of somewhere. Okay? Away from people. It'll be okay."

When the meal was over they all slept.

Nick did not wake up.

Sasha found him dead in the bed beside her. She held him for an hour until the others woke up.

"What are we going to do with him? We can't take him to that terrible Jeremiah," she said.

"Dad wants him there. It's what he told us to do. Love you, Nick," Rab said.

Sasha didn't dare say it.

"Can't we just bury Nick ourselves? No one'll know," Sasha said.

They heard Bevan singing in the shower.

"Surely that'll be okay. It'll be better," Sasha said. They talked in whispers, wanting to keep Nick to themselves for a bit longer. Bevan came out of the shower, rubbing his hair with a towel.

"Dad's already paid. He paid for all of us. He thinks it's important. Come on, Sash. You're talking crap. This is what has to happen."

"I guess, then. I don't want to go there, though. That Jeremiah makes me sick," Sasha said. She stroked Nick's hand.

"Rab and I'll do it, Sasha, with their Mum and Dad. You stay here and rest," Bevan said. He'd dreamt of being with a woman the night before. That always cheered him up.

"The thing that's killing me is how I'm going to tell Mum," Rab said. "She's downstairs thinking he's still alive."

"She's prepared, at least, knew it was coming. She'll be able to say he's not suffering anymore. But what about your Dad?"

Sasha held Rab's hand as he told his parents. The grief was terrible. Tired.

Mrs Albadara could barely walk from the desolation. Bevan had to carry Mr Albadara who looked different, and Sasha realised his teeth had fallen out overnight; his gums hard, protruding from his jaw.

Sasha watched them drive away, and, when she was alone, cried. She sorted through Nick's things while they were gone, her way of saying goodbye, and found his box of skeletons. The bird, the cat, a rabbit, the half-charred rat. Examples. His work.

Sasha stared at the box then picked it up and took it to a field. She held it for a while then began throwing the bones away.

Rab came up behind her.

"What are you doing?"

"They stink. These bones stink. I can't stand the smell of them. How was the funeral?"

Rab lifted his hands. "Yeah, great Sash. Happy day. They burnt him up, and Jeremiah couldn't even wait till we were gone. We heard it. The grinder. I swear I could smell bone."

"What did it smell like?"

"You wouldn't like it."

Rab's mother stood in the kitchen, screaming.

"How could this be right? This was not a burial. This was a desecration. My son, my son."

Rab's father was too stiff to hold her. She screamed at him, "How could you allow this to happen?"

"It's information that could save us all."

"My children are not information. They are sacred from my flesh. Will you consign me to the same fate? Rab? Our grandchild?"

Rab and Sasha stood in the doorway. Bevan was outside, washing his car.

Rab looked at Sasha. She nodded, her face white.

"This is our sacrifice for the human race. We are the intelligent ones. The educated ones. It is our responsibility," Mr Albadara said.

"I despise you. I hate you. I hate you!" Mrs Albadara screamed, then she collapsed at her husband's feet and wept, holding his legs.

Later, Sasha and Rab went to her bedside where she rested with a cup of tea, pictures of Nick and Rab as babies.

"How did you know?" Sasha whispered. Mrs Albadara smiled. "I wasn't sure. Where's your father, Rab?"

"He's with Jeremiah. At The Grinding House."

"Good. Now listen to me." She rose up, and her sudden strength was almost frightening. "You must get away. I cannot have you all left to Jeremiah. I don't want you to end up in a jar on the shelf. You must go before it's too late."

"It's already too late, Mum. It's over," Rab said.

"Go anyway. Just drive."

"But where?" Rab said. He was so tired he could hardly talk.

"I know a place," his mother said. "It's an almond grove, a beautiful place. I passed it once, with your father. There's a little cabin there. It seemed uninhabited but you'll have to see. Go there, all of you. Maybe take another woman. Pick someone Bevan likes. To keep him company. I worry about him a little. And tins of food. Water. Books. You'll think of things.

"Go to the almond grove. The place where the almond trees grow is very warm and there are no frosts. When it rains the water is slowly absorbed into the hard, dry ground. Did you know an almond tree looks like a peach tree? That a peach tree smells of bitter almonds? It is beautiful there.

"Now Nick is gone, I think you should go to the almond grove. Leave us. It is better for you there."

Rab said, "We'll go tomorrow. Spend tonight together. But maybe we should just go home to the city."

"Maybe we should try to find this almond grove. I don't think home's the way it used to be," Sasha said. "I think it's a good idea. We should go tomorrow. I'll tell Bevan."

"Do we take anyone else with us?" Bevan said. The only women he'd seen here were in their fifties. Too old even for him.

"Let's just go," Sasha said. "First thing in the morning."

None of them slept well, and before dawn Sasha and Bevan had packed the car. Sasha led Rab to the front seat. Then they drove, past fields of bone flowers marching like soldiers. They listened to the radio, music and ads, no news. An ad for Slenderise told them, "Now with added iodine."

"What the fuck's that for?" Rab said.

"Something for our own good?" Bevan said.

"There's iodine in kelp," Sasha said. She looked at Bevan. "And in that salt you pour on everything."

Bevan laughed. "So I'm a good guy?"

They had been driving for two hours when Rab clutched his stomach.

"I'm hungry. I'm so hungry."

Sasha ripped the ringpull on a can of spaghetti. "This'll fill you up till we get somewhere."

Bevan drove with his thumbs sticking out. Sasha sat with her feet tucked under.

"You're not stiff at all, are you, Sasha? You're not feelin' it even a little. That shits me," Bevan said.

Sasha shook her head. "I wonder how the others are going. The other vegans I mean. It's gotta be the animal products. Not all of them like kelp but none of them touch meat."

Bevan snorted. "Yeah, whatever. I'm not givin' up meat just cos you say so."

"I'm not asking you to. I don't care what you eat."

She closed her eyes.

The traffic was steady. Reasonably smooth. Police cars amongst civilians ensured the rules were followed. One man was arrested for driving with his arm out of the window. He was pulled over, his car taken away.

They passed through another toll booth, handing money to the uniformed cop there. "I wonder where Henri is. That nice cop. He's probably been killed by one of them by now," Sasha said.

"Let's hope he's all right," Rab said.

People stopped often at the roadside food stalls. There were hundreds of them, all along the road. People shovelling food in, ravenous. Some served food to the cars and that made it even easier. Everyone was so hungry.

"I'm still hungry. I'm still hungry," Rab said. They had to stop and get him food before the nausea set in.

Bevan pulled up at a roadside stand. Dust was thick in the air and they could see it settle on the food. Rab grabbed meat on a stick, six of them, smothering them with peanut sauce. The food slid into his mouth so fast the cook laughed and thrust more at him.

"Eat! Eat!" the cook said loudly as she turned away.

"I'll just have some rice, please," Sasha said. The woman didn't respond. Sasha spoke louder, shouted. Rab limped around the table and waved at the woman.

"I can barely hear," she said loudly. "My ears are closed over." Her voice was nasal. "Nice to be out in the country, hmmm? It sounds awful in the city now. The chaos. You don't get that kind of chaos here."

Bevan said loudly to the roadside seller, "You should meet us where we're going. It's an almond grove. It's supposed to be beautiful."

She nodded. "Okay. I'll visit." She smiled and they could see her teeth were just hanging on.

"Her jaw's pushing through," Rab whispered. He wriggled his own loose teeth with his tongue. As he walked back to the car he suddenly wasn't sure where the ground was, where the sky. He stumbled.

"Dizzy?" Sasha said. He rubbed at his ears until the dizziness faded.

"It's okay," he said, though he couldn't even hear his own footfalls.

There were four people parked at the next picnic rest spot. A young boy, an older girl, woman and man. A family. The son was curled up into a ball. The parents took it in turns to rock him.

"How are your kids going?" the father said. His shirt was like Rab's, fatherly.

"I'm not a father," Rab said.

The parents exchanged sorrowful glances.

"I wish we could look after you, too. But we're going to my parent's place. They have a built-in pool." The mother smiled. Her neck spasmed grotesquely. The boy groaned.

"Come find us at the almond grove if you can," Sasha said. She hugged the girl. "It'd be nice to have a friend."

"Yeah, we need more friends," Bevan said. The mother stared at him.

"It's a chance to rebuild," Rab said. "That's why we're going." He tripped over nothing, fell to the ground.

"We'll see," the mother said. Sasha tried to hug the girl again but the father pulled his daughter in close. "I'm sorry to be rude, but we're trying not to have physical contact with strangers."

"You don't get Spurs through touch," Rab said.

"They don't know how you get it." It wasn't the only time they came across this. People avoided touch.

The mother's phone rang. She answered it nervously. "Yes? Yes. No. He's still all right. Hang on, I'll check." She put down the phone and spoke to her son. "Darling? Can you hear me?" The little boy blinked at her, nodded. She picked up the phone. "Yes, he can still hear. Can we bring him to you? Can't you do something? Please?"

She put down the phone, weeping. The father said, "That the medical team? Are they coming to help?" She shook her head.

"God, that poor kid," Sasha said when they were out of earshot. "He's going to suffer like that little boy in the mall."

"They oughta shoot him," Bevan said. "Take him out of his misery."

"That's not funny."

Bevan drank a can of beer, slugged it straight down his throat.

"I wish you wouldn't do that," Sasha said. "It comes out of your pores and you stink." In answer he coughed.

At their next stop, a man sat surrounded by the debris of a feast. "You can feel it growing, hmmm? If you lie still you can feel the growth of it. Hmmm? The intensity of the calcium. The appetite of bones." He poured milk in. They could barely see him swallowing. It was like his bones absorbed it before it even left his mouth. He twitched and fidgeted, his legs shaky.

"Don't you love the sun?" the man said, though his skin was red and blistered. "Don't you just worship it? Feeding the bones. Helping them fuse." He lifted up a blanket with a flourish. The smell of old wool wafted over them. Beneath, he'd laid out row after row of rusty old cans of food.

"Buy some food," he said. "Good food." He had a price list, written on dirty cardboard.

"You are kiddin', aren't you?" Bevan said. "An old can of beans for five bucks?"

"I could charge ten. In fact, for you, it's ten. Per can."

"People aren't going to buy it."

"People already are, hmmm. The smart ones. Haven't you figured it out yet? It's the food. The milk, the meat. Even the vegetables, but not as much. You've got to eat pre-Spurs canned food until it passes. What else are you going to do? Look, it's the food. We want it too much, the need is too desperate for it to be healthy."

"We can't stop eating, mate."

"No. But you can eat this old canned food." Some of the tins were bloated, misshapen.

"Arsehole," Bevan shouted. "Takin' advantage of people."

"That's where the wealth is."

"Come on, Bevan. There's plenty of food around." Sasha grabbed his arm.

"I wouldn't eat it," the seller said. "I wouldn't."

"We're not buying your food, creep," Rab said.

"Hey?" the man said. "You speak too soft, mate."

"I said Fuck Off!" Rab shouted.

He limped away, leaving Sasha behind.

"It's because of how we treat the poor. That's what I reckon. The poor people live off food full of this super calcium. It kills them, they're burnt or buried in pauper's graves. We get this lush earth, these flowers, and it spreads. No one likes the flowers, do they? Couldn't sell those for free. You want to buy yourself some cans, lady. You really do. Fifteen dollars a can. Hmmmm?"

"Arsehole," she said, and walked to the car. Rab and Bevan watched her.

"Do you want to lie down in the back seat?" Sasha asked Rab.

"I'm not that bad yet," Rab said, though he slumped in the front, hating the constriction of the seatbelt but unable to sit up without it. His eye was caught by movement.

"What's that over there? That thing running?" Rab said.

"That's a tree, mate. You're seein' things," Bevan said.

"It's a bit blurry. That's all."

"You know, we should have done like your Mum said. Got supplies," Bevan said.

Rab said, "We're not going to arrange women for you, Bevan." Bevan didn't answer.

Later, Rab said to Sasha, "I can't trust any of my senses, Sash. I'm hearing things, now. I thought you said, 'I've never loved you. I hate you.'"

"I didn't say that," said Sasha. "God, Rab. I love you. I love you."

"You just loved Nick more."

"No, no, I didn't. I can't even express what that was. I honestly didn't think it would bother you. It was a mistake. I was a joke to him. But he felt bad about you. He really did. He thought you were taking it too well."

As they drove along, Rab said, "Stop the car. I think there's an earthquake."

Bevan said, "There's no earthquake," but he pulled over and waited until Rab stopped shaking.

"There's a roar in my ears. What's that?"

"Your ears are closing over," Sasha said loudly.

"I don't want Bevan's to be the last voice I hear."

Sasha sat and whispered in his ear until he fell asleep.

"We're gettin' close, I think," Bevan said. Two days had passed. He drove like a zombie, dangerously tired.

Rab held Sasha's hand. He couldn't release his fingers. He hadn't grabbed her too tight or her fingers would be bloodless. His eyelids were closed. He opened them to slits and she could see bone there, grown over. Bevan stopped at the side of the road and they carried Rab to the grass. Sasha slid her fingers out of his grasp. "I'll get you a peppermint. Wait there," she said. She walked to the car and Rab spoke urgently to Bevan through the small hole of his throat.

"This is for her, now. You're dead, too, and she's going to be all right. You've got to get her to the almond grove. Make her safe." He spoke loudly because he could barely hear himself.

For Rab, the feeling of immobility was terrifying. He could barely see, barely hear, and each breath was not enough. He seemed to project himself into the ground, he could feel the earth covering him.

Rab could feel his skeleton, his one-bone, leaching its calcium-rich marrow into the earth. The earth growing rich and loamy, good planting dirt. The grass growing lush and green vegetables so beautiful you desperately craved them, and all grown on the mutant calcium of his bones.

"Don't bury me. Burn me. And the others. Don't put us in the earth here. Burn us." He screamed the words but as he screamed the base of his skull closed over and the last thing he felt was Sasha's wet face against his cheek.

A rattle in Rab's throat made him fight for breath. He struggled and writhed in Sasha's arms as he tried to suck air in. She heard the cracking of his bones as he threw his arms up.

"How is he?" Bevan said.

"He's bad. He's so bad. Let's get him back in the car, and we'll go over some bumps or something." She slid a peppermint between Rab's lips.

Bevan drove off the road and the car shook and rattled.

When he stopped, Rab was dead.

Sasha looked at Bevan. She held Rab close.

"Petrol's pretty low, Sash. I'm thinkin' we should save it for emergencies. Not take him to Jeremiah."

"He wanted to be burnt properly."

Bevan coughed. "We'll do a better job than that creep. Really. It'll be all right. I don't want to be burnt by him either. When we get to the almond grove, I want to dig two holes. We'll put Rab in one. You can put me in the other."

"Maybe we should burn him."

"We'd never get the fire hot enough. We'd just burn his flesh off. I'd rather him go into the ground lookin' like that than seein' him as a one-bone."

"Yes. Yes. All right." She turned away. They opened their windows and Bevan drove until he found an open supply store. "We need things. Water, tin plates. All the things we'll need for campin'. Mrs Albadara gave me heaps of money."

"I guess you're under obligation after all," Sasha said. "Why didn't she give it to Rab?"

"She thought he'd waste it. Spend it on somethin' worthless. She trusted me."

They filled their car and Bevan started the engine. "Ready?" he said. "Let's go." It was further than they expected; six hours passed before Bevan said, "That's it. That's got to be it." It was beautiful. They both sighed.

He opened the door for her and she climbed out. As she walked toward the grove, he pulled Rab's body out, dry retching. "The stink'll never go," he muttered. He ran to catch up with Sasha.

As they entered the almond grove they fell to their knees and shovelled in almonds. Starving.

They walked through the grove, their feet crackling. "It's the nuts," she said. They heard crunching. A terrible sound. "It's just the almonds underfoot," Sasha said.

"Yeah," Bevan said, but he could feel the bones in his feet crackling.

They found a small cabin with two rooms and a fireplace. Thick sawn pieces of tree trunks for chairs and a packing case for a table.

"This is as sophisticated as our place," Sasha said. There were four chairs and she sat in one and cried, thinking all four chairs should be filled.

"Missin' the boys?" Bevan said. He tried the tap. Dark water came out. He walked outside to check the tank.

"The cover's blown off so God knows what's in the water. It smells pretty foul. I say we drain the tank, fix the cover and start again. We've got two cases of drinkin' water to go on with, and there's a runnin' stream I can hear. For washin'. Let's go check it out." Sasha shook her head.

"Sasha, you can't sit here thinkin' about the boys. All right? It's us, now. We need to decide on the water, find out what food there is about. Come on."

Bevan was right; it was a running stream and the water looked fresh.

"This is fine," Bevan said. "We'll be fine. Pick up any sticks you see. Dry ones for the fire."

"I'm not an idiot, Bevan. I can see what there is to do,"

"I know, Sash. But you've never been campin' before, have you? I know a little more than you, here."

Bevan's feet crackled. "Who would've thought I'd outlast those other bastards so you and me could get together."

"That's not going to happen, Bevan."

"But you were askin' for it. You told me."

"When?"

"In the car. When you massaged my shoulder."

"It wasn't a massage. I touched you on the shoulder for being so nice to Nick. I thought you understood. I wasn't leading you on, Bevan. Honestly. I haven't done anything to lead you on."

"You did, you bloody did, you were tellin' me." He walked towards her and Sasha felt suddenly afraid.

"Bevan, things don't happen so fast. Okay? You need to be patient. Now let's move on and pretend this never happened. All right?" she said. Her shoulders felt stiff.

"Did you hear about these lovers?" Bevan said. His voice was muffled as he hunched over. "Fused together, I heard. They were almost one-bone and she said, let's die together, so he was fucking her, I heard. And her gash fused over. Closed up. Snipped his dick off like a sausage."

"That's horrible. Why would you tell me a story like that? You don't even care about Rab or Nick. You couldn't care less."

"I'm happy being the last man alive, Sash."

He imagined his seed joining that of Rab and Nick. A child born with three fathers yet only one to call Dad. He held himself in, imagining it in such detail he had to turn away from her to hide. He didn't want to rape her. He wanted her willingness. That was part of it. He would wait, be kind, and she would learn to love him.

"Don't call me Sash," she shouted. "Never, ever dare to call me Sash." She turned and ran to the cabin.

"Fuckin' idiot," Bevan said to himself, clenching his fists. "Think before you speak, you fuckwit."

He left Sasha alone for a while. When he entered the cabin she smiled at him as if nothing had happened. Forgiveness.

A certain routine fell into place in the almond grove. Bevan fed Sasha, collected water for her, listened to all she said. He was so sweetly attentive Sasha wondered if she should wake him out of the fantasy. But he was so good to her she couldn't stop herself from taking advantage. He was all joky and jovial, trying to entertain her, make her laugh. It didn't work. He tried too hard.

He found an abandoned vegetable patch, and he cleaned it up before leading her there.

"It's gonna to be okay. Look. We can grow vegies. There's stuff sproutin' already."

"That's good. We can get it going in case more people arrive. Like Mrs Albadara."

Bevan was silent.

"We could go and see if she wants to come," she said.

"There's no petrol, Sasha. All we can do is go places close to home."

They put signs out on the freeway, hoping to make it easier for people to find them.

It was two weeks before a visitor arrived. Bevan was tending the tomato plants, already in fruit when he discovered the garden. Sasha washed their few dishes, loving the feel of the cool, fresh water running between her fingers. Birds sang overhead, and she had a moment of clarity; that this was okay. Then she heard a noise.

"Bevan! Can you hear that? A car!"

He stood up, wiped dirt across his sweaty brow. "They'll drive past."

Sasha stood up. "They're not. They're not. They're coming!" She dropped the plates and ran to their hut.

"I'll get the basket, fill it with nuts. They'll be hungry and thirsty. Bring the mugs, fill them with water," she yelled to Bevan.

He watched her go then shook his head. "It was nice with just us," he said to himself. He rinsed his hands and filled two mugs with stream water.

"Hurry, Bevan," Sasha shouted. She ran to the sound of the car, near where Bevan's was parked.

"It's stopped!" she said.

Bevan caught up to her. They heard one door slamming.

"Just one. Or the others too sick to get out," Sasha said.

They could see the car, now.

"Or Jeremiah," Bevan said."

"Oh, fuck, not that ghoul. He's come for Rab. I swear. Hide."

"We can't hide from him forever," Bevan said. "It'll be okay. We'll just tell him how it is with us and he'll have to fit in."

Together, they walked out of the grove to greet Jeremiah.

"Hello, Bevan. Still with us?" Jeremiah said as he reached them. "And Sasha." He bent and kissed her hand. She smelt decay and ground teeth.

He looked around. "Rab? Where is Rab?" Sasha and Bevan exchanged glances.

"You must be hungry, Jeremiah. Have some nuts. Water. And Bevan, any tomatoes ripe? Could we have some?"

Bevan nodded.

"Still feeding the masses, Bevan? You're the cook, aren't you? You are. Mrs Albadara spoke highly of your skills. Spoke highly."

Bevan felt sudden intense grief, like his brain filled with blood. He touched his nose, thinking he had a nose bleed.

"Here, a hanky," Jeremiah said. The linen was clean and crisp. "I cut up shrouds for them. The best of materials."

They sat to eat. Jeremiah placed another handkerchief on his log chair.

"Have you got any other suits? White might not work so well out here," Sasha said.

Jeremiah smiled. "You are not the arbiter of all good taste, young lady. Not by a long shot."

He reached into his bag and brought out a globe. "I had a presentation to make to Rab, on behalf of his father, but he is no longer here. I cannot imagine Mr Albadara wanted either of you to have this, so I will keep it myself until we locate Rab."

"What is it?" Sasha asked.

"Beginning, middle, end. Heaven, Earth, Hell. Three," Jeremiah said.

"What's three? What are you on about?" Sasha said.

Jeremiah watched her lifting food to her lips. She chewed a little stiffly.

"The eternal bone is shaped like a triangle. All things important are triads. This is an inheritance of many generations of the Albadara family. Many, many." He glanced sideways at Sasha's belly.

"You're looking well," he said. "Baby coming, is it, or have you taken to fattening foods? Baby?"

Tears ran down her face. She was bereft of all strength. Nothing left to stand up with.

"It's a baby," she said.

"If I could be assured that infant was next-in-line, I would pass this into your caring."

"It's one of theirs. Rab's or Nick's." Sasha felt her cheeks burning with shame.

Jeremiah tutted. "We'll have a sense when the child is born. Until then I'll keep the globe. Mr Albadara would have been very sad to know Rab is gone, too. On his death bed he told me, 'Go do what you need to do. Find them.' His wife had confessed where she sent you. Such an honest woman, at the end. She, too, wanted me to deal with Rab." He paused and smiled. The smell of decay hit Sasha and she had a sudden image of a toothworm swallowing the inside of his teeth and leaving waste to fill the hole.

"So where is he?" Jeremiah steepled his fingertips together in a triangle. "Where have you put him?"

"Would you like some nut milk?" Sasha said. She stumbled in her haste to get away. Jeremiah held her elbow to steady her. He pinched so hard she felt her bones bruising.

Sasha collected nuts, gathering them in her lifted skirt.

"You're like a little squirrel," Jeremiah said.

She screamed. "Don't sneak up!"

"You could use my grinder to make the nut milk," he said. "I brought a portable one. Not so portable, really. That would be much easier, little squirrel."

A soft pull and clunk made Sasha jump.

"So nervous," Jeremiah whispered. "It's only Bevan killing our dinner."

Bevan lumbered through the grove to them, holding aloft a rabbit in one hand, his home-made slingshot in the other.

"Got one!" he said. It made Sasha's shoulders heave, and with the heaving she felt stiff, and she knew Spurs was beginning in her.

"I'll store these nuts in the hollow tree, near the water tank," she said, lifting her skirt full of nuts. Bevan stared at her legs, his mouth open.

Jeremiah said, "Little squirrel."

Bevan felt in his pockets, fidgeted. He walked to his car and searched it meticulously. He ripped up the carpet.

"Fuck fuck fuck," he said.

"What's the matter, Bevan? Trouble?"

"I can't find any smokes. Not one."

"Ah, well, Bevan, in this little world of ours we all have to make certain sacrifices. I have left my business behind. Sasha has lost her brother lovers. And you have no cigarettes."

"Just get me some in town, will you?"

"It's possible. I intend to travel to the Pathology Department to deliver my jars."

Bevan sat down, tired. "Thanks," he said.

Jeremiah said, "When I come back we'll talk about Rab and his parents' final wish for him."

While he was gone Bevan and Sasha made plans to leave but in the end absolute lethargy and fear of the unknown kept them in place.

"I don't want to leave here just to get away from him," Sasha said.

"I'm just spewin' I'm not the last man left alive," Bevan said. "It'll be okay. He'll get bored and leave us, soon enough."

"Shouldn't we think about moving Rab? I don't want him found."

"Do you really want to dig him up?"

Sasha stared at Bevan in horror. "What are we going to do?"

Jeremiah returned five days later. "They refused to take delivery. Can you believe it? They told me to keep hold of them." He had been shopping, and emerged with bags of food. "I got some honey. You'd like honey, wouldn't you, Sasha?" he said. "You could rub it on your tummy if you won't eat it."

"No, I don't like honey. Is it even safe? The bees caused the cross-pollination of the bone flowers. How safe do you think the honey is?" Sasha asked.

"We don't know, do we, Sasha?" Jeremiah said. He sighed as if with deep exhaustion and began to walk the perimeter of the almond grove, seeking disturbed earth. "I'll find him, you know," he told Sasha as he passed her for the third time. "There's no point in hiding. Don't you understand this is important for the future of the world?"

"What future?" Sasha said. She held her belly. "I can't bear to think about the world my baby will be born into."

"I think the world is going to be a place you're happy with. Completely vegan," Jeremiah said.

"For the wrong reasons."

"Does it matter?"

A car drove past and Sasha looked up. Hoping.

"I keep thinking someone's going to stop. Someone else must come," she said.

"How would they know about it?" Jeremiah said, picking his teeth.

"We told people. We said this was the safe place. We told them to come."

"Maybe you gave them the wrong directions. Hmmmm?"

"We put signs on the road. Didn't you see them?"

Jeremiah shook his head. "Gone, I'm afraid," he said. "You know that Mr Albadara came to think that Spurs has happened before? He was quite certain by the end. There is nothing new under the sun."

Jeremiah sat with his portable grinder between his feet. It was a massive thing. Once in position it was hard to move. It was like it had taken root and would need to be dug up.

"They say that civilization can be traced back to the time we learnt how to control our environment," Jeremiah said. "And the grinding of the grain was part of that. Once they had their grinding stones, they were not so keen to move about. They stayed, planted crops, kept herds. Some people say that was the beginning of the end of the world. That all progression came from there, and that it all led to this." Beside him was a sack of bones. He turned the handle, grinding, grinding, dropping in a bone and singing as he ground away.

"Are you plannin' on stayin'?" Bevan said over the terrible noise.

"For a while," Jeremiah said, smiling. "For a while." His ivory teeth were like sharp bones sticking out of his jaw.

"What about your job?"

"The Grinding House is where you make it," he said. "And what you make it. This is our Grinding House, now."

He turned the handle. Sasha's teeth screamed at the sound, throbbed in rhythm.

Bevan muttered, "Fee Fi Fo Fum."

Jeremiah said to him, "It really should have been the Albadara boys here. That would have made for better symmetry. Rab, Nick, Sasha. Three. You never did quite fit, did you?"

Jeremiah asked Sasha to collect almonds as he worked. These he tossed in his mouth. The ash he bottled and labelled and added to his pile.

When the pile was complete, Jeremiah summoned Bevan.

"You don't have to do as he says," Sasha said.

"I know, but he seems to know what has to be done. More than we do. And now I've done one thing it's hard to say no to the next. Being a leader isn't for me."

"I thought you were a brilliant leader," Sasha said.

Bevan smiled. "I can't do it, Sasha. I can't take over again. Maybe when he's gone."

Sasha watched as Jeremiah demonstrated what he wanted Bevan to do. Bevan started to dig.

"He wants a bunker to bury the jars in. Somethin' deep and safe," Bevan told Sasha.

Jeremiah said, "I've got plenty more jars. There will be plenty more. We need another pit. More, Bevan. We need to preserve these ashes. Did you know we have cellular information from grain burnt in ten thousand BC? Preserved by the burning. This is what we're doing. Preserving information for the next inhabitants."

Using newspaper, he wrapped the jars carefully, reading the headlines and snorting. "'Slenderise Final Link to Spurs'," he said, shaking his head. "Skinny little fools." He rested the glass globe amongst the jars.

He placed the triangular concrete block he'd bought in town over the bunker. "A symbol, we need. Something which will make it clear in two hundred years what we meant today."

The next time Sasha looked, there was a symbol scratched into the surface:

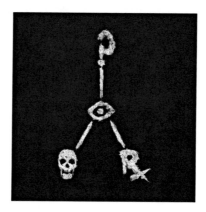

Sasha sat alone in the cabin listening to the grinding, the digging. She wondered when the others would start arriving, the hopeful ones who had heard of the almond grove.

She would welcome them, of course. This was a place of charity, of helping the poor and needy. She would tell them the rules; that all must be shared. That no animal products must be ingested.

She felt a great thirst, though. A terrible, terrible thirst. And a hunger she had never felt before. Belly aching hunger.

She didn't want to starve the baby in her womb. What she was eating was not enough. Her baby was telling her that. Her stomach ached with need.

There were cows in a field nearby, and a farm not too far away where she exchanged almonds for eggs.

Her first sip of milk made her gag, but she felt it in her bones, calming them.

The eggs she scrambled, ate with bread.

Then she slept, feeling like a good mother.

Sasha could hardly move. She relied on Jeremiah to feed her, clean her. Bevan had gone off in the car for food and never returned. Sasha imagined he had died; she knew he would not desert her. Her baby moved very little. Sasha slept a lot. She awoke one day to find Jeremiah staring at her.

"You know you won't be able to have that baby normally. Vaginally." She blushed at the word. "And you haven't got long. You need to decide what to do."

In the end the decision was made for her. She was so stiff she couldn't move, her arms fused by her side. She couldn't run, couldn't leave, and there was no one to carry her. She wept as Jeremiah came for her. "I'll look after it, don't worry," he said. "It'll get a good education." He had equipment collected on his last trip and he gave her pills to render her unconscious. "Say goodbye," he said. His foul breath filled her throat and vomit rose.

"Goodbye," she whispered.

Jeremiah sliced open her belly. Inside her womb the baby's bones had fused and merged until all that was left was an almost perfect oval inside a curled up body.

"The bones of the children," Jeremiah said, and he went to ready the fire and clean the grinder. He had work to do.

Green

Green

The blackish-green trunk of the tree shines as I approach. Nothing else grows nearby because a rich vein of copper deposits lies beneath the roots, leaching chemicals into the soil.

"Keep away from that tree, Doctor," the taxi driver had said. "The green lady haunts there. They buried her to make the tree grow. If you see her, all your money will turn to copper. Poor overnight."

"What happens if you have no money to lose?"

The green lady appears before me.

The air whirls, coppery and thick.

"She will take what is most precious to you," the taxi driver had answered.

I want to go home.

But I don't even know my name.

Sins of
the Ancestors

Sins of the Ancestors

Clients like to die in different ways. Yolanda was no longer surprised by the methods they chose. She pulled on thick gloves and stood, naked, in front of the mirror.

"I look ridiculous," she muttered. She glared at herself, trying to look like a killer.

He was waiting upstairs, sitting on the lounge, watching TV. A bowl of peanuts on his lap, large glass of white wine (not red. There'd be enough stains for his cleaners to deal with if she did her job right).

She pulled on a pair of boots for height, flexed her fingers, slipped on a robe and walked upstairs on the tips of her toes, not wanting to alert him. Some of them preferred a warning, others wanted sudden, choking fear.

His head was slumped forward and she could hear his deep, congested breathing.

Sleeping.

She nodded, steeling herself, then walked up to him and dropped her robe. He didn't stir.

She stepped sideways, poured herself a brandy, tossed it back, all while eyeing him off, placing him.

He wasn't a government man. Most of them were too scared of exposure to use a service like hers.

A company man, then. Sugar? She leant close to him and sniffed.

Tobacco. She recognised him now, from the social pages. His skin was sallow. You couldn't tell that from the photos. His hair was lank, sitting on his shoulders like old corn silk.

He'd paid good money to risk his life being with her, and he looked almost dead anyway.

She readied her fingers around his throat.

She straddled him. He stirred. She bit his lip, tightening her fingers around his neck. He shifted, but she had his arms pinned to his sides with her thighs.

"You should be careful who you bring home," she said, because that was part of his fantasy; he was a risk-taker, picking up a woman, not caring about her Ancestor ID, taking her home.

She squeezed tighter and he began to fight for real, now.

"You should have checked my ID. My ancestor was a murderer. Tried, convicted, dead by firing squad. What do you think that makes me?"

Her client's eyelids fluttered and she took that as a sign to stop. She loosened her grip on his throat, stepped off him and poured another brandy. It was the expensive kind; only high-level careers could afford it.

He lit a cigarette and turned the TV up.

"Money?" she said. He pointed at a sideboard, a huge pre-ID piece he must have inherited.

She and her brother Theo had only inherited bad blood.

The money, old, dirty notes which looked like they'd been used to clean a toilet. "Take it, you piece of shit."

She looked at him, sitting in his stained underwear, stinking of smoke and sweat, his fat white flesh unhealthy.

Yet I'm shit, she thought.

"You can fuck off now," he said, throwing the full ashtray at her. It hit her on the chin, bringing tears to her eyes.

She pulled on her robe. She'd shower downstairs, once he'd sunk into the TV.

He watched her. "You could have killed me. You don't look big enough to have strong fingers like that."

She mimed twisting. "I kill a lot of chickens."

It was what he paid for; the moment of fear when it could all end for him.

Because men like him, they really did believe that murderer descendants are easily capable of murder themselves.

"Next time you eat a chicken, think of me," she said.

She called Theo and waited for him under the small shelter the doorway provided. There were places in the world where you could be warm outside. She'd read about them. Places where they didn't judge you on who your ancestors were and what they did.

She checked her face in the mirror. The mark from the ashtray was clearly visible.

"How the hell did you get that? Don't worry. Don't answer. You need to stop what you're doing. It's bad for the body and for your soul." Theo drove angrily. She knew he was angry because he was helpless.

"Next client is Oster Wu," she said.

He tutted. "You should rest between, at least."

"Who has time to rest? You can wait downstairs. He doesn't mind. Use the shower, make a coffee."

Theo wrinkled his face. "But then I'll hear you. I don't like to hear you."

"You can block your ears. You need a shower and coffee will do you good, too."

The curtain fluttered as they arrived. Oster Wu liked to be ready; Yolanda took some heavy-duty painkillers, preparing herself for what would come.

Oster Wu picked up her shirt and cleaned himself up with it, then handed it to her.

"You should clean yourself, come to the Arena today."

"I can't afford to go to the Arena!"

He opened his wallet. "Here. A pass. For you and your killer brother, too." He smiled. He'd asked Yolanda to bring Theo along to their sessions; he liked the idea of more than one assassin.

She'd never agree. Shove the money.

"You don't need to protect me," Theo had said, furious when he realised what she shielded him from, while putting herself in it.

"Looking out for you is the only worthwhile thing I'm ever likely to do. So let me do it."

Oster waved money in her face.

"I really don't like these shows."

He moved quickly, grabbing her throat.

"I'll pay you. I want you to be there. To see it. There's two going down today. Both mine. I want you to see it." He was proud of his work at the Department of Unsolved Crime.

"All right, all right, I'll go."

"And you'll pay attention."

Yolanda scrubbed his blood off her arms, her face, her hair. He liked to bleed on her bare skin.

"So he's paying us? That's why we're going?" Theo asked.

"You know I'll do anything for money."

"I don't know why going to these shows bothers you so much, anyway."

"It's the implications," she said, as Theo drove. He liked to drive with just a finger on the wheel; only the fact that the car practically drove itself saved them three or four times.

She curled herself up in the front seat.

"What implications? What do you care if a killer dies?"

"Descendant of a killer. Of an alleged killer. This is an innocent person."

"With guilty blood. You can't deny that. They have the evidences."

"We have that blood ourselves, Theo."

"Yes, but our ancestor paid the price. We will not have to pay for it. God, would you look at that sky? Perfect execution weather," Theo said.

"It's always like this." Grey and cold, the sun a pale star. "What would it be like to live in a warm place, do you reckon?"

"Wouldn't be good execution weather."

They were six blocks from the execution hall when traffic blocked them. Theo looked for a parking spot.

"Drop me off at the door. I don't want to walk all that way."

"It's okay for me to walk so far, is it? I'll miss the show if I have to drive through that to drop you off. You'll walk with me."

"I'll get out here, then," she said. She didn't like to tell him, but this was a fine time to find new clients. Not so many men came to the executions. Of the ones who did, there was always one or two who would like to use her services.

Busloads of spectators arrived.

She watched Theo drive off, then turned and walked toward the arena. The footpath was slick and slimy with a reddish sheen to it as it often was after the rain.

Crowds of women walked past, rushing into the arena, not wanting to miss a moment.

What was it that made women so interested in the death of another? she thought.

Inside the arena, it was hot. Yolanda's hair went limp and her clothes were wet in a moment.

"Where's the air-conditioning?" someone yelled.

"Shut down. Can't cope with the heat," and that was all very funny, but who could breath in there?

The crowd roared, conversations piling one on the other until the din sounded like a chicken yard before the killing began.

The air smelt of pine needles. The smell of sweat, too, hundreds of bodies soaked through. Vomit, from the heat and the drink.

Yolanda tucked her arms into her body, made herself small. The jostle and press of the place was oppressive. She wished she was outdoors.

The lights dimmed and people quietened, lone voices shushed. A spotlight on centre stage showed a bright red armchair with large purple cushions.

The crowd hushed as the announcer spoke. "Sonny May, you are charged with your ancestor's unpunished crime of the murder of 13 women over a nine year period. You have chosen to die by dream sleep. What is your selected dream death?"

Sonny May's voice started creakily and he had to clear his throat. "I want to dream of dying while having sex with a beautiful woman."

The audience laughed, enjoying this.

In the next section she saw Oster Wu, his face bright, his clothing loose. She knew he'd had a lot to do with bringing Sonny May to justice. Oster liked her to break into his home, carrying a gun. He liked to disarm her, take her down.

She turned her head, not wanting to speak to him. She'd asked him for a favour; access to files she shouldn't see. She was waiting for his answer, but this was not the place to remind him.

Theo found her, gave her a wink.

The executioner entered the dream death and gestured Sonny May to sit in the armchair.

"This'll be good," Theo whispered to her. He was agitated. Excited. Most of the men were; she could tell by the way they fidgeted.

Sonny May sat down and was strapped into the chair. His hat was removed. He was bald, beneath.

The executioner applied lubricant to his temples then attached the transmitter, adjusting it so it didn't slip and choke him.

"Do you have any last words?"

Sonny May looked at the audience. "Just that this is my ancestor's crime, not mine, and that I have three children who are also innocent."

"Exodus, Chapter 20, Verse 5. "For I the Lord thy God am a jealous God, visiting the iniquity of the fathers upon the children unto the third and fourth generation of them that hate me."

Sonny May had lived an easy life. No label on him, because the crime had remained unsolved until recently. He could have done anything; gone anywhere.

And yet he'd wasted that freedom, staying in his own little place and doing nothing but have children.

At that moment, Yolanda hated him with jealousy-filled fury.

"Are there any registered descendants of the long-dead victims of this family?" the announcer called. One man stood up.

"I am."

"Do you wish to close-witness the death?"

"I do not."

The crowd hissed. What was he, an objector? He should stay home, then.

The executioner set the dreamer going. Sonny pulled back from the temporal impact, then relaxed into it.

His face slackened. His lips puckered. He wriggled in the chair.

The medic nodded. The executioner started the drip which would stop the blood in its tracks.

Some in the audience hissed.

"Why can't they let him die his own way?" Yolanda said.

"They think this dream death is too good for killers."

"If the Victims' Lobby Party say it's okay, they should accept that."

Sonny May stiffened. Close up shots of him showed that he appeared to be approaching orgasm. Then he slumped.

An extreme close up of his face showed a tear in his eye, and an expression on his face Yolanda recognised.

It was the look people give when a terrible truth dawns on them.

On the wall, above the commentary box, sat a counter, indicating the number of seconds it took for him to die.

Assistants dressed in black wheeled Sonny off stage, through the audience and out of the arena. Some leaned in for a better look; others pulled back.

Yolanda tucked her head under her arm.

She felt a tap on her shoulder. A big man stood there, two heads taller than she was. His shirt barely covered his stomach, which stuck, white and hairy, over the top of his pants.

He thrust a large wad of notes in her hand.

"Toilets. Now."

She shook her head. He leaned in.

"Oster Wu sent me. I'm a file clerk."

She was quick enough to know what this meant.

He had access to the files she wanted to see.

She nodded. "I'll be back soon," she whispered in Theo's ear.

The man handed her a knife. Security was always lax in the arena.

"He doesn't know you're coming. I want to give that bastard Oster Wu a scare, a real scare. You do this, I can help you out."

Yolanda hated unknowns. They were dangerous, because people thinking on their feet always were.

She needed the file clerk's help, though.

She slipped quickly through the crowd, knowing her only chance was surprise. Crouching down low, the knife ready. In the crowd she nicked a leg, saw the blood drip appear, moved on.

Oster watched the stage. He was short, had to stand on his toes to see.

She stepped up behind him, pulled his hair back and held the knife to his throat.

"Money, fucker," she whispered.

"Die, Bitch." He twisted out of her grip easily and punched her, full-fisted, on the face.

The pain blacked her out for a split second but she had the sense to turn and run.

The file clerk grabbed her around the throat.

"Kill her, killer, kill her." Oster Wu hissed. She felt wet all over. One of them pissed on her, one of them spat, no one noticed and no one cared.

The file clerk twisted her neck and she sucked air, suffocating.

"Let her go. Stop now," Oster Wu said. She fell, panting for air, to the floor amongst the vomit, piss, spilled drinks.

"Can't kill my best girl," Wu said.

The interval. A bar surrounded the arena with a hundred bartenders pouring good, solid, old fashioned drinks like gin tonic, vodka orange, brandy dry. Service was quick and efficient; you could easily manage three drinks in the interval if you drank quickly.

The lights flickered. "Testing the equipment," someone called. People laughed; Yolanda couldn't see how that was funny.

"Seats, please. Seats please. The execution of Mele Dova will begin in twelve minutes."

A rush for the bar; most people liked to sit down with a drink in either hand.

They heard the screaming first.

"This'll be interesting," Theo whispered. "When they fight it. The ones who just take it aren't much fun."

Forget about dignity in death then, Yolanda thought.

The announcer said, "You should all have a dream death in mind. The technology is available to citizens, not just convicted descendants. You can die in bed, on a mountain top, you can die with a mouthful of your favourite food. You can die after saying goodbye, making amends."

"None of us have that kind of money," Theo said.

Mele Dova screamed as they wheeled her down the aisle, strapped in a wheelchair. A brace held her head still, but they hadn't gagged her.

"What's wrong with her?" Yolanda asked Oster Wu, who had loosened his belt and had his hands down there.

"I heard she was useless below the waist."

But Yolanda could see her legs straining against the binding.

"With this death, we apologise for the sin of murder. We hope this apology will help to lift the curse on this country. Mele Dova, you are charged with the murders of eighteen patients, victims of your nurse-ancestor. You failed to select a method of execution, so it has been decided you should die in the manner of your ancestors. Are there any registered descendants of the long dead victims of this family?"

Two women called out, "We are."

"And do you wish to close-witness this execution?"

"Yes."

They ran to the stage, making people laugh at their eagerness. They stood in front of Mele Dova, staring into her eyes. She began to cry. "I'm sorry, I'm sorry, I'm sorry."

They always cried when confronted with the victim's descendants.

They wheeled the electric chair down the aisle.

The audience screamed, a contagion of noise which set them all off.

"I don't want to watch this," Yolanda said. She had seen many terrible things in her life; had done some, caused some. But this...

She hid her head under Theo's arm. Let him tease her about it later.

The minutes passed. The counter said 18.06 but it felt like a lot more than eighteen minutes, watching the woman die.

The victim descendants moaned and cried. Close up, it was even worse. Mele Dova had no dignity in death. She burned, fried, stiffened, stank, all with the audience watching, breathless. She ground her teeth so hard she dribbled spots of enamel onto her chin.

It was so cold outside Yolanda felt the wax in her ears crackle. She wanted to curl up somewhere and cry, away from the world.

She found the car and waited for Theo. Around her, people were enlivened, walking quickly, a bounce in their step.

"The air! The air is good! Cleaner!" they shrieked to each other.

"What dream death would you choose? I know some women would like to die in childbirth," Theo said, opening the car.

"Who wants kids? They'd only be labelled like we are."

"We have a right to children."

"Having a right doesn't mean you have to exercise it," Yolanda said. "I'd choose to die in a plane crash, on my way to some wonderful place. When it's still perfect, still about the possibilities."

"I'd die in the water. Warm water, the sun beating down, salty water you can feel on your skin. That's how I'd die."

"You did well at the execution," Oster Wu said. It was warm in his house. Wonderful to be warm inside. In the car, the wind chill factor dropped, but it was so very cold.

"Someone has to pay, isn't that right?"

He smiled. It was the police motto. Half the city's population were cops.

He unzipped his pants, and she hid her revulsion.

"When are we going to travel for the weekend? Or the week? Think of the danger you could be in, travelling with me like that," she said.

There were certain privileges awarded to All Clears. Access to restaurants high in the mountains, where she'd heard the food was made for the Gods.

Unrestricted Travel.

Air Travel.

There were benefits.

"You can't travel, Yolanda."

"You could help me to. I'll kill you in Venice. I'll kill you on the beach, in an old crypt, I'll murder you on a hilltop and slit your throat on an ocean cruise."

A red spot of colour appeared on his cheeks. "My mate was pretty impressed with you."

"So he'll help me?"

"He'll help me. But he was impressed. He'll arrange for you to look at the records. That's all. Just to see if there's a flaw somewhere. Some people have had their ancestors' convictions overturned. If you find a flaw, they'll do the molec test. They wouldn't have done it at the time."

She knew that the molec test read molecular vibrations. Each person has one, and leaves a trace very easily. Each one is unique and there is a unique crossover between killer and victim. It is unmistakable. Inarguable.

"I don't know why you're bothering. You're lucky. Your ancestor was punished for the crime. You won't be executed for it."

She said, "I'm uneducated, unskilled and the only men who'll sleep with me are the sick fucks who think I might just kill them. Some of them are disappointed to be still alive when it's all over, I think."

He'd already lost interest, though, and he flipped open a newspaper to look for mentions of himself.

It gave her some space. Thirty minutes alone, to sit in the warm and quiet, to think.

Weeks later, she went to the file clerk's house. She had to do him first, but he liked it simple, straight sex, no violence. One of the easy ones.

"I wanted to be a cop but they wouldn't take me, fat arse that I am. They're the fucken heroes of this world. I tell you. Look at the crime rates. Lowest since record-taking began. I'll show you how to log on. You'll look at your records, and your records alone. If you look at anybody else's records I'll be able to track your downloads and you'll be prosecuted, no doubt of that."

"But..." she stroked his hand. "What about you? I mean, this isn't a threat, but if I go down, they'll trace it to you."

He shook his head. "I'm logging you in through nine different routes."

Strange how the details of history are lost. The names of minor players, whose actions have great affect on the way events play out. The guards who let in the assassin who killed a king; their names are forgotten, though surely they affected the future with their laziness.

Decisions are blurred, too; small level politics which affect many major decision are not noted or registered. The lunch which won a vote, the accident which lost one.

Yolanda understood this as she read her ancestor's files. She could see poor research, interviews unfinished and a local area study questionnaire mostly marked "To Be Completed".

Yet her ancestor Paul Friedham had been convicted. Checking the dates against recorded events she saw that, during his investigation, there was sniper at large, targeting police officers.

Not only would this have distracted the police from other investigations, but there was mention of her ancestor as a possible associate of one of five suspects. Both of them homosexual and, in those times, therefore instantly untrustworthy.

That was enough, it seemed, to convict and put him to death.

But his elsewhere excuse was perfect. Someone had written 'unchecked' across the photo. All the photos were archived; Yolanda found the original event, a concert of musical opera, and there was the photo, with her ancestor in the audience.

Much was made in the press of how an uncle had taken Paul in as a teenager, against all warnings. "He's flighty, untrustworthy" people said. But the uncle took him in. The uncle, father to fourteen, a legendarily fertile man, was a great proponent of children in marriage and caring for blood.

Yolanda wrote her letter carefully, ensuring any hint of desperation was removed. She stated her case, presented the facts, enclosed copies of the evidence. Theo called her a fool to stir things up.

"You're happy enough, aren't you? You should be grateful for what we have." He had a new lover, and all was right in his world.

Then she waited. She carried on with her life. Days driving around, nights with customers. It was often Oster, forever a freebie after all he'd done for her.

She felt great self-hatred after each session. She wished she had the power, the guts, to really kill them, but she never would.

She'd go to Theo in the car and he'd hold her while she cried. He'd count the money and talk about what they'd spend it on, and he'd feed her little crumbs of chocolate he stole from a café.

Every morning she covered her bruises, dressed and checked her post office box.

No letter came. She'd been told, don't call, don't email, don't show up in person. Just wait. You'll know when you'll know and then you'll know.

Others had received their assessments (always no; almost always no) in nine weeks.

It was fifteen weeks later when she was awoken in the car by two Ancestral Police, in red uniforms.

"Step out of the car, please. Yolanda Friedham?" one said. His voice was soft and gentle; it made Yolanda smile. She nodded, climbing out of the car.

"Yolanda Friedham, your application for reassessment of ancestral crime has been received," the other said.

She smiled. Still smiling.

"The files have been assessed and molecular vibrations taken. I will read the result of the reinvestigation to you. Your ancestor, Paul Friedham, has been found not guilty."

Before she could speak, though, before she could cheer and jump, kiss the Ancestral Police (but why were they there? This ran through her head, right underneath the happiness, the thoughts of freedom), the AP said, "However, investigation of this offence and the reassessment has brought to light further evidence, leading to the identification of the actual perpetrator of the homicide."

Yolanda realized the other AP had stepped very close to her.

"And?" she said. Her voice felt hard in her throat.

"The identified perpetrator is Thomas Friedham, uncle of Paul Friedham, founder of Freedom Food, the charity. There is latter-day evidence of corruption at high levels in local government, the police department and the courts.".

The AP smiled, as if unsurprised by this example of human nature. He read, "As this renders the crime unpunished, under ancestral law Thomas Friedham's most direct descendant will be charged and executed."

The AP said, "We inherit the material wealth of our ancestors. We must pay for their sins, as well."

Yolanda had thought herself a strong woman. Unlucky and strong.

Now she realised she had been neither.

Yolanda sipped champagne, gazing out at the sea below. The flight attendant, realising this was her first flight, was very kind, explaining things to her, giving her drinks and food, making sure she didn't feel nervous.

Beside her, Theo flicked through a magazine, smiling at her every now and again.

"Happy?"

"Of course."

The plane dropped slightly, and the passengers gasped, grabbing each other.

The pain began in her toes, an ache she attributed to cabin pressure. Then her shins, her thighs, her hips, and once it hit her spine, the agony was too much to bear. The agony took her out, took her off the plane and into the arena where she knew, she really knew and had to admit that her plane would never land.

Doll Money

Doll Money

I am surprisingly agile as I search my father's house. That's what an observer would say, watching a woman with near-useless legs and long steel crutches squat, bend, twist, open, riffle, search.

I must find my father's doll. I started in his workshop, thinking that's where he would have made it. I found strange metal and twisted designs. Then I reached under his bed (three peppermints; a small piece of lace; handkerchiefs; a pair of underpants) and under the mattress. I looked there while he was still in the bath.

While I was scrabbling at the back of his cupboard (magazines I didn't want to open, mouldy shoes) the phone rang. I had been crying for an hour.

"Hello," I said, in my father's weak voice.

"Mr Branch, this is your confirmation officer. We'd like to see you for just a few moments within the next twenty-four hours, if you can manage that."

"Ooh, I can manage, all right. I'll send my daughter in."

"No, Mr Branch, we need to see you. We need visual and digital confirmation. There have been reports of your demise."

"Surely not. Unless you're chatting up a ghost." I chuckled, Dad's chuckle. I had been doing this for years, getting things done by phone for Dad.

There was no response, none, from the confirmation officer.

"So you want me to come in?"

"Actually, we'd prefer to come to you. That way we can complete an evaluation in the eventuality you do die."

"Cheery, very cheery," I said. I hadn't inherited my father's wit. With him died the last humour in the world. On my wedding day, Dad was so funny. He hated the skin-tight clothes fad which made it hard to breathe, so he wore a purple and white caftan. I kept giggling explosively, making a terrible impression on Darren's family. They thought Dad was mad; I knew he was just smarter than them.

I sat on Dad's bed in the big empty bedroom and looked at all I would soon lose.

All I'll have left this time tomorrow is my small collection.

The three dolls.

They are mine forever. They are my history. My life.

My mother dressed hers in her wedding gown, as many women did. That one moment in our lives, when things change.

I'm tired. I'm tired. This is insane. I know Dad loved me. Where would he hide the doll? I used the broom to clear down the high cupboard. My little baby dresses were there, and strange, uneaten pieces of cake.

I remember when I first saw Mother's doll. She brought it, crying, to show me. She called it Life Insurance and said she had to face facts. She sold our things, one by one, and slowly bejewelled her doll. She said she had to accept the diagnosis or Dad and I would be penniless.

It was dressed in woven gold. I still remember its glitter. She hugged it on her death bed.

They had to wait for rigor mortis to pass before they could remove the doll from her clutches.

So where is your doll, Dad?

Where is your doll?

There must be one. You were a good father.

He was senile by the time he died. He imagined he had a job; every day he'd leave the house, "Off to work!" cheery, with a kiss to me. I'd make him cheese sandwiches with pickles, just like Mum always made.

Before Dad died, the neighbours began to hang around the house. I could hear them in the yard. It was like they were animals sensing death. Watching, curious, at a distance.

I made jugs of cool drinks and left glasses on the door stop. I made biscuits and sandwiches. If they were going to stand vigil, they shouldn't do it hungry.

They came around with things for me to do, to take my mind off Dad.

I painted their portraits, tiny pictures on teaspoons and stamps they could keep snuggled in their pockets. I sewed as well, mended, created, made.

I did a little cleaning. Some phone research. It kept me busy. Everyone likes to be busy. No one wants to be a charity case—you have to work hard to avoid that.

Whenever Dad came in from his pretence at work, I poured beer and made a fuss.

I never mentioned the doll.

Now I wish I'd asked.

My own doll has been made for a long time and hidden in a box in my closet. I can only reach it with a struggle, so the temptation to take it out and fiddle with it is not so strong.

My doll is dressed in the clothes I was wearing the day I met Darren. To me, that day is the happiest, because it was the beginning of our short time together.

Dad wasn't going to work; he was hosting garden parties for the neighbours. I could hear them laughing out there.

Everyone always loved Dad.

I wasn't game to have a look in case someone said, "Come on out."

I hate outside. I'm safer here.

An hour before the confirmation officer was due my bag was packed. My mother's doll, denuded, her dress and jewels sold and spent on my education. My wedding ring, which I was allowed to keep because it was mine by law. Darren's grey T-shirt doll. That's all. A small suitcase.

I was ready for when the confirmation officer came.

I would hear his van from up the street. Only they have big cars like that now. People use small, safe runabouts, or they don't drive at all. We don't like sudden death. We like to be prepared.

Darren loved to drive. He said it was safe, with everyone else being so careful. He tried to live without a car but he didn't have the patience.

"Waiting is a waste of time," he said, wrapping my scarf around my head like a shroud and drawing me onto the street. "I want to be there, not here."

His parents blamed me for his death. They thought I was wild, untested.

When I first met Darren, I was impressed by his family's doll collection. They had dozens. His father had selected to dress himself in his first school uniform. His mother wore the clothes she had worn to give birth to Darren, thus indicating how important he was. They made their dolls even though they outlived Darren.

It was a resting home for dolls because they sat there and were left alone. Some were old; they oozed pink chemicals from their eyes like strawberry tears, and their smell made your nose wrinkle.

There were rooms of them. Still are, I imagine; I'm not welcome in that home.

Perhaps if I had given birth to one of their own they may have taken me in.

All those people with time to prepare for death. Darren had only seconds after he crashed the car. His grey t-shirt was torn and bloody. I was in shock, watching it all like a dream.

"Take off my t-shirt," he said, and I hurt him doing so. He twisted it till it puffed into head and shoulders.

"My doll," he said.

I had that, at least. We could bury him properly. I feel sorry for those souls who don't complete their dolls or even begin. Bodies thrown onto the furnace for fuel. Souls drifting in the atmosphere, seeking purchase.

Where is your doll, Dad? I don't want you left unburied. I looked behind the fridge. Old magnets. Old cheese, grease.

After the accident, there was no doubt I should move home with Dad. Darren's parents didn't want me, that was clear, and Darren's little grey t-shirt doll would not buy me any food.

I could not expect anyone but my father to care for crippled goods.

We lived happily for years. Dad would stumble off to the shops with notes from me, I would stay in the house and never, ever leave. He made me work, though. No invalidism for me. If I slept past nine he'd stamp about, shouting songs which entered my dreams.

"All right, Dad," I'd say. "I'm up."

"So's the price of wool," he say, and together we'd roll some dough for breakfast.

I shuffled down the stairs to Dad's tiny cellar. He kept wine down there. Rarely drank it. All that would be taken. The stairs were hard work. I rested in Dad's armchair, smelt his aftershave in its texture, and I slept and dreamt of him and Mum, the way they loved to sit and talk.

I couldn't climb the stairs. I searched again, found shortbread biscuits. They went quite well with Dad's old wine. Why save it for the confirmation officer, I thought.

In the morning I had more strength so I dragged myself up the stairs.

I searched in the bathroom and in the toilet cistern. Nothing. I ignored the phone when it rang, and breathed through my shirt when I imagined Dad's scent filling the house.

I searched pockets of clothes, and even the seams, in case the doll was a solid gold miniature.

Nothing.

I had no inheritance. And Dad would not be buried.

The confirmation officer called at 9am. I used my own voice.

"Just confirming my appointment with your father," he said.

He knew perfectly well Dad was dead. He would roll up in his big van, throw me inside and chain me there while he assessed my belongings. Then he would drop me without my crutches somewhere far from home.

"Why can't you leave us alone?" I said.

"Miss Branch, do you have any idea of the high cost of social services? There are young families waiting for blankets and you begrudge them. If your parents failed to make adequate arrangements and you haven't made a suitable marriage, there's nothing we can do."

How can you argue with charity?

I answered the door. I'm good at it, can swing it open like anybody. I get a lot of deliveries. A confirmation officer in a grey jumpsuit (don't they realise how foolish they look? How fat?) stood on my step, his mouth open.

He smiled.

Actually smiled.

"I have an appointment with Mr Branch," he said.

I mirrored his smile, couldn't help it.

"I'm afraid he's dead," I said. There was nothing more to do. I had my small suitcase packed. I planned to sit on a street corner until someone took pity on me. Or killed me.

"Yes, I can see," the confirmation officer said. He was smiling. Then he laughed. I had not heard a laugh since Dad died. Not live, anyway, and the laughter on TV is so perfectly calibrated it chills me. Dad died quietly, in his sleep, then filled the bed with piss and shit. He had been so continent before that.

It took six hours to move him, clean him, stuff the bedclothes into garbage bags. One of the children took the bags away. I don't know where my rubbish goes. I used my wheelchair. I could balance that way, use my solid arms to lift and turn him.

I washed Dad in the bath, dropped myself into the warm water with him. I cried, then, because we had bathed together when I was a child, wonderful, warm memories, my mother sitting on the side of the bath washing our backs.

I talked to Dad and answered in his voice. We talked until the water went cold. Then I left him there to clean his bed. Then I laid his body on the bed and began to look for his doll.

"It's not funny," I said. "Dad's dead and I can't find his doll."

The confirmation officer stared at me. His jumpsuit was wrinkled from the nipples to the crotch.

"When was the last time you went outside?" he said. He was playing with me.

"A while."

He reached out his hand. I imagined it would be sweaty from clinging so hard to his briefcase, but it was smooth and dry. "Come on, I'll help you."

"I don't need anything outside," I said. I would step outside and he would run behind me and lock the door.

"Come on," he said. He tugged me gently. I shuffled my feet and my sticks until I was over the threshold. Sunlight flashed, hurting my eyes, and I realised how long it had been since I was outside. I don't like outside. I fear that the door will slam shut and I will be alone, my doll upstairs in its box.

I hadn't packed it.

I had forgotten my own doll. "Let me back in," I said.

"Onto the street," he said. I concentrated on the ground, checking for bumps and cracks. I would not fall in front of the neighbours.

They were all out to watch. They were good people; I found bread and eggs on my doorstep. They looked after me.

The confirmation van sat idling on the curb. I'd heard they left them running because people were often abusive and the officers needed a quick get-away. I would never behave so badly.

He led me to the front gate. I was suddenly sure he wanted to push me into the van, take me somewhere where they liked cripples like me, liked weak people to rape and murder. I would not cry, though fear made me spin back towards the house too quickly. I lost my balance and he centred me, his fingers digging gently into the strong muscles of my arms.

And I gasped as I saw for the first time what Dad had been working on. That clever, clever, funny man.

On the roof was a giant balloon with his face. Draped around the whole house was purple and white material, bringing back my wedding day. Somehow he'd hung arms from the eaves, and legs were mounds of dirt covered with flowers.

"There's your doll," said the man, and he helped me back into the house which would be my home for the rest of my life.

The Gibbet Bell

The Gibbet Bell

The dead woman's house stank of smoke. The reek of it seeped through the dusty fly screen door, waves of stale cigarette fumes assailing Jane as she knocked on the wire door again. The whole frame shook but the rattle seemed muffled.

"Hello?" she called. Not too loudly, not too rudely. "Mr Martin? Are you there?"

She listened for signs of movement. Heard the clatter of cutlery, like someone looking for a knife in the top drawer.

It went on for a very long time.

"Hello?" Jane said, louder this time. She waited for a quiet moment then shouted, "Mr Martin?"

The cutlery noises stopped altogether. Jane pictured him waiting with his hands in the drawer, pretending he wasn't there.

"It's Jane Ruse, Mr Martin. I'm here to see how you are."

She heard the sound of silverware dropping. A grunting noise. Jane pictured a pig, snuffling on all fours, but she kept a straight face as he appeared.

He was short and fat.

"What's that?" he said.

"I'm Jane Ruse. I'm here to see how you are."

He wore thick glasses and blinked at the light coming in.

He pulled his grey cardigan to cross over his chest, as if he was cold, though the sun warmed Jane's back.

"May I come in, Mr Martin? The Department has sent me to see how you are."

"I'm all right. I'm having my lunch."

It was 10am.

"What's for lunch, then? Are you a good cook?"

"Not as good as Mum is," he said. He swallowed, his adam's apple rising and falling as he stretched his neck forward.

"May I come in and see what's for lunch?" Jane said. He tugged the door back. It caught on the thick, soft carpet. Jane saw the man had bare feet. He flexed and squeezed his toes in the softness of the wool.

"Shoes off?" she said. He recoiled.

"No shoes," he said. "No dirt." Jane eased off her shoes. She felt thankful she'd worn stockings that day. Bare feet on this man's floor worried her.

She stepped inside.

The smell of old cigarette smoke was even thicker there. The lounge room was dark, thick curtains closed against the sun.

"Should we get some fresh air in here? Open the curtains? The windows?"

He shook his head. "It'll fade the carpet," he said. He flicked on a table lamp. The stand appeared to be cement, inset with animal teeth.

"I made that," he said, "when the cats died."

Jane glanced down, away from the lamp.

Parts of the carpet stood in wet peaks. Like a sheepskin rug sucked by a kitten.

Mr Martin caught her looking.

"It's a lovely carpet," he said.

He led her to the kitchen, which smelt of old, burnt cheese. Cheese stick wrappers, ends of cheese, a grater speckled with cheese; these things littered the bench. Apart from that, the room was clean. The sink shined. The fridge door was bare, unmarked.

"You clean up well," Jane said. She smiled at him, noticing a dark, greasy stain on his yellow tie. She touched her handbag, itching to make notes, write down what she was seeing, but she didn't want to worry him.

"You've got a nice backyard. Flowery and leafy," Jane said. She leaned on the bench and gazed out.

"You can go out if you want to. I don't like it so much. It makes me think of Mum, now."

Jane saw the deckchair. She'd made a mistake, forgetting about that. Even from a distance, she could see the dark stains marring most of the brightly striped material.

"Would you like me to organise a clear out? Take the chair away for you?"

He shuddered. "I don't think so. That was her last resting place." A resting place she had sat in for two weeks after her death. The body must have been foul.

"All right, Mr Martin. Things look okay here, but I think we need to get you some groceries. Some fresh fruit and veggies, what do you think?"

"Mum used to get them delivered."

"How about we organise a weekly delivery of the things you need?" She glanced in at the toilet and was glad she didn't need to go. "Toilet paper and the like. Or you could come with me on a little shopping trip. I'll take you in the car. It might be nice to get out."

"We don't go out much," he said. He pulled his cardigan close. Jane knew he was 43. His face was unlined. Pink. Just his mannerisms seemed old.

"How about we take things as they come?" Jane said. "Now, let's see what you need in the bathroom." Jane stepped down the hall. She smelt stale perfume, thick and sweet. It made her think of clothes hung back in the cupboard without being washed.

"Mum's room," Mr Martin said, whispering very close to her. His mouth reached her shoulder and she thought she felt his breath against her throat.

She glanced in, curiosity overcoming any sense of the dead woman's privacy.

"Her things," he said. Jane stepped inside.

The bed was unmade, the pillows askew, the sheets rumpled. A patchwork quilt, dull colours, lay creased at the foot of the bed. On the bedside table, a mug which, Jane could see as she stepped closer, contained solidified hot chocolate. A romance novel, bookmarked. A book never to be finished. False teeth resting in a glass of cloudy water. An overflowing ashtray.

"It's all just how she left it," he said.

One drawer of the solid mahogany chest was slightly opened. The sleeve of a thin grey jumper poked out, hanging like a thick ribbon. On top was a brush with some white hairs.

The bed was massive, oak, Jane thought. One of the bedposts was larger than the others, a shelf, and in the centre of it was a lace doily. On the doily was a beautifully ornate brass bell with a wooden handle. There were carvings in the handle.

"Oh!" said Jane, charmed. She reached for the bell.

"*No!*" Mr Martin stopped her arm. The contact was shocking to both of them.

"Don't ring the bell," he whispered. Jane felt her heart skip. He was panting, panicked.

"What is it?"

"The bell. Don't ring it."

Jane tucked her hands in her pockets to make it clear she wouldn't. She backed away.

"I just wanted to have a look at the handle. It looks so beautiful. Is it very old?"

"It's as old as the bed," he said. "They made it from a gibbet. Do you know what that is?" He leaned toward her. She nodded, not trusting her voice. "They hung you from it," he said. He lifted his tie above his head. Jane recoiled, her hand over her mouth. He said, "They let you rot on it. My aunt died on it, Mum said."

"Surely not your aunt? Perhaps a great-great aunt?"

"My Mum said aunt."

"Anyway, the bed and bell are beautiful," Jane said, picking on the detail of the story, not wanting to think of that long-hanged woman.

"Don't ring it. You can't ring it."

"I won't," Jane said. They stood staring at each other.

"Ringing the bell calls back the dead," he whispered. "If you ring that bell, Mum will return." He started to shake.

Jane broke all the rules and put her arm around him.

"Come on. Let's go out. This room upsets you. Let's close the door now."

He nodded. "Close the door."

Jane's relief on leaving the room surprised her.

Later that week Jane spoke to her supervisor. She enjoyed these weekly meetings. They were a chance to make someone else listen for a change, and to share the responsibility of care.

"We're fairly certain the relationship wasn't abusive, just very strange," Jane said. "The mother hadn't left the house for 30 years, and the son looked after her. He's very sweet, actually. Just not used to people."

"And do you think he's okay there? He's looking after himself okay?"

"The surface stuff is fine. The house looks clean enough and he's eating, though mostly cheese."

Her supervisor grimaced.

"I've arranged for shopping to be delivered," Jane said, looking at her notepad, "and I'm going to see if I can get him to at least step out to collect the mail. Benny, the little boy next door's been taking it to him since the mother died. Everyone feels very kindly towards him."

"Likabilty helps," her supervisor said. "Perhaps you need to start by taking a little of the outside to him. The local paper. A flower from his garden. Maybe something of yours."

Jane nodded. "I can do that. I'm going to see him tomorrow. The only thing that worries me is that bell. Listening to him I almost believed him. I was scared to ring the bell."

Her supervisor nodded. "It's good not to mock his belief, especially one so complex. It's a chilling fantasy he's got going there."

Jane nodded. Her supervisor said, "I think we leave the bell problem for now, until we figure out what it really means to him."

Jane nodded again. "Thanks," she said. "I'll let you know what happens tomorrow."

Jane went home to her cluttered, warm home, her scattered, warm husband. She said to him, "If someone was to assess us based on our house, they'd probably think we were crazy."

Her husband, stirring curry, said, "Probably."

Mr Martin was waiting by the door when Jane arrived.

"I made a cake," he said. Jane could smell incense; she'd brought him some last visit, suggesting it might smell nice in the house. She'd told him she used it at her place.

"I just have to ice it," he said.

"And a cup of tea, too, I hope," Jane said. She knew he had tea because she'd made his shopping list.

He let her in.

His hair was neatly combed and he was wearing a suit. It was too small for him and the underarms were faded. The tie he wore was poorly knotted and bulky around his throat.

"Where are you off to, all spiffied up? Do you need a lift?" Jane felt an unwanted sense of urgency, as if her pet bird was about to fly away.

"It's Dad's suit. Mum likes me to wear a suit for special occasions."

"And today?"

He looked at Jane steadily.

"Today will be special." He led her to the kitchen where the table was set for two. He placed the flowers Jane had given him into a cut-glass vase, a beautiful thing like most of the items in the house.

The plates were laid out perfectly atop a bright red tablecloth. Jane blushed. *Ohmygod*, she thought. *He wants us to eat together.*

He opened the cutlery drawer and jangled about in the mass of silverware. The noise hurt Jane's ears but she held herself back from helping him. He found the pieces he wanted and laid them carefully on the table. He poured hot milk into a mug and stirred it with a silver spoon.

"I think my husband might be a little jealous if I sat with another man at such a romantic table," she said. *How difficult*, she thought. *How very difficult and embarrassing.*

"You've gone to so much effort," she said. "Thank you." Mr Martin stared at her.

"It's not for you," he said. Years away from society leant his words their bluntness. "It's for Mum."

Jane gasped. She glanced out of the window. The stained deck chair was still there.

"But Mr Martin, your mother..."

He nodded. His lips twitched and she wondered if that meant he was smiling. "You can watch if you like," he said.

She was bewildered. She felt very slow.

"Come on," he said. She followed him to his mother's bedroom. He'd made the bed. Cleaned the bedside table. Changed the water in the false teeth glass. Emptied the ashtray. Put some flowers in a vase on the chest of drawers.

The curtains remained closed. Mr Martin put the mug and spoon down beside the bed.

"I'm going to ring the bell," he said.

Jane prayed she had the right words.

"Mr Martin, I know you miss your mother terribly. I know she was your dearest friend. But..."

He sat on the edge of the bed. His feet dangled, not quite reaching the floor. "I thought you were frightened to ring the bell," she said.

"Not frightened. Just not ready."

"And you're ready now?"

He nodded.

Jane sat beside him, her stockinged feet resting flat. "We'll ring the bell, then we'll have a nice meal together. Would you like that? I'll call my husband. I'm sure he won't mind. We'll sit down at that lovely table you set and..." He reached for the bell. Jane was certain the air suddenly chilled; she shivered.

"I..." she said.

"Shhhh," he said.

He picked up the bell and rang it. Jane expected a tinny sound to match the size of it, but the toll was like that of a grand church bell, deep, resonating. She felt it in her belly, the whole shake and ring of it deep in her gut.

Mr Martin put down the bell.

Jane could not speak.

She heard the ticking of a clock.

They didn't move.

She heard a rustle behind them in the bed. Jane squeezed her eyes tight. *It's nothing, of course it's nothing*, but the smell, the smell, of that perfume, that cigarette smoke. She felt the mattress sink, just a little, as if someone had sat down at the head of the bed.

Mr Martin wept without turning.

"Is she there?" he said. "I can't look."

"She's not. Of course she's not," Jane said.

But then they heard a deep, deep intake of breath. Someone sleeping.

Mr Martin turned his head. He coughed tears out, crawled around. Jane turned then, because she had to see.

There was an old woman lying in the bed. As Jane watched, she seemed to emerge, as if from water. Her hair was white. She had glasses tied to a cord around her neck.

She slept.

Jane screamed.

"Hush!" Mr Martin hissed. "Don't wake her. She needs her sleep," but the woman's eyes blinked open. Her mouth flapped gummily but no words came out. She looked at Mr Martin and smiled, a stiff grimace which made Jane scream again.

"Mum," Mr Martin said. He crawled over and laid his head gently on her chest. She jerkily stroked his hair.

"No," Jane said. She tried to stand, but felt her legs stuck to the bed. Her feet no longer touched the floor.

She heard a clicking noise and turned to see the woman snap in her false teeth, snap click of the teeth.

Jane felt herself sinking into the bed. Her mind blanking. Mr Martin stared into her face.

"The bed is hungry now," he said.

Jane choked. She felt nothing but terror. No pain. She felt like she was sinking into quicksand. She waved her arms, tried to push herself upwards, but the sucking in, the swallowing, was too great.

"Help me," she said. "My husband needs me. My clients. My sister."

"Let them ring your bell," Mr Martin said. "If you've got one." He smiled, a definite smile, his teeth white and wet with saliva.

"We'll have lunch in a minute, Mum," he said.

There was a banging on the wire door.

Jane tried to scream but her chest was so constricted the noise she made was minimal. "Help me!"

Mr Martin shoved a hanky into her mouth. She could barely breath through the cigarette and perfume stench.

"That must be little Benny," Mr Martin said. "Come with the mail."

"Good," said another voice. Not Mr Martin's. "Ask him in. I think it's time to wake up Grandma too, don't you?"

In the Drawback

In the Drawback

If he flared his nostrils and breathed deeply, the drummer boy could catch the deep salt tang of the ocean, its seaweedy stink hinting at vegetation and food. He glanced down to where a group of men were collecting firewood. They worked in silence; no voices reached him. But they were companionable. Compatible. The drummer boy knew that if he joined them they would be agitated. "Be quiet," they'd say. "Stop your fidgeting," and they'd ask him to fetch something from the caravans, something difficult to find and unneeded.

Sitting on the rocks, he gazed out at the water, far away in the distance. He stared without blinking and chewed on a piece of salt fish until thirst drove him to stand. He blinked then and saw it.

"There's something out there," he said. "Hey! Hey! There's something out there! Something big!" Thomas, down on the beach collecting wood, stopped working and, shielding his eyes, stared out. He stared for some minutes, then shook his head.

"There's nothing there" he shouted through cupped hands. "Maybe a tangle of ropes if you're lucky. Go claim it for yourself, boy, bring it to show us tonight."

The inhabitants of Sunlit Waters rarely looked out to sea. Months could pass without anything being revealed and they grew bored watching the drawback. They had found many treasures in the past; old boats and bone, rubbish, bits and things discarded and lost over the centuries. Once, they had anticipated the revelations and scavenged the goodies, looking for clues to the past.

But the drawback was slow. The drummer boy knew that, yet still he never failed to be amazed by it. "The water will never touch that place again," he'd say to the others. "It won't come back." The men shook their heads, used to it and bored. Decades now, the water had been drawing back. Long enough for it be normal.

The drummer boy walked out on the sand with his sack over his shoulder. He found some smooth glass for Miles' collection, seven plastic lids for Tom. He found a circle of material that he guessed was once the neck of a t-shirt. He filled his bag with little treasures and walked on.

As he approached the pile, his step slowed. It was nothing; he could tell that now. Just a tangle of bottles and the sort of seaweed that looks like human hair. He wrenched the bottles out; everything was useful in some way. They knew that at Sunlit Waters.

There was something smooth, though, right at the water's edge. Smooth and brown, like a rock, but shaped unnaturally even. The drummer boy's bag was heavy and the light was falling, so he left the mystery. He knew it would be revealed when the tide went out.

Three of the men had been to the city to shop. There would be a feast tonight. Food was always shared equally, salty food to make them thirsty. They would sit together in the games room and make what conversation they could. There would be no fish, and they would pretend not to hear the crash of the waves, clearer in the night but still far away.

The walls in the games room were covered with mould from the roof down to where the tallest man could reach with a scrubbing brush. From there, mould spread in patches and stripes. The smell of it was dirt and vegetable in one. When the men first entered the room, they breathed though their mouths, but soon grew used to it.

They sat around a massive metal table, circular, scratched and dented. A find from in the drawback.

The drummer boy sat on an upturned boat in the corner and thumped his feet against the wood, thumping thumping until the men turned and noticed him.

"Be quiet, boy," one said.

"There's something out there. I know it. In the drawback. I saw a glimpse of it today."

"Be quiet, boy."

And he was, for a while. The men who'd been to the city spoke of the noise there, the low hum which made them all queasy.

"It's busy, though. Colourful with women. And they laugh in the city. You know, funny ha ha."

"Did any of them speak to you?"

They shook their heads. "They looked at us as if we were crazy," they said. "And their faces are thin, like this." The man sucked in his puffy cheeks and the others laughed.

The drummer boy glanced at their faded clothes, the salt sheen on their skins. Pale eyes in brown faces.

The men drank wine, great mugs of it. The drummer boy found a mug for himself and filled it. He sipped the thick red liquid and felt nothing. He sipped again and again until the numbness set in.

"Look at the boy!" someone said, and they all laughed at him, slumped in his chair dribbling onto his chin.

He lifted his head and saw their faces, disgust showing through the drink.

"I'm not a boy," he mumbled. Thomas spat on the floor.

"You're the closest we've got, so wear it," he said. They all sat back, their feet up to ease swollen legs.

The drummer boy went into a frenzy then, whirling and drumming on every surface he could find; the table, heads, bottles and glass.

"Attaboy," they said, being nice to him, wanting him to keep playing the child because they missed children so much, they missed their little darling over-protected faces.

"Hey!" the drummer boy shouted. He started on a run to the cliff's edge, then turned to climb down, slipping and losing his grip in his eagerness. He reached the bottom and ran towards the path through the ti tree shrubs, terrified that whatever he had seen would sink and disappear before he could show the others.

"There's something out there," he shouted.

Everyone was in the caravans. Thomas slammed the door of his, bored with the news. "It's history," he said. "Who cares about what's done?"

Miles had been tending his flowers but grabbed his coat and nodded. "Time was, everyone'd join in," he said. "Time was, you'd be left behind the pack if you didn't hurry."

Fred shouted at them, do it yourself, find it yourself ya buggers.

So Miles and the drummer boy walked alone. The drummer boy knew the sighting was his, once confirmed by Miles. He would receive the greater share of whatever bounty was found. Why else would he sit and watch on that lonely, windy cliff top?

The flat expanse of sand stretched out before them, almost unchanged over many months. Only wind and the occasional scavenger bird digging for worms changed the landscape now. Once the water drew back it did not return.

Far out, near the water's edge, they could see a great mound.

"Is it a ship? It might be ship. It will be full of treasure if it's a ship," Miles said. He loved trinkets and shininess, loved anything that glittered, even if it fell apart in his fingers.

"We won't know until we walk out and see," said the drummer boy.

They walked.

"It's not a ship," the drummer boy said.

"It's a whale," Miles said. They smiled at the thought of a whale, unseen for decades, suddenly showing itself. "A shark, then."

"We'd smell if it was a shark. We'd smell the stink of it and the birds..." They glanced up, watching for circling seagulls. There were a small few, as always when people walked. People on the move meant food to a bird.

"Anything dead would stink. It must be some kind of ship. From space. A space ship that landed and sank and they never got out," Miles said.

They were silent as they approached the giant mound.

It was a man. A huge man, as big as four men. They could see his heels. He was face down.

There was a massive chain around both ankles.

The drummer boy and Miles stared at the man until they shivered. "You run get the others," Miles said.

"You go. They won't believe me."

So Miles went and fetched the men to come before the tide returned and covered the titan to his heels again.

They crowded around the huge man. The tide was out to his head, but they knew it was on its way in again. They stepped closer, took off their shoes and rolled their pants up to stand over him and look hard. His clothes were rotten, still damp from being covered.

"It'll be a year before the drawback reveals him," Fred said.

"We can see him when the tide's out," the drummer boy said. "We can get the other caravan parks to help us drag him."

"Let's just leave him for now," Thomas said. "There's no hurry. He's not going anywhere."

"But what if the tide takes him?"

The chain around his ankles, corroded almost to dust, sank into the sand.

"What's at the end of it? It may have been protected by the sand," Fred said, screwing up his eyes.

They brought spades and large digging shells, and slowly removed the sand. It was still very wet, and filled the hole they dug like quicksand. Working quickly, they revealed glimpses of what lay beneath.

"It's a rock. The chain is caught in a rock. They must have used some massive force to press this rock."

"The woman on the hill says once they all were tall. Strong, like this one," said the drummer boy, tapping on the rock with his sticks, tap tap.

They found skeletons about him. Weapons. A buckle.

"Why are they skeletons and he is flesh?" the drummer boy said.

The giant had remarkably little stink about him. It was almost pure brininess, so salty the drummer boy could barely breathe.

"We're not going to be able to turn him on our own," Miles said.

Many years ago, a whale had beached itself and two or three caravan parks had joined to turn, cut and remove the meat. Better to share than to have the carcass left behind. They still had the whalebone cutlery, the needles. They would never kill a whale; they didn't need to kill anything. The shore was always littered with dead fish as the drawback continued. The older men said the fish was saltier now. Chewier. They talked of soft-fleshed fish that melted in your mouth.

The giant's skin was white from being under water.

They poked and prodded, tore off bits of the rotten cloth to use back at the caravan park for stopping drops.

"Someone needs to tell her," said Fred. "She'll want to know."

"I'll do it," said the drummer boy. He didn't mind visiting her on the hill. There was a smell in there the men didn't like. A dried fishiness and they didn't know if it came from her or the things about her

"She'll give you treats tonight and someone will come fetch you in the morning," Thomas said. The men laughed. Tears came to the drummer boy's eyes.

"Baby," sneered Fred. The drummer boy knew he didn't fit in. They wanted him to pretend to be a child but hated him for it. Despised that he made them think of children.

The drummer boy walked back to shore and up the hill to the caravan belonging to the woman, Petra. She wore a floral dress and had him do her hair. "A lady has to look after her hair," she said. The men didn't like to touch it. It was thick and greasy like seaweed, and their fingers felt coated with grease for days.

As he did her hair, the drummer boy told her of their discovery. He said, "They want to wait for the drawback to turn him over."

She shook her head and tiny specks flew off. One landed in the drummer boy's eye. "Nonsense. They'll drag him out. They'll get the neighbours to help and drag him out of the water. What are they waiting for?"

"I think they're frightened of him."

"Well, they should be. They know my stories. The terrible time of ancient dreams. Once there were many people like him. Men and women so tall they used caves high in the cliffs to store their treasures. That table in the games room was a gong," she said. "Can you imagine the size of the mallet? You could dissolve a limb to liquid with one hit. It was used by the giants."

"What happened to them? Did they all die?"

Petra shook her head. "No one knows." She pointed to her most prized cup, a huge thing with a piece like a bite out of the rim. "All we know is, they were here."

The drummer boy had explored some of these caves. He could not reach them all. Inside them he found perfect spheres, papers long past reading, shiny bowls and things that glowed. Petra salvaged nice things, remains of the past she didn't like to use. Mugs on hooks, cracked and yellow. A little stack of books, pages glued together from their time in the sea.

The drummer boy collected remnants of toys. He had the head of a plastic action figure. The axle of a toy car. Seventeen mismatched building blocks.

Petra fed him a delicious soup and made him talk about things he didn't want to talk about.

The drummer boy said, "How do you know the past?"

She said, "It's the books and the things we find and the stories I remember. I try to pass the knowledge on but they don't listen. They don't care about the terrible time. They don't want to learn from the past. A great wave begins with a sudden drawback. Something must follow." She muttered, losing her point, and it was frightening to the drummer boy to learn she didn't have all the answers.

All the caravans were falling apart, long past their holiday glory. Rusty. A metal smell about them all. A mustiness. The flooring all white, sanded away by years of walking.

She said, "Did you hear about the fire at Tree Shady Park?" He shook his head, horrified to think of the children who may have died there.

"It's alright. No one died. Places can be reborn, too. They can drown and be reborn. Changed." She squeezed her eyes shut. "You tell Thomas to get the others and drag that thing out of the water."

The next morning, the drummer boy told Thomas of Petra's instructions. The men spent half the day discussing how it would be, then sent runners to the other caravan parks to ask for help. They agreed the apex of low tide was the best time.

Thomas said, "Drummer boy, you guard tonight. No one is to begin without we're all here."

They left him a campfire. He boiled a pot of water and dug his fingers in the sand to collect pipis. He cooked them and ate them, hot and tasty, straight from the shell.

He could not remember a time when he felt happier.

He collected rocks and threw them at the birds swooping down seeking a beakful of meat. Rocks landed with a splash in the water. The ones on sand sank down, and some landed on the giant's back

There was something almost delightful about hearing the bones of this titan clunk, and the drummer let a few more rocks fall until there was a small mound on his back.

He slept, curled sitting up in a ball, and was woken by birds. In the distance he could see the groups walking towards him.

He walked to the water's edge, which pulled rapidly to the shoulders of the giant. The drummer boy washed his face and wet his hair, slicking it back out of his eyes. Then he saw movement.

He turned, thinking one of the men must have run forward.

"We won't begin," the drummer boy said. There was no one there. It must have been a fish, he thought, lifting out of the water, or a low-flying bird.

As the men approached, he quickly removed the rocks nestled on the giant's back. They looked shoddy in the daylight, weak and pathetic, and the drummer boy was not proud of his actions.

As he lifted the last rock off, the giant's shoulder twitched.

The drummer boy shouted and stepped backwards. He fell over, landing in the sand and wetting his trousers.

He wriggled backwards away from the motionless giant.

"He moved," he shouted to the men. "He moved his shoulder."

They snorted. "He didn't move. He's probably caught a fish in his shirt."

"It's only the parasites. New food for them all. Word will get out and they'll come from everywhere to feast," Tom said.

Miles said. "Time was, we'd shoot those birds."

The giant lay on his stomach, his arms beneath his body. It took the men from three caravan parks in shifts to drag him out and turn him. Others had heard the news and were travelling up and down the coast.

This was something which never happened and it made most of them uneasy. They were not comfortable with community. Community insisted on modes of behaviour, saying the right thing.

Providing for visitors.

Thirty men heave ohed on one side, twenty tugged on the other. The giant's flesh was surprisingly firm, the drummer boy thought. He marched around the grunting men, tapping his slow rhythm as they worked. He felt proud of his drumming. He did not miss a beat, he would not, he would drum and drum and drum while the men toiled to turn the giant over.

Other bodies they'd found were either dissolved to bone, or the flesh turned greenish and jelly-like. Usually you grabbed the arm of a revealed body and your fingers sank to bone. You could slide the meat off the bone and collect it in a bowl. Even the dogs wouldn't eat this sludge, though the woman on the hill swore by its efficacy as fertiliser. She sold the vegetables grown on this stuff (she called it sea sludge) for a higher price, saying it cured ills of the mind. She said that when you defecated next, your shit would contain tiny worms, too small to be seen. These worms drawn down from your brain by the scent of the sea sludge in your belly.

The drummer boy would rather keep his sadness than eat anything grown from that stuff.

The giant's body was not like that. His flesh was firm. The ropes they used dug into his shoulders, and the drummer could see the flesh reddening.

"That can't be right," he said. "His flesh should not change colour." The drummer boy drummed one-handed and pointed at the markings on his back. "Why is his skin marked?"

They shook their heads. "Who knows? Let's turn him over then worry about it."

The drummer boy marched around and around. The tide was coming back and would cover the giant to his ankles this time. The men rested and debated whether to come back as the tide drew back.

"If we wait a year the water will draw back, anyway," one said. "There's no hurry."

But as he spoke the carrion birds circled above, rawking down at the people stealing their food.

They set back to work. It was tough going, and they took it in shifts, collecting water and cooking pipis and fish to eat. They all talked, theorised about the man.

"So, did he walk out into the ocean, dragging or carrying his rock, until he could no longer walk?"

"Or did they drop him off a boat and he couldn't move?"

"And who dropped him? And why?"

Finally they had the leverage to turn him over.

"One, two, three," they chanted, and with a strain and a push, he was over.

Water lapped at his hair, softening it into baby fineness. His arms were crossed tightly and he held something there, an armful of something. His wrists were chained. His eyes were closed and his mouth was so tightly pressed he looked like he had no lips. He was terribly scarred, marked.

"His lips are sewn together," someone up that end said. "And his cheeks are puffed out. Has he got jewels in there?"

They had heard tell of people who were buried with their jewels or money in their mouths, their lips sewn shut to scare off thieves.

"Shut up," someone further down said. "Shut up and look at his arms."

The drummer boy pushed through the knees of the men. Some of them were weeping.

"It's children," he said. The giant held, close to his chest like he would not let them go, five small skeletons.

"Children!" the men said. They began to wail with fear and sorrow. "It's children!"

They all stepped back, wondering what to do. Where to go from here. They stared at the children's skeletons.

"They'll need a proper burial," said one. "At least that."

There were nods, agreement. They were good at burials. There were thousands of bones in the dirt behind the caravan park, all carefully laid in a stack and words said over them.

The woman on the hill trundled down on her electric car. When she saw the lips sewn, she spoke. Her eyes were closed, chin to neck, voice muffled.

"They did it at sea. Did it once to the master of a captured ship." She waved her arm at the sea, as if they would find evidence of this under the waves. "He moaned so much the pirates sewed his lips together and tossed him into the sea."

She tossed her arm and her fingertips flicked at the drummer boy. "Don't you remember we found that boot once, with a needle imbedded?"

This was proof to no one but the drummer boy and the woman. The men hissed, "Shut up! Shut up!"

The giant was covered with sucking, biting things. One burrowed into the eye of his penis, which they could see through his torn pants.

The drummer boy stared at the giant till his eyes watered.

"I saw his finger move," he said.

"Be quiet now, boy," said Fred.

And then they all saw it. One finger flicked stiffly. Then another. Then his shoulders shook.

The men ran, shouting. The drummer boy behind them, not as fast in the sucking wet sand.

They stopped a ways off and stared back.

He couldn't be alive.

They watched as his fingers unclasped. The children's skeletons tumbled about on his chest as he released his grip, and he lifted his great hand and swept the bones off like crumbs. His shoulders shook and the men ran shouting to the cliffs as the giant slowly sat up.

They watched him through binoculars from the cliffs. Petra was there, and the other women, too. He took hours to stand, his movements slow and careful, as if his body reawakened slowly. He seemed so human when he stretched some of the men murmured, "We should talk to him."

Then he lifted his hand to his mouth and touched the stitches there. He looked towards the cliff and began to walk, each huge footstep sinking into the sand and being lifted out with a sucking noise they could hear from the beach. The ancient chain broke away.

He thundered on. He searched the ground as he walked, fingering the stitches.

"What's he looking for?"

"Something sharp."

They moved further back as he approached, wanting to run but wanting to know as well.

Then he reached down and lifted up a shell. He'd found his sharp object.

He was close enough now they could see the barnacles clinging to his ears.

"Stop him," Petra said. Her voice came in gasps. The drummer boy had never seen her scared.

"Who is he?" the drummer boy asked.

She shook her head. "I don't know. I don't know."

"But who sewed his mouth? How?"

She slapped him, the fat fleshiness of her hand softening the blow.

She looked at him sidelong. "I don't know," she said. She began to shake, to quiver, like her body knew what was coming.

Feeling the stitches with one hand, the giant used the sharp with the other and soon his mouth was loose. He bent over and spat a mouthful of rocks to the ground.

He dropped the sharp.

His nose screwed up, his lips kissed out then peeled back in a grimace. His teeth were smaller than they could possible have imagined; like an adult with baby teeth.

There was the beginning of a sound, a low-pitched noise which made the drummer boy feel sick to his stomach. The giant opened his mouth wider, wider, and his jaw seemed to dislocate itself as he stretched his mouth out so wide they could see deep inside his throat. He began a noise, one long echoing note which shivered the drummer boy to his core.

One man began to cry, then another.

The woman wailed. "We don't want to hear it," but the giant stepped closer, closer, and it filled their world and that of everybody nearby.

To a man they began to weep. The drummer boy was filled with such complete sadness he saw no room for the future, but he was used to sadness. Used to absorbing it, ignoring it.

Miles fell over, dizzy, disoriented. He wailed, "I'm drowning! I'm drowning!" though water was nowhere near. The drummer boy felt his vision blur and he reached for Petra. She was slumped in her electric car, vomit covering her chest.

The giant stood, his head back, mouth open, as men turned to jelly about him. Far out on the waterline, whales beached themselves and those still capable of seeing shouted in surprise at the sight.

The drummer boy heard crashing, cracking, and he saw the cliff collapsing onto a dozen men below.

Men cried salt tears and the drummer boy watched as they staggered towards the water, seeking out the drowning in droves. Thomas lead them, striding as if he was in control, but the drummer boy saw him falter in every step. Petra rolled till her wheels stuck then she threw herself down and crawled like a worm out to the water.

How did the ancients stop him? the drummer boy thought. *How did they sew his mouth without dying on approach? Did they numb themselves? Sacrifice themselves for the children?*

The children. There was a small family of them in Tree Shady Park. The drummer boy's stomach pained him so much he couldn't swallow. He had to spit it on the ground. He wanted to run to the children, gather them up and take them to safety.

The giant wiped spit from his mouth and was silent. He looked around at the deserted beach. The drummer boy thought, He sees me. I should run to warn the children, run my fastest and beat him there.

The giant stepped towards him. The drummer boy thought, *no. No. I'll lead him away. I must lead him away.*

So he began to run. He ran. The giant stepped after him, walking slowly, each step ten of the drummer boy's.

The drummer boy ran inland, rhythmically, counting the beat in his head as he ran. He knew the giant would catch him. There was no doubt of that. But the further he could lead him away the better he would feel.

He ran for a full day before he sank to the ground in exhaustion.

The giant stepped forward, picked him up and held him close. The tenderness of it crushed the drummer boy's ribs and made him wish for just...one...more...breath.

The Census-Taker's Tale

The Census-Taker's Tale

The middle-aged man (life expectancy in modern day England being 65 for men, 68 for women) listened, nodding his head, writing carefully in a small notebook.

"You listen very well," one of his fellow passengers said, "and yet you have nothing to say. What are you writing in that book of yours? Are you a spy, looking for secrets to take to Londonstan?"

The man smiled. "No, I am not a spy, although I have spoken to three. I am, rather, a census-taker."

There was little uproar in the carriage following this announcement. Most of the other passengers continued with their earlier conversations. One young woman, a neat girl with hair cut short in the fashion of the day, continued to watch him. She was of the innocent breed—the adults who never fully become adults. They could do a day's job without complaint and so were tolerated.

"I never met a Census-Taker," she said. "I met farmers and builders and once I met a man who worked at the Council."

"We have just over 100,000 council workers by last count. You'll probably meet a few in your day. Especially if you're going to Canterbury."

The girl's mother looked him up and down.

"She's not staying in Canterbury, so lift your mind out of the bedroom. She's stopping off to get the train down to Dover. They need seamstresses down in Dover." The woman sniffed. "Don't meet many Census-Takers."

"There are 53 of us working in this country. I can't answer for elsewhere."

"Elsewhere!" The woman snorted at the thought of such a place. Most people didn't travel far from where they were born. Only the drunks moved a lot, because they were not welcome in their homes.

"Not too many of us are happy elsewhere. I see a lot of that in my work," the Census-Taker said. "My name is Romulus Remus Jones. My father read history at Oxford and was sure I would be one of the founders of the new England. He thought the weight of the future rested happily with me." The man smiled. Cleared his throat. "I do a lot more listening than telling. People give me their stories. Even as a child, I always listened. I remember more about my parents' childhood than my own. My mother's first memory is of sitting in her push chair, surrounded by her aunties and uncles. She says her mother put her there on purpose, to keep her quiet. The aunties and uncles were all dead with the plague, and here's this little girl with all the hopes and dreams, sitting amongst them."

"Are you the only Census-Taker? Are you married?" the young girl asked.

He laughed. "You think I can count five million people plus ghosts myself? I am no Santa Claus."

"Have you seen a lot of houses? How other people live?"

"People live in similar ways. You'd be surprised. Bottles are precious everywhere, filled and refilled and filled again. Many houses are built out of rubbish, gaps plugged with more rubbish, glass houses. I went to one home with forty rooms, so many rooms I didn't know where to sit and there was a ghost in every room. This was the home of the Banker. I heard his son's story. The son was the guard at the bank, but he fell asleep, drunk. The money was stolen and the son was hung."

The man nodded his head at each of the travelers, counting them. He said, "I was married once, but my wife was not what she was supposed to be. She did not support a head of household. We need rule in the house, while we have no strong rule of law outside. I followed the way of Londonstan; I simple said, 'I divorce you,' three times. I have not married since. I am married to my job, I always say. Can't have a father who's never home. You'll end up with drunkards for children."

"I know a woman doesn't remember how many husbands she's had," the girl's mother said.

"Records are lost. Not everyone remembers all the spouses."

The Builder's Labourer, whose tale had drawn the women of the carriage to him in horror, said, "So you'll tell us a story then, Number Man? A story of counting sheep, perhaps."

The rest of the carriage laughed, but the Census-Taker did not seem bothered by the mockery.

"I am more of a listener than a teller, but I will do my best. I could tell you plenty of stories which have happened to other people; love gone wrong ending in bloodshed, love too strong, love unrequited. Murder and betrayal, lust and magic; these things all happened to other people. I am not an investigator. I ask the same questions of everyone. It is the answers which make all the difference. I like people who can't read or write because I write their answers. Otherwise I'm not supposed to know.

"The story I will tell you is a frightening one and I hope it won't upset you too much."

He was rewarded with a slight opening of lips from the ladies, a shifting in the seats.

"My parents are both what is known as plague babies. Babies born during the plague years who never fell sick, but who prospered and flourished. Most who survived those years are thin, unhealthy beings, exhausted from a short walk out for milk and bread. They managed to have children; some of you are that issue—and the children are weakfish, too.

"Not my parents. They grew up pink-cheeked and bouncy, on opposite sides of England.

"The doctors noticed them early on, and the few others like them. Twenty, perhaps, around the country, standing out from their fellows.

"There came a time when somebody, a doctor who studied and read the past, thought perhaps that the blood of these children, taken as a dose, could cure, or at least protect from the plague.

"So this is how my parents met. All the Plague Babies brought to Eastbridge Hospital, here in Canterbury.

"My mother still talks about the arrival. They had been taken from what remained of their families and transported by carriage. They were treated well. My mother saw many families along the way, some walking, the children dragged on wheeled carts when they needed to sleep. Others crammed into old carriages, babies hung out the windows on improvised hammocks. It made my mother tired to watch, and she slept a lot on her journey.

"She said she wasn't worried about where she was going. It was an adventure to her, something different. The small village she lived in bored her. The only thing she found interesting were the ghosts which clung to the village like the dags on a sheep."

The ladies sat forward again. They liked a ghost story.

"My mother could hear the ghosts when the rest of them were deaf and blind to it. She found out all about the villagers, especially the ones who would prefer their secrets kept.

"The schoolteacher, an ignorant, angry woman who taught only as much as she knew, which was very little indeed, always stood on her step and screamed at passersby. "Look at your wife, her body hanging out," or "Some learning wouldn't go astray, Mr. Plod." Yet my mother knew, through the radiant ghost of a baby which crawled the streets crying for her, that the schoolteacher had more than one child and she had drowned them all. These are the things my mother learned from the ghosts in her village.

"Meanwhile, my father grew up on a farm, where three uncles not much older than he ran the cattle in a very efficient way. None of them had book learning, but they were smart in the ways of animals and the sun and were rarely surprised. My father swears there were no ghosts, though my mother says she has seen plenty there. That everyone has secrets."

" 'Not these men,' my fathers says. 'They were too busy with their cattle for secrets. Too busy Feeding the Nation.' "

"Whenever I heard 'Feeding the Nation' I knew it was time to make myself scarce. A full-blown argument was brewing, wherein they would insult each other's families. Deride each other's knowledge, mock each other's perceived ailments and then move to the next phase; violent love-making. If I was still there at this point one of them would have the presence of mind to thrust a coin at me, tell me to go to the village for a puppet show. Mostly I took the coin for myself before it got to that point. If I was lucky there would be something other than

Punch and Judy. If I saw Punch and Judy, I expected to come home and find one of my parents murdered with a rolling pin.

"So my parents from different sides of the country and with different lives, came together at Eastbridge Hospital."

"I went knocking there one time," one of the passengers said. "When I broke my arm falling out of a tree. They said they couldn't do me unless I paid. 900 years they've been there, and they can't fix one measly arm?"

"They were not set up as a medical facility when my parents arrived. It was a home for old, wealthy citizens. And for travellers and pilgrims. It surprises me they turned you away, sir. They have never been known to turn a needy person away. In my opinion that hospital is one of the reasons Canterbury was chosen as the new capital. Its spirit of giving and helping is one we would all do well to adhere to."

"Well, all I know is they turned me away. I had to go to a local man and my arm's never sat right since."

It was true; the man's arm sat at an odd angle.

The Census-Taker nodded. "We all take impressions differently. That's why numbers are important. Numbers are what they are and cannot be argued with. We have this many men, that many women, this many children. That is why I count. To have something to rely on. Why, did you know that of our population, there are...." Here, the Census-Taker drifted into number talk, little realizing that his audience was not interested.

"Tell us about the ghosts," the young girl interrupted.

"Hear, hear," the others agreed.

"The twenty plague babies, the children, were treated very well. Each had their own room, but they were lonely and often ended up sleeping three or four to a bed. My mother was the only one to see the ghosts and she kept everyone awake repeating the stories they told. Can you imagine? 900 years of the sick and the people who cared for them. There was no end to the stories.

"It was a time of adventure. They had a small amount of schooling, but mostly they were subjected to one medical test and examination after another, until they felt like museum specimens. Apart from that, they were free to explore."

"I've been to the museum. Smelly, dusty place it is. I wouldn't go there again," the girl's mother said. "What's the point in all that history, anyway? Doesn't mean a thing."

"I agree with you there, Good Lady," the Census-Taker said, smiling. "In all my questionnaires, the one about the level of historical education draws the most confusion. What is history, indeed? It is opinion, nothing more. Ask any two people about the fall of London and you will get two different stories. Ask ten and you will get ten stories.

"My parents and their friends thrived and grew. My mother in particular was never bored. She had the other children, but she also had the ghosts, who told her all kinds of wondrous things. She tried to teach the others how to see the ghosts and, after five years passed and they were sent back to their ordinary lives of struggle, some of them could indeed discern movement. They could not hear the voices though.

"The tests became more invasive as time went on. There was an air of desperation. This was in 2058 when my mother was five and my father eight. An air of desperation as the plague continued to kill.

"Finally, one morning the children were given a particularly fine breakfast of bacon and eggs and herded into what was once the kitchen. It was vast and still full of the items of the past. Rusting machines, the use of which the children could not imagine. They were gathered in the corner and told, "We have a very special man coming to see us. Who has heard of Prince Charles?"

There was a clamour in the carriage. "What year was this again?"

"2058."

"Fifteen years before he became king, then."

"Yes. He was just a young man. But with great vision, even then."

"You say he's got vision? What about the workers? What's he ever done for us?" the Builder's Labourer said.

The Census-Taker shook his head. "He has done more than you know. He was reading medicine at Oxford at the time. I think they held the school open for him, or near enough. Anyway, he came to the hospital to talk to my parents and their friends. My father never forgot the speech, being old enough to listen. Whereas my mother was more interested in his formal mode of dress and in contemplating what would be for lunch.

" 'Now is the time for sacrifice,' the Prince told them. 'The future of all of England lies in your veins. You are the strong. The fit. You are unaffected by the plague which is slowly but surely destroying us. I ask of you a sacrifice, but this sacrifice will not kill you. And you will be compensated, both with money and with fame. Your names will be known now and forever.' "

"What are their names?" the Builder's Labourer said.

The Census-Taker named his parents and some of their friends. The passengers all shook their heads.

"You see? History is bunk. The great sacrifices are forgotten."

"What sacrifice was it?" the young girl asked. "Did your parents die?"

The passengers spluttered into laughter. "If they'd died, they couldn't have had him, right?"

Tears came to her eyes and the other passengers consoled her. Disabled children were always treated very well, because they were considered to be a punishment for bad behaviour and, as a message from God, very worthy.

There were not many disabled in modern England. The weak died early, premature or ill babies were not kept alive. There were more miscarriages, called a blessing from God. God taking the punishment.

"No, they didn't die. Three of their friends did through miscalculation. Are any of you old enough to remember the medicine taking of 2060?"

An older gentleman nodded.

"That serum, given to every man, woman and child of Great Britain, was made from the blood of the Plague Babies. It is because of my parents, their blood, and King Charles V, that we're here today at all. She still makes me my lozenges, Mum does, with drops of her blood, to suck on. Keep me healthy."

"The plague simply died out. Everyone knows that. You can't claim hero status," the Builder's Labourer said.

"Not me, no. But my parents and the other children spent five years in that hospital, giving their blood to the cause. They were not unhappy; any cache of toys or books found were allocated to them, over and above the Royal family. They got used to a rich diet, unlike anything we know. And the doctors worked to use the inoculation. There is still a stock somewhere, of the blood. Kept underground, I believe, somewhere in Scotland, where the ice rarely melts.

"My parents and the other children disliked being back at home. They felt displaced, as if the world had shifted slightly while they were in the sky-high world of Eastbridge Hospital and their feet had landed in an unfamiliar place. Things were the same; in fact life had gone on without them all quite well. They were different, but not in a good way. People walked around with their inoculation scars, little realising it was my parent's blood which had saved them. My parents didn't really realize this themselves until later when they read together at Oxford.

"For yes, they did meet again, as young adults. The others fared both well and ill; some went to an early death (though none through the plague) and others had turned to a life of crime, seeking the riches they had known as children. My parents both accepted their lives in a way which meant they would change it at the first opportunity. The Prince made sure they were all looked after, but it was not enough.

"They kept in contact through long, increasingly personal letters. One of their members (she is a writer for the newspapers, has been for 30 years. King Charles is not always pleased with what she has to say, but that is by the by) built them a newsletter, a very private sheet only ever seen by the Plague Babies. In this way those capable amongst them plotted to meet up at Oxford, where they would learn enough to save the world. Rule the world. Change the world. Again."

"Who are these people?" demanded the mother. "More names. You say they changed the world yet we know nothing of them." She gave the Census-Taker a good look and seemed to decide he might be good material after all. With the new morality, the rewritten religions, sex for procreation was good in and out of marriage. "You should sit up straight. Strong men don't slump."

He shrugged his shoulders back. "I always carry forms with me. They're heavy." He gave them more names, of a writer, an architect, a historian, people whose names were in the newspaper. He unrolled a roti with curry and was looked on with suspicion by the others. "It's tasty and handy food. It doesn't mean I am Indian."

"None of us care what you eat, mate. It's the fact you're eating. Dead people out there. Ghosts in here. Most of us couldn't manage it," the Builder's Labourer said.

The Census-Taker ate his roti.

"My parents were quieter in their achievements. And, before too long passed, they gave birth to me. Well, my mother did. She said that around the birthing bed clustered all the women who had died in childbirth. They didn't want to see her die. Shift this way, now that, they told her. They knew the best way to get a baby out. I was fine, they knew. Strong and healthy, ready to claw my way out. 'Slow him down,' they told my mother. 'Not too fast.'

"I was one of 40 babies born in England that day. I can give you the statistics on the others. All of the Plague Babies expect great things of their own children. Hard work, no illness, no foolish thoughts. My parents expected great things of me. They taught me to respect difference and risk. They expected me to be perfect, a great creator. I am neither of those things. I believe in a complete count, and that my numbers matter, but I don't believe I am the one they think I am. They even opened me up to see if I would be a priest." Here, he lifted his shirt to show his belly; a jagged scar, angry and red, across the front. "Priests have a small, hard stone in their stomach, to remind them to think of God at all times. I've known men to swallow a stone in order to be chosen as a priest.

"My mother became a faith healer. She sucks up the poison in a person's soul. She always smells awful. Oh, the stink of her after a day at work. She comes home, dusty, dirty, wanting to squeeze me tight to help her forget about death and disease. But I can't stand the sour-sweet smell of her.

"I tell you all of this so you will understand how very accepting I was when I entered the village of Beddington and found everyone dead.

"There are some who say that people like me, children of Plague Babies, attract death. Or can sense death in large numbers."

The Builder's Labourer said, "You people, people like you, you got everything."

"If I have everything it is because my parents gave everything. Don't you understand that?" He took a lozenge from a small bag and sucked on it.

"From the start, my mother was determined to teach me to see ghosts. She said that ghosts took advantage of the ignorant, that they stole thoughts away and memories, too. It's happening to my father. Most days he knows where his hat is, but others he'll spend an hour searching and there it is on his head all along."

"That happens to all people as they get old," the older gentleman said.

"Not my mother. She snarls at those ghosts if they come reaching for her. She thought she had failed in her lessons because for a long time I couldn't see what sat right in front of my face. I could hear them, though, small voices telling me if someone was lying or not. It was only once I started work I could see them. If people left out information, the ghosts would laugh. They like liars. They like people who leave information out of their census answers which would help the country. That makes me very unhappy."

Here he stared at the Builder's Labourer, who had, perhaps embellished his tale just a little.

"I have been working as a Census-Taker since I left school fifteen years ago. In that time I have spoken to people of many walks of life. I have seen fresh-born babies and noted their birth defects. I have watched people say goodbye to their loved ones as the priest calls last rites. These things bring ghosts, chattering creatures who fill me with their own important nonsense. My awareness grew stronger, to my mother's delight. The ghosts began to appear as a shimmering apparition then, as I learned to focus, as formed humans, albeit unstable ones. They sit with us now, in this carriage."

The young, slow girl squealed in horror and leapt to her feet. "Where? Where do they sit?"

"There, there and there. They are raggedy creatures and bloody. Victims, I would say, of the terrible accident which has caused our delay. And you," he said to the mother, "You have a radiant boy by your side, watching over you. We only see radiant boys who have been killed by their mothers."

"You act as though this was ordinary."

"It is to me. I'm not telling the story very well if you don't understand that. Seeing and hearing these things was ordinary in my household. You know that some evolution seems damaging to the creature, but it takes that creature forward. Hyenas give birth through a pseudo penis. Peacocks' tails, nightingales' songs, cardinals' plumage; all this attracts the mate, but the predator as well. I think ghosts are evolving like that. They are damaging themselves, but evolving. Most ghosts will stay at home, except for the men who like the travel, looking for a host body. They move further from home, seeking purchase, but they weaken as they do so You can tell them by their foot fall. Heavy, slow steps. They might be body-less, but they have all the weight of the world on their shoulders."

They heard this noise soon after and there was panic in the cabin. "He wants to take my body," the young girl screamed. So she had understood that much. But it was an old woman walking to the lavatory.

"I had been asked to take the census on the road from Canterbury to Brighton, taking in Ashford, Rye, Hastings..." This time he did notice the bored shuffling. "Some of the villages I stopped at had no numbers recorded there for 30 years. Partly this was due to the isolation of the countryside in this direction; it was three days journey to get there from the nearest major road and I needed to take all my own supplies. There were no shops along the way. Not even a roadside stall. There was barely a roadside. Lack of travel meant the cowslips and grass had grown, the rocks and pebbles washed over by the rain were not cleared, the pot holes were not filled. More than once I felt despair. I pulled a small cart behind my bicycle with few comforts in it, and I peddled hard to get to my destination. I believe the future of Great Britain belongs in the counting, and that the first civilized nation to account for its people will be the one to hold sway over the rest.

"After close to four days travel and thousands of questions, a great downpour forced me to shelter for close to eight hours inside a derelict cow shed. I would guess the abandonment occurred during the heat wave of 2078, because there were old newspapers lining the windows dated around this time. People tried to keep the heat out in such ways but these cows died like so many of them at the time. There was bone here; nothing but. Well, nothing until evening fell and with the storm still raging outside, I settled in for the night.

"As I warmed some beans over a Bunsen flame and sorted through my forms to ensure none were damp, I heard a whispering in the corner.

"One of the things we learn before we go on the road is how to defend ourselves, but from a sitting position this was not easy. Still, I shifted carefully, as if I were preparing for sleep, in order to catch a glimpse of who I was up against.

"The glow told me it was nothing alive. Ghosts can affect you at a spiritual and emotional level, if you let your guard down, but not at a physical level, so I stood up cautiously.

"These children were very, very clear. I assumed they had died in the shed along with the cattle, because the closer the place of death, the clearer the apparition. Your boy," the Census-Taker said to the mother, "is very blurry, so I would say he died a long way from here."

The mother began to cry quietly. Her daughter didn't seem to fathom what was happening, and no one chose to tell her about her dead brother.

"The radiant children crouched in the corner over a small piles of coins, playing some simple game. They were not yet aware of my presence. Like all children, they were too thoroughly absorbed in themselves to be observant, but I didn't want them to discover me as I slept, so I walked over to them.

"Radiant children rarely speak. I think it is because they do not want to talk about their mothers. There is great shame and sorrow in such a death; I think by not speaking they avoid the subject.

" 'I am the Census-Taker,' I said. 'I would like to record your details for the files.'

"So we did just that. Using sign language, and fingers, and pointing, we filled out a form for their barn as place of residence. I was cold, but they were not. Ghosts don't feel the cold. When I asked them if this was their place of birth, they flapped their hands about, shook their heads until I produced a map of the region.

"They pointed to a small village some ten kilometres from our position. On the map it was dominated by an Anglican Church. My map was quite a new one, but I knew it had not been updated in all these regions for many years. The church could well be long gone and the road impassable.

"My final question on the Census for the dead is cause of death. I understand the many causes of death. One I hear often is the loss of sanity. The inability to feed oneself. The loss of desire to survive. The lack of intention to work.

"No one admits to suicide in the family. It is considered the worst sin after infanticide. I know the suicides, though. They have a reddish glow, and they smell of wet dog. They wander, causing havoc. Sucking the will to live from others.

"The children didn't want to answer this question, but as we communicated, their stomachs glowed blue and I checked 'poisoning'."

"I knew that a visit to their village could well lead to my loss of employment. My supervisor frowns on sidetracks, prefers us to stick to the job at hand. He doesn't understand just how many sidetracks there are. He moves from his neat, clean home in Canterbury to his neat, large office in Canterbury, wearing a sheltering hat and barely noticing the world passing him by. He knows how many steps take him from place to place and he knows, according to the figures, how many people should pass him by. But he doesn't care to look any of them in the face.

"It seemed important to me to count this village. I would not be back this way again; my route was a circuitous one, moving up past Croydon on my return to Canterbury. Yet here was a whole brood of children, killed by their mothers far from home. I needed to know their number.

"So in the morning I orientated myself and, trying to avoid the thickest puddles of mud, I set off on my detour.

"As I approached the village, just on lunchtime, I heard a low hum. I rode into the village mud-spattered and hair awry. I must have looked quite a sight.

"I called out as I walked, wary to be a stranger in a place which hadn't seen such a thing in a long time. I heard women's voices, no men's. This is not uncommon. Whole villages, sometimes, all the men gone. Those women are old, though, old widows. These voices sounded younger.

"The voices of young mothers.

"I found them clustered around the communal cooking pot. I called again and didn't realize until I was close that they glowed. Every one of the six women glowed."

He stopped and closed his eyes. "Go on," the mother said. "Tell us about the ghosts."

"I admit to being a little shocked to find them all dead. The radiant children hadn't warned me about this. Perhaps they didn't realize. It was not surprising to find the women around the cooking pot, though. Ghosts like to be in the place they were happiest, most cohesive. I wished my mother was with me, to help me speak to them, take their count. But she had taught me well.

"I took out my forms and began to ask my questions. They told me their children had turned into fire-breathing monsters who burned all they touched. They said they had lured the children to the barn, telling them a puppet show was there, and that they had given them poison in sweet, cold drinks.

"It was all they could do, in order to put out the fire, they said.

"I don't think it was the only place this happened. I think villages lost sense like that all over the country. The children are often the first to go."

"So what did you do? What will you do?" the older gentleman asked.

"I will enter my census forms. I will account for each and every village left. I will note ages and I will note cause of death. I will add 'abandoned' for the domicile question.

"Did none survive?"

"None in this village. I can't speak for the other places. The church no longer existed. It burned down, with all the remaining villagers in it. Caused by the children, the mothers said.

"I noted cause of death as insanity brought on by the heat, the weather."

The Census-Taker took a sip of water without offering any around.

"So that is my tale," he said.

"English people don't treat each other that way. It must have been the Indians. Or the Pakis. It was the Chinese. The Bangladeshis. They're like that."

"When it comes to survival, we are no different to anyone else.

There was silence in the carriage. Outside, the land was green and pleasant as it ever had been. The young girl took his hand.

"Anyone going to the Olympics? I would if it wasn't in Birmingham. That place is a fucken hole," the Builder's Labourer said, and they spoke of sport, and competition, and tried not to think about villages of dead children around the countryside.

His Lipstick
Minx

His Lipstick Minx

Mike's lipstick minx sat on his shoulder, twitching and waiting with her lipstick brush. She was a good one, bred small through natural means. She came with her family's growth chart, each generation smaller than the last. She wouldn't have children. Her womb was too small and Mike didn't want to risk tearing her apart. Though something in him wanted her baby. It'd be tiny. So tiny. Its little fingertips on your mouth would take an hour, filling each pore with a tiny plug of lipstick. You'd rarely need to reapply.

Mike's lipstick minx said, "I think we should go tangerine for this evening. You need to make a splash. Stand out."

She was right, of course. Every bloke on the base would be at the bar tonight, each wanting to be noticed.

He sat down and bent forward to rest his chin on the table. She hopped off his shoulder and went to work.

She was painstaking, his lipstick minx. She wouldn't be rushed. When he glanced at the watch set into his wrist, she tutted at him.

"I'll stop if you're bored," she said in her high little voice. She squatted, the brush between her knees. She sucked the tip. All she liked to eat was lipstick. He had to buy the expensive brand, less chemicals, more palm oil. She said it kept her hair sleek. Mike wondered if her insides were tangerine tease, purple power, ravishing red.

He glanced at the mirror. She had one small patch to go.

"Just that one bit," he pleaded.

His lipstick minx sighed. She knew she was lucky to be with Mike. He had such pride in his lips that he appreciated her work. Other men made their lipstick minxes work naked, dance, they made them play.

Mike wasn't like that.

His lipstick minx jumped up and finished his mouth. He pursed his lips.

"How do I look?" he said.

She nodded. "Very fine," she said. She plumped up her hair. He knew she wanted to come out with him, that staying in the room was dull for her.

But if there's one thing the men have learnt it's this; women talking is dangerous. Even lipstick minxes, with their pipsqueak little voices, peeping at each other about conditions and colours.

He gave her a biscuit to nibble on and left his spare phone with the connection to a sitcom tuned in.

"Watch that while I'm gone," he said. "And clean the brushes."

She sighed, hunkered down and sucked the lipstick brush. She smiled at him, her teeth tangerine. Mike's lipstick minx was very kind to him. She picked special colours out and she painted his lips perfectly. Once she dragged a wet cloth across the room and tried to clean his fingers, but it annoyed him, tickled him, so he backhanded her away. He found her against the wall an hour later, panting softly. Her back recovered but always gave her pain after that, and she walked with a limp.

Mike's lipstick minx could mix a lipstick which made his lips tingle as if they were being kissed. He wiped a smear onto his finger once and that tingled too.

He thought too much about that lipstick.

Mike pushed open the heavy metal door to the bar and braced himself for the smell of working men. He felt greasy between the toes and wished he'd washed more thoroughly. He was too eager to get going, though, and he'd scrubbed his pits, wet his hair, washed his balls with soap. You gotta have that bit clean. If he scored one of the Big Girls, he'd keep his socks on.

His mates spotted him, called him over. They sat on high, hard stools. Doug's fat arse spilled over the sides.

"Hold the stool when he stands up," Mike said. "It's slipping up his arse and when he walks it'll knock the drinks over."

Doug rolled his lips back. His teeth had smudges of lipstick, pale pink, like the inside of a worm.

"You've got lipstick on your teeth," Mike said. "There's your basic difference between minx born to it and a man-made minx. You never see a smudge on my teeth."

"You call mine man-made if you like. She's got more spunk than yours."

Doug was very proud of his minx, how he got her. He paid for his minx while she was still in her mother's womb. He paid for the drugs and cigarettes, all the stuff to stunt the growth, keep the birth weight low.

It meant a minx who'd die young. Mike had seen Doug's minx twice or three times. She was beautiful in an ill way. Distorted by the bindings. Mike's minx was perfect.

"So are the Girls here yet?" Mike asked.

"What d'you reckon? Would we be talking to you if they were?"

A bus load of Big Girls was due to arrive, and the men were keen. They saw so few Big Girls on the base. Outside the base, too; there just weren't enough women to go around.

Bernie joined them with a round of beers, elbowing a big dirty man out of the way. "Sorry, mate," he said. They all nodded. Yeah, sorry. Mike remembered a time when it would have been all in for such an act. Before the minxes arrived at the base.

"Jeez, I'm tired," Bernie said. "I just pulled a 24-er. If one of 'em picks me, I'm gonna be no use to them." Bernie's lipstick minx had done a good job, purple lipstick thick and glossy, barely damaged since application. It bled into the lines and cracks of his lips, but with an artistry Mike believed was deliberate.

The men nodded, mumbled in their beers. It was a concern, though not one they discussed; could they cut it? If they were picked, would they have the juice to follow through?

"I was on tanks," Mike said. "I feel like I've got grease coming out my ears. It was two inches thick, some places!"

"That's what you get paid for, right? Makes it all worth it." The base was a no-wheeler. What they meant by that was you had to walk everywhere, no matter how tired you were. After a 12 hour-er you walked to your room and fell into bed. You were too tired to shower.

One bloke, Denny, while ago, he'd showered after an 18 hour-er. Fell asleep, tipped forward, banged his head, drowned in the puddle. He pissed himself, they said, and you couldn't mention Denny's name after that got out. They were tough blokes, but drowning in your own piss? You'd rather be on tank-cleaning duty for a year.

Mike bought a round of beers.

They told stories for a while, tall tales with a drop of truth, stories of animal cruelty and female misbehaviour which made them all laugh and feel good. Then the bus arrived.

The men combed hair back, sat up straight, tried to look unconcerned. But the breeze of the Girls coming in the door, the coolness of the breeze and the sweet, sweet smell of them made jaws drop and brains freeze.

There was a fight to get the Girls drinks.

Mike never fought for the Girls. He didn't know how. It wasn't in him. He pressed his lips together, knowing the orange of them would get attention at least.

When a Girl sauntered over to him, he put down his beer and placed his hands on his thighs to stop them shaking.

She looked him up and down.

"Orange?" she said.

His mates all laughed, and so did she. Mike stood up, grabbed his jacket, left the bar.

He poked his minx awake roughly.

"You picked the wrong colour!" he hissed. "They want red! They're dressed all in red and black. Paint them again."

There wasn't much point to it, but he wanted to go back there and show he wasn't a fool. His minx painted his lips quickly, without her usual care, and he glared at her without thanking her.

"You come home safe," she said.

It was too late, though. The Girls had chosen. The bar was full of quiet, rejected men.

When he got home, his minx lay asleep on the kitchen table, curled up and shivering slightly. He wondered what she dreamed about. She'd seen so little, knew so little it was hard to imagine what lay in her subconscious.

He poured whisky into a large glass and sat at the table, watching her. He left a remnant of lipstick on his glass, a faint trace of red, ugly in the bright light. His lips felt dry from being out in the cold.

He picked up his minx carefully. She fitted along the length of his arm, her cheek nested in his palm, her bottom in the crook of his elbow, her feet tickling his underarm. He put her to bed. She didn't wake.

In the morning, he awoke to find her mixing a paste for his lips. Her tiny fingers rubbed his mouth, finding dry flakes of skin and rolling them off.

She painted his mouth with aloe vera and lanolin, a strong smell which made his stomach heave, the memory of beer and whisky returning.

He vomited in the sink then ran the water, hard. The water was brown, polluted, and he vomited again, thinking of the glass of water he'd skulled at dawn, desperately dry-mouthed.

Doug shoved his way in. Mike's lipstick minx scurried to hide; most of them disliked other men. Doug's mouth was bright red and shocking.

"Bernie got picked," Doug said, taking a loaf of bread and tearing a chunk off.

"When?"

"This morning. He got home and she was waiting for him."

"Duty calls," Mike said. "Duty calls for us all." He reached for a protein shake.

His lipstick minx stood in the cupboard, her hands pressed together, her eyes wide.

"What happened to his lipstick minx?" Mike said. "Who's taken her?"

Doug shrugged. "She went with him, I think. You need lips at war, mate." Doug tore more bread. "Anyway, I'm off. Just wanted to let you know. It'll be us before long. Don't worry. We'll get a shot at it."

The minx came out and swept up the bread crumbs. She pressed them into a ball which she popped into her mouth.

"You hungry?" Mike said. He got down the cheese spread for her.

His lipstick minx seemed taller. It was disconcerting; they were not supposed to grow. She stomped her foot, hands on hips, and he saw she had boots on with heels as high as her forearm was long. She wobbled, so he reached out a finger for her to grab. "It's okay. No trouble walking for me," she said.

The Girls were at the bar the second night. The Girl who'd laughed at him the night before was there, her lips so pale they were almost invisible. Mike imagined smearing his lips over her face, colour on her cheeks, splotches on her lips. He imagined he and his mates ganging up to kiss her. Leave her sprawled, panting, multi-coloured.

The Girl came up to him. "Red is good. I like red."

So he took her home.

They didn't speak as they walked. Mike cleared his throat twice, wishing words would come. If it was Doug walking alongside, or Bernie, they'd be yakking about work, how they'd spend their money, what the boss said.

"You been on a base before?" he said.

She looked at him sideways. "You're better looking if you shut up. Where's your room?"

"Nearly there."

As they entered the building, Mike knew other men would be watching, wishing they were him, wishing they could share, steal, wishing they were the ones with the Big Girl.

"This is my room." He pushed open the door and waited for her to enter. She pushed him inside.

"Your minxes paint you tame and nice. I want wild," she said. She scrabbled in her handbag for a stick of lipstick. Hot pink.

His minx climbed up onto his shoulder.

"No, Mike! You don't want that feeling," she squeaked.

The Big Girl picked her up by the ankles, tossed her. "Lie down."

The Big Girl straddled Mike and painted his lips.

He felt virile but rage-filled. His minx called, "Mike, Mike" in her horrible voice.

He did the job.

He did a good job.

His lipstick minx waved her lipstick brush, its tip bright purple, over the sleeping Girl.

"You can't paint her lips," Mike whispered. "She won't like it."

"You help me. This lipstick is to make the blood rush. Give her more sexy thoughts for you."

His lipstick minx winked and Mike was not sure at that moment if he should trust her.

He nodded. She carefully painted the sleeping Big Girl's lips. Mike had to look away. It didn't look good. The lips were bright purple, bruised, horrible.

The Girl sat up. She blinked, wrinkled her nose. She saw the minx and roared, "Get away from me, freak." The lipstick minx cringed, covered her ears.

"She doesn't like loud noises," Mike said. "I'll take you to the bar. Buy you a drink."

The Big Girl stared at the lipstick minx. "What's she done to me?"

"Nothing. Nothing."

The Girl wiped her mouth, then looked at the purple smear on the back of her hand. "She painted my lips!" She reached out and grabbed the minx by her ankles, hoisting her into the air and flicking at her.

"These things do you blokes no good. You realise that?"

The lipstick minx twisted her body sharply, bent at the waist, managed to stab the Girl's wrist with her brush. The Girl yelped; blood on her wrist angered her. She wiped her hand across her mouth, adding blood to the purple.

The minx tried to stab her again, and Mike said, "No!"

The door opened and other Big Girls came in, always ready for trouble. A skittering sound; the minxes were there as well.

The Girl swung his minx back by her ankles and bashed her hard against the bed post. Mike, too late, stepped forward to stop her, but three Big Girls held him back, pushed him down and sat on him. He tried to shout but one of them kissed him, covered his nose with her hand and kissed him big and hard, so he couldn't breathe or talk.

The Girl threw Mike's lipstick minx to the ground and stomped on her.

"These freaks are no good for working men."

The minxes ran around the room wanting to stop this but their owners scooped them up and tucked them into shirts, hid their faces, whispered, whispered, whispered.

The Girl kept stomping until the minx was a fat greasy smear of lipstick on the dirty carpet.

The siren went for night shift. One of the other lipstick minxes, Bernie's, Mike thought, scurried over to him and lifted her brush.

He shook his head.

"Paint your lips, big boy," said the Girl. She wiped her mouth and tossed her head at the other Girls. Mike watched them walk through the lipstick puddle of his minx.

"I can't work today," he whispered. Bernie's minx began painting his lips; he didn't know what colour. It calmed him, though, whatever colour it was, and he closed his eyes while she finished.

He felt numbed when she was done.

"Let's get on site, mate," Doug said. Mike put on his work boots and stood up.

"I'll do the grease tanks today," Doug said.

"Thanks, mate," Mike said.

It would be a good day, if he didn't have to do the grease tanks.

Polish

Polish

The car was smooth, air-conditioned, and completely wrong.

"We should be suffering," I said to Callie. She was driving, sucking barley suger, silent. "We should be hot and only half as far. We should have changed a tyre." I drank a mouthful of water. "And I should be desperate to turn around, go back home to the city. Instead, I'm looking forward to getting to the old homestead."

Callie smiled at me. "Things are different now. Your parents are dead. All the ghosts are gone." It was a strange thing for her to say, because I had never told her about Yessmiss. There was something familiar waiting for me at the homestead; something I had not seen for years.

"Yes," I said. "Yes, Miss." I used my sleeve to polish the dashboard. "Yes, miss," I said. The smell of furniture polish haunted me as a child; I smelt it when no one else did. I only use a cloth when I polish.

The smell of polish surely didn't get stronger as we drove further away from the city. I sniffed, though, sniffed again, and I could smell Yessmiss, my childhood ghost, as we drew closer and closer to the place of my birth.

Callie didn't speak. She drove, just crunch crunch of the road, crunch crunch of the barley sugar until her eyes watered. Without asking me, she pulled in at a pub. "Let's have a drink," she said.

She wasn't a country girl, she didn't realise what these places could be like. The social centre of a small town, where people behaved in established ways. Two women together were sluts looking for a root.

Pubs don't welcome strangers.

"Well, don't order a martini," I said. "Just a beer. Don't even specify which kind, just say beer."

Callie laughed. She grew up in the inner-city; she thinks she's tough. She leaned over and kissed me on the mouth. Her lips were sticky with barley sugar juice. I polished them with my tongue.

"Yes, miss," she said. I had never explained my silly saying. Didn't need to with her. She just accepted it, embraced it. As she embraced me and my skittishness, my temper, my passions, my goals.

"This isn't the place to be out," I said.

"Der," she said, squeezing my thigh. "Really, you think you've cornered the market for narrow-minded. Mate, I've been abused in more places than you've..."

She couldn't think of a clever ending and I laughed.

"Than I've had trips around the world. Which is none."

"Won't be long," she said. We were travelling together in three months time, my last chance before the next career move tied me up for years. It would be our honeymoon, in advance.

But first I needed to watch the demolition of my childhood home.

There was a buzzy murmur as we entered the pub. Callie behaved beautifully, but I could see it annoyed her. I had suffered so much, I knew how cruel, how *blind*, these people could be.

There is always a young one in the pub, who gets a little sex every now and then from someone who isn't his wife, shoots more kangaroos because he can still steer and aim at the same time, he's a legend for his drinking. He's been brought up at the pub, there with his Dad from the age of five, rather than home with Mum, because all she does is whinge. If Dad gets a bit pissy he might belt you one, but he'll give you a dollar with it. He'll give you sips of beer, get you pissed till you chuck at twelve, then you'll beat the crap out of him on the day you turn eighteen and take his place at the bar.

I know this; this is the story of my father and my brother.

They never heard Yessmiss. I was the only one. It began with the smell of furniture polish. We didn't use it in the house; we used spit.

I could read by the time I was three. Dad read the paper aloud, he had to to understand it, and I sat on his knee and followed his moving finger. Mum taught me all she knew, but I was desperate for more. I read everything that came into the house; Reader's Digest was my favourite, because it lasted a little while, and there were hundreds of them piled up in the dunny.

I never saw Yessmiss. I imagined her round and cuddly, taller than me. At night I dreamt she crawled into bed with me, and we held on tight while the usual noise went on. Just before I left home at sixteen I thought I saw her; I woke with my heart racing, darkest before the dawn as I often did. I glimpsed a bent figure, fumbling at my bedhead. "Yessmiss," she said. "Yessmiss."

That was all.

The carpet in the pub was green, though it could once have been beige. A dishrag was close by and I dried a puddle of beer, rubbing it, rubbing.

"That'll do, thanks, love," the bartender said. "You'll make someone a good wife, elbow grease like that."

"Can I have some chips, please?" I said. "A coupla packs of salt 'n' vinegar and one barbecue." He tossed them on the counter and I paid, munched away, because I didn't want to talk to Callie. They'd *know* if we talked. They'd be able to tell.

"Just passin' through, are yous?" It was the young guy; he could have been my brother.

"Just seeing a bit of the countryside," Callie said.

"God's country, here," he said, and the bar murmured. I glanced around; the door was propped open with the fire extinguisher; brilliant sunlight poured in, a broad strip. A black dog lay sleeping there, his ears flicking away the flies.

Apart from that the place was in darkness. There were no windows, only advertisements for beer, boxers, guns and Penthouse.

"God's country," I said, and raised my glass. Callie glared at me; she knows better than me when to put a stop to things.

The young guy took the stool next to me at the bar.

I polished the bar. "Yes, miss," I said.

"Sorry, love?" said the young guy. He leaned close and I could see he wasn't so young. Mid 30s and nowhere to go.

"Buy you another?" he said.

"Nah, look, we've gotta head off," I said, and Callie and I downed our beers and stood up. I didn't know, until we were in the car, if they would let us go. I had forgotten how frightened I could be.

"Fuckin' lezzos," they said after us, which made us smile, then laugh, made it all worth it.

"So, what was all that about?" I said to Callie. "Why the tearing need to get our heads kicked in at a country pub?"

"I just needed a break."

"Oh, from me? Thanks a lot. I won't say anything if that's it."

We drove in silence while she thought of what to say.

"It's just that I don't always understand you. I thought if we broke it up a bit, you'd stop worrying."

"Well, it didn't work. It's worse."

"Well, I only tried." She was right; I had thought I was happy to be heading home, but she saw through my pretence. Yes, miss, she did.

We were still five hours from the homestead, and I wanted energy for what came next, so we pulled into a motel, just three rooms, coffee and tea facilities and a huge fat candle to make things romantic.

The owner didn't flinch, putting us in the same room. We're such good friends, Callie and I, people don't assume we're lovers as well. And he had that tired look, that bored look, he didn't care anymore, he just wanted it to be over.

The bed sagged in the middle so we rolled together all night. We lay, lip to lip, breathing each other's air until we were dizzy. Then we kissed, lazy, salty kisses, and we touched warm fingers to warmer skin, we threw off the blankets and watched the candlelight against our lovely bodies. Nobody grunted and I didn't polish a thing. I do it in meetings; they mimic me, the others. Polish my glasses, or anything I can touch, the table, the coffee cup. They say if I stop polishing watch out!

I asked Mum once if she ever saw or heard Yessmiss, and I described her. Because she was clear in my mind. I knew what she looked like although I hadn't seen her.

Mum told me I needed to stop eating cheese, it was giving me nightmares. In fact, she said, I needed to cut back all round if I was to be a lovely bride.

"Can girls marry girls?" I said, because I didn't ever want a husband, I wanted a wife. A wife would laugh with me and be my friend. A wife would smell nice.

Some things never change.

At school, I realised I was somebody; I was a Robey. My family had been in the district forever. We were the richies; we had servants, once. We were known for toughness, meanness, cruelty. If I ever asked anyone to do anything, they'd say, "Oh, yes, Mistress Robey, immediately."

Callie was very good to me. Very patient. She calmed me when I panicked. She talked to me a lot, the last five hours of the trip, made me laugh, let me be quiet and think. Yessmiss was waiting for me. I polished the windows to make sure we got there safely.

It was my first time home in fifteen years.

As we approached, I thought the front door was open, and I drew my breath, the fear of intruders too much.

"What is it?" Callie said. It was a favourite saying. "What is it?" I saw so many things she didn't see.

"There's someone in the house," I said, but when I looked again the door was closed.

"It's okay," I said. "It's all right. I'm just remembering things. Let's go in."

I had a sticky key; it had hidden in a desk drawer these fifteen years. The door had not changed in that time; it was like I was returning from a week at school.

The front verandah hadn't changed.

"There's Dad's chair," I said. The imprint of his bum, decades of fat-arsed relaxing, had not left. He worked without cease, my Dad, until my brother was old enough, and then he sat down and hardly got up again.

"Once he stopped going to the pub he sat there for hours, drinking, shouting out at some ghost no one else could see."

Callie smiled at me, held my hand, tugged me close, kissed my cheek.

"I didn't realise you two had so much in common," she said.

"You'll have a ghost of your own one day, me, dead from neglect."

"Hardly."

The front door key was hot in my palm. I had had it ready to use for an hour now, my fingers pinching it, my wrist turning. I used it at last, and pushed open the door to my family home.

The smell of furniture polish would have made me gag if I were not so used to it. It made me remember how much I had forgotten about my childhood friend.

The house gleamed, shone, it was cleaner than I'd ever seen.

"Ooh, bit of dust there," Callie said, sarcastically. She didn't understand, so she joked.

"Yes, miss," I heard.

It was Yessmiss. She was there.

Callie turned on the lights and we saw the stain in the thin, old carpet at the foot of the stairs where my mother had landed. I would have imagined my father pushing her, because he'd done it before. But they were certain his heart attack had killed him three hours before she died; in that time she had fallen, dragged herself to the phone, and stayed alive long enough to reach hospital. She hated hospitals. They always asked questions about her injuries that were none of their business.

Callie explored the house. There was not much to look at; my siblings had cleaned the place out after the funeral. Piles of old Reader's Digests, a broken toy or two, furniture nobody would ever want, that's all they left. I sat upstairs, alone in my bedroom and waited for Yessmiss.

"Are you there, Yessmiss?"

"Yessmis," my childhood ghost said. She was louder than I remembered, and a trick of the light showed her to me. She was short, and broad, and familiar.

Callie and I ate toast cooked in the fire and drank red wine from plastic cups we found under the sink.

My old room had barely been touched. We slept that night in my single bed, where I had spent so many nights dreaming of this; a beautiful woman holding me perfectly. Callie always sleeps by the wall if there is one. Our king-sized bed at home has only one free side. She feels protected that way. She knows what's coming. Callie, I think, has stories of her own she doesn't tell.

I was woken in the night by Yessmiss. She was clearer in the moonlight. She polished the brass knobs of my old family bed, the one which had belonged to a spinster aunt when the house was first built and the family rich, a hundred years before.

That aunt was the main cause of our family's reputation.

Yessmiss polished and polished. "Yessmiss," she said, and "Yessmiss." Then, and I could see this clearly now, I knew it wasn't a dream, she raised her hands to protect herself and fell to the floor.

I threw off the doona, crawled to the end of the bed. She was not there.

My heart was beating quickly, too fast. Yessmiss had woken me out of deep dreaming, shocked me, and I wondered for a moment if she had appeared to my father as suddenly, and made his heart fail.

Callie loved the heat, sat out in it till her clothes sizzled. We ate sandwiches and toast, drank cuppa after cuppa sitting on the verandah.

Time passed. We were happy, unhassled, though we snapped a little at each other in the quiet of it all.

Then one morning we were woken by banging downstairs. I pulled on some clothes and covered Callie with the doona. It was the wrecker, wanting to come look. My brother owned the house now, because girls didn't own houses. He hated it. Hated the age of it, so he was having it pulled down. A new house built, modern, with pastel colours and man-made materials.

The wrecker was a small, smelly man, neatly dressed in polyester. His men were giants and worked in shorts, their backs bare, brown and marked with melanomas.

"Didn't think anyone was here," he said. He nodded at me. Not his place to judge. He did a quick scout around the house, a first impression, he called it, while his assistants smoked, leaving the cigarette butts in a neat campfire pile. He caught Callie and me kissing in the kitchen; he rapped on the window.

"Hello, hello," he said. "Don't let us stop you."

"How do you do?" said Callie, turning to face him. Her voice is strong but gentle. The wrecker stared at her, then me.

"Well, well," he said. And that was it for niceties. "We'll be back next Thursdee."

Yessmiss appeared again and again. Callie couldn't see her at all; she watched me watching, and I caught her crying.

"She's there," I said. Yessmiss polished every night, I could see her. Had she always been there to be seen? As Callie and I tasted and touched, I heard her mutter, and there at the foot of the bed she was, she polished the ancient brass knobs then her hands flew to her head, her eyes locked with mine, she collapsed.

I stared at the space thinking it was real.

"What is it, love?" Callie said. I loved her for not adding, "this time."

"Murder," I said. "Murder."

I thought again about my father and how my mother would have found him and run down the stairs. Naked, I walked there; stood at the top and slid my feet over the smooth, slippery polished surface. I had my mother's habit of wearing socks to bed.

Yessmiss watched me. She held her head; seemed to be crying.

"Yes, miss," I said. She walked towards me. I remembered how I had dreamed of her, those lonely nights in my antique bed. She held her arms out to me but I didn't fear being pushed. I held my arms out and somehow she was whole, I hugged her and her flesh was sweet.

She passed her hands across my face and I was her, and my name was Agnes, and I worked for the spinster, the one who's photographic image was sour and unhappy.

I was her servant, my jobs were many, but mostly I had to polish. The Miss loved her things shiny and they were never shiny enough.

My ears were boxed, my legs pricked with pins, she said, "Agnes, let's get a nice shine up. A nice shine," and I said, "Yes, miss." That's all. I didn't have other words.

Some days she was even meaner and I was terrified for my life. And she slept in the bed with the brass knobs, and she liked them shiny first thing, shiny like the sun, and I get up in the dark to polish and polish, and one morning it's dark and she groans in her sleep, and the master of the house is within the bed, and he shouts at my presence when the moonlight strikes.

And she strikes me; and again.

And I polish and polish, as is my job. And I see a young girl, lonely like me, different like me, and she hears me.

She hears me.

She is the only one who does.

Agnes takes her hands away and is gone. Callie calls me and oh, how she loves me. She says, "Never mind, never mind," without needing to know what's wrong, and I realised she often spoke to me like that, warm short words like pats of comfort.

I promise myself to be good to her, understand her, allow her to be weak sometimes

But I know I'll forget.

We packed all the things from my room. Dismantled the bed and strapped it to the roof. I whispered, "You shouldn't have killed them, Agnes. Not for me, anyway. But I wish you well. I hope you find another little girl."

Agnes paced back and forth across the room, her hands flapping.

I watched her until my eyes felt gritty with sand.

Callie and I sat in the air-conditioned car for three hours and watched men demolish the house. I thought of Agnes; I pictured her there, on her knees, polishing the floorboards. She was about to die again.

We went into town for lunch, came back, the house was almost gone. Such a simple, destructive thing. My brother wanted the land cleared. He wanted every last bloody stick off it.

We drove away.

As we left, I felt something nestle around my neck, a cool, soft wreath I could lie my head against. I thought how much Agnes would have loved our house in the city; made of wood, full of it, and it's a warm, comfortable place. We allow things to pile up. Callie says often, "For someone who loves to polish, you're a pig!" but she is like that too. We both love a mess.

We were nearing home, after many hours, when Callie sniffed the air. Her brow creased, a rare sight.

"What is it?" I said.

"I smell furniture polish. Why would I suddenly smell furniture polish?"

I had never told her about the smell of Agnes. I had mentioned her, not her polish.

"I can smell it too," I said. I wondered how Agnes could possible have known we were approaching her new home.

I would never bring her killer to justice, but I mourned her death and I felt the guilt for my ancestors.

That, it seemed, was enough. She forgave me, and my family, and once we were home I rubbed Callie's feet until she moaned.

The
Coral Gatherer

The Coral Gatherer

Claire arrived at the resort pale-skinned, nose and shoulders pink from the trip across the water to the resort.

"Hello, Madam. Can I help you?" A quick flick of the eyes behind to check for a companion.

"Single room, Claire Yates."

"We have no single rooms," the receptionist said. Some kind of foreign pity all over her.

"It's a double, then. Lots of room for me." Claire was too happy to be here to let an ignorant woman doing a menial job disturb her.

The porter loaded her suitcases onto his trolley. He would be surprised to know what was inside.

"Thank you, thank you," she said a dozen times over, polite to the point of would you shut up.

Her room was beautiful; opening straight onto the beach, painted sea blue, sand yellow, a huge bed draped with a mosquito net. The porter flirted with her, and she found his muscular, brown body attractive. But that could wait; she needed to gather the coral before anything else. She unpacked her suitcase and stowed the other in the space provided. She hadn't known what to pack; casual? dressy? so had gone with both. A trip to the resort's shop bought a horrendously expensive swimsuit and a chiffony wrap-around which felt soft and sexy. Buckets, too, three of them. Again, the glance, looking for children who didn't exist.

She charged it all to her room.

To begin with, Claire greedily filled her buckets, almost sick with the abundance of the coral. On the first morning, she collected three buckets full. She walked carefully, not wanting to crush any of the almost transparent crabs which covered the sand in wispy movement. Or the coral; the crunch of it beneath her feet made her ill. It sounded like the bones her dog ate, cracking them with his strong, dangerous teeth.

He'd love to have a man around.

She sat down in the sand with her pile of coral. She chose a position near the wall. Dry sand meant the tide didn't reach here, and the curve of the coast meant she wouldn't be seen from the bar or restaurant. She didn't want any helpers.

She began with the spine. She wanted to be as accurate as possible, so propped the medical handbook she'd brought with her on the sand, not caring that it was being damaged.

She built the spine, notched and straight. The shoulder blades; she managed just the collarbone before running out of coral.

The work made her hungry. She'd promised herself to stop for food, drinks and sleep, not be too eager. She had a week here and she could extend if she needed to.

For the next three mornings, she gathered coral and built her man. She finished the broad shoulders and built strong hips, long legs, thick, strong knees and big feet.

She made long arms, long fingers. The skull she built with high cheekbones and a strong, jutting chin. Claire became adept at choosing the right shaped coral. She knew she needed a nose bone; she found the perfect piece.

Standing back, her fingers criss-crossed with tiny cuts from the coral, she liked his length and width.

He was tall. She liked tall men. He would be strong, once he had flesh, and smart, once he had a brain. She was hoping he would make her laugh, teach her how to be funny. That he would find a job with lots of travel, or that he would care for her while she worked such a job.

She hoped for a sensual man would adore her, worship her, never leave her. Could cook. Loved to read.

She built a man she hoped was perfect.

She finished the coral skeleton on the third day. She needed five things to finish him; blood, hair, muscle, flesh and organs.

She took a taxi into the town, carrying her large handbag lined with plastic.

She'd done her research; knew where to go. One part of town was so overpopulated nobody could count the people there and they all lived under one great connected roof, a swarming mass.

She asked for a guide and it was a young man who stepped up. He was blind in one eye and had lost the toes off one foot, but his basic material was all she needed.

She'd brought a cane knife for a few dollars at the market. At home she'd practised on animals, slicing their throats with ever-increasing efficiency.

She killed her guide and removed the bits she wanted.

Taxi back to the resort with her precious parcel.

Guests were gathering for pre-dinner drinks and a couple of the men, drunk and brave in a group, called out to her.

They had no idea how little interest she had in them.

It was still light enough for Claire to see on the sand. Her man glowed and from 12 paces away she thought he was rising up.

She dug a small pit where his stomach would be and buried the things she'd harvested.

She went to have dinner, wanting to be satisfied for the night vigil. Steak, a salad full of indulgent, imported ingredients like fetta cheese and sun-dried tomatoes. A carafe of house wine, sharp and bitter but effective. A slab of dry chocolate cake she didn't finish.

She made herself move slowly. There was no rush. She showered in her glorious bathroom (studded with sea shells, tiles a sky blue) and pulled on her chiffon wrap-around. Nothing underneath. Might as well start out as you wish to continue.

She took a bottle of water and a towel to lie on, and settled herself in the sand beside her man, waiting for him to wake up.

It was dawn before there was any movement. She thought she'd imagined it at first. Her eyes were gritty and the air seemed blurry as the sun rose.

She sat up.

He formed. First the coral melded, formed the skeleton. Then the sinew, the muscle, and the organs, growing as coral does, blossoming, expanding. Then the blood vessels, the veins and the blood started to flow, sluggish at first then faster.

Claire felt her own blood flowing, could hear the beat of it in her ears.

The flesh filled in, then, slowly, the skin formed.

He was pale pink. His hair was white, very fine. She shifted so she lay next to him. All normal; just a couple waking up on the beach after a romantic night.

Nothing odd.

Movement; he shuddered. His shoulder lifted. Heaved. His hands arched. She stroked his sweet, soft chest and he turned his head to look at her.

"Hello, darling," she said, because that's what lovers called each other.

He opened his mouth. Inside, his teeth were coral; jagged, pointy, filled with miniscule holes. He pulled up onto his elbow, smiling his coral smile at her. His breath was salty, fresh fishy, not bad.

He sat up. Creaky, the sound, but nothing broke.

Tears pricked her eyes. He lifted his hand, placed a finger under her eye, catching the tear. Sucked his finger. Smiled. Lent forward and licked her face, little grunts and he sucked the tears. She had to push him gently away and she thought, *I must never let him know how salty my blood is.* A precaution; nothing more.

She led him to the room and showed him the bed, the chair, his suitcase full of men's things. She gave him water but he didn't like it until she ordered room service with a salt cellar and salted up the water.

He sat stiffly, not speaking. She would have to teach him the words.

She kissed his fingers, and he took her hand and bit gently on her fingertips. She pulled away but too late. The taste of her excited him and he grabbed her arms and pushed her onto the bed.

Even then, even though she knew, she thought, *My wedding night. All I've dreamed about.*

Then she screamed, screamed, as his coral teeth bit into her throat, opening her jugular and letting the sweet, salty drink pour out.

Bone-Dog

Bone-Dog

In the porn industry, models don't usually get to choose the venue for photo shoots. I guess "Fat Slits" has to be a bit more flexible than other magazines; some of us just can't get too far from home. They agreed to send the photographer to me, agreed to my price; their attention brought tears to my eyes.

When I heard the photographer's van at the end of my long driveway, I walked slowly to the vast tree stump where I sometimes display the gifts Bone-Dog brings me. I had the tree cut down and turned into doors—very solid doors that will never slam shut and lock me inside the house.

I like my doors open.

I could see the photographer's lips twitching as he walked towards me. Controlling his laughter. Bone-Dog growled deep in her throat. I motioned her away.

"I'm Melody," I said as I gave him a beer and he drank it in one. He was not a talker. He wiped his mouth with his shirt; I could see silvery snail trails on the sleeve. This was a man who did not bother with a handkerchief. He was bony, too. I hate bony, skeleton showing through.

"Where do you want me?" I said, winking. He squinted, as if he wasn't sure what he'd seen. I couldn't be flirting with him. Not possible.

"Just there'll be fine," he said.

I waited until he was set up, then let my robe fall.

He didn't actually shiver; he was protected by the camera lens.

He lifted his head, though, as I began to arrange my bones. I know so much about bones I can hear my own glide and click as I move. Naming them is easy. All you need is a good memory. My memory is very good.

He lifted his head and stared.

"Oh, yeah," he said. It's nice when their voices sound like that. I leaned against the stump. It creaked a little.

His breathing reached me. He wasn't looking in the lens, but he was clicking, shooting me.

I arranged my bones this way and that for him. My fans would love these ones.

I like to get fan letters. It keeps the postie coming, every day, and if I don't collect my mail from the box he'll tell someone. That keeps me safe from being locked inside the house with my Bone-Dog. Even though I've taken precautions, I don't want to be locked in.

"Your film's run out," I said. He stepped from behind the camera and towards me. He reached for me. Touched me, stroked my forearm, the childhood scar there shiny and puckered. Blood and fat and bone and I screamed when it happened.

"Ha ha, scared of blood," kids said.

I had to tell them the truth. I said, "No, I'm scared of bone."

I wanted more photos afterwards, but he was ashamed and out of film. He stumbled about packing up; he almost stepped on Bone-Dog.

"Sorry, little fella," he said, glad of the distraction.

"She. Baby."

"Baby the dog?" he said. I nodded. I liked him for seeing her. He couldn't have known how kind that was. Not many people admitted to seeing her. Hearing her rattling. It's not in my head. That little dog found me, sniffed at my ankles and followed me home. At my feet, snap snap, bones jumping like a little dog.

It would be a good set of photos. He had seen Bone-Dog; he understood me.

He bent to pat her but she trotted over to me and squatted at my heels.

"Pretty, isn't she?" I said. "Prettier than me?"

He nodded. Shook his head.

"Another beer?" I said. I wanted him to stay. I wanted to suck his fingers, lick his ribs.

He shook his head. "Gotta develop these." He lifted the camera. I saw his elbow flinch. He wanted to snap Bone-Dog.

"You're out of film," I said.

Bone-Dog was on her haunches, ready to bite. Snap snap go her teeth. I can hear it even if she's not with me. Snap snap of a little sister wanting her bones back.

He leaned down to pat her.

"I wouldn't. She doesn't like strangers."

He ignored me. Leaned closer. Stepped back when he saw, it became clear, that she was a Bone-Dog.

He sucked breath. She leapt at him, bit his little pointing finger off and spat it out, sucked clean of flesh.

The wound didn't bleed. I could smell burnt flesh. He stared at his cauterised hand. He walked backwards to his truck, "You should control that thing," his jaw snapping, and he left me with her.

There was plenty of food but I didn't feel like eating. Sometimes, after I have my photo taken, I don't feel like eating. I want to stop being a fat woman. Bone-Dog lay at my feet, all bone, skeleton, and I went to the kitchen and made an eight-egg omelette and ate it standing there.

We've lived here many years, the perfect place for us. Paid for with porn. Bone-Dog doesn't approve of my work, but she is happy to sleep in the house I paid for, sleep in my bed, refuse my shameful food. She found the place herself, bringing me the paper and staying so quiet as the real-estate man showed us around I almost forgot she was there. It was a quick, eager sale; most people were put off by the old graveyard, partly uncovered, so close by. Not Bone-Dog; she loved the sense of all those bones, so close. I allowed myself the fantasy that our mother was buried there, and in the early days would visit with offerings of food, laying it at the collapsed brick entrance to the graveyard. I haven't been back for a long time, but I remember the mess of it, the jumbled, forgotten nature of it.

I slept until the moon and Bone-Dog woke me. Looking out my bedroom window I could see the bones in the yard, how well I've lined them up. They shone silver in the moonlight. If I stared long enough my eyeballs quivered and the bones jerked and danced.

Those bones, so carefully laid out. "Thank you, Melody, for being so careful with our bones," their thin voices said. Whistling like the wind so Bone-Dog howled at the noise. "Melody, Melody," their voices tuneless. Melody and Baby. My little sister was Baby because Mum hadn't thought of a proper name yet.

I called her all the names I could think of but she didn't blink. Dolores. Jemima. Janina. Godliness.

Bone-Dog leapt at my feet. I reached down to pet her and she snapped her jaw together. She hadn't forgiven me for letting her die. She thought I let her starve to death. She thought I let her bones be jumbled up, and that I should have escaped earlier.

Bone-Dog thought I liked being locked in that childhood house, but the smell of it has never left me.

I have a very sensitive sense of smell. A hint of rot and I have to leave the room, waste the food. Mould on bread, rotten meat and vegetables, sourness of milk. Fresh food is all I can abide. The smell of rot is a warning. Do not eat this. Do not be near this.

Bones left in the sun for long enough will lose their smell of rot.

My mother left when I was five. Went out for a run to get back in shape. Gotta get back in shape. I was old enough to stay by myself. She deadlocked the door so we would be safe and she ran away, her smooth long legs tan against her shorts, her shoulders muscular but slim, the keys hooked to her waistband.

"Back soon. Gotta get back in shape," she said. I'm still not sure it was an accident. Perhaps she left us there because she wanted me to be thin when she got back. She ran away, a long run, because she had not been since Baby was born

It was a hit and run driver. I hit and ran at school, once I got my weight back. I could hit hard and run fast for my size. I still can. I can run and surprise people so their jaws drop.

It's not good for my ankles, though. The driver hit and ran and moved her body to a river or a lake.

They didn't know who she was and no one claimed her. I knew who she was; I saw her once on TV and told my little sister. She stared at me. She didn't blink. She didn't move after the first three days, just lay there. She was one month old.

There was food in the fridge. I liked to eat. There was some cake and chicken and cheese. There was beetroot, pickles, potatoes and one carrot. There was plenty of food. There was chips and chocolate and lemonade.

I gave the carrot to my sister but she wouldn't eat it. I didn't want to eat, either, once the things started to rot. I put off opening the fridge because of the terrible smell, but the house smelled bad, too.

I didn't eat very much. I chose from the fridge the least rotted thing and ate that. I gave a little to my sister every day, an offering to her to make some noise.

It was quiet in the house. I could reach the kitchen sink with a chair. I couldn't use the can opener.

Watching my sister was like watching a TV show. A slow one. She slowly changed. The smell of rot was terrible. I never got used to it. I watched her every day, watched her change.

I was only five.

I cried a lot, but no one heard. My Dad was gone away and my little sister was a mistake with a stranger. I had no aunties or uncles or grandparents.

I cried a lot.

Our phone wasn't connected, Mummy said we didn't have the money for it. I have one in every room. I have a huge freezer, well-stocked. My cupboards are full of tins, and in each cupboard I have a can opener and a fork. In case my legs break under my weight, I can crawl around and eat until someone saves me.

Mummy said, "Don't leave the house. You stay here till I get back."

I knew I had to be naughty the day I opened the fridge and all that was left was a piece of green sausage. Very hard and I couldn't chew it. I knew I had to be very naughty and find a way to leave the house.

I tried doors again. Then the windows. The only one we had without locks was the one in the toilet. Mummy didn't want any men coming into the house or ringing up.

I couldn't reach the window. Even standing on the toilet, and the cistern was slippery.

So I covered the cistern with the mat from the bath by standing on the toilet seat. Then I put Mummy's tool box on the seat so I could climb onto the cistern.

The window opened when I pushed it. People asked me that. "How long did it take to open the window?" I learned to lie, to say it took days. I learned to say I had tried to get out from the moment Mummy went away.

I walked along the road in the direction I'd seen Mummy run. It took me so long I was sure I'd see Mummy running back, and she'd pick me up and carry me home. She'd have icecream and apple pie and a piece of bacon to eat on the way home.

I love a fresh-killed pig.

I walked. My sister was in my knapsack and I could smell her, but it wasn't so bad outside. There were other smells.

I walked until I came to a house but it was a stranger's house. I couldn't go there. I didn't know, but I put the knapsack on upside down, and my sister's bones with her flesh still on them dropped out along the road. They could never find them all.

So I sat on the wall and had a rest. I told my sister we would have some dinner soon. I didn't know she'd already gone out of the knapsack.

I sent Bone-Dog away. "We need ear-bones. And this one is missing some spine. And we need three thigh bones," I said.

Bone-Dog snarled. She liked to bring what she liked to bring. I had no say.

She rattled up the street; I worked hard while she was gone. I cooked more food for the freezer. The X-rays I pasted all over the kitchen windows cast a greyness. When the sun was out their shadows bone-danced on the floor and the table, keeping me company as I cooked.

She was gone a long time. I sorted out the bones on the lawn, reshaped them, rearranged. Then she returned and dropped her offerings at my feet. A finger bone and a shin bone and a jaw and a skull.

She pushed the bones towards me with her nose then trotted two steps, three, wanting me to follow her, to say how clever she was. She jumped and leapt, bones slipping in and out of joint.

Bone-Dog brought me a small foot bone. I placed it in the pile. Bone-Dog snarled.

"I'll put it in place properly later," I said. "I'm tired now." Bone-Dog whined. She knew more than anyone that bones should be together.

Bone-Dog snapped at me all night, hungry for my bones. I could smell rot on her. It gave me nightmares of being locked in the house, my skin scraping off as I climbed through the toilet window, my sister waiting below, quiet in the knapsack.

I awoke to the stink of her in my throat and I kicked out, rolling her smash onto the floor.

Her old bones scattered, rolling under my bed, into the corner, into the hallway. I heard a hungry moan. I lay there, knowing I needed to take her bones and spread them far and wide, give myself some space. But the thought of such activity made my heart crash. It took the bones ten years to come together the first time.

I was fifteen. I wanted to leave school because no one liked me, and I needed a job, money to get away from my foster mother. She was one of those skinny women who find obesity frightening. That house always smelled of packet chicken noodle soup.

Bone-Dog appeared on the day which became my last at school. She found me, snap snap, and expected me to know who she was. She bit through to bone on my ankle, luckily, because the kids were going to lock me in a box and see if anyone missed me.

Bone-Dog saved me. She didn't want me to be locked up ever again.

I have the first bone Bone-Dog brought me on my shelf of special things. Up there with the prizes I carried in my pocket when I climbed through the toilet window; a rock; a little doll; a very small can of fruit.

The first bone was a finger. I didn't see the significance of the offering for a while; it was only when Bone-Dog brought me another finger bone, a thigh bone and a smooth elbow that I wondered if she was bringing our mother's bones together. If perhaps my fantasy had been realised and we were living by my mother's grave.

But we still haven't collected a full set. She doesn't listen to me when I tell her we are missing the pelvis, a toe or a knee. She brought me a man's pelvis, then a child's, then distracted me with shiny old bones, meaty new ones.

I felt bad, pushing her off the bed. I'd taught her a lesson, though; she brought me the bones I'd asked for. She jumped and leapt, bones slipping.

I had assumed Bone-Dog and I had the same plan in mind. But when she finally brought me a knee-bone and I made a low cry of joy she blinked at me.

"Mother's nearly finished," I said. "Only a couple more pieces." She blinked again, then bared her teeth in a slow snarl of outrage.

I realised I had misunderstood her. She wanted an orderly bone-yard full of skeleton companions, not a bone-mother.

"It can't hurt," I said.

She jumped and leapt, bones slipping.

"All right, I'll follow you," I said. Big sister martyr making up for disappointing little sister. And I thought perhaps I could find the final pieces to our mother's puzzle myself.

Bone-Dog looked at me. She knew I had two hundred and six bones in there.

And she was hungry. She never forgave me for letting her die.

She looked at me, choosing which bone she wanted first. I laughed at my paranoia.

She nipped at me, her skull clicking. Herding me to the gravesite.

I didn't want to visit there, but she was keen to show me. She wanted me, big sister, to be proud.

She was very patient. We had to rest a lot. I hadn't walked more than one hundred steps, the distance to the mailbox and back, in years.

I took a brown bag of food with me and ate snacks on the way. I offered her some, as I always did, and she turned her snobby nose up.

"You should have eaten what I gave you," I said.

There were many bones, though just four gravestones. The others were all unmarked, mixed up, in piles. Perhaps bastard children were buried there without a stone, and murderers, adulterers, the ones they chose to forget.

So many bones.

It was quite a hike; my bones screamed.

Bone-Dog grinned at me, a snarling hateful grimace, and I knew she sought revenge for her stolen life.

"Go away," I said. I had no name for her. "Leave me alone. I don't want any more bones."

She leapt at me, her bones growing, an adult skeleton leapt at me. I turned to run, tripped, fell flat on my face in an open grave. I didn't sink. I was too fat. I stared down into the darkness, smelling the rot, the wood, the flesh, the bone.

"Help," I said. I could hear nothing but my air sucking in and blowing out. I could not control it.

God, the stink of that rot.

"No," I said. No. And Bone-Dog danced a victory jig across my fat back.

Tontine Mary

Tontine Mary

New Ceres Tontine Group, seventh meeting

The President of the New Ceres Tontine Group opened the seventh meeting with the litany. "Two dead by hanging. Three by knife. One by gun, five by carriage, eight by illness, two by drowning."

The people murmured softly, concealing their delight.

Mary scuffed her feet, bored already. She had expected a celebration; the seventh meeting was only three days after her seventh birthday and she had stepped into the great hall in her new button-up boots proud as a peacock and ready to be celebrated.

Her mother had some sweet ginger for her and hissed, "Mary, don't be a goose. You're done with birthdays for the year."

Her brothers, the five of them, all older, sat around her, keeping her safe in their circle. They spoiled her each birthday. They made her toys, found her treasures money can't buy. There was not a lot of wealth in the family, which was why only Mary was signed up to the Tontine.

The coffee men walked around the auditorium with their pots, dozens of them in shiny satin coats, pouring the coffee with stony faces.

"Look at that fool," Mary's father said. "Does he think we don't know he's working his father's business? There should have been a test for quality of character for entry to the Tontine, and that fellow would not have passed."

The man's name was Calvin, Mary thought. There was a boy at school called Calvin, and he often tried to hold her hand, although the teachers had asked him not to.

Calvin marched between the coffee pourers, watching them as if looking for errors. These workers did not make errors. They knew how important the coffee was.

"Hot coffee! Hot coffee!" Calvin called. The adults tutted and looked away.

"Why he thinks he needs to sell I don't know. His father never sells. He lets the business sell itself. It's coffee, for Ceres' sake."

Mary felt sorry for the man. He had no friends, no parents with him.

"At his age," her mother said. Mary thought he must be more than 25, because her oldest brother was 25 and this Calvin looked older.

Her father was distracted as ever. Other fathers shook his hand; they said, "Good job of a tough business, Charles." Mary knew they called him an Alienist, and sometimes "New Ceres' foremost alienist", but she was not sure what that meant.

"I want to go to the Market. They are handing out sweeties, my teacher said."

"Hush, Mary. Your great-grandmother will give you a sweetie at home if you listen carefully here."

The President glared at them. "And greetings to our own Tontine Mary, the youngest of us all. Don't the newshounds love you, young one? You make us proud, won't you?"

Mary shrank from the expectations of the people in the room. She was too young for such responsibility.

It was late when they came out. Mary was so tired the lights of the street seemed to twinkle like stars.

She loved the stars.

She didn't like the newsmen surrounding her, asking her questions about her favourite doll, why she wanted to be rich, silly questions for men to ask a girl.

Her father said, "The next person to come near my child will find themselves arrested and up before the courts."

At home, Mary's great-grandmother clapped her hands in Mary's face. "Don't blink," she said. She was so weak the effect was lost; her hands were slow and barely created an impact. Mary had time to prepare. The old woman told her, "You've got good blood. No reason you won't live forever. The women live long in our family. Much longer than the men. And we can look after you, Mary, keep you safe. Nobody can keep boys safe. The only thing I ask you, Mary, is that you birth healthy children to keep our line. We've got Coopers going back to the French Revolution."

Mary squinted at her. If she asked what that was, she'd tell her for a very long time.

It frightened her, the idea of great age. She felt nothing but horror and revulsion at her great-grandmother. How angry her parents were at her demonstration of such.

"She's sacrificed a lot to buy you a place in the Tontine. You should be grateful."

The woman was so old, her skin was almost transparent, and Mary felt ill at what she called 'the insects' inside her; her beating heart pushing blood through her veins, crawling.

Her hair was still dark and thick, though.

"You have a direct, verbal link going back hundreds of years. The main thing you can bring, Mary is long life. You need to stay safe, for the sake of the Coopers."

She winced; her stomach gave her pain.

"I'll bring you a cackeral, grandmother," Mary's mother said. Mary decided to hide away. She hated cackeral, the fish they made for those who needed to go to the toilet and couldn't. She thought the fish was full of bowel motions, and she couldn't understand why anyone would eat such a thing.

She sat on her swing outside, feeling sorry for herself.

Her family loved her dearly, and she knew that should give her a warm place in her heart. People told her love keeps you warm and your belly full, but she had to disagree.

New Ceres Tontine Group, twenty-fourth meeting

Workers on high stools lined the entrance to the hall, great urns behind them. They poured coffee for the members as they entered. A meeting without coffee did not go smoothly.

Calvin, now in control after the death of his father, had learnt to trust in his product. He was popular; Mary could see that. The ladies giggled around him, the men nodded at him.

"Amazing what inherited wealth gives you," Mary thought.

"One dead by hanging, three by knife, four by gun, one dead by illness, two by suffocation, six by amputation and one by bee sting," the President said.

Mary tried to block her ears. She hated this litany of death they had to listen to every year.

Mary's new husband Philip hummed in her ear, one of the beautiful songs he had to keep her happy.

His band (and she knew full well they were her bodyguards also) tapped fingers and toes, a natural rhythm they often found.

"We are attended today by representatives of the coffer holders, who keep our funds safe and ensure all is above board."

The members nodded soberly.

"And who ensures they are above board?" Phillip said. He was as cynical as her father. The two got along well.

"How was the visit to your father?" he whispered.

"He hates it there," she whispered back. She had come to the Meeting from Traitor's Gate, where her father was imprisoned for his crimes against the refugees. He was a weeping mess of a man, filled with bitterness for the oscillating opinions of New Ceres. Mary had told him, "You'll be a hero again, Father. Before your future grandchildren are adults, you will be seen as a great man again."

The newspaper hounds followed her to the jail, of course, and would make sure her sad father's face was on the front cover of every edition. *Haven't they got anything better to write about?* she thought, though her father would be pleased with the attention he received.

He made the place his own, as he did any place he stayed. He told her, "It's all about superiority and survival. Nothing should stand in the way of the survival of the family."

The way Phillip played music made him seem like an angel and that took him far in New Ceres. Like any land filled with refugees, the collective skills were a wonder to behold. Many great musicians gathered from elsewhere; unlikely to fight, considered worthy of rescue, they were first on their ships. Phillip taught in the College of Pure Music, an institution where, like the rest of the planet, technological advances were not admitted. Some of the musicians remembered a time on Earth of recorded music, where you could listen over and over without the presence of a player. Not so on New Ceres. Music was precious and fresh.

Mary was assoted by him; adored him beyond all else. The 'paper hounds had followed the courtship as they followed everything else, dubbing them "The prince and princess of the Tontine".

The wedding was beautiful; lights in all the trees, dancing, music and wine. Mary was secretly glad the newspaper hounds were there; they took a good photograph.

Phillip hated the attention and was often tempted to behave outrageously, just to shock them and give them something to write about.

Phillip's family had chosen him as the Tontine holder, Mary suspected, because of his talents, his looks; they knew he was best placed to make a good match. Even at a young age, he was very clever.

Many of the Tontine holders married within their own ranks. Other Tontine holders understood what it was like; and the joining of the tickets could only help.

Mary first noticed Philip at the 15th meeting. He said he'd noticed her before that, but was too nervous to do talk to her. She didn't remember him; she'd been distracted by her father's odd behaviour. At the end of the meeting, he'd clapped his arm around the shoulders of one of the younger members. Mary wondered what he was doing. He should be on his way home for the late dinner her mother made them.

He came home very late, after Mary was asleep. The fighting woke her; her mother was furious.

"You're so blatant about your infidelity. How does it make me look?"

"I would never be unfaithful to you, my love. This was Tontine business."

"You men and your Tontine business."

Look as she might, Mary never saw the young member again.

When her great-grandmother told her, "Keep your enemies close," she did not imagine how literally Mary would take the advice. Perhaps Mary was too close to Phillip; she could see the small beads of sweat clinging to the fine hairs on his arms. She smoothed her hand across his skin and he sighed, a deep, satisfied sigh which made her wish he would wake up and look at her with his intense, dark eyes again.

She rolled off their high bed, her toes just stretching to the floor. She would get used to sleeping in her new husband's bed. He'd let her have the side by the door, (though he slept there now, had sunk there and was far too heavy to move) but he loved his high bed. She teased him about monsters hiding under the springs and he laughed along with her.

"I fear nothing, my love, except losing you," he said, kissing her fingers, her palm, and the crook of her elbow.

Phillip took her to the zoo, a place she had never enjoyed, not even as a child. It seemed to her a barbaric practice, one which should have been left to die on Earth. There was a wild cat which frightened her. Its eyes glared luminous red, glowing from the darkness of its cave like a miniature demon.

"Why do its eyes glow like that? I don't like it."

A zoo keeper whispered, "There'd be hell to pay for it. I'm going to La Policia tomorrow. The owner's put the Preserve on the poor creature. The red eyes, and if you get close enough you can smell lavender. I don't know how it works, but I know it's against God and against the laws of New Ceres. And the clean up of their cave? I wouldn't discuss that in front of a lady."

"That's terrible," whispered Mary.

"Don't you want to live a long time?" Phillip said.

On the slow journey back, he held her hand tenderly and kept her well-supplied with little treats from his picnic basket. She wondered if he would be ready to discuss children with her.

Not far from home, their coach driver stopped the horses.

"Why have we stopped, man? We want to be home," Phillip called through the window.

"Sorry, sir. I have a business to attend to." The driver climbed down and opened their door.

"You'll attend your business on your time, not ours," Phillip said. He exchanged a smile with Mary to temper his harsh words.

"Your business is my business, sir. You see," and here, he tilted his hat back so they could see his face.

"You won't know me, sir and madam, because your type doesn't notice my type."

Mary grasped Phillip's hand, suddenly nervous.

"My family and I, we all put the cash in. All we had."

"Phillip!" Mary whispered.

"And you can't blame me for wanting to win the big prize."

He stepped back from the carriage and, raising his whip, sent the horses away, riderless.

"Phillip!" Mary screamed. Phillip, frozen momentarily, at last moved. The carriage rode smoothly, steadily; the driver had not counted on the habits of the workhorses. Phillip carefully pushed open the door, his hand out to steady Mary in her seat.

"Be careful!"

He climbed out onto the step then, stretching his long body in a way Mary could admire even in such a circumstance, reached the driver's seat and pulled himself up.

"Hiya!" he called, pulling the horses gently into his control.

Mary's father would never forgive Phillip for placing Mary in such a situation, going so far as to accuse him of trying to kill her.

"Never, Charles. I worship Mary."

The horses were retired and allowed a soft and easy life as reward for their great actions.

NEW CERES TONTINE GROUP, THIRTY-FIFTH MEETING

Mary had a new dress made for the Meeting. Turning 35 bothered her more than she admitted to Phillip. There were lines on her face and a softness about her body she didn't like.

It was childbirth. The children. It was all the worry of a family; are they eating, are they being well educated, do they have the right friends.

Her son Michael had come home only days before (in fact, on her birthday, so his timing couldn't have been worse) saying,

"Dominic's grandmother had the Preserve put on. But they caught her. She's in jail!"

The community was abuzz with it. Mary thought, "Why do they wait till they're old? Why not Preserve youth?"

On the way home from collecting her dress, Mary stopped at a chirographist. She did this sometimes if Phillip wasn't about. If he was there, he mocked the idea of reading the future, of palms being able to predict what would happen in time coming.

The chirographist told Mary all she wanted to hear. All they ever told her; your life line is long, my dear. You will have a long life.

"Your mother looks like a young girl tonight," Phillip said to the children at the table, "She doesn't dress for me, it's only for the Tontine, you know." He was jealous; she understood that, so wasn't angry with him.

"How long will you be gone?" their daughter asked. She didn't like her mother to be gone long.

"We'll see the Passion Play tomorrow if you're good," Mary said.

The meetings were an enjoyable outing for her and Phillip. The members knew each other well, and had lost some of the politeness of society. It meant for some frivolous behaviour, and Mary usually came home with her cheeks aching with laughter.

"Are you ready, Aunt?"

Her nephews guarded her now, doing it grudgingly for the money and the promise of more.

Keeping Mary alive was the family business.

The media wasn't so much of a concern. They lost interest around the twenty-fifth year. Mary had proved a dull teenager, and once she'd married, even less newsworthy.

The meeting was held in a large conference room above the hall.

"One dead by defenestration, two by bee sting, two by hanging, three by knife, five by gun, ten by carriage and fourteen by drowning," said the President.

Her father, retired now and just an old man, stood beside her and Phillip. Sometimes she looked at her father and thought he seemed so ordinary, not the person responsible for the deaths of hundreds of illegal aliens. She had been right, though; on his absolute pardon from Traitor's Gate he had been compensated greatly, and a small statue stood of him in Proserpine Square.

Calvin announced that he wanted to set up a museum in his flagship coffee shop. A collection of items from the Tontine; things left behind at meetings, and the great book they'd all signed thirty-five years earlier.

"I don't see why you should take charge of these things," Mary's friend Elizabeth called out. "Why you?"

"Is anybody else interested in the enterprise?" Calvin said. "I didn't think so."

"He'll never amount to anything," Phillip said. "Except for dilettantism. The man is a fool." Her husband was so very sensible, reliable, kind to those who deserved it. "The problem with an expected inheritance is that some people will use it as an excuse to achieve nothing with their lives."

"You're a fool," Phillip said. "A whacking great goose of a man."

Yet Calvin was determined. He was a wealthy man, so wealthy people wondered why he bothered with the Tontine at all. Most of them had risked all they had, all their families had, for the chance to better the lives of future generations.

Calvin had all the money he needed.

No family.

It was a gamble to him.

By the 36th Meeting, he had transformed his coffee house. A display cabinet filled one wall, hundreds of small compartments with treasures nestled inside, coffee beans in each space to absorb the smells. He placed small mementoes of those passed in each small compartment. Mary didn't like it, being reminded of the dead like that, but others seemed to think it a worthy exercise.

Her father leaned heavily on her, and she looked at him, surprised. It was very unlike him to engage physically with anyone. "Father?" she said. "Phillip!" Her voice stopped the meeting, so there were many witnesses as her father fell to the floor, his face red, his hands to his chest.

"Father!" She knelt beside him, putting her head on her chest. "Mary, I couldn't be more proud of what you've achieved. Better than any son a man could have."

Someone took her arm and moved her away so the medical men could do their work.

And other work was done, too; Mary saw her older brother lead away a woman five years her senior. Doing Father's work.

The next morning, she could not bring herself to talk to the children of their grandfather's death. Instead, she pretended all was well and took them to the Passion Play, performed each year for New Ceres Independence Day. It began well enough, and Mary was glad to be distracted from the truth.

Huge puppets of the Lady-Governor dancing with famous war heroes, hilarious costumes making them all laugh at old Earth.

Then came the Cautionary Tale. Mary had forgotten how frightening they could be; the last few years had been humourous lessons in greed and sociability.

This year it was a lesson against putting on the Preserve. A man, glowing red eyes, sat in a barrel of his own waste, pulled on wheels by his doctor. A sign above his head said, "Against God and the laws of New Ceres."

"The Devil! The Devil!" her children wailed, and Mary cursed the officials who decided terrifying the young was a good idea. The smell of lavender was cloying and made her ill.

She made Phillip tell the children the news of their grandfather that minute, when they already felt so bad they couldn't feel any worse.

NEW CERES TONTINE GROUP, FIFTIETH MEETING

Mary attended the fiftieth meeting as an orphan. She felt she would never be used to her mother not being there. Her son tried to make her take action, saying, "You understand, mother, that the family finances are now your concern. We are not to rely on the uncles; they have their own families to be concerned about. You and father had better ensure your wills are up to date, unless you want the coffers of New Ceres to receive the lot."

Tears welled in her eyes, and he had the sensitivity to quieten. He put his arm around her.

"Mother, we're all doing our bit, you know. All helping out."

She squeezed her eyes tight to bring a buzzing in her ears. She did not want to know.

The worst thing about losing her mother, and she felt selfish in this, but needed to be honest with herself, was that now she was old. She was the older generation.

Yet she felt as if life happened to her, and that she had always been safe in her cocoon.

Philip asked her what she imagined she might have done differently. Where she might have gone; what she might have done.

"I don't know," she said. "And I'm happy with you and the children. But what if my brothers had let me out more? What if my father had said, this week you'll go away, alone, you'll have an adventure without someone watching you."

"And me? You wish I'd let you alone?"

Mary closed her eyes. She felt tears there, trying to explain what she meant without hurting him. "No. Not that. But I feel sometimes I've never made a decision alone."

"But you're not alone. You're my wife, the children's mother. You're a sister and an aunt."

"And everyone is relying on me to grow old whether I'd like to or not, in order to win wealth and comfort for a future I won't even see."

The look Philip gave her surprised her, and made her realise people only liked her when she were doing what they considered the right thing. "It's not much to ask, Mary."

One newshound waited at the meeting place, having heard of her mother's death and looking for tears. They liked her to show emotion, although she rarely did.

Calvin watched from the doorway as Mary answered the foolish, shallow questions. As she walked up to him, he nodded.

"Good evening, Calvin."

He indicated the newshound. "They're always after you. The youngest. Never the richest, the smartest."

"You don't really want that kind of attention, do you?"

"Of course not. Why would I want that?"

But he did, and she could not understand why. It was as if he thought the star belonged to him.

The President read the litany; "Fifteen to elderly causes, nine to heat exhaustion, three to undisclosed illness, four to unnatural causes," (here her son nudged her. She twisted her shoulder away from him) "two to Preserve gone wrong."

Mary had never seen a Preserve go wrong, but she'd heard about it. Strange how names come to suit, even if they didn't to begin with. When a Preserve goes wrong, the blood thickens, like jam gone well. It sluggishly fills the veins and begins to ooze out of the pores. Once that happens, they say, your death is days away.

Yet people persisted, ignoring law, punishment and repercussions. There were great warnings of loss of the memory of happiness; these warnings were ignored.

Her friend Elizabeth sat next to her. "I'm seriously thinking about putting on the Preserve," she said. "A neighbour had it done," here she looked around to ensure La Policia were not listening, "and she hasn't aged a moment since. Seriously; you do it now, or you're preserving something past worth preserving."

Mary held her chuckle in. At 67, Elizabeth still felt young. Good for her, Mary thought.

"Of course," Elizabeth added, "The rest of the neighbours hunted her down and strung her up, once they realised the Preserve had worked. So perhaps it's not so useful for extending life, after all."

Mary looked at Calvin. He seemed barely to have aged, these last meetings. The rest of them; you could see the aging clearly, once a year. He was such a recluse, though, so careful of public appearances, she wondered if anyone else had noticed.

NEW CERES TONTINE GROUP, SEVENTIETH MEETING

Phillip died just before the 60th meeting. "You hang in there," he whispered to her, his breath foul with disease and wet in her ear. "Don't let them win."

He had been a protective husband, taking over the role from her father, keeping her away from the sick, and from any dangerous pursuit, and out of the company of anybody troublesome.

Her son filled the role next, bravely stepping into his father's shoes whether Mary wanted him to or not.

Five of the grandchildren came to take her to the meeting. Four boys. One girl. The girl she was interested in, not the boys. They were there as muscle, nothing else. They found her sorting, as she liked to do, throwing out anything she thought too old to keep.

"Gran! You can't throw this out! It's a new chair! We gave it to you for Christmas three years ago."

"Three years is old," she said, pffing with her mouth, waving with her hand.

The boys carried weapons she could not name. They were more worried, this generation. They seemed to think the danger was greater.

The 70th annual meeting took place in the anteroom of the great hall.

"Nine dead of old age," Calvin said. Just ten of them left. Mary's friend Elizabeth, strong as an ox, sat with her stitching, sucking on a mintoe.

Calvin gave them coffee to try. "This bean was named for you two lovelies," he said. "The beautiful Mary-Elizabeth."

"You always were a charmer," Mary said.

"Thank you, my woman," Calvin said. He looked sidelong at Mary as he kissed Elizabeth's hand. Mary could care less for his shenanigans. Calvin's eyes were red and tired. Mary remembered her great-grandmother saying, "You'll be old like this one day." It was like a curse, yet here she was, frightening children herself now. What was so horrifying about age? Was it the decay? The uselessness? The inevitability?

Calvin's face was a bright shiny pink with tinges of blue. He smelt of lavender, a hard-grown flower on New Ceres. Mary thought his hand felt a little lumpy as he took hers to kiss it, and his lips were so cold she felt the chill up to her armpit.

"Calvin, you're looking well."

"As are you, my lady. As beautiful as ever."

Mary was no more convinced by his flattery than she had been 40 years earlier, and 30, when he made the rounds of all the women members, seeking matrimony. Most had laughed at him, but Carolyn Merino had not. Their baby was born dead, though, a terrible tragedy from which Carolyn never recovered. She sent herself into the Devil's Arms, taking her own life with a terrible dose of untreated lum.

Calvin did not marry again. The ladies of the Tontine whispered that his seed was poison, and no one would touch him.

Mary and Elizabeth sat and remembered the early days, when the great hall was full, standing room only, and out on the pavement, too. It all seemed like fun, then; the bustle and the wit, none of the desperation of later years.

Calvin shook his head sadly now and again. "Of this I remember nothing. Nothing. All memory of the good is gone from me."

Calvin wrapped a cape around his shoulders and waved his hand at his bodyguards. Three of them, quiet, strong men dressed in neat black suits.

"Surely you don't expect one of us to hurt you, Calvin? I think we can wait it out now, don't you?" Elizabeth said.

Calvin covered his head. "I look forward to seeing you again next year," he said.

"Why do you care so much, Calvin?" Mary could not help asking. "You will do anything to win, yet you have no wife or child."

"My lady, I may not have your great achievement of a large and healthy family. But I have a great coffee empire, which I hope to take to our neighbours."

He turned to the window. Out there the planets twinkled. "And I will be the one to open the door."

Elizabeth invited Mary out for a meal, as she did every year, saying, "Come on, Mary. We've got something to celebrate," but her oldest grandson shook his head.

"Need to make our way home, grandma. It's late, and you know how the lights upset you."

"That's a shame." Elizabeth leant to Mary's ear. "What do you suppose Calvin is doing? He's barely aged."

"I'm sure I don't know," Mary said, but she knew very well. He had put on the Preserve. He would do whatever it took to win and he had the money to pay for the treatment and the bribes.

Still, Mary couldn't understand why the authorities didn't just arrest Calvin. Did they not realise? Or did his influence reach that far? Was he such a recluse that only she, Elizabeth and their guards ever saw him?

Mary called for the carriage to take her home. She liked to look through the window, watch the world as they travelled. She could not see too far into the distance, but the close sights of New Ceres reminded her of the sheltered life she'd led. Street urchins playing with a filthy ball (she had never played in the street. Never been dirty). A woman beckoning passers by, her skirt hem twitching (Mary had never met a strange man, never taken one). The street vendors, with their apples, their seafood, some of it stinking, some of it pale with age.

But to get through that transaction, to live it even the illness which may follow...

There was a scuffle. Her bodyguard glanced out. "It's the Preserves. The ones who've failed are left on the streets. It's an absolute disgrace."

He moved to pull down the blinds, but she stayed his hand.

"Let me see," she said. Outside the window three men staggered. Their thickened blood oozed from their fingertips, and they wept red tears, they wept so loudly it was like the din of a cattery.

"They say you lose your memory of happiness," her guard said, pulling down the blinds.

NEW CERES TONTINE GROUP, NINETIETH MEETING

"Mother, I've got some news." Her eldest son always spoke slowly which annoyed her. Was she some great fool who didn't understand a thing? She understood plenty.

"Elizabeth Jones just passed away," he said. He smiled at her, wanting her to smile back. Instead she cried, tears pouring down her cheeks and running, salty, into her mouth.

"She was a good woman. A friend. She could stitch a rose you could smell and feel the thorns. Calvin will be..."

She wasn't quite sure what Calvin would be.

"And her death leaves you one of two. Calvin Arnold is 24 years your senior though he is remarkably well-preserved."

"Perhaps he made a deal with the devil. An extra deal. I mean. All of us signed our souls away when we became members of this Tontine."

"It's a simple exercise in life insurance, Mother. That's all."

"But we've every last one of us spent the last 90 years wishing each other dead. That kind of thought is bad for the soul."

"You can't think that way, Mother. Think of what you've done for Proserpine, for New Ceres. For the family Cooper."

Two young men carried her in to the meeting, lifting her into a brocade chair. She could no longer keep track of who was who; they had a vested interest in her, though, she was sure. Mary had agreed to meet in Calvin's flagship coffee ship. Her grandsons, were they?

took the chairs near about, ever watchful. They bought her coffee from outside, fearing poison.

The newshounds were there, two young cubs sent on this annual, newsless assignment.

"One dead, old age," Calvin said. He smacked his hands together. "And that's just about it, eh, Mary? Just the two of us now."

Calvin was a man in his dotage, now, a second childhood overtaking him. He sucked on coffee beans and seemed hard pressed to concentrate.

Calvin held her chair and she sat. He sat beside her, his legs stiffly in front of him.

"Are you in pain?" she whispered.

"No pain at all, my dear lady," he said. He made a gesture as if to take her hand again and kiss it, so she quickly scrabbled in her purse for an imaginary item.

Her suspicions of the last few years were answered. It was clear what he was doing, and she wondered no one had acted on it yet. Perhaps no one else noticed. He was a lonely, friendless old man and perhaps she was the only one who saw him with any regularity.

Calvin said, "It has come to this. A meeting of equals." The blueness around his nostrils darkened.

"Equals, indeed."

But she knew that wasn't true. If the money went to her, it would mean any number of possible futures, guided by her offspring in myriad ways. Calvin would spend it all on his business. Not taking coffee to those who couldn't afford it or anything worthy like that. Expanding his empire to give his name a chance at immortality.

The smell of lavender made her feel a little ill to her stomach. She was queasy so easily now; a simple smell, or a slightly rich meal, or sudden movement, could make her stomach rise. She didn't like to talk to the children or her physician about it, because they would panic and cause all sorts of strife. Her apothecary understood her and would never speak out of turn. He would be remembered in the will.

Calvin's jaw fell slack to one side and Mary looked at him with great pity.

"How long have you been dead, Calvin?"

Calvin said, "Ah, so you've noticed at last."

"I've known for some time, Calvin. I'm just too polite to say so."

"It's been near on 20 years. A good job, wouldn't you say? They're better now."

Calvin started to leak from his ears. He seemed in great pain, struggling to take a breath. His fingertips were stained red with thick blood.

"One thing they don't tell you is your memory is shattered. I remember only ill, the deaths, the guilt, the cruelties. I remember the smell of my new-born dead-born, already on the rot. I don't remember the smell of my wife's hair, or of roast meat cooking to welcome me home. Only the ill."

Mary shook her head. "You've made a mistake," she said.

"Yet I am still here, matching you. You will need to put on the Preserve yourself, Mary."

"It's too late for me to put on the Preserve. I need the Reverse. I need something to take me back forty years, to when I was young."

"For that you'll need great wealth. Wealth beyond imagining."

"Oh, I've imagined it. Believe me."

"As have I," Calvin said.

"Yes, but I have children, grand-children. I will have great grand-children before long."

Calvin rapped the bottom of the table with his knuckles. "I admit defeat to you, dear lady. Your clean, good living is your long life."

His shoulders slumped; his guards came forward.

"The Preserve has failed," one of them whispered, and they looked at her differently.

With that, Tontine Mary, Mary Cooper, mother of three, grandmother of nine, won the First New Ceres Tontine.

Mary stroked the hair of her favourite great-grandchild. Black, straight hair Mary recognised. It was like her great-grandmother's

"You have a great responsibility, dear child. There are Coopers going back to the time when Earth was home; you must ensure we continue."

The girl looked at her, horrified.

"You need achieve nothing else in your life."

She thought of the life she'd led; cautious, protected, always thinking of the end rather than the journey.

She wished she was strong enough to release her granddaughters from a similar life, but she was not.

The Cooper family, wealthy now beyond all imagining, would go forward, generation after generation, into the future of New Ceres.

A Positive

A Positive

Not long after my father killed my mother, I removed him to a special home.

"I'm taking you somewhere nice, Dad. They've got big TV and lots of food."

"Why can't I stay with you?" I thought of the shit in the seams of his trousers, the smell of him. He was so helpless. Such a child.

"It's for the best."

I carried his empty suitcase to the front door.

"Got my Agatha Christie books in there?"

"Yep."

"And my photos? And my postcards? And my pyjamas?"

"All there, Dad."

I patted him. "You'll love it. I'll visit often," I said. I couldn't wait to see him settled in his new home.

The house was mine at last, and I didn't bother with a garage sale, didn't sort a thing. I called the Salvation Army and told them to take the lot. Everything. All my belongings were those of the man I used to be.

They marched up and down the stairs with load after load, and they were friendly at first, making jokes.

After a while they were dead silent, and they worked quickly.

They wouldn't look at me.

They carried out boxes of clothes, books, ornaments. Clocks and crockery. Glasses, flags, beakers, needles, syringes, stainless steel bowls, drips, magazines, photos. Papers they would burn or read. They carried out furniture.

They carried out bedspreads, sheets, towels. Toaster, fridge, TV, stereo.

"Shower curtain," I said, and they even took that. I went on inspection when they finished; they wouldn't come in.

I brought out one last armful of things; toothbrushes, soap, a hula hoop, jewellery, a bucket still crusty with blood, a pair of shoes and a teapot. I passed these over the threshold and waved my past goodbye.

It was still there, though, in the walls, the carpet, the ceiling, the smell of the place. So I hired a wallpaper stripper and a carpet remover and a floor polisher and I bought some paint and that was a full month's work for my girlfriend and me.

Then it was time to go see Dad. The pathetic little marks he'd scratched into me were gone, the memory of his light weight, too. He was always a small man. Smaller than Mum, although that made no difference to their happiness.

They married soon after they met, then spent fifteen years living the life. They never wanted kids. Kids would interfere. Kids didn't travel well or eat well and they were no good in restaurants. They cried and were dirty. They couldn't speak for years and when they finally learnt it was only to abuse you.

Mum and Dad plannned to remain childless.

As I was growing up, people often said, "Were you an accident?" because Mum and Dad were so old when they had me. I eventually gathered that "accident" meant "unwanted", and truly did not want to know the answer. Thinking they were comforting me, my parents said, "No, you were the most planned baby ever," and told me why I was born. I realised then we were not a normal family; that not everyone shared blood with their father.

My parents exchanged fond glances as they told me the story of my birth. I always felt they cared about each other so much, one day they would both love me together. I was well-treated, properly schooled, impeccably fed, but the giggles and the games they saved for themselves.

"You were planned for very carefully, because your father got sick after a lifetime of being healthy. We just didn't know how to cope. We couldn't do the things we used to; he tired so easily."

"So you had me to keep you company at home," I said.

"Not quite," Mum said. "We went to so many doctors, and none of them could tell us how to bring him back to life. After weeks of tests, all they said was, 'It's middle age.' It really was a terrible time."

Dad was silent.

"So we started trying the other doctors, the ones you didn't see at hospital. Now they were a funny lot."

Dad smiled now. "They had me naked for the night air, eating raw meat to clear the toxins, swallowing by-products I wouldn't like to discuss. And there was always the sex, of course."

"But none of it worked. He was still lethargic, so tired. He drooped about the house, driving me mad."

Mum always hated it when I was tired and weak. "Get a move on! Show some life!" she poked at me. She thought I did it on purpose.

"And then there was the doctor who made us young again," said Mum.

"And caused you to be born," said Dad.

"So you had me to keep you young?" I said.

"Yes."

"It was his blood that was the problem," Mum said. "It was old and tired. That's all. I would have given him all of mine, but we didn't match." Again, the fond smile. They sat together on their couch. I was on my chair in the corner; I had to twist to face them.

I said, "But you do match." It was one of the rare times I impressed them.

"Everything but our blood," Dad said. "My family were no use; they either had different blood or they were diseased. And the hospital wasn't interested in helping us."

I didn't know much about Dad's side of the family. There was a big fight years ago, around when I was born, and they didn't talk anymore.

"Is that why you hate them?" I said.

"One reason," Dad said. He and Mum had only ever needed each other.

"We were often at the doctor, begging him to help us," Dad said.

"Demanding, really," "Mum said. "How could we live like that, with death? We couldn't."

"Lucky you didn't die, Dad," I said. He wasn't much of a believer in luck. He always said, "Luck is what you do with your opportunities," which was okay if you got opportunities. If your parents took them all, how much luck could you expect to have?

Mum said, "The doctor told us it was a shame we didn't have a child, because it would probably have blood which wouldn't clump his. That was when the planning began."

Dad wanted a transfusion whenever I was able to provide one, so I have never been strong. As soon as I felt rich with blood, I'd be drained again. It was all they asked of me, though. I had no chores; no cleaning, cooking, visiting, politeness for me. Just that look in Dad's eye, that need, and the pain, and the life going out of me. Our special room was called the theatre. I thought that was normal, "I went to the theatre," people said, until I realised there were two kinds. I no longer boasted about having one. People only laughed, anyway.

I always knew when it was going to happen. I'd be the centre of attention, have favourite meals. We'd go for a drive one month, shopping another. I could never enjoy these special days though. I knew what was coming. And all day Dad would pinch and squeeze at me, wanting me pink and tender.

I never had an imagination, so I had nowhere to go while the transfusion was taking place. I wished the ceiling was a story book, all the cracks and lines making rabbits and bears. All I ever saw were cracks and lines. I knew them very well.

Dad liked to hum along to a bit of music in the background. I still hate anything classical. There was always that silence, between the movements, when I'd hear Dad's bad blood drip drip into the bucket, as mine was slowly entering his veins. It was perfect, that rhythm, and I imagined I could hear it over the crashing cymbals and roaring chords of Dad's favourite music.

Mum's favourite was the garden and she threw the full buckets over the flowers. I couldn't understand why she never answered when people asked her how she kept it so nice. Why didn't she tell them? So I answered for her. Just the once.

"Dad's blood," I said. I was locked in my room that day, all day, and the shock of being a bad boy kept my mouth shut for a long time. I liked it better as Mum's good boy, Dad's blood boy.

It was a private, quiet life. My pleasures came when they took their excursions. Dad would fill up, jovial and magnanimous as he took my strength, and Mum cooked my favourite casseroles and desserts for the freezer.

I was left to pretend the house was mine. Sometimes I dreamed a crash, their caravan folding in two and their blood pouring out when rescuers freed them.

And then things changed.

"Poor Old Girl needs to save her energy," Dad said, though he was the pale and shaky one. He liked to joke people thought Mum was his mother. "Old Girl," he called her. *Never thought to let her have a go at me.*

He lost his license, was the thing, and she'd never had hers because he did the driving. They took my pleasures away. Now, they never left the house. They sat quietly with me, listening to the blood pulsing through my veins.

Dad wanted blood every three weeks then. It got so I couldn't bear those nights at home, all three of us waiting for the others to talk, and almost the only thing we had to talk about was the next visit to the theatre.

Sometimes they discussed grandchildren as if I wasn't there. Never, I thought. I knew how they would treat a grandchild. They thought my blood was getting old. I'm not one of those types who feel better when they do the same things to the next generation of innocent children.

I began to go out at night, leaving the house without a word, slamming the door like a teenager. I wasn't sure what people did, out. I tired very easily, and would sometimes just sit in a place where there was a lot of noise, and absorb the energy.

I found there was an undertow in the city. It dragged me, without a fight, to kindred spirits. Damaged people without armour.

I went to one of those bars where people are whipped and manacled, because I knew about receiving pain. I'd been strapped down, pierced, drained, all my life, but I'd never liked it. They gave me a whip to use but I wasn't strong enough. Under the lights you could see my thin arms. It was very warm in there although I'm usually cold. You could see how many times I'd saved my fathers' life, a record of tracks.

Someone was impressed. It was a woman, with a black cowl over her face to cover the criss cross scars there, her body shrouded, her voice low, her fingers cool. I wouldn't take her offered drink, but allowed her into my car. I agreed to drive her home.

I stayed with her for two days. It was the longest I had been away from my parents, and I felt breathless without them.

We ate pizza and drank wine, and I told her my life. She was sickened. Sickened, a scarred woman hiding in black.

She said, "Why do you agree to it? You're an adult."

I had often tried to answer this question, alone, in the dark, thinking terrible thoughts in the middle of the night. When I was young, it had all seemed so normal; when I realised it wasn't, I was embarrassed, like an abused child, or children in a strange religion. Now, it's the guilt, mostly, and the fact that I've never lost my need for approval. They liked having me close by and I was too weak to move away. I didn't finish school, which Dad found irritating. He said intelligence was only a matter of looking and learning. They learnt how to give transfusions, didn't they, by watching? Mum going to hospital once and watching the whole thing. It was Mum who did it; Dad hated the sight of blood. He always kept his head turned away.

I didn't need a job either. They gave me plenty of money. I never wanted for anything.

"I don't know," I said.

I began to suffocate in her arms. She was draining love from me, swallowing it in breathless gulps. So I returned home.

I had never heard my father raise his voice; now he screamed, screeched, called me a killer. I said, "Who am I supposed to have killed?"

"Me, me," he said. He took my wrist and tried to lead me to the theatre.

"No," I said.

"What do you mean?" Mum said. Her face looked dark, damaged.

"I'm not giving blood anymore. I need it all for myself."

My father wailed. My mother cried. "Where were you?" Mum said.

"With my girlfriend."

My father stopped wailing to snort.

I went to my room.

Each day my mother grew fearful, my father begged and drooled, and I yearned for my girlfriend. So I went to my girl in black. I never imagined my mother was in danger. Their blood didn't match.

I stayed away for two nights. She wanted to meet my parents. I said, "Soon." We went for a drive in the country, to the old boarding house where she kept her mother and we watched her mother take a bath.

It was very quiet when I returned home. Quieter than usual; I could hear no pottering. The house seemed darker, and colder. But I could be inventing. Could be the house was the same as ever, and it was only afterwards I turned it into something else.

I found Dad lying on his bed in the theatre, waiting for his transfusion. The room smelt so very clean, compared to the world outside its walls.

Dad told me the story. He told it in a wheedling tone, he told me the truth, hoping it would make me help him.

"You hadn't been here for weeks," he said. To him, I only existed in the theatre, or when we were preparing for it. "And I was very ill. So I wanted your mother to do that one small thing for me. Just once. It's not like I ever asked her before." He led me around the house, indicating a wall, a room, making me look at nothing.

"But her blood was no good for you."

"That's what she always said. But I thought, maybe she's lying. Maybe it was always good. And when she said no, no, no, all I could see was red. She was cooking the potatoes how you like them, in case you came home, and I said I'd do it. But I saw red.

"I just scratched her, I thought, so I could see the blood, see if it was OK, but it wasn't."

And neither was she. My father wept and snuffled in a corner in the kitchen, denying what he had done, not looking at the proof before his eyes.

I had no time to prepare myself. I felt greater grief than I could have imagined; this woman had cared for me, kept me alive, kept me clean and fed.

We were always good at secrets. We took Mum's body away to the country and buried it. We were the only ones who would miss her.

Dad never got another drop of blood. He was probably addicted to it; he suffered. He seemed to get old very quickly. Was it Mum's death, or having to live with his own blood?

Dad finally paid attention to me. He followed me around like a little lamb, and I loved ignoring him. He didn't complain. He shrugged and sighed.

He became quite tender towards me, remembering things which never happened, emotions we never shared. Then one day he reminded me of the truth.

"Sometimes you just have to be patient. We had to wait those first few months while you grew your own blood, to take the place of your mother's. I didn't want anybody else's blood. Only yours." He said it casually, as if we had all been involved in the decision. I think he thought he'd talk me into going back to it.

We had a lovely time alone, Dad and I. He'd talk and I wouldn't listen. I cooked food he disliked or couldn't digest, and I locked the door of the theatre and kept the key on a nail out of his reach. I never washed him, till he hated the stink of himself. I sprayed him with after shave and perfume, toilet deodoriser, and laughed as he cringed from me.

None of it was enough.

It was never going to be enough. I wanted him used, drained, sucked out.

I took my girlfriend home to look at Dad.

We stood outside his bedroom window as the sun rose and watched him struggling from his bed to greet the day. He slept naked; I wouldn't help him into his pyjamas.

My girlfriend thought he was perfect. She helped me get the suitcase down from the cupboard, and watched from the car while I cajoled him out of the house. We laughed all the way there, her hand on my thigh. We felt committed; both our parents would be in the same home.

It brought tears to my eyes. It was only a small place, just a few mothers and fathers, ancient things; this one guilty of sexual abuse; that one of beatings; that mother nagged still, her purple tongue swollen from some unprescribed drug. My girlfriend's mother had her skin scrubbed in the bath. And scrubbed. And we could visit any time. We could watch it, stare at them, hate them even more.

I dropped him off and went to my own home. He saw something he didn't like before I left; his own greedy need perhaps, in someone else's eyes.

I said, "You'll fit right in, Dad. "They'll love you."

He fought like a demon to come back home with me.

My girlfriend and I visited often. We joked about our parents falling in love; everyone loved Dad there. The other residents and their occasional visitors. People loved to make him bleed, because he hated the sight of it. They pinned open his eyes and made him watch as they cut off a little toe and sold it to the highest bidder. They took his blood, plucked his white stringy hair, shaved his body. We watched from the gallery, my girlfriend and I, and we talked quietly about love and revenge.

You just have to be patient. You just have to wait until they're old and helpless.

Dad was in good company. One old man was daily raped and forced to perform orally. He liked it at first, I was told, but soon learned fear. A woman was hit every time she opened her mouth and sometimes when she didn't. She soon learned to bite her tongue.

In the dining room, hungry old people sat in front of food they hated. Some of it was mouldy, all of it was cold. They had to eat what was in front of them.

All the rooms were small and dark.

I felt unwonted tenderness when they let Dad wander the grounds in his nightshirt, a small figure with a painted face, laughter drawn in red around his mouth. He stroked and patted every part of his body. I imagined he was memorising it for the day it would be taken away from him completely.

The
Capture
Diamonds

The Capture Diamonds

Sarah's bedroom glittered with diamonds. Her eyes shone, too, as she held out a bandaged hand. I dropped two Capture diamonds into her palm, one pale mauve, one pale blue.

"Provenance?" she said. She read the pale blue sheet first. "48 year old male. Car accident. Meat eater." She sniffed his Capture diamond.

"Heat and pressure," I said, "turn human ash to diamonds. You can't smell anything." She smiled at me. The pale mauve Capture diamond was a 12 year old girl. Dead by stabbing. Known masturbator.

"Add this to the next one," Sarah said, passing me a small box. Inside was her pinkie finger, her last digit. What next? A foot? And who would she ask to amputate?

Ghost Jail

Ghost Jail

Rashmilla arrived early at the cemetery, knowing she would need to battle the other beggars for a good place, not too close to the grave of the much-loved leader, not too far away. Cars stretched for a kilometre, spewing exhaust as they idled, waiting to park.

Rashmilla's face was dirty because the water didn't run every day. She waved a laminated letter at the people, a piece of paper which proved her house burned down and her five children, too. Many carried such a letter. They shared it. Once, a house did burn down with five children, but it was not Rashmilla's house. Not her children. There was a fire, when Rasmilla was seven, her mother's house, her twin sister burned to death. Her childhood ghost, now, always seven, always with her.

Rashmilla had a sack full of dried peas to sell. Most people refused the peas with a wave of a hand. "Please, for my children," she said, holding out her hand. Her childhood ghost wreathed around her neck like a cobra.

People gave generously; they always did at funerals. It was the fear of punishment in the afterlife, punishment for greed or cruelty. Rashmilla waved peas at the outer mourners and was about to push her way further in when she noticed a young child trapped in a closed circle of gravestones. Whimpering. His family ignored him; they did not like to think about how he could be saved.

Rashmilla stepped in, ignoring the whirl of angry spirits, letting her twin sister snarl at them. She told the child, "It's okay, I can help you," then stepped out again. He kept whimpering and Rashmilla hissed, "Sshhhshhh, they don't like voices. Voices make them envious and wild."

She walked slowly around the circle, reading the dead names in a stilted, cautious way. Then she worked at each gravestone with her fingers, finding the one which was the loosest. This, she pried up and tipped over.

The circle broken, the boy stepped out, silent now. He glared at his family, as if to say, "A strange woman had to save me." Rashmilla put her hand out to the mother. "Please," she said. The woman ignored her. Rashmilla stepped forward; she would be paid for helping the boy.

"You need to say thank you." It was the Police Chief, come himself for the important funeral. He stood beside Rashmilla, twice as broad across, two heads taller than her.

The boy nodded, his mouth open. He glanced sideways, looking for his mother to help him out of trouble.

"Saying thank you would be a good idea," the Police Chief said, his voice gentle. "Give her money."

The boy ran; Rashmilla shook her head. "It doesn't matter," she said. "I didn't do it to be thanked."

"Why then?" The Police Chief leaned closer, intent.

"Simply that those ghosts need to be told."

"What about this man's ghost? Whose death we mourn?" Police Chief Edwards said. He led her to the graveside, pushing through as if the other mourners didn't exist. Her childhood ghost muttered in her ear.

"Did he die in peace?" Rashmilla whispered. Her childhood ghost nodded, much braver.

Police Chief Edwards didn't smile or respond. Rashmilla thought he would beat her. She said, "His peaceful death will give him quiet," and the police chief smiled.

A small man, dressed neatly, threw himself into the mud. "Murder! Murder!" he wailed, and he threw both arms up, reaching for the Police Chief, as if beseeching him to take the act back.

Out of nowhere, men appeared, police sticks in hand.

"Such bitterness," Police Chief Edwards said to Rashmilla. "Such anger. It was an unfortunate death."

"Who killed this great man?" the small, neat man shouted. "Who silenced his great voice, who stilled his tongue and stopped his hand? Ask the question, ask it! Murder! And the guilty dare to stand here!" He squealed as the policemen dragged him away.

Rashmilla shut her eyes, not wanting to see, but the men were close, so close she could smell hair oil. She stepped back from the conflict and tripped over a stone, too fast for her childhood ghost, who leaned forward, wanting a better look.

"I want to talk to you. Don't be frightened." Chief Edwards looked at her ghost, not at her. "In the van. We'll sit in the van and I will buy all your peas. Your day will be done." He held out his elbow to her. "Come on," he said. "I have tea in the van. I will read your letter."

He was being very kind to her. Nobody read her letter; no one cared about her house fire. He held her arm with gentle firmness.

In the van he poured her a tin cup of tea. It was black and strong and she felt the energy of it filling her as she sipped it.

He watched her, a smile on his face she didn't like. He said, "There was a man buried here today. I will not lie and say that he was a good man; for all I know he beat his wife and spent his children's school fees on beer. But he still deserves to rest easy. Lies will send him to a restless grave. That mourner should not tell lies about how he died."

The van had thick walls, Rashmilla thought. She could not hear the prisoner in the back. She nodded. "I heard what he said. He said this man was murdered."

"He wishes to discredit the very people who save this country."

She closed her eyes, but her childhood ghost watched, sitting on her lap.

"I saw what you did for that young boy."

"I don't need a thank you."

"What you both did for that young boy."

She blinked at him.

"I can see her. Your ghost."

"Most can't."

"It's a talent which can be learned. It can be useful."

"Not useful. A nuisance. Always the one to tell those bad ghosts what to do."

"Yes, I saw that. You have a way with them."

"I know them."

Chief Edwards considered her. "You come to the barracks in three days and ask for me. I think I have a job for you."

"A job? At the barracks?" She imagined herself with a bucket, a mop, hot, bloody water.

"The job is not at the barracks, no. At the Cewa Flats. We are helping people to relocate. You must have heard. You come in three days, and I will tell you what I need you to do."

"Selena in the Morning here, DJ to the disaffected. Up and at 'em, people, we can't change the world from bed." Her voice was sexy, deep. She liked to talk in that way, like silk between the fingers. "I hear they've cleared the Cewa Flats because beneath them are the remnants of early settlers. Treasures, power. Police Chief Edwards wants it cleared because he wants that shit for himself. He's willing to risk the cancer, I bet."

She played a message from him: "*Because the breath is all that remains when we die. All that remains of us. The body can be burned, can be buried. The breath exhaled is the very essence of us. If that is tainted, cancerous, then no passage from earth will be gained.*" His voice sounded so reasonable. "*It's for your own good to leave this place. This is no place for families. Children don't belong here.*"

Lisa Turner, already at the computer, getting an hour in before leaving for the newspaper office, listened and smiled. She liked to start the day with Selena.

Lisa wondered how she managed to stay sharp, out of their reach, when she spoke the truth. They didn't like the truth.

Selena whispered in her heart-felt voice, "He's gonna rip up that yard for something buried. His Great Malevolence is gonna dig the crap out of it and we all know what he's gonna find. A few old stones the museum would be interested in, nothing else. The man is a fool."

Selena launched into her soap opera, names changed to protect the innocent, but she went too far with it, and the next morning Lisa tuned in like she did every day, only to hear the dull voice of a company man, playing sweet tunes and letting the words rest. "We don't need words," he announced. "Now is the time for music."

Lisa's editor Keith led the protest to bring Selena back to the airwaves. He used the newspaper and printed sheets, on the street, in letter boxes, no names on there, no trouble. He used his contacts, his power. "Freedom of Speech the Victim," the campaign ran. Enough letters in, brave people willing to risk arrest to have their say and it was "Thank you, all of you," from Selena. A week after her removal she was back on the air. "I laughed so hard I split my pants when they banged on my door. No one wants to see my split pants. I have to be serious for just a moment. Thank you for wanting me back. I'll try to make it worth your while. I've got this for you; I've heard there's only one place in the city where electromagnetic interference means no bugging devices can be used. Cewa Flats. So if you're making a plot or think someone's watching you, this is the place for you. Sorry. I said I'd be serious and I lasted about a minute. Carry on without me for three minutes forty-five seconds," and she played a local song of Hibiscus flowers and the river running clean.

Lisa and Keith arrived at the Cewa Flats to cover the evacuation of the families. She'd driven past the flats many times. At first she'd felt guilty, in her good car with her warm clothes on, seeing the children in torn singlets, bare legs. Rubbish piles. She'd felt all the guilt of privilege. But that faded; she got busy, distracted by bigger stories. She drove past without even noticing now. The flats were so small you could see through the front window and out the back. Four storeys high, ten rooms on each storey, six buildings. All the corners broken off, and a great crack running down the middle of building C, so broad she could see sky through it. Graffiti, written and written again, illegible and meaningless. The bricks, once pale yellow, were dark-red. Lisa knew it was a chemical reaction within the pigment, but it looked blood-stained.

The children ran barefoot, in shorts too small, shirts too big.

Plastic bags full of belongings, the people waited for buses to transport them to their new homes. Lisa helped one woman with five children, each carrying two bags.

"We have nothing more," the mother said. Lisa had some canvas shopping bags in the car, and she gave them to the woman, helping her transfer the things. Grey, beige, some washed out colours. Wrapped in a torn shawl was a hard box; the woman nodded at it. "All we have. My grandmother's coin of release."

Lisa knew a lot of these people came from kidnapped slaves.

The mother spoke with her hand over her mouth. Others did, too, and some wore masks covering half their faces.

The children were mostly covered with head scarves.

"I can't breathe," one skinny little girl complained. "And this doesn't smell like air."

"You don't want to breathe until we leave. You don't want to catch Cancer of the Breath," the mother said to her.

Lisa shook her head. "You know there is no such thing. You can't get cancer of the breath."

"Oh? Then what is in my mouth to make this?" The woman dropped her bags, reached up and grabbed Lisa's ears, pulling her close.

The breath was awful, so bad Lisa gagged.

"You see? Even your white girl politeness can't stop you."

"That's not cancer of the breath. It's your teeth and gums."

"If you had children you would understand. You would not risk your child's breath to stay here."

"You should wear a scarf," the skinny little girl said to Lisa. "Your face is ugly and pink and shiny too much."

Lisa cared little for taunts about her burn scars. She was proud of them, proud of where they came from, though she never spoke of what she had achieved in getting them.

Other children rolled an old tyre to each other, a complex game with many a side.

A policeman gestured to the family. "The bus. Come on."

The mother gathered her children and they squeezed into the bus on laps, arms out the window.

"I'd like to come, see where you're being settled," Lisa said. The woman waved her away with a handflap.

Keith had been helping another family. He said, "I'm imagining where they're going has to be better than this." He patted her shoulder. "I'm looking into the land reports. You chase this story up."

Lisa followed the buses to the new settlement, forty-five minutes away. The air was cleaner out there, and the shacks lined up neatly, each facing away from the door of the next. There was the sense of a village about it.

Lisa watched the children run around and explore. The parents calling to each other, laughing.

"It seems okay," she reported back to Keith.

"What did you expect? A work camp?"

"You never know. I haven't figured out his justification for getting rid of them."

Three days later, Keith's house was seized, under the "Uncontrolled Verbiage" ruling. He had written his editorial without restraint. He'd lived life too easy; he didn't know how it could get. He wrote: *No one with any critical assessment thinks the transfer of families from Cewa Flats is solely to benefit the children, although anyone can see that the people are far better off. Their new place is much finer; it is the motivation I call into question.*

He rang Lisa, told her he was going to stay at Cewa Flats before they came to arrest him. "Last place they'll expect me to be. And I can do some good there, you know. Prove this breath cancer bullshit isn't true."

"And if you're there, others are there, they won't be able to go ahead with the redevelopment. It's not like they can pull the place down around you. People will be watching. I'll be watching."

"You be careful, Lisa. You write only the truth. Give the rumours to Selena."

They both laughed.

"Truth in print. Gossip on the radio. As it should be."

Lisa understood about covering up; many days she buried small pieces of information, anything which might connect her to the long-past fire. She did not regret her actions, but she was terrified of the results.

Selena in the Morning said, "I've got it here. The land assessment report of the Cewa Flats, and I'm not going to tell you who gave it me. It's real, though. You know I said there were treasures buried? It's a little more than that. According to the report, the land itself is worth something, and the dirt, it's full of some sort of shit we need. Why should The Government get it, just like that?" The radio went quiet for a moment. Then music.

Selena was silent for three days, then Lisa pushed her way in for an interview with Police Chief Edwards. She lied; said it was a piece about mothers' cooking, how good it is, favourite recipes.

He was a big man, charming, with a dazzling smile. If she'd met him at a bar, any pick up line would have worked.

He was furious when he realised where she stood. "How dare you? I am not a monster. I want families to be safe from people like you and your cancerous words." He threw her out, hissing, "Write nothing. Say nothing."

That night, Lisa heard a crash of glass downstairs and reached for the phone. Voices, and she knew for sure there was someone in the house.

She dialled Keith but his mobile didn't work; all she heard was a high-pitched squeal. Then she dialled her neighbours, hoping one would at least look out the window, shout at the invaders. No answer. Finally, in desperation, she called the police. She flipped open her computer and logged on at the same time.

The phone rang a dozen times. She heard the men downstairs, moving around as if they were looking for something. She quietly shut her bedroom door, then moved to look out of the window. It was barred; she had no chance of getting out that way.

"Hold, please," the operator said.

Music, some old pop song, played on bells. "Help," she whispered. She hid in the cupboard. She didn't care what the men took; they could have it all. She didn't want to disturb them. They carried machetes, these home invaders, and guns. They would not always try to kill, but she knew that many arrived out of it on booze or drugs.

"Hello?" she whispered into the phone. Footsteps on the stairs.

"Can I help you?" The cold, hard voice of the operator.

"My home is being invaded," she whispered. She gave her address. "Hold, please." The operator was remarkably calm; unaffected.

"Lisa Turner?" This came through the door. They knew her name.

"Lisa Turner, we have a warrant for the repossession of your home due to uncontrolled verbiage activity."

Lisa felt deep relief. Every day she spent in fear that her moment of activism would catch up with her, the grieving relatives perhaps would track her down and ask her why people had to die for her cause. Lisa did not regret the fire. The building had been on sacred ground and the activities inside destroyed the souls of the true residents of the country. She was sorry that people had to die, but it had been necessary. She had lost contact deliberately with those who had instigated the attack; they had considered the deaths a victory, whereas she felt great pain, great guilt, and knew that she would have to atone for it one day.

The police operator hung up on her. As the men entered her room, Lisa hit send, and her notes went out to a dozen journalists and activists around the world.

She expected to be interviewed, locked up, but they gave her thirty minutes to pack her bag and leave her home.

They recommended a hotel for her to stay in, which made her laugh. They would watch her every move, listen to her every word.

Before he ran, Keith had told her, "We can't put friends or family at risk. If you need to, come join me. Don't go anywhere else. If they take your house, go there. It's the first stop. We'll get the bastards."

They confiscated Lisa's car, too, so she hailed a taxi to take her to the Cewa Flats. They passed through a roadblock at the end of the street; Lisa wondered who it was they were keeping out. All the way the driver cleared his throat, spitting out the window. When they arrived, he turned and smiled at her. His teeth were red. "I'll be out of this country soon. I keep my mouth shut. I'm just waiting for my visa to come through."

"You know it won't, don't you? You know they're not letting anyone out. They've cancelled all visas, all passports."

He shook his head. "University Girl. You don't know how this country goes. You shouldn't tell lies to us."

Lisa climbed out, paying him a generous tip. "Good luck with it," she said. He gave her such a look of hatred she mis-shut the door and had to do it again.

The flats were dirty and huge up close. She stepped forward, over a grey, cracked path. The front dirt area was empty of people, a rare thing. Even after the families left, the young men remained, and they would hang together in clumps, moving as one large mass, always something in their hands to be tossed up and down, up and down.

None of the young men were here. In their rooms? Lisa looked up at the many dark doorways. Doorless.

An old woman took her hand and squeezed it. "I am Rashmilla. I will guide you through the spirits." She had an odd shape, lumpy around the chest, as if she had a child hidden in there.

"Up there," she pointed. "You find a room up there. You scream if they bother you and I'll send my sister to talk to them."

Lisa saw the lump in Rashmilla's chest wriggle.

"You can see her?" Rashmilla whispered. She began to unbutton her dress; Lisa backed away, wanting to escape.

"If who bothers me?" Lisa said. "I have friends here, you know. They don't bother people. They speak the truth."

"I'm not talking about your friends, dear," Rashmilla said. "You will know when you meet one."

It was hard to tell a vacated room from an inhabited one. Families had left in a hurry, leaving rubbish, belongings behind. Small clay pots, some with grey ash to the rim, sat in many corners. Mouldy cushions, piles of mice-infested newspaper, remnants of clothes.

Lisa poked her head through a door on the top floor, saw a man sprawled on a mat and pulled back.

"Who's there? Who is it?" he called. "I'm at home."

Lisa backed away. He hadn't seen her and she didn't know him. He sounded desperate; too eager.

She changed her tactic after that; walked slowly past each door and tried to have a sideways peek through the shuttered window. The walls had posters, dismal and ancient attempts to bring colour and life to the small, dank rooms. They seemed embedded, welded to the walls.

She carried a small suitcase. She'd left the rest of her things behind in her house; she imagined the police would have been through everything by now and taken what they wanted. She found a room with a mat and a pile of empty, rusted tins, each with a dry residue at the bottom. She put down her suitcase and tried to find comfort. The rooms were three metres square, space for a mat and a sink which also did as a toilet, she could tell.

Looking from her window, all she could see were buildings; dark, rank, decrepit.

It was late—past eleven—and quiet. She curled onto her mat. It was hard and thin with smooth stains at either end. She pulled out a shirt and used that as a shield for her face.

In the morning, people started to emerge. A sense of community filled her. Of possibility. She could hear people talking quietly, and footsteps, people moving around, making breakfast, and, she hoped, coffee. She recognised faces; people she knew. From the inside out the room didn't look so bad. She had a view, when she stood on her toes and squinted, of a small shrove of trees which would bear fruit during the wet season. With a small breeze she fancied she could smell the fruit. It was intoxicating, like the first sniff of a good wine.

She liked wine. Felt an emptiness for it. That first sip around the dinner table, already knowing that the conversation would become free the more people drank. That soon they would be shouting, making plans, talking of outrages, human rights and moving the country forward.

She saw Rashmilla one floor down in the building to her left. She called out but her voice seemed muffled. She tried again but then... She opened her mouth to call out again and from her feet, from through the floor rose a tall thin ghost, a man with red lesions along his cheekbones. He raised his fist and she flinched, unprepared.

He thrust the fist into her mouth and out, so fast all she felt was a mouthful then nothing but the taste of anchovies left behind.

She reached to grab him but he leapt over the balcony, over so fast he blurred in her eyes.

She heard nothing.

She looked over and there was nothing, only Rashmilla looking up, her face serene.

Lisa ran; got to the stairwell, turned around and the ghost was right beside her, fist raised. With his other hand he shushed her, finger to lips.

She hated to be shushed. "I won't..." she started, but the fist again, in and out of her mouth again, how the hell? She couldn't even get her own fist in there.

She watched him this time over the side and down to the ground where he seemed to...disintegrate.

Lisa dragged herself down the stairs. There were people in many of the rooms, most with their hands over their ears. Others moved up and down the stairs, purposeless. She knew some of them, had sat and talked all night with them, but none of them acknowledged her or seemed willing to even meet her eyes.

Rashmilla slid up to her as she reached the bottom step. "I don't want peas," Lisa said, waving her away.

"Have you understood?"

Lisa's eyes adapted; she could see a young girl, the ghost of a young girl, resting herself on Rashmilla's chest. Lisa could see her face, her teeth, she could see the dirty scarf she wore around her neck.

"I understand I won't stay here." Lisa stepped away. Rashmilla grabbed her arm, reached out and touched Lisa's scarred cheek.

"You were burned badly in a fire. I look at you and think of loss. Of all the things gone in the fire."

Rashmilla had the skin of a child. Soft, pale brown, unblemished; it was wrong for her.

Lisa pushed past; Rashmilla hissed, "You behave ugly, you get the cancer of the breath."

"I don't believe you."

"It doesn't matter if you believe or not. This is not about belief." There were deep holes here, dug by bored children.

Lisa reached the stone path and trod carefully this time, lifting her foot over it.

Something grabbed her ankle, both ankles, and pulled her back. No time to prepare, she landed with a crack on her chin and lay there, pain blurring her thoughts of all else.

"You can't step over the gravestones," Rashmilla said, shaking her head. She dabbed at Lisa's chin with a filthy rag. "They moved them so carefully, laying them down one by one. It doesn't matter, though. The ghosts don't care about how gentle they were."

Lisa crawled from stone to stone and saw that Rashmilla was telling the truth; the names, the dates of the long-dead, the recently-dead, their stones laid close together.

Lisa pushed herself up and ran to her room, ignoring the whisper of the ghosts around her.

She turned on her laptop to send some emails, get some action. The outrage at such desecration; surely that would get a response. Her first message was to Selena. There was a woman of power, with a voice. Selena needed to know the place wasn't safe, that it wasn't a good place to meet. There were ghosts.

The battery was dead though, and she felt a sense of great disconnection.

Rashmilla knocked at their doors one by one. "You will listen to the speech," she told everyone, "You will listen when he speaks."

"Listen," her childhood ghost echoed, "Listen to the man in the van."

Police Chief Edwards, broadcasting through the speakers of his large white van, said, "Language is a violence. You lepers bring cancer of the breath to the people; it is best you are kept away from the deserving, the good people of this land who support what we are doing and accept it."

Lisa saw Keith, waved at him, wanting his help. *Look at me, look at me.* He scratched under his arms and went back inside.

She circled around Rashmilla then up the stairs to Keith's room. The smell of human waste was terrible. Did they all use the sinks? With barren ground surrounding the buildings, she couldn't see why people would use sinks for their toilet.

Keith lay on his mat. She had never seen him inactive; it looked odd. Even when he rested he would read, take notes, do something. He lay there, almost motionless.

"Keith," she said. "It's me. I'm here."

There was a stirring around her, like bats she couldn't see.

"They don't like you to talk loud," he said. He got up. "I'd ask you in but there's not really any room."

"There isn't. This place is awful, Keith. It's haunted."

"It's safe," he said, but his eyes were closed as he spoke.

"It's not safe. There are ghosts here who don't want us to speak."

"They don't like noise. They don't mind quiet talking."

"What about talking about our situation?" she said. Keith curled up away from her, blocking his ears with his shoulders, his hand over his mouth. At her ankles she felt a tugging, and she looked down to see the ghost of a legless man, his fist drawn, his face livid.

"Quiet," Keith whispered.

"I'm not staying here, Keith. This is not a haven. Haven't you realised that?"

The look he gave her made her feel shallow and empty.

Keith turned his back to her, curled up on his mat and hummed softly.

"We'll get out of here," Lisa said. "I'll find a way and we'll get out."

Keith gave a low moan, blocking his ears. Lisa felt a cool breeze behind her and turned to see a gelid old ghost of a woman, shaking with fury. The woman lifted her arms and flew at Lisa, clutching her fingers at Lisa's throat.

Lisa choked, trying to suck in air. It smelt like old potatoes.

The old woman thrust her thumbs into Lisa's mouth and pinched. The pain brought tears to her eyes. Her terror was so complete she felt as if another word would never come from her.

The old woman vanished in a faster-than-light flash. Lisa turned to see Keith, sitting up, hugging his knees.

"Shhh," he said.

She left him and went to lie on her own mat, to think. Surely she was able to think.

The moment she closed her eyes her head was filled with voices, a mess of noise she couldn't make sense of. The voices were flat, dull; it sounded like thirty people reading the newspaper aloud in language unfamiliar to them.

She lay with her eyes open, letting her body rest. She felt a deep exhaustion. She had not felt such sustained fear since the fire. That, at least, had been a tangible threat with an obvious course of action; if she was caught, she would confess and never give any names away.

Here... but there was something she could do. She scrabbled for her phone and found it. The battery was fully charged but she could get no signal except a high pitched squeal which made her want to jump out of the window.

Lisa tried again, and again, and once more to step over the stone path, but she couldn't. The ghosts screamed in her ears; she felt a pop, as if her eardrums had burst, and a sharp pain which felt like a knitting needle in one ear and out the other.

"Can you call someone to visit? I have a friend I want to contact."

Rashmilla shook her head. Her childhood ghost laughed, spun around.

"You can't leave."

"Will you call her for me? I'll pay you."

Rashmilla shook her head. "You don't want me to leave the ghosts alone. They are nice when I'm here."

"Nice?" Lisa looked at her to see if she was making a cruel joke.

"They behave for me."

"Why can you step out?"

"They don't know if I'm a ghost or a woman

"If we lift the stones will the circle be broken?" Lisa felt nausea and pain when trying to talk. The ghosts of two young boys with yellow eyes pulled her backwards.

"They are set in concrete. Cannot be lifted. You could read the names but they don't want to be released."

"Her name's Selena. She's on the radio."

Rashmilla nodded. "I know that lady. The Police Chief calls her Sell. He says, Sell, what do you think, but he doesn't listen to her answer. I see through every window. Sell lies naked with the Police Chief."

"Selena?" Lisa had never felt so stupid, so naïve, so ill-informed and betrayed. Her career was a joke; she could not research, write or investigate to save her life.

"How do we stop the ghosts?" she asked, looking over her shoulder. The ghosts rose up, snarling, teeth bared in fury.

"There is no way," Rashmilla said. "They don't like noise, they don't like talk, they are caught by the endless circle of stones."

A taxi pulled up, and a young man stepped out. Lisa knew him, the editor of a local "radical" magazine. She'd met him a few times at drinks, and they'd spoken of change, of affecting change. She'd emailed him at the moment her house was taken. She didn't know if he'd responded or not.

"Don't step in," she tried to shout, but the ghosts of the young boys kicked her shins, knocked her to the ground and hovered their filthy faces in hers. There were bleeding cuts on their cheekbones.

Rashmilla stepped out to greet him, then helped him into the circle. Her childhood ghost ruffled his hair, looked into his ears.

"Dale," Lisa said. One of the ghost boys grabbed her tongue, spat in her mouth. "Dale, lift the stones," she said, but he didn't hear her, didn't recognise her in the dirt. He caught his toe on a jagged corner and tripped. He broke his fall with the heel of one hand, and a sharp edge sliced into the soft mound and blood oozed out.

He walked his arrogant, hip-thrusting walk, past her to the stairs. Rashmilla helped him, but Lisa could see the ghosts hovering behind her, waiting for her to release him.

A scream came, harsh and odd in the silence.

She still had the energy to step forward and look, see what had caused the noise. Other people did too, men and women dragging themselves out of their small, stinking rooms to see Keith, fallen or pushed, splattered on the ground.

There was a sigh, a collective sigh, not of sorrow but of pure envy. "Lucky lucky lucky lucky lucky," Lisa heard, the people whispered, "Lucky lucky lucky" but none of them leapt over, none of them had the strength or the power to die.

Lisa opened her mouth to let the noise out, but around her the ghosts waved their fists and she swallowed it down.

Lisa thought of all the silenced voices and how many more there would be. Soon this place would be empty again, starved husks removed or left to rot or to be buried by anyone who had the strength.

She felt a great sense of impetus, of gravity.

Lisa said, "Do you have any matches?"

Rashmilla said, "Give me money." Lisa gave her all, gave her everything she had.

She thought clothing would burn well, so she went upstairs and put everything from her suitcase on. The t-shirt with "Bali - Party Town" on it that she wore to bed. The scarf her mother knitted her. The jeans she bought in Hong Kong and wished she'd bought ten pairs, because they were perfect.

She put all that on. She collected a can of fuel from under the stairs and stood there, out of sight. She struck a match.

The ghosts were furious, ripping out her hair, tearing it out in chunks, tripping her. The ghosts came at her and she felt her energy leaving. She had to finish it.

Lisa struck another match. She heard whining behind her. Rashmilla said, "What are you doing? You have made them angry." Her childhood ghost clung to her, hiding her eyes in the torn material of her dress.

Lisa set fire to her scarf, to the long sleeves of her shirt, to the cuffs of her jeans. She fell to her knees as she burnt, screaming with pain, so full of it she no longer noticed the ghosts. From the great heat to cold. She had been under anaesthetic three times before and this felt like it; the cold starting at the entry point, in the arm, and pumping with the blood till her heart was chilled to stillness.

She grabbed a gravestone and she felt something shifting, moving inside her. Her ghost lifting. The body slumped; her ghost flew up.

"You won't last. You are not meant for here," Rashmilla said. "You can't escape. We have tried." Her childhood ghost shook her head.

"Shhh," Lisa said, and thrust her fist into Rashmilla's mouth.

Keith joined her, fresh ghost, lacking bitterness, unconfined. They moved together, waiting for Police Chief Edwards, for Selena and others like them. Ready to fill their mouths with fists and hair, ready to stop their words and change the world.

The Gaze Dogs of
Nine Waterfall

The Gaze Dogs of Nine Waterfall

Rare dog breeds; people will kill for them. I've seen it. One stark-nosed curly hair terrier, over-doped and past all use. One ripped-off buyer, one cheating seller. I was just the go-between for that job. I shrank up small into the corner, squeezed my eyes shut, folded my ears over like a Puffin Dog, to keep the dust out.

I sniffed out a window, up and out, while the blood was still spilling. It was a lesson to me, early on, to always check the dog myself.

I called my client on his cell, confirming the details before taking the job.

"Ah, Rosie McDonald! I've heard good things about your husband."

I always have to prove myself. Woman in a man's world. I say I'm acting for my husband and I tell stories about how awful he is, just for the sympathy.

I'll bruise my own eye, not with make-up. Show up with an arm in a sling. "Some men don't like a woman who can do business," I say. "But he's good at what he does. An eye for detail. You need that when you're dealing dogs."

"I heard that. My friend is the one who was after a Lancashire Large. For his wife."

I remembered; the man had sent me pictures. Why would he send me pictures?

"He says it was a job well done. So you know what I'm after?"

"You're after a vampire dog. Very hard to locate. Nocturnal, you know? Skittish with light. My husband will need a lot of equipment."

"So you'll catch them in the day when they're asleep. I don't care about the money. I want one of those dogs."

"My husband is curious to know why you'd like one. It helps him in the process."

"Doesn't he talk?"

"He's not good with people. He's good at plenty, but not people."

"Anyway, about the dog: thing is, my son's not well. It's a blood thing. It's hard to explain even with a medical degree."

My ears ring when someone's lying to me. Even over the phone. I knew he was a doctor; I'd looked him up.

"What's your son's name?"

The silence was momentary, but enough to confirm my doubts there was a son. "Raphael," he said. "Sick little Raphael." He paused. "And I want to use the dog like a leech. You know? The blood-letting cure."

"So you just need the one?"

"Could he get more?'

"He could manage three, but your son..."

"Get me three," he said.

I thought, *Clinic. $5,000 each. Clients in the waiting room reading* Nature *magazine.*

There are dogs rare because of the numbers. Some because of what they are or what they can do.

And some are rare because they are not always seen.

I remember every animal I've captured, but not all of my clients. I like to forget them. If I don't know their faces I can't remember their expressions or their intent.

The Calalburun. I traveled to Turkey for this puppy. Outside of their birthplace, they don't thrive, these dogs. There is something about the hunting in Turkey which is good for them. My client wanted this dog because it has a split nose. Entrancing to look at. Like two noses grown together.

The Puffin Dog. Norwegian Lundehound. These dogs were close to extinction when a dog-lover discovered a group of them on a small island. He bred them up from five, then shared some with an enthusiast in America. Not long after that, the European dogs were wiped out, leaving the American dogs the last remaining.

The American sent a breeding pair and some pups back to Europe, not long before her own dogs were wiped out. From those four there are now about a thousand.

The dogs were bred to hunt Puffins. They are so flexible (because they sometimes needed to crawl through caves to hunt) that the back of their head can touch their spine. As a breed, though, they don't absorb nutrients well, so they die easily and die young. We have a network, the other dealers and I. Our clients want different things at different times so we help each other out. My associate in Europe knew of four Puffin Dogs.

It's not up to me to ponder why people keep these cripples alive. Animal protection around the world doesn't like it much; I just heard that the English RSPCA no longer supports Crufts Dog Show because they say there are too many disabled dogs being bred and shown. Dogs like the Cavalier King Charles Spaniel, whose skull is too small for its brain. And a lot of boxer dogs are prone to epilepsy, and some bulldogs are unable to mate, or are unable to give birth unassisted.

It's looks over health. But humans? Same same.

The Basenji is a dog which yodels. My client liked the sound and wanted to be yodeled to. I don't know how that worked out.

Tea cup dogs aren't registered and are so fragile and mimsy they need to be carried everywhere. Some say this is the breeders' way of selling off runts.

Then there's the other dogs. The Black Dogs, Yellow Dogs, the Sulphurous Beast, the Wide-Eyed Hound, the Wisht Hound, and the Hateful Thing: The Gabriel Hound.

I've never been asked to catch one of these, nor have I seen one, but godawful stories are told.

The only known habitat of the vampire dog is the island of Viti Levu, Fiji. I'd never been there but I'd heard others talk of the rich pickings. I did as much groundwork as I could over the phone, then visited the client to get a look at him and pick up the money. No paper trail. I wore tight jeans with a tear across the ass and a pink button up shirt.

He was ordinary; they usually are. The ones with a lot of money are always confident but this one seemed overly so. Stolen riches, I wondered. The ones who get rich by stealing think they can get away with everything. Two heads taller then me, he wore a tight blue Tshirt, blank. A rare thing; most people like to plaster jokes on their chests. He didn't shake my hand but looked behind me for the real person, my husband.

"I'm sorry, my husband was taken ill. He's told me exactly what I need to do, though," I said.

The client put his hand on my shoulder and squeezed. "He's lucky he's got someone reliable to do his dirty work," the guy said.

He gave me a glass of orange soda as if I were a child. That's fine; making money is making money.

I told him we'd found some dogs, but not for sale. They'd have to be caught and that would take a lot more.

"Whatever. Look, I've got a place to keep them."

He showed me into his backyard, where he had dug a deep hole. Damp. The sides smooth, slippery with mud. One push and I'd be in there.

I stepped back from the edge.

"So, four dogs?" he said. "Ask your husband if he can get me four vampire dogs."

"I will check." My husband Joe had his spine bitten half out by a glandular-affected bull dog, and all he could do was nod, nod, nod. Bobble head, I'd call him if I were a cruel person. I had him in an old people's home where people called him young man and used his tight fists to hold playing cards. When I visit, his eyes follow me adoringly, as if he were a puppy.

My real hunting partner was my sister-in-law Gina. She's an animal psychologist. An animal psychic, too, but we don't talk about that much. I pretend I don't believe in it, but I rely on the woman's instincts.

The job wouldn't be easy, but it never is in the world of the rare breed.

My bank account full, our husband and brother safe with a good stock of peppermints, Gina and I boarded a flight for Nadi, Fiji. Ten hours from LA, long enough to read a book, snooze, maybe meet a dog-lover or two. We transferred to the Suva flight, a plane so small I thought a child could fly it. They gave us fake orange juice and then the flight was done. I listened to people talk, about local politics, gossip. I listened for clues, because you never knew when you'll hear the right word.

Gina rested. She was keen to come to Fiji, thinking of deserted islands, sands, fruit juice with vodka.

The heat as we stepped off the plane was like a blanket had been thrown over our heads. I couldn't breathe in it and my whole body steamed sweat. It was busy but not crazy, and you weren't attacked by cabbies looking for business, porters, jewelry sellers. I got a lot of smiles and nods.

We took a cab which would not have passed inspection in New York and he drove us to our hotel, on Suva Bay. There were stray dogs everywhere, flaccid, unhealthy looking things. The females had teats to the ground, the pups mangy and unsteady. They didn't seem aggressive, though. Too hot, perhaps. I bought some cut pineapple from a man at the side of the road and I ate it standing there, the juice dripping off my chin and pooling at my feet. I bought another piece, and another, and then he didn't have any change so I gave him twenty dollars. Gina couldn't eat; she said the dogs put her off. That there was too much sickness.

I didn't sleep well. I felt slick with all the coconut milk I'd had with dinner; with the fish, with the greens, with the dessert. And new noises in a place keep me awake, or they entered my dreams in strange ways.

I got up as the sun rose and swam some laps. The water was warm, almost like bath water, and I had the pool to myself.

After breakfast, Gina and I took a taxi out to the latest sighting of vampire dogs, a farm two hours drive inland. I like to let the locals drive. They know where they're going and I can absorb the landscape and listen while they tell me stories.

The foliage thickened as we drove, dark leaves waving heavily in what seemed to me a still day. The road was muddy so I had to be patient; driving through puddles at speed can get you bogged. A couple of trucks passed us. Smallish covered vehicles with the stoutest workers in the back. They waved and smiled at me and I knew that four of them could lift our car out of the mud if we got stuck.

The trucks swerved and tilted and I thought that only faith was keeping them on the road.

The farm fielded dairy cows and taro. It seemed prosperous; there was a letter box rather than an old juice bottle, and white painted rocks lined the path.

There was no phone here, so I hadn't been able to call ahead. Usually I'd gain permission to enter, but that could take weeks, and I wanted to get on with the job.

I told the taxi driver to wait. A fetid smell filled the car; rotting flesh.

"Oh, Jesus," Gina said. "I think I'll wait, too." I saw a pile of dead animals at the side of a dilapidated shed; a cow, a cat, two mongooses. They could've been there since the attack a week ago.

"Wait there," I told Gina. "I'll call you if I need you."

Breathing through my mouth, I walked to the pile. I could see bite marks on the cow and the animals appeared to be bloodless, sunken.

"You are who?" I heard. An old Fijian woman, wearing a faded green t-shirt that said, 'Nurses know better' pointed at me. She looked startled. They didn't see many white people out here.

"Are you from the *Fiji Times*?" she said. "We already talked to them."

I considered for a moment how best to get the information. She seemed suspicious of the newsmakers, tired of them.

"No, I'm from the SPCA. I'm here to inspect the animals and see if we can help you with some money. If there is a person hurting the animals, we need to find that person and punish them."

"It's not a person. It is the vampire dogs. I saw them with my own eyes."

"This was done by dogs?"

She nodded. "A pack of them. They come out of there barking and yelping with hunger and they run here and there sucking their food out of any creature they find. They travel a long way sometimes, for new blood."

"So they live in the hills?" I thought she'd pointed at the mountains in the background. When she nodded, I realised my mistake. I should have said, "Where do they live?"

It was too late now; she knew what she thought I wanted to hear.

"They live in the hills."

"Doesn't anyone try to stop them?"

"They don't stop good. They are hot to the touch and if you get too near you might burn up."

"Shooting?"

"No guns. Who has a gun these days?"

"What about a club, or a spear? What about a cane knife? What I mean is, can they be killed?"

"Of course they can be killed. They're dogs, not ghosts."

"Do they bite people?"

She nodded. "If they can get close enough?"

"Have they killed anyone? Or turned anyone into a vampire?"

She laughed, a big, belching laugh which brought tears to her eyes. "A person can't turn into a vampire dog! If they bite you, you clean out the wound so it doesn't go nasty. That's all. If they suck for long enough you'll die. But you clean it out and it's okay."

"So what did they look like?"

She stared at me.

"Were they big dogs or small?" I measured with my hand, up and down until she grunted; knee high.

"Fur? What color fur?"

"No fur. Just skin. Blue skin. Loose and wrinkly."

"Ears? What were their ears like?"

She held her fingers up to her head. "Like this."

"And they latched onto your animals and sucked their blood?"

"Yes. I didn't know at first. I thought they were just biting. I tried to shoo them. I took a big stick and poked them. Their bellies. I could hear something sloshing away in there."

She shivered. "Then one of them lifted its head and I saw how red its teeth were. And the teeth were sharp, two rows atop and bottom, so many teeth. I ran inside to get my husband but he had too much *kava*. He wouldn't even sit up."

"Can I see what they did?" I said. The woman looked at me.

"You want to see the dead ones? The *bokola*?"

"I do. It might help your claim."

"My claim?"

"You know, the SPCA." I walked back to the shed.

Their bellies had been ripped out and devoured and the blood drained, she said.

There were bite marks, purplish, all over their backs and legs, as if the attacking dogs were seeking a good spot.

Insects and birds had worked on the ears and other soft bits.

I took a stick to shift them around a bit.

"The dogs will come for those *bokola*. You leave them alone." She waved at the pile of corpses.

"The dogs?"

"Clean-up dogs. First the vampires, then the clean-up. Their yellow master sends them."

"Yellow master?" She shook her head, squeezed her eyes shut. Tabu subject.

"You wouldn't eat this meat? It seems a waste."

"The vampire dogs leave a taste behind," the woman told me. "A *kamikamica* taste the other animals like. One of the men in my village cooked and ate one of those cows. He said it made him feel very good but now he smells of cowhide. He can't get the smell off himself."

"Are any of your animals left alive?"

The woman shook her head. "Not the bitten ones. They didn't touch them all, though."

"Can I see the others?" I would look for signs of disease, something to explain the sudden death. I wanted to be sure I was in the right place.

One cow was up against the back wall of the house, leaning close to catch the shade. There was a sheen of sweat on my body. I could feel it drip down my back.

"*Kata kata*," the woman said, pointing to the cow. "She is very hot."

It looked all right, apart from that.

I could get no more out of her.

Gina was sweating in the taxi. It was a hot day, but she felt the heat of the cow as well. "Any luck?" she said.

"Some. There's a few local taboos I'll need to get through to get the info we need, though."

"Ask him," she said, pointing at the driver. "He's Hindi."

Our taxi driver said, "I could have saved you the journey. No Fijian will talk about that. We Hindis know about those dogs."

He told us the vampire dogs lived at the bottom of Ciwa Waidekeulu. "Thiwa Why Ndeke Ulu," he said. Nine Waterfall. In the rainforest 20 minutes from where we were staying.

"She said something about a yellow master?"

"A great yellow dog who is worse than the worst man you've ever met."

I didn't tell him I'd met some bad men.

"You should keep away from him. He can give great boons to the successful, but there is no one successful. No one can defeat the yellow dog. Those who fail will vanish, as if they have never been." He stopped at a jetty, where some children sold us roti filled with a soft, sweet potato curry. Very, very good.

The girl who cleaned my room was not chatty at first, but I wanted to ask her questions. She answered most of them happily once I gave her a can of Coke. "Where do I park near Ciwa Waidekeulu? How do I ask the Chief for permission to enter? Is there fresh water?"

When I asked her if she knew if the vampire dogs were down there, she went back to her housework, cleaning a bench already spotless. "These are not creatures to be captured," she said. "They should be poisoned." To distract me, she told me that her neighbours had five dogs, every last one of them a mongrel, barking all night and scaring her children. I know what I'd do if I were her. The council puts out notices of dog poisonings, *Keep Your Dogs In While We Kill the Strays*, so all she'd have to do is let their dogs out while the cull was happening. Those dogs'd be happy to run; they used to leap the fence, tearing their guts, until her neighbour built his fence higher. They're desperate to get out.

They do a good job with the poisoning, she told me, but not so good with the clean up. Bloated bodies line the streets, float down the river, clog the drains.

They don't understand about repercussions, and that things don't just go away.

The client was pleased with my progress when I called him. "So, when will you go in?"

With the land taboo, I needed permission from the local chief or risk trouble. This took time. Most didn't want to discuss the vampire dogs, or the yellow dog king; he was forbidden, also. "It may be a couple of weeks. Depends on how I manage to deal with the locals."

"Surely a man would manage better," he said. "I know your husband doesn't like to talk, but most men will listen to a man better. Maybe I should send someone else."

"Listen," I told him, hoping to win him back, "I've heard they run with a fat cock of a dog. Have you heard that? People have seen the vampire dogs drop sheep hearts at this dog's feet. He tossed the heart up like it was a ball, snapped it up."

The man smacked his lips. I could hear it over the phone. "I've got a place for him, if you catch him as well."

"If you pay us, we'll get him. There are no bonus dogs."

"Check with your husband on that."

I thought of the slimy black hole he'd dug.

"They say that if you take a piece of him, good things will come your way. People don't like to talk about him. He's taboo."

"They just don't want anyone else taking a piece of him."

We moved to a new hotel set amongst the rainforest. The walls were dark green in patches, the smell of mold strong, but it was pretty with birdsong and close to the waterfalls which meant we could make an early start.

We ate in their open air restaurant, fried fish, more coconut milk, Greek meatballs. Gina didn't like mosquito repellant, thinking it clogged her pores with chemicals, so she was eaten alive by them.

"Have you called Joe?" she asked me over banana custard.

"Have you?" We smiled at each other; wife and sister ignoring him, back home and alone.

"We should call him. Does he know what we're doing?'

"I told him, but you know how he is." She was a good sister, visiting him weekly, reading to him, taking him treats he chewed but didn't seem to enjoy.

We drank too much Fijian beer and we danced around the snooker table, using the cues as microphones. No one seemed bothered, least of all the waiters.

The next morning, we called a cab to drop us at the top of the waterfall. You couldn't drive down any further. In the car park, souvenir sellers sat listlessly, their day's takings a few coins that jangled in their pockets. Their faces marked with lines, boils on their shins, they leaned back and stared as we gathered our things together.

"I have shells," one boy said.

"No turtles," Gina said, flipping her head at him to show how disgusting that trade was to her.

"Not turtles. Beetles. The size of a turtle."

He held up the shell to her. There was a smell about it, almost like an office smell; cleaning fluids, correcting fluids, coffee brewed too long. The shell was metallic gray and marbled with black lines. Claws out the side, small, odd, clutching snipers. I had seen, had eaten, prawns with claws like this. Bluish and fleshy, I felt like I was eating a sea monster.

"From the third waterfall," the seller said. "All the other creatures moved up when the dogs moved into Nine Waterfall."

I'm in the right place, I thought. "So there are dogs in the waterfall?"

"Vampire dogs. They only come out for food. They live way down."

An older vendor hissed at him. "Don't scare the nice ladies. They don't believe in vampire dogs."

"You'd be surprised what I believe in," Gina said. She touched one finger to the man's throat. "I believe that you have a secret not even your wife knows. If she learns of it, she will take your children away."

"No."

"Yes." She gave the boy money for one of the shells and opened her large bag to place it inside.

He said, "You watch out for yellow dog. If you sacrifice a part of him you'll never be hungry again. But if you fail you will die on the spot and no one will know you ever lived. If you take the right bit you will never be lonely again."

I didn't know that I wanted a companion for life.

As we walked, I said, "How did you know he had a secret?"

"All men have secrets."

The first waterfall was overhung by flowering trees. It was a very popular picnic site. Although it took 20 minutes to reach, Indian women were there with huge pots and pans, cooking roti and warming dhal while the men and children swam. I trailed my hand in the water; very cool, not the pleasant body-temperature water of the islands, but a refreshing briskness.

Birsdsong here was high and pretty. More birds than I'd seen elsewhere broadbills, honey-eaters, crimson and masked parrots, and velvet doves. Safe here, perhaps. The ground was soft and writhing with worms. The children collected them for bait, although the fish were sparse. Down below, the children told us, were fish big enough to feed a family of ten for a week. They liked human bait, so men would dangle their toes in. I guessed they were teasing us about this.

The path to the second waterfall was well-trodden. The bridge had been built with good, treated timber and seemed sturdy.

The waterfall fell quietly here. It was a gentler place. Only the fisherman sat by the water's edge; children and women not welcome. The fish were so thick in the water they could barely move. The fishermen didn't bother with lines; they reached in and grabbed what they wanted.

Gina breathed heavily.

"Do you want to slow down a bit? I don't think we should dawdle, but we can slow down," I said.

"It's not that. It's the fish. I don't usually get anything from fish, but I guess there's so many of them. I'm finding it hard to breathe."

The men stood up to let us past.

"There are a lot of fish," I said. Sometimes the obvious is the only thing to say. "Where do they come from?" I asked one of the men. "There are so few up there." I pointed up to the first waterfall.

"They come from underground. The centre of the earth. They are already cooked when we catch them, from the heat inside."

He cut one open to demonstrate and it was true; inside was white, fluffy, warm flesh. He gestured it at me and I took a piece. Gina refused. The meat was delicate and sweet and I knew I would seek without finding it wherever else I went in the world.

"American?" the man said.

"New Zealand," Gina lied.

"Ah, Kiwi!" he said. "Sister!" They liked the New Zealanders better than Australians and Americans because of closer distance, and because they shared a migratory path. Gina could put on any accent; it was like she absorbed the vowel sounds.

I could have stayed at the second waterfall but we had a job to do, and Gina found the place claustrophobic.

"It's only going to get worse," I said. "The trees will close in on us and the sky will vanish."

She grunted. Sometimes, I think, she found me very stupid and shallow. She liked me better than almost anybody else did, but sometimes even she rolled her eyes at me.

The third waterfall was small. There was a thick buzz of insects over it. I hoped not mosquitoes; I'd had dengue fever once before and did not want hemorrhagic fever. I stopped to slather repellant on, strong stuff which repelled people as well.

The ground was covered with small, green shelled cockroaches. They were not bothered by us and I could ignore them. The ones on the tree trunks, though; at first I thought they were bark, but then one moved. It was as big as my head and I couldn't tell how many legs. It had a jaw which seemed to click and a tail like a scorpion which it kept coiled.

"I wouldn't touch one," Gina said.

"Really? Is that a vision you had?"

"No. They just look nasty," and we shared a small laugh. We often shared moments like that, even at Joe's bedside.

Gina stumbled on a tree root the size of a man's thigh.

"You need to keep your eyes down," I said. "Downcast. Modest. Can you do that?"

"Can you?"

"Not really."

"Joe always liked 'em feisty."

Gina's breath came heavy now and her cheeks reddened.

"It's going to be tough walking back up."

"It always is. I don't even know why you're dragging me along. You could manage this alone."

"You know I need you to gauge the mood. That's why."

"Still. I'd rather not be here."

"I'll pay you well. You know that."

"It's not the money, Rosie. It's what we're doing. Every time I come out with you it feels like we're going against nature. Like we're siding with the wrong people."

"You didn't meet the client. He's a nice guy. Wants to save his kid."

"Of course he does, Rosie. You keep telling yourself that."

I didn't like that; I've been able to read people since I was 12 and it became necessary. Gina's sarcasm always confused me, though.

At the fourth waterfall, we found huge, stinking mushrooms, which seemed to turn to face us.

Vines hung from the trees, thick enough we had to push them aside to walk through. They were covered with a sticky substance. I'd seen this stuff before, used as rope, to tie bundles. You needed a bush knife to cut it. I'd realized within a day of being here you should never be without a bush knife and I'd bought one at the local shop. I cut a dozen vines, then coiled them around my waist.

Gina nodded. "Very practical." She was over her moment, which was good. Hard to work as a team with someone who didn't want to be there.

What did we see at the fifth waterfall? The path here was very narrow. We had to walk one foot in front of the other, fashion models showing off.

There were no vines here. The water was taken by one huge fish, the size of a Shetland pony. The surface of the water was covered with roe and I wondered where the mate was. Another underground channel? It would have to be a big one. It would be big but confining. My husband is confined. I'm happy with him that way. He can't interfere with my business. Tell me how to do things.

At the sixth waterfall, we saw our first dog. It was very small and had no legs. Born that way? It lay in the pathway unmoving, and when I nudged it, I realized it was dead.

Gina clutched my arm. Her icy fingers hurt and I could feel the cold through my layers of clothing.

"Graveyard," she said. "This is their graveyard."

The surface of the sixth pool was thick with belly-up fish. At the base of the trees, dead insects like autumn leaves raked into a pile.

And one dead dog. I wondered why there weren't more.

"He has passed through the veil," Gina said, as if she were saying a prayer. "We should bury him."

"We could take him home to the client. He already has a hole dug in his backyard. He's kind of excited at the idea of keeping dogs there."

Is there a name for a person who takes pleasure in the confinement of others?

We reached the seventh waterfall.

We heard yapping, and I stiffened. I opened my bag and put my hand on a dog collar, ready. Gina stopped, closed her eyes.

"Puppies," she said. "Hungry."

"What sort?"

Gina shook her head. We walked on, through a dense short tunnel of wet leaves.

At the edge of the seventh waterfall there was a cluster of small brown dogs. Their tongues lapped the water (small fish, I thought) and when we approached, the dogs lifted their heads, widened their eyes and stared.

"Gaze Dogs," I said.

These were gaze dogs like I'd never seen before. Huge eyes. Reminded of the spaniel with the brain too big.

"Let's rest here, let them get used to us," Gina said.

I glanced at my watch. We were making good time; assuming we caught a vampire dog with little trouble, we could easily make it back up by the sunfall.

"Five minutes."

We leaned against a moss-covered rock. Very soft, damp, with a smell of underground.

The gaze dogs came over and sniffled at us. One of the puppies had deep red furrows on its back; dragging teethmarks. I had seen this sort of thing after dog fights, dog attacks. Another had a deep dent in its side, filled with dark red scab and small yellow pustules. Close up, we could see most of the dogs were damaged in some way.

"Food supply?" Gina said.

I shuddered. Not much worried me, but these dogs were awful to look at.

One very small dog nuzzled my shoe, whimpering. I picked it up; it was light, weak. I tucked it into my jacket front. Gina smiled at me. "You're not so tough!"

"Study purposes." I put four more in there; they snuggled up and went to sleep.

She seemed blurry to me; it was darker than before. Surely the sun wasn't further away. We hadn't walked that far. My legs ached as if I had been hiking for days.

At the eighth waterfall we found the vampire dogs. Big, gazing eyes, unblinking, watching every move we made. The dogs looked hungry, ribs showing, stomachs concaved.

"They move fast," Gina whispered, her eyes closed. "They move like the waterfall."

The dogs swarmed forward and knocked me down. Had their teeth into me in a second, maybe two.

The feeling of them on me, their cold, wet paws heavy into my flesh, but the heat of them, the fiery touch of their skin, their sharp teeth, was so shocking I couldn't think for a moment, then I pulled a puppy from my jacket and threw it.

Their teeth already at work, the dogs saw the brown flash and followed it.

They moved so fast I could still see fur when they were gone.

I threw another puppy and another vampire dog peeled off with a howl. The first puppy was almost drained, its body flatter, as if the vampires sucked out muscle, too.

"Quick," Gina said. "Quick." She had tears in her eyes, feeling the pain of the puppies, their deaths, in her veins.

I threw a third puppy and we ran down, away from them. We should have run up, but they filled the path that way.

I needed a place to unpack my bag, pull out the things I'd need to drop three of them. Or four.

We heard a huffing noise; an old man coughing up a lifetime. We were close to the base and the air was so hard to breathe we both panted. Gina looked at me.

"It must be the alpha. The yellow dog."

It seemed to me she stopped breathing for a moment.

"We could try to take a piece of him. We'd never be lonely again, if we did that."

The vampire dogs growled at us, wanting more puppies. The last two were right against my belly; I couldn't reach them easily and I didn't want to.

"I don't want to see the ninth waterfall," Gina said. I shook my head. If the vampire dogs were this powerful, how strong would he be?

"It's okay. I'm ready now. I'll take three of them down quietly; the others won't even notice. Then we'll have to kick our way out."

She nodded.

We turned around and he was waiting. That dog.

He was crippled and pitiful but still powerful. His tail, his ears and his toes had been cut off by somebody brave. Chunks of flesh were gone from his side. People using him as sacrifice for gain.

Gina was impressive; I could see she was in pain. Was she feeling the dog's pain? She was quiet with it, small grunts. She walked towards him.

The closer she got to the dog the worse it seemed to get. "I want to lay hands on him, give him comfort," Gina said.

The dog was the ugliest I've ever seen. Of all the strays who've crossed my path here, this one was the most aggressive. This dog would make a frightening man, I thought. A man I couldn't control. Drool streamed down his chin.

He sat slouched, rolled against his lower back. Even sitting he reached to my waist.

All four legs were sprawled. He reminded me of an almost-drunk young man, wanting a woman for the night and willing to forgo that last drink, those last ten drinks, to achieve one. Sprawled against the bar, legs wide, making the kind of display men can.

His fur was the color of piss, that golden color you don't want to look at too hard, and splotched with mud, grease, and something darker.

One ear was half bitten off. The other seemed to stand straight up, unmoving, like a badly made wooden prosthetic.

One lip was split, I think; it seemed blurry at this distance.

He licked his balls. And his dog's lipstick stuck out, fully 12cm long, pink and waving.

Thousands of unwanted puppies in there.

He wasn't threatening; I felt sorry for him. He was like a big boy with the reputation of being a bully, who has never hurt anyone.

But when we got close to the yellow dog I realized he was perfect, no bits missing. An illusion to seduce us to come closer. Gina stepped right up to him.

"Gina! Come back!" but she wouldn't.

"If I comfort him, he will send me a companion. A lifetime companion," she said.

"Come live with me!" I said. "We'll take some gaze dogs, rescue them. We'll live okay."

He reared back on his hind legs and his huge skull seemed to reach the trees. He lifted his great paw high.

Around our feet, the vampire dogs swarmed. I grabbed one. Another. I sedated them and shoved them in my carry bag.

The yellow dog pinned Gina with his paws. The vampire dogs surrounded him, a thick blue snarling band around him.

I threw my last two gaze dogs at them but they snapped at them too quickly. I had no gun. I picked up three rocks and threw one, hard. Pretended it was a baseball and it was three balls two strikes.

The vampire dogs swatted the rock away as if it were a dandelion. I threw another, and the last, stepping closer each time.

The yellow dog had his teeth at Gina's throat and I ran forward, thinking only to tear her away, at least drag her away from his teeth.

The vampire dogs, though, all over me, biting my eyes, my ears, my lips.

I managed to throw them off, though perhaps they let me.

The yellow dog sat crouched, his mouth covered with blood. At his paws, I thought I saw hair, but I wondered: *what human has been down here? Who else but me would come this far?*

I backed away. Two sleeping vampire dogs in my bag made no noise and emitted no odour; I was getting away with it. They watched me go, their tongues pink and wet. The yellow dog; again, from afar he looked kindly. A dear old faithful dog. I took two more vampire dogs down, simple knock out stuff in a needle, and I put them in my bag. A soft blanket waited there; no need to damage the goods.

I picked up another gaze dog as I walked. This one had a gouge in his back, but his fur was pale brown, the colour of milk chocolate. He licked me. I put him down my jacket, then picked up another for a companion.

It took me hours to reach the top. Time did not seem to pass, though. Unless I'd lost a whole day. When I reached second waterfall, there were the same fishermen. And the families at first waterfall, swimming, cooking and eating as if there was no horror below them. They all waved at me but none offered me food or drink.

The souvenir salesmen were there at the top. "Shells?" they said. "Buy a shell. No sale for a week, you know. No sale. You will be the first." I didn't want a shell; they came from the insects I'd seen below and didn't want to be reminded of them.

I called a cabbie to take me to my hotel. I spent another day, finalizing arrangements for getting the dogs home (you just need to know who to call) then I checked out of my room.

The Doctor was happier than I'd thought he'd be. Only two dogs had survived, but they were fit and healthy and happily sucked the blood out of the live chicken he provided them.

"You were right; you work well alone," he said. "You should dump that husband of yours. You can manage alone."

I'd just come from visiting Joe and his dry-eyed gaze, his flaccid fingers, seemed deader than ever. The nurses praised me up, glad there was somebody for him. "Oh, you're so good," they said. "So patient and loyal. He has no one else." Neither do I, I told them.

A month or so later, the Doctor called me. He wanted to show me the dogs; prove he was looking after them properly.

A young woman dressed in crisp, white clothes answered the door.

"Come in!" she said.

"You know who I am?"

Leading me through the house, she gave me a small wink. "Of course."

I wasn't sure I liked that.

She led me outside to the backyard; it was different. He'd tiled the hole and it was now a fish pond. The yard was neater, and lounge chairs and what looked like a bar were placed in a circle. Six people sat in the armchairs, reading magazines, sipping long drinks.

"He didn't tell me there was a party."

"Take a seat. Doctor will be with you shortly," the young woman said. Three of the guests looked at their watches as if waiting for an appointment.

I studied them. They were not a well group. Quiet and pale, all of them spoke slowly and lifted their glasses gently as if in pain or lacking strength. They all had good, expensive shoes. Gold jewelry worn with ease. The Doctor had some wealthy friends.

They made me want to leap up, jump around, show off my health.

The young woman came back and called a name. An elderly woman stood up.

"Thank you, nurse," she said. It all clicked in then; I'd been right. The doctor was charging these people for treatment.

It was an hour before he dealt with his patients and called me in.

The vampire dogs rested on soft blankets. They were bloated, their eyes rolling. They could barely lift their heads.

"You see my dogs are doing well."

"And so are you, I take it. How's your son?'

He laughed. "You know there's no son."

He gave me another drink. His head didn't bobble. We drank vodka together, watching the vampire dogs prowl his yard, and a therapist would say my self-loathing led me to sleep with him.

I crawled out of the client's bed at 2 or 3 am, home to my gaze dogs. They were healing well and liked to chew my couch. They jumped up at me, licking and yapping, and the three of us sat on the floor, waiting for the next call to come in.

Afterword

Afterword

When the editor asked the writer, "Where do you get your ideas?", Ms Warren vanished. Where she had stood was a ball of string, $4.35 in coins, three polystyrene cubes, a single square of dark chocolate wrapped in gold foil, and the following notes.

Dead Sea Fruit

This story started cruelly. I was bored at a folk music evening. I don't mind folk music but this night was really awful, full of talentless musicians and body odour. I had to stay to the end because a friend was playing then. So I distracted myself, as I do when bored, by looking around the room and inventing stories.

I saw wreathes of smoke crawling up the wall and sneaking out one small open window. Did I mention it was very smoky and warm in this place? I envied that escaping smoke.

There was a woman, moving from table to table, throwing her head back, laughing. There's a woman like that in every social group; one who knows everybody, who is the centre of it.

This sentence came into my head: I kissed every man in the room until I found the one who tasted of ash.

As the story developed, both the line and the woman disappeared. But the taste remained.

WOMAN TRAIN

I wanted to capture the rhythm of the train in this story, so wrote it line by line, like a poem. I wasn't sure whether to present it that way or not, but in the end thought it interrupted the story if I did.

I wrote it after an Anzac Day dawn service in Canberra. These early mornings are very moving; you get a strong sense of the lost sons and husbands. Less of the lost daughters and wives.

DOWN TO THE SILVER SPIRITS

I feel very lucky to have my children, but I also understand those who choose not to have children. They're lucky, too.

The unlucky ones are those who are desperate to have children and can't. It took me three or four months to fall pregnant with my son and that seemed like a very long time. Some people struggle for years and it never happens. Even after four months, I felt the beginning of desperation and despair.

Taking this feeling to the extreme led me to the men and women of this story. They are not like most others; their obsession takes over their lives and they are no longer functioning members of society.

I took this story away with me on a writer's retreat, and it was helped greatly by the input of the others, especially Deborah Kalin.

FRESH YOUNG WIDOW

This is one of the rare times the title of the story came to me first, and I wrote around it. The image of the dead being encased in clay came to me as I imagined the lonely young widow.

COALESCENCE

I wanted to create a really creepy character in Schizo Blogger. The idea of personality being transferred from one person to the next isn't new, and I think I have another four or five variations of the idea ready to be written.

Cooling the Crows

This is one of the first stories I wrote while living in Fiji, and I can see the influences easily. Along the main road which travels along the coast from Suva to Nadi is a huge pile of decayed cars, and even in three years the nature of these cars changed as the plants took them.

Also, before we left we took some 'self-protection' lessons, and mostly what we were told was that in order to stand up to violence, you had to accept it. Allow it into your life. This philosophy fascinated me and I wondered about a man who really lived by violence.

The pub itself was inspired by a country pub just out of Canberra. It was a bikie's hang out for a long time; then it burned down. We drove past it a month or so later, and the bikies were there, in the carpark, next to the burnt out building. Still drawn to the place even though it no longer existed.

Buster and Corky

Autobiographical stories? Never! Except this one. Something very like this happened to my Auntie.

Edge of a Thing

This is another Fiji story and I can trace much of what I saw and learnt while living there when I read it.

The killing stone which opens the story sits in the Fiji Museum, a small, underused but fascinating place. You really can see a dark bloodstain around the smooth curve at the top.

The story of developed land being cursed is not a new one, but it was one told to me again and again while I was there.

Fijians are known for their very long weddings which can start quite late. I went to an Indian one; my friend and I arrived about half an hour late, thinking we'd have to sneak in guiltly. The hall was still half empty and for the next three hours, people drifted in and out while a long service was held on stage. I loved it; I could sit and stare, listen, observe. And we got fed too; I've never had a better gulab jaman.

GUARDING THE MOUND

I loved writing this story. It was one of the first stories I wrote after having my second child. I was exhausted, physically on the go all the time with barely any time to read, let alone write. This story came to me and I wrote it in a frenzy, writing while rocking the pram, stirring the bolognaise, and, in my head, while reading a kids' book for the fiftieth time. It reminded me I was a writer, that I loved to write, and that stories did come to me easily sometimes.

STATE OF OBLIVION

My sister and I came up with this setting together. She imagined a world above the clouds at the same time I was reading about lost mountain families. I wondered about the isolation and so did she; I merged the two together.

THE SOFTENING

I have a gorgeous piece of art from Canberra sculptor Stephen Harris. http://harrison.mogkat.com/html/praguecastle3.htm

Stephen's work fills me with ideas. I sat with notepad and pen, the sculpture on the table and I free-associated the basic story line of "The Softening".

THE GRINDING HOUSE

I did a lot of walking when my kids were little. Really, a fuck of a lot. My left heel started to ache, then it caused me real pain. Eventually, I forced myself to see a podiatrist, who thought I had spurs in my foot.

I'd never heard of them before and the very idea made me feel ill. My bones, growing inside my flesh?

Ugh.

My spurs went away, but the idea for "The Grinding House" was born.

It's odd how you remember small things. Sometimes they pop into a story and I don't realize until later. The character of Nick, I say, "Smells of milk." I always remember a boy at a school holiday program. I must have been about 9. He smelt of milk, sweet, fresh milk. I wished I smelled like that but I never did, no matter how much milk I drank. When I wanted to create a sweet character in Nick, I made him smell of milk.

GREEN

In Fiji, there are trees that are considered haunted. Some of these look very inviting; a wide canopy with space underneath for a pleasant picnic. While researching this story, I read about tests for copper in the soil, and that's where the idea for "Green" came from.

SINS OF THE ANCESTORS

I had the idea for this story a while ago, and it's been percolating ever since. I like the idea that we pay for the sins of our ancestors, because in a way it's true. Each generation is stronger or weaker because of the actions of the parents and the grandparents.

DOLL MONEY

One of the few stories in which the protagonist appears to be quite happy.

In this story I talk about a daughter hoping to pretend her father is alive. So much of fiction is reflected in reality; a news story has just been released of a Japanese family who kept their father's death a secret for thirty years. He was actually registered as the oldest man in the world, and he'd been dead for thirty years!

THE GIBBET BELL

After my mother-in-law died, her bedroom was left as it was for over a year. We spent a night there once, and I felt her presence strongly. There was a bell on her dressing table and I wondered what it was for. I wrote this story in my head, lying in the bed. My mother-in-law was nothing like the woman in the story.

IN THE DRAWBACK

Don't you love the shore? The way the water pulls back and returns, pulls back and returns, and the way the mood changes by the minute as you watch and breathe in the salt smell. I love what is revealed as the water draws back, and this story imagines what a world would be like if that water did not return.

The cities of Bruge and Lympne both suffered permanent drawback, I've read.

THE CENSUS-TAKER'S TALE

When Dirk Flinthart put the word out for shared-world stories inspired by Chaucer's *Canterbury Tales*, my first thought was that I'd love to read the book but didn't think I'd be able to come up with anything suitable. I remembered something, though, that I'd noted years earlier; Chaucer was a census-taker.

Thinking about this sparked a story, as did reading about the ghostly beliefs in parts of England.

Of course, when I found my original note, I realized that Chaucer was actually a Customs' man, not a census-taker.

Now that would have been a different story all together.

HIS LIPSTICK MINX

I wanted to capture the sense of a woman enslaved, men caught in hateful jobs and the feeling of a stomach full of lipstick. It was inspired by the story of a woman arrested as a prostitute because she carried lipstick in her handbag.

POLISH

I use the Australian country pub a few times in my stories. I think it's the fact it acts as a microcosm of the local society.

The idea for the story came when I was visiting a friend's mother, and the house smelt very strongly of polish. For some reason I imagined a ghost, polishing, polishing. Maybe I was bored and imagining stories again? I can't remember.

THE CORAL GATHERER

Another of my Fiji stories. This one was written while sitting in a resort. Most people would likely not write a story like this at a resort, but that's just me.

BONE DOG

The plot device in this story is a mother who doesn't return to her children, who leaves them alone in an apartment. When I wrote it, I didn't think a mother doing this deliberately would be believed, so I added in a hit and run driver to kill her off. Of course, mothers like this are in the news all the time. Not long after the story was published, there was a news item about a woman who left her kids in the house to go to a casino for a couple of days.

TONTINE MARY

The Tontine was a popular form of life insurance in England and France in the 17th and 18th centuries. Members entered a large sum of money; the last person left alive won the lot.

The first French Tontine was won by a 96 year old woman just before her death, and the first English Tontine was won in a similar manner.

Tontines were made illegal once the authorities realised how many unnatural deaths, unlikely accidents and unfortunate incidents occurred amongst the members.

I've been fascinated by Tontines since I was about nine. I can't remember how I first read about them, but I did read widely then as I do now. I always wanted to write a story about one and the shared world setting of New Ceres was the perfect foil.

A POSITIVE

I've seen the short film Bearcage Productions made of this story. When I watch it, I think, "Jeez, I really am a bit weird, aren't I, to come up with that?"

Kirstyn McDermott had very early input into this story, when I submitted it to a horror magazine she worked on. It was inspired by my mixed feelings about couples who have a second child to act as a donor for their first. The image of an old man moving into a new home, thinking he was talking his favourite things but taking nothing, I found really sad and conflicting with the usual way children treat their aging parents.

THE CAPTURE DIAMONDS

I'm sure there are more stories about this now; turning your loved ones into jewels once they die. I'll be using the idea again, that's for sure.

GHOST JAIL

Fiji again. This one is inspired by the censorship in place in Fiji, that people really do not have a voice. Web pages are blocked and the newspapers are muzzled.

I talk about the woman, Rashmilla, waving a piece of paper claiming to have lost her children in a house fire. Many people on the streets of Suva do carry papers like this, and they wave them at you to read. I always carried pockets of change to give them. One time, I'd just been to my favourite second hand clothes shop and had a bag of clothes. A woman waved her paper at me. "All my clothes are burnt, all gone," she said, so I gave her a gorgeous red t-shirt. She pulled it on straight away and did a dance for us on the street.

GAZE DOGS OF NINE WATERFALL

There is a waterfall in Suva called Colo I Suva, meaning heart of Suva. People loved it; I hated it. I found it claustrophobic and awful. Plus you're warned about the robbers who hang out there. So it was a perfect setting for a horror story.

The yellow dog is not only representative of many of the stray dogs in Fiji; I actually saw a dog like this, malevolent and huge.

Story Acknowledgements

"Dead Sea Fruit" copyright © Kaaron Warren. First published in *Fantasy Magazine*, 2006. Edited by Sean Wallace.

"Woman Train" copyright © Kaaron Warren. First published in *Outcast*, CSFG, 2005. Edited by Nicole Murphy.

"Down to the Silver Spirits" copyright © Kaaron Warren. First published in *Paper Cities*, Senses Five Press, 2007. Edited by Ekaterina Sedia.

"Fresh Young Widow" copyright © Kaaron Warren. First published in *The Grinding House*, CSFG, 2005. Edited by Donna Hanson.

"Coalescence" copyright © Kaaron Warren. First published *Aurealis* 37, 2007. Edited by Stephen Higgins and Stuart Mayne.

"Cooling the Crows" copyright © Kaaron Warren. First published in *In Bad Dreams*, Morrigan Books, 2007. Edited by Mark Deniz.

"Buster and Corky" copyright © Kaaron Warren. First published in *Scary Food*, Agog! Press. Edited by Cat Sparks.

"The Edge of a Thing" copyright © Kaaron Warren. First published in *British Fantasy Society Yearbook* 2009. Edited by Guy Adams.

"Guarding the Mound" copyright © Kaaron Warren. First published in *Encounters*, CSFG, 2004. Edited by Maxine Macarthur.

"State of Oblivion" copyright © Kaaron Warren. First published in *Elsewhere*, CSFG, 2005. Edited by Maxine Macarthur.

"The Softening" copyright © Kaaron Warren. First published in *Shadowed Realms Redback Issue*, 2005. Edited by Angela Challis.

"The Grinding House" copyright © Kaaron Warren. First published in *The Grinding House*, CSFG, 2005. Edited by Donna Hanson.

"Green" copyright © Kaaron Warren. First published *Shadow Box*, Brimstone Press, . Edited by Shane Jiraiya Cummins.

"Sins of the Ancestors" copyright © Kaaron Warren. Appears here for the first time.

"Doll Money" copyright © Kaaron Warren. First published in *Fables and Reflections*, 2004. Edited by Lily Chrywenstrom.

"The Gibbet Bell" copyright © Kaaron Warren. First published in *Borderlands* 8, 2006. Edited by Stephen Dedman.

"In the Drawback" copyright © Kaaron Warren. First published in *The Glass Woman*, Prime, 2007.

Thank you

The publisher would sincerely like to thank:

Elizabeth Grzyb, Kaaron Warren, Lucius Shepard,
Olga Read, Jonathan Strahan, Peter McNamara, Ellen Datlow,
Grant Stone, Jeremy G. Byrne, Sean Williams, Garth Nix,
David Cake, Simon Oxwell, Grant Watson, Sue Manning,
Steven Utley, Bill Congreve, Jack Dann, Stephen Dedman,
the Mt Lawley Mafia, the Nedlands Yakuza, Angela Slatter,
Shane Jiraiya Cummings, Angela Challis, Donna Maree Hanson,
Kate Williams, Kathryn Linge, Andrew Williams, Al Chan,
Alisa Krasnostein, Lewis Shiner, everyone I've missed ...

... and *you*.

CPSIA information can be obtained
at www.ICGtesting.com
Printed in the USA
FSOW02n0118251217
42730FS